LOVE ME AGAIN

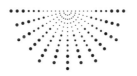

SHAYLA HART

Love ME AGAIN

WRITTEN BY

SHAYLA HART

A SHAYLA HART NOVEL

Copyright

Acknowledgements & Dedications

First of all, I would like to thank my husband and my children for giving up precious time with me and waiting patiently, supporting me while I finished writing this book. Secondly, I want to thank my family, friends, and my beautiful supporters for all the love and support you have shown me through the first book to this one. Without your encouragement, none of this would have been possible. Thank you from the bottom of my heart. You all mean the world to me.

Chapter 1
COLE

"Happy birthday!"

I look up from my desk and see Shayla standing in the doorway to my home office--naked, a cupcake with a candle in her hand, looking all kinds of sumptuous. I grin and lean back in my chair and admire my wife. Four months pregnant with my baby, and she's absolutely glowing, literally the most beautiful thing I have ever laid my eyes on. She's got a cute baby bump where she's finally starting to show. "Lord, have mercy. Show me a more desirable birthday gift than you, baby. Get your sexy bum over here, Mrs Hoult." I tell her, and she smiles and saunters over to me.

"Make a wish, baby." She expresses, holding out the cupcake with the candle to me. I lift my gaze to hers over the flame and smile.

"Honey, what more can I possibly wish for? I have you. We have a baby on the way and all the success I can ever dream of." I tell her, and she smiles amorously and bites her lip.

"You forgot the most important thing—health. You can wish for health, bebé." I sigh and gaze into her eyes. This is why I love her so damn much.

"You're right. There is nothing more important than our health and the health of our baby." I declare, placing my hand on her stomach where my unborn baby lay. Shayla lays her hand on mine, and I close my eyes and make my birthday wish, which was a lifetime of health and happiness-- Oh, and a little girl. Of course, I'll be happy, whatever the gender, but I really want a little princess with Shayla's gorgeous eyes, her smile, her long dark hair, and my dimples. My heart melts at the thought of her running around, shouting Daddy.

"What are you thinking about?" Shayla questions, watching me with a grin on her face. I blow out the candle and beam at her.

"I can't tell you, or it won't come true," I say, pulling her into my lap and kissing her soft lips. Shayla presses her forehead to mine and caresses my jaw.

"Happy birthday, love of my life." She whispers, and I smile, closing my eyes.

"Thank you, light of my life." I cup her face and kiss her deeply. Shayla jumps and pulls back from the kiss, her eyes wide.

"What is it, baby?" I question, concerned, and she shakes her head and looks down at her stomach. Shayla lifts my hand and presses it on her belly, and I frown when I feel something tap against my palm. "Whoa, is that..."

"The baby is kicking." She smiles, nibbling her lip. I rub her stomach affectionately and press my forehead to her temple, gleaming.

"Shayla, you've given me so much to be grateful for. Your love has truly changed me and made me a better man." I tell her earnestly, and she smiles, grazing her thumb over my knuckles.

"You were always a good man, Cole. You've always had a good heart. That's all on you, not me." She replies and pulls back to look at me. "Now..." She utters, picking up the cupcake and licks the frosting with the tip of her tongue, and looks at me sultrily. I lean in, grasping her jaw in my hand, and suck the buttercream off her tongue.

"Mm," I moan and watch as she slips off and walks back a little, her eyes hot on mine.

"What do you say, birthday boy, want to get down and dirty?" She purrs sexily, smearing the frosting of the cupcake all over her breasts. I bite my lip and watch her with hungering eyes.

"Oh, I'm going to devour you, Mrs Hoult," I growl and slap my laptop shut before I get up and walk over to her. Shayla squeals laughing when I haul her up into my arms and carry her to the kitchen, my face buried in her chest, licking, and sucking the buttercream off her body, while I lay her down on the marble island in the middle of our kitchen. "Have your breasts got bigger, or have my hands shrunk?" I ask when I cup them, and they don't fit in my hands any more.

Shayla lifts her head laughing. "They're certainly bigger. One of the perks of being pregnant. Enjoy." I look at her breasts wide-eyed and grin like a child in a sweet shop.

"Oh, just try to stop me." I groan, burying my face in between them, and Shayla laughs. I kiss down to her stomach where our baby was growing and kiss it. "Hi baby, Daddy can't wait to meet you." I lift my eyes to Shayla, watching me with a beautiful smile on her face while brushing her fingers through my hair. "Do you think it can hear me?"

Shayla nods, smiling, "The book that I'm reading says the baby starts to hear sounds at sixteen weeks, which I am now. It's the size of an apple at the moment." She tells me, pushing out her bottom lip.

"So, you've got a little apple in here." I coo, nestling her stomach, and she grins, nodding.

"Yes, our little apple is blissfully floating around in there." She sighs, content as I rub her stomach. "Mm, that feels nice." I watch Shayla as she closes her eyes while I caress her tummy. I still find it incredible that a little person is growing inside her right now--a small bundle made of our love combined into a tiny human. Frankly, I've never felt so inferior to her or any woman, for that matter. We men really are lesser creatures. "Honey," I lift my gaze to hers, and she smiles dotingly at me. I feel my heart swell. I'm so in love with her.

"Yes, baby?"

"Make me yours." She whispers, and I give her a hundred-watt smile before I push her legs apart and enjoy my birthday treat. By the time we were done, there was buttercream everywhere, and we were covered in colourful frosting. We both lay on the kitchen floor panting with satisfied grins on our faces. "I'm sticky in places I definitely shouldn't be," Shayla laughs, and I chuckle.

"Hey, you wanted to get messy, so messy we got, baby." I pant, smothering her face with frosting I had on my hand, and she slaps my hand away, snickering. I roll onto my side and look at her. "Let's always do crazy shit like this, okay?" I say, reaching over and writing my name on her stomach with a heart.

Shayla rolls onto her side, imitating my action, and writes her name on my chest over my heart.

"Always." She whispers, and I pull her to me, kissing her passionately. "We better go shower." She mumbles against my lips, and I nod.

"Mm, let's." I stand up and gently help her up, making sure she doesn't slip on all the buttercream all over the floor. Once we got away from the buttercream over the floor, I scoop Shay into my arms, and we go to the bathroom upstairs. We spend a good twenty-five minutes trying to get all the buttercream off our body, which was more difficult than I imagined it would be.

"You're not going to work in the morning, right?" Shayla asks, running her hands down my back. I shake my head while washing the shampoo out of my hair.

"No. I'm with you all day," I answer, opening my eyes to look at her, and she smiles, nibbling her lip coyly. "Why do I have a feeling you've got something more planned?"

"Because you know me too darn well." She croons, wrapping her arms around my neck, and gazes into my eyes.

"That I do, baby. What are we doing?" I ask, intrigued, and she shrugs impishly and presses me back against the wall.

"Well, first, I'm going to make love to you." She whispers, running her hands over my chest. I groan and watch her excitedly. "And then..." She kisses my jaw softly. "We're going to have breakfast with your parents." She smiles and trails her lips along my jaw. "After that, I'm going to kidnap you, and we're going on a little trip to Amsterdam with Aimee, Jo, Josh, and Sam."

I laugh and kiss her temple. "Boy, I've not been to Dam in an awfully long time. Last time Josh and I went, we got so baked we ended up on the blue light district." I tell her, and Shayla's eyes go wide, and she laughs.

"No!"

I laugh, nodding, "Luckily, I realized, and I stopped Josh before he did something he would have needed a shit load of therapy for later." Shayla throws her head back and laughs hysterically.

"Well, as bummed as I am that I can't get 'baked' with you guys, I'll be sure to keep you all away from the blue light district." She promises, and I chuckle, shaking my head at the fond memories I had on that trip. This was on Josh's twenty-first birthday, we took a boy's trip with all our friends, and it was a memorable one at that.

After our shower, Shayla and I went to bed.

THE FOLLOWING morning Shay kept her promise and woke me up with soft loving kisses on the lips. We made love before we had to pack for our two-day trip to Amsterdam and meet my parents for breakfast.

"I cannot believe we're going to Dam. I am so excited!" Jo chirps as we walk into the jet. I wrap an arm around my wife and nuzzle her neck tenderly, and she nestles into me. Aimee pops the champagne and pours us all a glass each.

"Sorry Shay, you're having apple juice, babe," Aimee teases, handing her a glass of apple juice, and she grins. "I'll drink in your place, don't worry." She adds with a cheeky grin.

"Lucky for you bitches, I don't need alcohol to have fun." She shrugs, and I kiss her jaw lovingly while I rub her stomach.

"All right. Toast time." Josh says, holding up his champagne flute. "To Coles birthday, you may be getting older, but you're still one sexy son of a gun." He toasts. I laugh, holding up my glass. "Happy birthday Cole!" We all clink our glasses and drink. I'm so incredibly blessed to have such a wonderful life. A great group of friends surrounded me. I have the most beautiful woman in the world by my side, who is having my baby. I was just so happy. The lights in the jet dim, and music starts playing, and we all cheer.

The girls pull Shayla off my lap, and they all start dancing. Josh and Sam start handing out shots of Patron. They were on a mission to get me drunk, that much I knew for sure. "Drink up, bro!" Sam sings, handing me another shot and slapping my back. Aimee pulls Josh to dance with her as Sam walks over to Jo. Shayla looks at me, grinning beautifully. I walk over to her and wrap my arms around her waist, drawing her against me. Shayla wraps her arms around my neck as we sway together to the music. "You love makes me dizzy, baby." I drawl in her ear, and she giggles.

"That's the tequila, Bebé."

I shake my head, smiling down into her upturned face. "No, it's not. I have you, but I still want you desperately. How is that possible?" I growl, and she smiles, her cheeks flushing.

"That's a good thing because I still want you, and I always will, you sexy beast." She tells me and draws my lips to hers, and kisses me hot and hard. I moan when she sucks and flicks her tongue over mine.

"Oh gross, I don't want to see that. Oi, get a room, you two." Sam grumbles, disgruntled at watching me sucking faces with his baby sister. I flip him off while I continue to kiss her while we continue dancing together.

WE LAND in Amsterdam an hour later. We hire tandem bikes and cycle through the city together--which wasn't easy to do while tipsy. Sam and Jo fell off twice, and it was rather amusing watching Jo scold him. He's like six-foot-four and built like a tank, while she's five feet two and petite. Such a miss-match, but she seems to keep him under control. After our bike rides, we walk through the city and visit the Anne Frank museum, where Shayla spent a good forty-minutes sobbing.

"Honey, come on, please stop crying." I urge, wiping her tears away. She sniffles and hiccups adorably.

"It's just so sad." She whimpers, and I wrap my arms around her tighter. "I read the book but seeing it just..." She sobs again. I smile and brush her hair away from her face and kiss her forehead.

"Look, baby, do you want a cinnamon pretzel?" I ask, trying to distract her, and she nods as we walk to the stand. I hand her the pretzel, and she eats it as we walk along the river.

"Dude, what was that?" Josh inquires, referring to Shayla's emotional outburst. I smile and shake my head.

"Hormones, bro. She's like a bloody yo-yo. One minute she's happy, and the next she's crying her eyes out." I explain, glancing at her laughing along with the girls like she wasn't just sobbing seconds ago. "I've noticed she likes to eat, so whenever she gets upset, I give her food, and she's happy again," I say with a shrug, and Josh cracks up laughing.

"Awe, but that's cute, though. How do you feel about the whole baby thing?" He questions, taking a sip of his coffee.

I sigh and bite my lip. "I'm excited, man. I felt the baby kick for the first time last night, and it was just the best feeling in the world. Watching the girl you love, carry, and nurture your baby inside of her is just so magical--despite all the hormones." I tell him, and Josh smiles, nodding.

"I'm thrilled for you, bro. I can't wait to settle down and have a baby." Josh confesses, looking over at Aimee. I follow his gaze and smile fondly.

"How are things with you two?" Josh nods, biting his lip.

"We're great. Aimee's, unlike anyone I've ever met. She's fierce and passionate about everything she does, and I love that about her. She keeps me on my toes, that's for sure." He chuckles, looking over at her. "Do you ever wonder where we would have been right now if that night you met Shayla, you went over to Aimee instead, and I went for Shayla like we were supposed to?"

I frown and try to picture myself with Aimee and shake my head with a grimace. "Nah. I can't imagine that. I honestly can't picture my life without Shayla or how I ever lived without knowing her."

Josh chuckles and shakes his head. "I think we both ended up where we were supposed to be. Shayla's like a sister to me now. It's weird to think that I was attracted to her once."

I smirk, "Yeah, let's not open up that can of worms again. I'm just thankful everything worked out for us in the end." I sigh, and Josh nudges my shoulder, nodding.

I never want to imagine my life without Shayla in it. She's my whole world wrapped up in a beautiful five-foot-six package.

Chapter 2

SHAYLA

"OH, HELL YES," I moan as I pick up my caramel latte from the coffee machine. I bring the cup of delicious coffee to my lips, just as I'm about to take a sip, it gets taken out of my hand, "Hey, I was about to drink that," I complain and lift my gaze to my sexy husband who was scowling at me.

"No caffeine while you are pregnant." He scolds me, and I sulk, looking at him.

"But--"

"Ah!" Cole cuts me off, holding up a finger, silencing me. "Herbal tea," He smiles, handing me a hot mug of steaming crap. I glance down at the tea and back at him.

"What the hell is this?" I question, wrinkling my nose, and Cole smirks.

"Decaffeinated tea. It's camomile. It's relaxing." He informs me, and I stare at him blankly.

"Honey, if I wanted to relax, I would have stayed in bed. I got the coffee because I need to wake up." I argue, and Cole shrugs while he sips my latte and moans in delight.

"Mm, this is so good." I watch him, not amused in the slightest, and Cole leans in close to my face. "Drink your tea." He whispers and kisses my nose.

"Fine, when I fall asleep in the meeting, you'll only have yourself to blame." I fume and stalk off toward my office while Cole laughs, shaking his head.

"I love you."

"Bite me!"

"Just say where baby!" I hear him call out after me, and I look back at him, sipping *my* delicious latte, while he watches me with a sexy grin on his face.

God help me. I love him.

I take a sip of the tea, and my stomach lurches unpleasantly. I run out of my office toward the bathroom, where I empty the breakfast I had earlier.

"Sweetheart, you okay?" I hear Cole's voice behind the door, and I sigh.

"Yes. The baby and I agree—we hate the tea." I hear him chuckle as I wash my hands and rinse out my mouth with mouthwash. I open the door and see him leaning against the wall. He pulls me into his arms and kisses my forehead.

"I'll get them to look into some decaffeinated coffee that's safe to drink while you're pregnant. How's that sound?" I close my eyes and sigh.

"Anything is better than that tea," I mutter with a shudder, and Cole chortles.

"All right. Anything to keep my baby and my little apple happy." He coo's rubbing my stomach. I smile and gaze up into his eyes.

"All we need to be happy is you, baby," I declare, and he grins before he kisses me softly.

"You've got me forever, sweetheart." Cole parts my lips, kissing me slow and deep in the middle of our office while our employees watch us. We pull apart when they all hoot and whistle. I blush furiously and bury my face into Cole's chest, who laughs. "All right, shows over, back to work you lot." He tells them off before he pulls me toward the conference room for our meeting.

We spent over an hour reviewing the ins and outs of this new project with a client who didn't seem to have a clue what he wanted. I had to stop myself from laughing at the expression on Cole's face when the client was explaining what he was looking for.

"All right. I've got all the notes of what you've requested, Mr Collins. I'll work on this design and come back to you in a few weeks?" Cole tells him, and the client nods with an assured smile. We shake hands, and he leaves the conference room. Cole looks at me somewhat bemused, and I giggle.

"You haven't the slightest clue what he was asking for, do you?" I question, amused, and Cole shakes his head whilst scratching his chin.

"Not a clue." He sighs. "He was fucking waffling the whole time. We will figure something out, though." Cole utters with a shrug, and I smile.

"That we will, honey." I check the time on my watch and get up. "Oh, I gotta go. I've got a call with my lecturer." I inform him and walk out of the conference room back to my office. I was so excited to be back at University to finish my degree. Cole was super supportive and helping me, though he wasn't pleased that I was taking on so much work while pregnant. It was a little tiring, but it's so going to be worth it when I graduate and finally get my degree in a couple of months.

FOUR WEEKS GO BY, and it was time for us to find out the sex of our baby. We did discuss letting it be a surprise, but I was too impatient to wait and wanted to find out, and so was Cole.

"How are we feeling, mama?" My midwife questions when I lay down on the bed.

"I'm terrific. Other than my hands and feet swelling, I'm feeling great." I tell her, and she smiles.

"That's completely normal. Just try to keep your feet elevated and avoid wearing heels." She advises, and Cole nods, pointing to his ears, indicating for me to listen to her advice. "Are we finding out the sex today?"

"Yes." We both say together, and she grins, pressing the receiver to my stomach. Cole takes my hand and looks at the screen when our baby comes up.

"Good. First, I'm going to do a couple of checks to make sure everything is all right with the baby." I nod and look at Cole, who was staring at the screen in awe. "We're growing nicely. The water looks good. Your baby is now the size of a small banana." I grin, and Cole chuckles, biting his lip. "Right, let's see if the baby will give us a peek." She states, shaking my stomach a little, and the baby jumps and kicks. "Oh, we've got a feisty one.

"Just like its mother," Cole teases, and I slap his arm playfully. He laughs cheerfully, pressing a kiss to my temple.

"Well, guys, say hello to your...baby girl."

"Yes!" Cole exclaims excitedly, and the midwife and I jump, startled at his sudden outburst. I look up at Cole, and he kisses me. "I'm so frigging happy."

The midwife laughs, "Well, we can see Daddy is pleased. How about you, mummy?" I nod and look at the screen, my eyes welling up.

"I'm thrilled," I cry, and Cole looks at me with his green eyes wide

"Oh no, no, not the tears again. Do you have any food?" He asks the midwife, who frowns, looking at him bemused. "It's the only way to stop her from crying." He whispers to her and hisses when I elbow him in the ribs. "Ow. What? *It is.*"

I scowl up at him. Eyes narrowed, "Is that why you keep feeding me?" I ask, affronted, and Cole shrugs sheepishly.

The midwife laughs out loud. "You two are adorable. It's completely normal for her to get emotional from time to time as her body is currently going through many changes every day. You've got one job, daddy, keep mummy happy, so baby is happy."

Cole sighs and smiles at me. "I'll do whatever it takes to keep my girls happy." He whispers, brushing a kiss on my lips and wiping away my tears of joy. The midwife gives us a video of the ultrasound and a couple of photos to take with us.

∾

"Have you thought about any names?" Cole inquires as we get into the car. I shrug, pulling my seatbelt on.

"I have a couple of ideas. What about you?"

Cole nods, grinning as he backs up out of the parking spot. "A couple."

"Let's hear it then."

"Well, I like the name, Sienna."

"Sienna Hoult." I nod, grinning but frown suddenly. "Wait, is that a name of an ex or..."

Cole laughs, "No. I just like the name. Let's hear yours."

"Alaia is at the top of my list," I say, and he grins.

"Alaia Hoult. It's perfect, baby. I love it." Cole says, taking my hand and kissing my knuckles.

"You do?"

"Yeah, it's such a beautiful name. Alaia."

"Actually...I thought we could give her a middle name. Alaia Mae Hoult." Cole repeats the name, smiling.

"Alaia Mae Hoult, get your butt down here." He mutters with a frown and then laughs. "I like it. You need to try it out when you're full naming her for when she's in trouble." I laugh and squeeze his cheek.

"You're so cute. Although, I think she's going to have you wrapped around her little finger, my love." I grin, and he nods, licking his lips.

"Damn right she will, especially if she comes out looking like a miniature version of you." He grins, giving me a side stare while he drives. "My beautiful queen and my mini princess."

Cole and I went to get something to eat before we went home. I'm currently sprawled out on the sofa, reading a book, while he was on the phone to someone at the Miami office. I can see him pacing back and forth in his office, looking rather irritated. Twenty minutes later, he came over to me and flops down on the sofa with a heavy sigh. "What's going on, baby?" I question, putting my book down. Cole opens his eyes and looks at me.

"I'm leaving for Miami in an hour." He tells me with a tired sigh, and I frown, sitting upright.

"What? Why?" I ask, and he lifts his head, rubbing my thigh.

"There's a major fuck up with that project for the new airport. The client is enraged and wants to meet with me tomorrow morning." He explains, brushing his fingers through his tousled hair.

"How long will you be gone for?"

Cole licks his lips and looks at me. "It shouldn't be longer than a couple of days. I doubt it will take much longer than that, baby. Do you want to come with me?" He suggests, and I pout, shaking my head.

"I wish I could, but I've got that meeting with the Bryson twins for their swanky new club tomorrow afternoon," I tell him, and he nods with a groan and pulls me to him, so I was straddling him. "Can't you send someone else?"

"No. It's a billion-dollar project. I have to go and calm the client down before he pulls the plug on it and gives it someone else." Cole explains, placing his hands at my hips.

"Well, it's only a couple of days, baby. It will give us time to miss each other a little." I say with a playful smile, and he presses his forehead to mine.

"Are you sick of me already?"

I cup his face with my hands and look into his eyes. "Sick of you? Are you kidding? It's not possible to be sick of you with all the tricks you can do with that tongue of yours." I drawl with a coy smirk, and his lips curl into a haughty grin while he watches me.

"Careful now, I might start to think I'm only good for one thing." He murmurs, sweeping his nose over mine.

"Two things," I whisper impishly. "You're good with your little sausage too." I correct him, and he laughs deeply. "Why do you think I married you twice? Good dick is difficult to come by nowadays." I tease him and gasp when he lifts me and lays me down on my back on the sofa while he crawls up over me.

"So is good pussy," Cole breathes, staring hungrily into my eyes. "Looks like we're both privileged in that particular department." He declares austerely, his emerald green eyes gleaming.

"I believe we are." I kiss him softly while I snake my arms around his neck. "We can use this time apart to do all the fun stuff that we missed out on doing. We skipped the whole dating part of our relationship. *Twice.*"

Cole looks at me questioningly. "I'm listening..."

I grin and kiss along his jaw, "Well, we can have phone sex..." I whisper in his ear, and he moans. "I can tell you all the things I will do to you when you get back home." Cole squeezes my hips a little and rocks his own up against me. "I can send you some racy pictures of myself, and you can send me a dick pic."

Cole laughs gruffly, "Baby, I have never sent a dick pic to anyone." I bite my lip, smiling wickedly.

"Well, then, here's your chance, big boy." Cole chuckles, and I pull his mouth to mine, kissing him ardently. We've not been apart since we got married, so sending him off was hard. I've got so used to having him around, and I had this niggling feeling in the pit of my stomach. Cole wraps his arms around me and pulls me against him. "You call me as soon as you get there. I don't care what time it is." I say, peering up at him, and he nods before pressing his forehead to mine.

"I will, I promise." He replies, cupping my face in his hands and kissing me slowly and deliberately as if he were trying to carve every inch of my mouth into his brain. "I love you, baby. I'll see you in a few days. If you need anything while I'm away, you call Josh, understand?"

I nod, "I love you so much. Finish up and hurry back home to me." I wrap my arms around his neck, and he hugs me tightly in return. "I wish you didn't have to go." I sigh, and he squeezes me and buries his face into my neck, inhaling deeply.

"Me too, but I'm going to be back home with you and our princess very soon," Cole assures me, and I nod, pulling back. Cole kneels in front of me, places his hands on my belly, and presses his lips to it, closing his eyes. "Take care of your mummy for me, princess. Daddy will be back before you know it. I love you, baby girl." I watch him with a pout, and he smiles lovingly at me as he stands and kisses me one last time before he walks out. I sigh sullenly and watch him open the car door. Cole looks at me, smiling handsomely; he kisses his fingers and places them over his heart. I smile and do the same back to him, we stare at one another for a lingering moment before he gets in the car, and they drive off.

I close the door and lean against it with a heavy sigh. I look down at my stomach and press my hand against my baby bump. "Looks like it's just the two of us for a couple of days, baby girl." I sigh sullenly and smile when I feel her kick. I couldn't sleep the first night without Cole next to me. I missed him terribly, so I hugged his pillow and waited for him to call me. It was a nine-hour flight to Miami—he should have landed by now. It was past three in the morning in London. I jump when I hear my phone ring and answer it in a flurry. "Cole?"

"Hi baby." I sigh when I hear his voice. "I just got to the hotel. Please tell me you didn't stay up all night waiting."

"I couldn't sleep without you," I tell him, and I hear him sigh on the other end. "I got worried when you didn't call."

"I'm sorry, sweetheart, I wanted to call you as soon as I landed, but my phone signal is playing up over here." He explains, shuffling around. "You should get some sleep, honey."

I shake my head. "The house is so empty, and our bed is cold without you," I sigh, getting emotional again. "I really miss you."

Cole sighs. "Oh, baby, I miss you too so much. Please don't cry. I'm going to be back in two days, okay? I nod, biting my lip. "Let me see that gorgeous face." I pull the phone back when it beeps, alerting me that he was requesting a video call. I accept and wait for it to connect. I smile when I see his handsome face appear on my screen. He grins sexily, "There's my baby."

"Hey stud." I sigh, laying down on the bed. We spoke for a couple of hours--he even let me watch him shower. "Hey, the camera is steaming up. I can't see anything." I giggle as he steps out of the shower, dripping wet, and wipes the lens so that I could see clearer.

"Better?" He laughs, running back to the shower again.

"No, better would have been me being in that shower with you,"

"You're telling me. I can't wait to come back home." After his shower, we both lay in bed and spoke until my eyes grew heavy, and I finally fell asleep hugging his pillow.

∿

THE FOLLOWING day creeps on and on, especially without him around the office. Every hour that passed by, I missed him more and more and was getting anxious for him to come back home. We face time at lunch, and I fill him in on my meeting with the twins while he listens to me, eating his salad. I told him I was feeling lonely in that big house by myself, and he suggested I get the girls to stay over till he comes back home the next day.

I called them, and they kindly agreed to keep me company while he was away. "Bish, I haven't the scoobiest idea what I'm doing here, by the way," Aimee declares, whisking the batter for the cake we were attempting to make.

I frown, looking at the recipe on the tablet. "Is it creamy?" I ask her, and she shrugs diffidently.

"If by creamy you mean lumpy, then yes, it's creamy." I chuckle and lean over, looking at the lumpy mess she's made of the batter.

"Aimee, you had one job. Cream the butter and sugar. How did you fuck it up?" Jo scolds her while looking into the bowl.

Aimee looks at her with an arched brow. "All right, Betty fucking Crocker, you do it then!" I shake my head, laughing at the two while they bicker. "And what are you laughing at?" She chuckles, throwing flour in my face. I cough and sputter, waving my hand in front of my face to clear the flour cloud. Aimee and Jo both laugh as I glare at them with a face covered in flour.

"Oh, it's on now." I grab a handful of flour and throw it at them, which then turns into a full-on food fight in my kitchen. We were all covered in flour, eggs, and batter. I rush over and answer my phone when Cole calls me. The look on his face when he saw the state of me was priceless.

"Jesus, what the hell happened to you?" Cole chuckles while the girls and I laugh.

"We're attempting to bake a cake for you," I tell him, wiping the flour out of my eyes, and he laughs out loud.

"Honey, the ingredients go in a bowl, you know that, right?" I smile and shrug.

"Blame Aimee. She started it by cocking up the batter." I tease, and she throws more flour in my face.

"Here, eat that!" Aimee cackles wickedly.

Cole watches me with a grin while I slap Aimee's bum. "I called to say good night, baby. Have fun with the girls. I'm expecting to be back home tomorrow afternoon. I love you."

I smile. "I can't wait. I love you, too." Cole blows me a kiss before he hangs up. I sigh and stare at the phone sadly. My heart felt heavy, and I wasn't sure why.

"Bish, are you all right?" Jo questions when she notices the gloomy look on my face.

I nod and force myself to smile, "Yeah, I just really miss him." I utter and try to shake off this uneasy feeling that was making my chest feel all tight. After we clean up, the girls and I snuggle up in my bed, and we watch a film till we fell asleep.

THE NEXT DAY I woke up feeling animated. My baby would be home in a few hours. After breakfast, I had a shower and got dressed, anxiously waiting for Cole to come home. I was counting down the minutes.

Hours went by, and he didn't come home.

It was gone past six in the evening; he was supposed to be home hours ago.

"Shayla, babe, why don't you sit down? You're burning a hole through the floor." Aimee sighs, watching me pace back and forth while redialling Cole's number for the two hundredth time.

"I can't sit down! Cole should have been home by now. Where is he?" I snap irritably as I pace frantically.

"Shay, maybe his flight got delayed," Jo suggests, walking over to me, and I shake my head.

"Then why hasn't he called me?!" I shout and take a deep breath, closing my eyes. "He knows I would worry. Something's wrong. I can feel it." I whisper. My chest was getting tighter, making it difficult to breathe.

"Shayla don't say that. Cole's going to walk through that door any minute, babe." Aimee tries to reassure me, and I shake my head.

"I've had this horrible feeling in the pit of my stomach since he told me he was leaving. It just didn't feel right, and it's getting worse. Something is wrong." I tell them, and Aimee wraps her arms around me.

"Shay, try and calm down, babe. You're pregnant. All this stress isn't good for you or the baby." She tells me, and I gasp when the door-bell rings. I pull away from Aimee's hold and run to the door. I pull it open, hoping to see Cole standing there, but it wasn't—it was Josh. He stood there staring at me, his blue eyes rimmed red, full of despair.

"Shayla..." Josh whispers, his voice breaking, and I shake my head.

Oh God...

"Josh, no."

"I'm so sorry," Josh mutters, taking hold of my upper arms. "Cole's plane has crashed.."

Chapter 3

SHAYLA

"Noooo!" I scream, and Josh caught me as my legs give out as if someone just yanked the floor out from under me. Josh cradles me in his arms, and we both hit the floor. Aimee and Jo come running over to us. I keep screaming Cole's name over and over again.

Cole wasn't gone. He wasn't.

He promised me...he said he was coming back home. Cole wouldn't lie to me. "Josh...Josh, he wouldn't leave me, he wouldn't! Please say he's not gone. Please, tell me he's coming back. TELL ME!" I scream at him, sobbing, pushing at his chest. Josh cries, shaking his head.

"I wish I could, Shayla." He whispers, and I weep into his chest as he rocks me. Aimee and Jo both come closer, and they all hold me while I weep. Josh's phone rings and he reaches down to answer it. "What?" He snaps angrily at whoever it was on the other end.

Josh looks down at me, sobbing in his arms. "Where? Okay....okay. Thanks." He heaves a sigh and nods before hanging up. "Shayla, hey, hey, they found him. He's alive. Cole's alive." He tells me, taking my face into his hands. I open my eyes and look at him.

"What?"

"He's in critical condition, but he's alive," Josh tells me, and I cover my face with my hands and wail helplessly.

"Oh God." I whimper. "Josh, please, take me to him." I plead, curling my fingers in his shirt, and he nods. They help me up, and we all leave the house. I sat in the back seat of Josh's car, my head in Jo's chest, crying while she brushes her fingers through my hair.

I was praying with every bit of faith I had in my heart for him to be okay.

He has to be okay.

If anything happens to him, how am I supposed to survive? I wouldn't. I couldn't go on without him.

That brief moment, I thought he was gone. I was ready and willing to join him. The pain was unlike anything I've ever felt in my life. When we pull up outside the hospital, I open the door and run to the reception desk with Josh and the girls on my tail. "Tristan Cole Hoult. Where is he?" I ask, sobbing, and the nurse looks at me and blinks.

"What's your relati—"

"I'm his wife! Where is he?!" I yell, slapping my hands hard on the desk. The nurse types away on her computer while I pace frantically.

"He's just been brought in by an air ambulance. Go to the Intensive Care Unit on the third floor. The nurse's station will give you more information." I don't even wait for her to finish before I take off running down the corridor.

"Shayla, slow down," Aimee calls out as they all chase me down the corridors of the hospital. Josh grabs my arms and pulls me to him as I pant.

"Shayla, hey, slow down. You're pregnant!" I fight in his hold and shove him away from me.

"Let me go!" I shout and push the door to the stairs and race up as fast as my legs would let me. I look around the signs and run to the end of the corridor where the ICU was. I stop when I see a team of doctors and paramedics rush through with a stretcher toward me.

I felt my soul leave my body when I saw it was Cole. "COLE!" I scream and race over to the stretcher. He was unconscious and had a deep cut on his head where he was bleeding severely, leaving a trail of his blood on the floor in the corridor as they push him through. "Cole, baby, I'm right here, I'm right here. You're going to be okay. You have to be okay. Please, I'm begging you, don't you give up on me. I love you so much." I wail.

"Miss, please step aside." The doctor utters, and I take hold of his bloodied hand.

"He's my husband. Please, save him, please don't let him die." I sob helplessly, and he nods.

"We'll do everything we can, I promise, but you need to let him go now." I weep and let go of his hand—following them till they rush him off into the OR.

"Cole!" I whimper, shouting out to him as Josh wraps his arms around me to stop me from running through the doors to the operating room. I look down at my hands stained with his blood and cry.

My knees shook under my weight, and I fall into Josh's arms, my screams echoing in the corridors.

"Shayla, hey, shh, shh. Cole's going to be okay--he's going to be okay. Look, he's fighting to stay alive for you and your baby. Now you must do the same for him. You need to be strong for him." Josh kept whispering in my ear as I sob, unable to catch my breath.

"Josh is right, Shay. You have to be strong for him and your baby. He's going to pull through this. Cole will never leave you, babe." Aimee comforts me as I sob and shake my head.

"Why us?" I whimper. "Why does this keep happening to us? We were finally so happy. Why can't we just be happy Aimee, why?" I sob, and she hugs me.

"Shayla, it was an accident," Jo tells me, brushing my hair away from my face. I shake my head.

"I should have gone with him," I whisper, staring at my trembling hands. "I should've been with him."

"Shayla?!" I look up and see Cole's mother running toward me, looking every bit as wrecked as I was. She falls to her knees in front of me, and we both sob.

"Is he okay? Please tell me he's okay?" She cries desperately, and I shake my head weakly.

"I don't know," I whisper, closing my eyes. "He doesn't look good, mum." I cry, holding my hands up, and when she looks at the blood on my hands, she weeps. Elaine cups my face in her hands and wipes my tears away.

"He's going to be okay, darling. I believe that with my whole heart, and you **need** to as well." I close my eyes and nod. She places her hand on my stomach. "He won't leave you both, not when he loves you so much." She consoles me, and I whimper.

"Oh God, I'm so scared. I don't want to lose him."

"Hey, look at me. We're not going to lose him." She tells me sternly, and I nod. I had no other choice but to hold onto those words, but inside I was dying, and no amount of words or assurance could stop the torment in my chest.

Hours went by with no word from anyone. My mother and brother came too as soon as Jo called him. Josh was pacing up and down the corridor anxiously while Sam leaned against the wall staring at the floor. My mother was comforting my mother-in-law, and I just sat there staring at my hands. "Shayla, let's go wash your hands and splash some water in your face," Jo suggests, and I shake my head numbly.

"Can we get you anything?" Aimee offers, and I sigh, closing my eyes. An endless stream of tears just kept rolling down my face.

"No." I untangle myself from the girls and stand up. My bladder was so full it was starting to hurt.

"Shayla, where are you going?" My mother questions and I tell her I have to use the bathroom, and she gestures to the girls to follow me. I stop outside the toilet and turn to face Aimee and Jo.

"Girls, give me a minute. Please?" I plead, and they nod in response. I needed to be alone for a bit. I walk into the bathroom and stroll into a stall. I close the lid of the toilet and sit on it.

I cover my mouth with my hand to smother the whimper that escapes me. I sat there sobbing for a while, just rocking back and forth. "God, please, please, I'm begging you don't take him from me too." I pray, laying my hand on my chest. "Please give him back to us, don't let my daughter grow up without her father like I did please, please, I'm begging you," I beg forlornly. "Don't make us live without him." I place my hands on my stomach and close my eyes. "Pray for your Daddy angel," I whisper distraughtly.

After hours of surgery, the doctor comes out. I lift my head off Sam's chest, who was holding me, and jump up when he walks over to us. "Mrs Hoult?" Both his mother and I answer simultaneously, and the doctor looks at us both, taking off his surgical mask. "His wife?"

"That's me," I whisper, stepping over to him. "How is he? Is he going to be okay?" I question in a flurry, and he sighs, looking at me sullenly.

"Mrs Hoult, your husband is very fortunate to be alive, given the state he was in when he was brought in. He has eight broken ribs, a ruptured kidney, and a punctured lung. On top of all of that, he took a hard hit on the head and fractured his skull." He explains, and I choke on a sob. "It's truly a miracle that he's held on this long."

"Oh, my God."

"Doctor, what does that mean? Is my son going to be okay?" Coles father queries, wrapping his arms around his sobbing wife.

"We can't say for sure at this point. He's fighting to stay alive, but with the injuries he's sustained, it would be a miracle if he made it through the night. We've done all we can for him medically. We'll continue to monitor him closely, though the next twenty-four hours are critical." He explains and looks at me. "He's a strong lad, and he's putting up a hell of a fight in there."

"Can I see him?" I ask, and he sighs. "Please, just for a second?" I sob, and he nods.

"Okay, but only for a second." He agrees and gestures for me to follow him.

"Shayla?" I turn and look at his mother; she looks at me pleadingly. "Tell him I love him." I nod and turn to follow the doctor into the O.R, where they gave me gowns and masks and helped me disinfect my hands before they led me in the ICU ward to see him.

I hear machines beeping as soon as I enter the room, and my heart begins racing. I stop by the door and release a tremulous breath. The doctor stops and looks at me. "Come on, sweetheart, it's okay, don't be afraid." He assures me with a nod of his head. I nod and creepingly walk into the room. I intake a sharp breath when I see him.

"Oh, God." I pant, holding my chest. Tears blur my vision and roll down my cheeks when I see the state of my husband--my Cole. "Oh,... God." I couldn't catch my breath. He didn't even look like himself.

Cole's head was bandaged up, face and eyes bruised and swollen. His once smooth and tan body was covered in cuts and bruises. They had him hooked up to ventilators. I.V drips on the one hand and a blood transfusion on the other. I whimper and shake my head, turning away from him. I couldn't bear to see him in that state. The doctor takes hold of my shoulders and looks down at me.

"Sweetheart, he's pretty beaten up, but he needs you now more than ever." He tells me reassuringly. I nod and turn to look at Cole again. My heart hurt to see him like this. I force myself to step closer to him, and I take his bruised hand in my trembling one.

"Hi baby," I mutter quietly, brushing my thumb gently over his knuckles. "I don't know if you can hear me, but I'm right here with you. Please, baby, keep fighting and come back to me. Come back to our baby girl who needs you." I weep, kissing his knuckles. "I'm going to be right here with you until you open those gorgeous green eyes and look at me again. We're all waiting for you to pull through this baby. You promised me you would come back, so I'm holding you to that promise." I tell him and kiss his hand again. I lean close to his ear and whisper. "I love you, love of my life."

"Shayla," I look back at the doctor, and he nods, informing me it's time to go. I look back at Cole and bite my lip.

"Your mum said she loves you very much," I tell him and place his hand back down carefully. "I'll be right outside, baby," I whisper and kiss my fingers and press them over his heart. I back away falteringly, my eyes never leaving him until the doctor guides me out of the room. The door closes, and I press myself against it, my face pressed to the glass looking at him. "Please, baby, don't give up. Fight for me," I breathe, closing my eyes, tears flowing down my face.

Once I take the gown and masks off, I walk out of the ICU back to where everyone was waiting. They all get up to their feet when they see me standing there, staring ahead with vacant eyes. I couldn't get the state of Cole out of my mind--that image would haunt me forever. Aimee and Jo come over to me, wrap their arms around me and walk me to the chairs. "Sit down, babe," Jo directs me down into the seat.

"Are you okay, sweetheart?" My mother asks, kneeling in front of me and cupping my face in her hands. "Shayla?" She shakes me, and I look at her.

"I think she's in shock," Josh states, standing next to her. He kneels beside her and turns my face so that I could look at him. "Shay, say something."

"He's so broken," I whisper, tears of despair rolling down my face. "He doesn't...he doesn't look like... Cole." I look into Josh's blue eyes and sob. "He doesn't look like Cole!"

"Hey, listen to me." He lifts my gaze to him when I hang my head. "What did Cole hate more than anything when it came to you?"

"To see me cry," I whisper, and Josh nods.

"Exactly, so you're going to pull yourself together for him and your baby. Do you hear me? Because when he wakes up and sees the state of you, he's going to beat the shit out of me for not looking after you." I close my eyes and shake my head with a heavy sigh. "Let's go get you some air and something to drink. All right?"

"I'm not leaving him." I refuse, shaking my head. "I promised him I'll wait out here, and I am till he wakes up."

"Shayla, Josh's right. Get some air. It will do you some good, Sis. We're all here, don't worry." Sam assures me. I look at Josh and the girls, who nod in response.

I sigh and allow them to walk me down to the cafeteria. We got some coffee, and I had a hot chocolate while we sat outside. "He's going to make it, right?" I ask no one in particular while staring down at my plastic cup.

"Of course he is," Aimee reassures me while taking my hand into hers. "You heard what the doctor said. He's fighting to stay alive."

I close my eyes. "I keep picturing Cole in that plane all alone. How terrified he must've been. I should have gone with him. I should have been there by his side."

Josh takes a seat next to me and rubs my back supportively. "Shayla, don't blame yourself. If you were there, all three of your lives would've been in danger. When I spoke to air control, they said the pilot reported turbine engine failure mid-flight just as they were crossing the North Sea and flying over Germany. The pilots had no other choice but to crash-land in an open field just over Germany to avoid colliding into the city and harming more people. Both pilot and the co-pilot died on impact, but Cole is so remarkably lucky to be alive right now."

I shake my head, "I would have rather been on that plane with him and died than live with the fear of losing him and having to face being without him." I tell him glumly. I wouldn't be able to bear going on without him. It sounds selfish, but it is what it is. I understand now more than ever how my mother felt after losing my father and why she couldn't face the world without him. You genuinely feel like a big part of yourself dies right along with them.

"Shayla, don't talk like that. What about your baby? No matter what, even if the worst happens, you will always have a part of Cole with you through your baby." Jo says, reaching up and wiping my tears away. "You conceived her through that fierce love you and Cole have for one another."

"And how am I supposed to look at her and not see Cole or remember what I've lost?" I cry, looking down at my stomach.

"Shayla, stop talking like you've already given up hope that he will pull through. Cole is in there fighting to stay alive for both of you." Aimee states and I sigh.

"Aimee, I'm scared." I sob, shaking my head. "I have this feeling of dread deep in my heart, and I can't seem to shake it."

"It's all going to be okay. You'll see. Cole's going to wake up, and you're both going to be blissfully happy again." Jo soothes me, and I exhale heavily.

"Oh God, I hope so."

$$\sim$$

OVER THE NEXT TWENTY-FOUR HOURS, Cole's parents, myself, and Josh stayed at the hospital. We sent the girls and my mother and brother home to get some rest after sixteen hours of no sleep. My mother tried to convince me to go back to hers and rest too, but I refused. There was no way I would leave Cole when he's in such a critical state. I'd worry even more being away from him. We all waited with bated breaths for the next forty-eight hours.

Thankfully, he was out of the woods, and the doctors told us that he would make a recovery physically, but they were still concerned about the slight swelling of his brain, so they kept him in an induced coma till the swelling goes down.

Cole was out of the ICU and in a private ward where I was allowed to stay with him. I refused to leave his side for ten days straight. I was only going home to shower and change and coming back to the hospital again.

Cole started to look like himself again, the wound on his head beginning to heal, and the bruises were clearing up.

On the eleventh day, Cole finally woke up. I was asleep in the chair beside his bed and jump awake when I hear him cough. His eyes were still closed, but he was moving his head and groaning. "Oh my God." I reach up and push the red button to get the doctors.

"Cole?" I say, moving over to his bedside. I take his hand in mine as he tries to peel his eyes open and blinks a couple of times. "Oh baby," I cry, kissing his hand when he looks at me. I heave a sigh of relief and brush my fingers through his hair as he blinks up at me, still disoriented. "Thank God you're okay." I declare, pressing my lips to his forehead.

The doctors come rushing into the room a couple of seconds later, along with Cole's parents and Josh. "He's awake." I sob, and his mother comes hurrying over to him.

"Oh, my baby." She whimpers, and Cole looks around the room, wincing. "It's so good to see you. You had us all so worried, sweetheart." Elaine tells him, brushing her hand delicately over his face, and he closes his eyes.

"Ladies, we'll need to examine him. If you could step aside for a couple of minutes, please." The doctor states, moving over to Cole. I let go of his hand and stand back as the doctor examines him.

"Welcome back, Cole. How are you feeling?" Dr Bennet questions and Cole shakes his head.

"Water." He croaks, wincing. I pick up a cup with a straw and move over to him.

"Here, baby." I slide my fingers at the nape of his neck and lift his head carefully so that he could drink through the straw. Cole's eyes meet mine, and he observes me as he drinks. Something's wrong. Cole isn't looking at me like he usually does. He blinks and lays back down, averting his eyes from me to the doctor.

"What happened to me?" Cole rasps, glancing around the room, perplexed.

"You were involved in a plane crash. Do you recall any of that?" Dr Bennet inquires, and Cole shakes his head slowly. "Okay, follow the light for me." He instructs. Cole follows the light, wincing. "Good. Are you feeling any dizziness or nausea at all, Cole?" Cole shakes his head again.

"My entire body hurts. I feel like I've been hit by a train."

"That's normal after the injuries you've sustained, son." The doctor utters, lifting his hand. "I'm going to check your reflexes. Tell me if you feel this." He adds, running a pen over his palm. Cole nods. "Wiggle your fingers for me?" Cole moves his fingers.

"Excellent. Do you feel this?" He brushes his pen over the bottom of his foot, and he nods. "Try to move your toes for me?" Cole moves his toes, and the doctor smiles, seemingly pleased. "Brilliant. Well, physically speaking, you're healing nicely, Cole. You will experience some discomfort when you pass urine the first couple of times—this is due to your ruptured kidney. One of your lungs was punctured by your broken ribs, and you have a hairline fracture on your skull. You have no idea how incredibly lucky you are to be alive. Someone up there must really love you. I don't know how you managed to fight through given the extent of your injuries, but we're all thrilled to see you up."

"How long have I been in here?" Cole questions looking around the room.

"Eleven days. You were in an induced coma. You've been through quite an ordeal, but you should be up and about in the next six to eight weeks." The doctor says with a smile while he looks at Cole's charts. I move over to Cole's bedside and take his hand into mine. He lifts his eyes to look at me with a frown, then at his hand in mine.

"You scared the hell out of me, baby," I say, and he lifts his gaze to mine again, tugging his hand out of mine.

"I'm sorry, do I know you?" He utters, looking at me blankly. I blink at him, look around the room, and laugh a little.

"Cole. Come on, baby, that's not funny," I chuckle, reaching for his hand, but he pulls it away with a deep frown. I look over at the doctor, watching us intently.

"Sweetheart, that's Shayla, *your wife*. You remember her." His mother tells him, and Cole looks at her and back at me, shaking his head, while his eyes rake over my face.

"Wife? I don't..." Cole mumbles. "I don't have a wife. I don't know her." I take a step back as I gaze into his eyes. No. There's no way. I look back when I feel Josh's hands on my upper arms, steadying me when my step falters.

"Cole, what's the last thing you remember?" The doctor questions moving toward him, and Cole frowns thoughtfully.

"Um, I remember leaving the office and meeting up with Josh and a few of our friends at The Shard--"

"Oh, my God," Josh whispers. "That was four years ago. That's around the time you met--"

"Sophie." Cole glances around the room. "Where is she? Why isn't she here?" He queries, looking at Josh again, who was looking down at me horrified.

"Cole. What year is it?"

Cole blinks, "It's 2016."

"What the hell is happening?" I utter, looking at the doctor, and he sighs, rubbing his forehead pensively.

"It seems Cole is suffering some memory loss."

"Some? He's missing four whole years of his life, Doctor. How could this happen?" His mother questions. I look over at Cole, who was staring vacantly at the wedding band on his finger. I move over to him, and he looks at me, his green eyes narrowed. I reach over and brush my fingers along his jaw.

"Do you really not remember me?" I ask him, and he stares at me and shakes his head.

"I'm sorry, I don't." I search the eyes that once looked at me with love and devotion, and when I see him staring back at me expressionlessly, my vision blurs, and I felt my heart snap and fall at my feet.

Cole watches me as I drearily turn and walk out of the room.

"Shayla." I hear Josh call my name as he comes after me. "Hey, hey, come here. It's okay." I fall into him, and he wraps his arms around me as I gasp, trying to catch my breath.

"Oh God. Josh, he doesn't remember me. How can he not remember me?" I cry. "How could this happen?"

"Shayla." I look over at the doctor, who places a hand on my shoulder. "I understand how devastated you must feel right now."

"Dr Bennet, please tell me this is only temporary, and he will remember again soon, please." I plead, and he sighs and takes his glasses off.

"Sweetheart, head injuries are very unpredictable. It's common that some impairments occur when a patient suffers a head injury. I can't tell you how long it will be before his memory returns, but I'm positive he will gradually start to remember. The swelling of his brain will cause confusion and erratic mood swings or personality changes plus the trauma of the incident--all of these things will have an impact on what he remembers and when." He explains, and I sigh. "I know it's not ideal, but you have to be strong and stick by him through this. The sooner Cole goes back to his old routine, the better it is for him." He adds, and I look over at Cole through the window.

"What do I do?" I inquire, averting my gaze from Cole to Dr Bennet again.

"Try and do things that you used to do together. Go to memorable places, do activities you would do together to try and jog his memory." He suggests and squeezes my shoulder. "Don't be angry or resentful toward him because it's not his fault he doesn't remember you. Keep telling yourself it's just a symptom of his injury. Just try to empathize with his situation; he's feeling very overwhelmed right now." I nod, closing my eyes. "He's alive. That's the main thing."

"Okay."

"I'm going to order a CT scan and run a couple of tests to see what we're dealing with, all right?" He tells me with a reassuring smile, and I nod, turning my gaze to Cole again, listening attentively to whatever his mother is telling him.

"He's going to remember you, Shay. How can he not?" Josh states with a frown looking over at his best friend.

"And if he doesn't? Then what, Josh? Do I just let him run off back to Sophie again?" I glower, pacing back and forth. "I don't know if I have the strength to do this all over again. At least last time he loved me, now he doesn't even know me." I cry, shaking my head despondently.

"Shayla, listen to me. If anyone can pull Cole through this, it's you. He fell in love with you before without even knowing it, and he will again, I promise you. You just be your beautiful self with him, do all the things you did together the first time around." I sigh deeply and close my eyes.

He did have a point.

After all, the mind may forget, but the heart never will. Right?

Chapter 4

COLE

"Cole, come on, one more bite." I shake my head with an agitated sigh, glaring at the forkful of food being shoved in my face.

"I don't want any more." I snarl, and Shayla glares back at me with those dark green eyes of hers. "I don't want it." I push it away from my face and roll my eyes.

"Cole, you need to eat so you can build up your strength. Come on, finish your food." She urges stubbornly, and I sigh, closing my eyes. I've never met a more stubborn and annoyingly persistent person in my life.

How the fuck did I end up married to her?

"Christ. Will you stop mothering me. I said I don't want it." I grit out, and Shayla exhales heavily, narrowing her eyes at me. "And while you're at it, you can stop glaring daggers at me too."

Shayla rolls her eyes, "Cole, the doctor said--"

"I know what the goddamn doctor said! I was in the room when he fucking said it. I don't need you to be persistently clucking around me. I get enough of that from my mother."

"Would you rather I let you starve? Or let you try and do it yourself and wind up hurting yourself more? Is that what you want, Cole?"

"What I want is to be left in peace for a goddamn minute without you fussing over me."

Shayla drops the fork and pushes her chair back, getting up furiously. "You can't take care of yourself in this state, Cole. You can barely move, for crying out loud! Unless you'd prefer your mother come in here and give you your sponge baths?" She argues, crossing her arms over her chest and looking at me expectantly.

I stare up at her, and when I don't say anything, she snorts and takes her seat again.

"I'm really struggling to understand why we ever got married in the first place. Remind me why I married you again?" I hiss testily, and she rolls her eyes in exasperation.

"You weren't such an arsehole the first time around. You also married me not once but *twice*." She retorts with a smarmy smile and proceeds to shove the forkful of chicken and mushroom pie in my face again. "Eat."

I push her hand away, scowling at her. "I must have been delirious," I utter cuttingly. "You still haven't told me how we met," I ask, staring at her questioningly, and she looks at me, wetting her pink lips

"I'll tell you what, for every forkful of pie you eat, I'll answer a question or give you a piece of information." She answers, lifting her brows challengingly, and I scoff.

"Stop treating me like a fucking child,"

"Then stop acting like one." She hisses back, dropping the fork on the tray and brushing her fingers through her hair in frustration. "Cole, I'm trying to help you. And all you've been doing is snapping at me."

"Did you ever stop to consider that I might not want your help? No one is forcing you to be here." I retort irritably and watch as she gets up and paces the room.

"Cole, I'm your wife!" Shayla grouses hotly. "Of course, I'm going to be here. Where else am I going to be?"

"How many times am I going to keep repeating myself? I don't know you—therefore, you're not my damn wife. I have a girlfriend! Sophie!"

Shayla stares at me for a long moment and shakes her head before she starts pacing again, her fingers curled in her dark hair while she mutters incoherently to herself. I watch her as she strides over to me and takes my face into her small hands, and she stares deeply into my eyes.

"Cole, listen to me. You do not have a girlfriend; you have a wife. *I'm* your wife, and I'm so in love with you, and you love me back. We're having a baby. Look..." She takes my hands and places them on her stomach. "That's our baby girl, our Alaia Mae, please, just try and remember *me*, remember *us*, Cole." She pleads, tears flowing down her pale cheeks. I avert my gaze, and she turns my face so I could look at her again. "Look at me, Cole." She cries, gazing penetratingly into my eyes. "Look into my eyes and feel the love I have for you, please." She sobs.

I search her green eyes and pull my hands away from her stomach and fist them by my side. "Shayla, I can't force myself to remember you," I state, pulling her hands away from my face. "I don't know you. I can't place you anywhere in my mind or my life. You've never existed to me before now...I'm sorry, but you don't." I tell her sincerely, and she takes a couple of steps back and shakes her head, her slender fingers trembling as she wipes away her tears.

"You'll remember, I know you will. You can scream and shout at me all you want, but I'm not giving up on us. I can't, not after everything we went through to be together. We fought too hard to be together just to throw it all away."

I rub my forehead and sigh tiredly, "Shayla, I can't fight for something I don't recall ever having. There's no saying when or even if my memory will ever come back. There's a chance I might never remember you or the life I had with you."

Shayla shrugs, sighing.

"Well, that's too bad because you're stuck with me. I'm not giving up, so I suggest you get used to having me around, *Lord Hoult*." She retorts back, placing her hands on her waist, and stares at me decidedly.

I close my eyes and tilt my head back. I was so beyond frustrated with everything. I've been awake for two days, and all I keep hearing from everyone is how much I love this girl and how we had this intense, magical love, but if it was so great, why was it wiped from my memory? Why don't I remember her? I should remember the girl I'm in love with-- especially if she's pregnant with my child--at least that's what everyone keeps telling me.

"It's time for your walk," Shayla says, walking over to me and pulling the covers back. I study her for a moment while she pulls her long brown hair over her right shoulder. I rack my brain for something familiar about her, but I draw a blank.

"When did you get pregnant?" I blurt out, and she looks at me startled, her olive-green eyes wide, and I swear she blushes a little.

"On our honeymoon." She answers, her voice barely over a whisper, and averts her gaze after holding mine for a touch too long.

Shayla has her hands out to me to help me out of bed. I wince and groan when I feel a surge of pain in my ribs whenever I move. "You okay, bab--" She starts to say but stops hastily, catching herself before she calls me 'baby' yet again.

She does that a lot.

I was getting the feeling we would call each other that quite a bit. "Hold on. Your gown is untied." She sighs and reaches behind me to tie the strings together.

Shayla's soft hair touches my cheek, and I turn my head when I smell something exotic and sweet. Where have I smelt that before? It felt vaguely familiar to me. "All right, come on."

Pulling back, she holds her hands out. I frown and take her offered hand and stand up. I hiss when I straighten, and the pain catches my breath. "Slow breaths Cole, Doctor Bennet said to avoid deep and sharp breaths. Short and shallow." Shayla speaks tenderly as she allows me to hold her arms as I take a couple of steps.

"Ahh fuck," I groan when a surge of pain ripples through me, and I stagger. Shayla steps closer to me, and I press my forehead to hers, trying to catch my breath.

"Do you want to stop?" She asks, lifting her eyes to mine. I shake my head and pull back a little.

"No." Shayla nods, and each time I took a step forward, she took one back, supporting me the entire time.

This was our routine for the next few weeks until I was able to move on my own. Shayla helped me with everything despite me snapping at her continually. I'd catch her eyes well up, but she blinks the tears away and exhales.

I was truly fed up with being cooped up in bed. After we left the hospital, we went back to the place I supposedly share with Shayla. Josh and two other girls-- Shayla's best friends Aimee and Jo helped bring me to the house. I look around the house and frown when nothing felt familiar to me. It felt as though I was in a stranger's home, despite the photos of Shayla and me on the walls. It didn't feel like home to me. I felt nothing.

I stood there staring at the enlarged photo of Shayla and me above a fireplace. We were dancing at what I'm assuming was *our* wedding, considering I'm in a tux, and she's in a bridal gown. I'm gazing into her eyes, and she's looking up at me lovingly, both of us smiling happily at one another with our arms wrapped around each other. "That was the happiest day of your life, bro." I look at Josh when he comes and stands beside me, looking up at the photo.

I shake my head and sigh. "I feel like I'm looking at an entirely different person. That person there looks like me but doesn't feel like me." I look at the photo and stare at Shayla's face. "How can I go from looking at her like that to feeling nothing at all?" I sigh, rubbing my hands over my face. "Josh, where is Sophie? I was happy with Sophie." I express, and Josh looks at me, shaking his head.

"Cole, that was four years ago. Sophie walked out on you and broke your heart, and then you met Shayla and fell out of your mind in love with her. You tried again with Sophie after you and Shay got divorced. You even almost married her despite being in love with Shay because she lied to you and tried to tell you that her ex-fiancé's baby was yours. She tried to trap you." Josh tells me, and I stare at him bewildered. "When you found out you were livid, you left her on your wedding day and went running after Shayla to stop her from leaving for Canada."

I sigh, rubbing my hands over my face, aggravated. "Everything you're telling me just feels so unfamiliar to me. This whole thing I had with Shayla sounds fucking messy and so unlike me. I ran off and married her in Vegas the night I met her? *Me?*" I press incredulously, shaking my head. "I would never do something like that. Period."

"No?" Josh nods and unlocks his phone, scrolling through it before he hands it to me. "Watch that." I take the phone and watch a video of Shayla and me in a chapel laughing hysterically. "That's the night you met her. Shay has changed your whole life for the better, man. You may not remember this, but you put her through hell, so much so that she was running away halfway across the world to disappear from your life." I watch the video of myself carrying Shayla out of the chapel kissing. "The whole world was in awe of your love for one another."

I rub my temples tiredly, "Enough, Josh, I'm tired of hearing about this great fucking love. I don't love her. I don't even fucking know her! She's just a girl I've never met in my life." I shout angrily and turn to walk off when I see Shayla standing there. Our eyes meet across the room, and even from afar, I can see the hurt and tears gathered in her eyes at my outburst. I shake my head and walk off toward the front door. I yank it open, ignoring the pain in my ribs, and storm out of the house.

I'm fucking fed up with people telling me what I should be feeling or how I should be feeling about everything. Does no one give a shit about how I feel? I almost fucking died, and all everyone keeps blubbering on about is how much I loved this girl. She's a girl. No different from all the bloody others. Did I feel a little bad for her? Sure. It can't be easy on her, but I can't force myself to feel something for her when I don't.

I wander around aimlessly for a while before I go back to the house. Josh and the two girls had left, and the place was quiet. As I walk through, I wonder if Shayla left with them until I heard noises coming from the first floor. I follow the sound, making my way up the steps one at a time, groaning at the pain of my ribs. I stop outside the door when I hear the distinct sound of someone crying. I wouldn't even call it crying, no, it was sobbing, like when you're in absolute agony, and you can't catch your breath. It was Shayla. I press my forehead to the door and close my eyes, my chest got tight, and my breath constricted the longer I listened to her weeping.

Something deep inside my gut made me push the door open and walk into the bedroom. Shayla was curled up on the bed in the foetal position crying, her whole body shaking with hoarse sobs. I feel like a real arsehole for hurting her. I walk to the bed and sit at the end, my head cast down while I stare at the floor. "I'm sorry," I apologise and glance over at her. I couldn't see her face with the way she was lying. She doesn't say anything for a while, only sniffles quietly.

"Please leave me alone." Comes her whispered reply, her voice breaking. I close my eyes for a second and turn to face her properly.

"Shayla, I'm sorry, I didn't mean for it to come out like that. I just--"

"You don't love me. I get it." I bite my lip. "I'm fine, just please... leave me alone." She weeps wretchedly, burying her face into the pillow. I sigh, defeated, and stand up. "Your bed is ready next door. If you need anything, you can shout." She whispers, and I stare at her back for a moment and nod before I walk out of the room, leaving her alone.

I lay on the bed staring at the plain white ceiling all night. I had so much on my mind, so many questions I couldn't find the answers to. The doctor said the best place for me was with Shayla because that's my routine, but it didn't feel normal. I couldn't stop thinking about Sophie and everything Josh told me about her. I should be with Sophie-- my girlfriend right now. I wince at the ache in my head--nothing makes any sense. I look over at the wall separating my room from Shayla's and wonder if she's asleep. With a frustrated sigh, I push myself up and opt for a long hot shower. I walk out of the bedroom and look around for the bathroom. My ribs were killing me. Where the hell did she put my painkillers? I see the light under the door to Shayla's room and notice the door was ajar.

I push it open and look around the bedroom. The shower was running in the en suite. "Shayla?" I call out, holding my ribs as I move over to the bathroom. "Shayla," I call again and get nothing. I feel a surge of panic rise in my gut when I get no answer from her. What if she's hurt? The door swiftly opens, and she appears in front of me naked and dripping wet. Shayla jumps, startled, and lets out an adorable squeak, looking up at me, her green eyes wide.

"Cole." She breathes, clearly surprised to see me standing there.

"Uh..." My eyes rake over her body, and she shrinks back a little under my gaze before picking up a towel. "Pills," I mumble when she wraps the towel around herself, her cheeks pink. Oh damn, that's cute as hell.

"Oh, they're in here." She tells me and turns to walk into the bathroom again. She comes back two seconds later, holding a bottle of pills.

I take them from her and nod. "Thank you. Would you mind if I shower? I can still smell the hospital on my skin." Shayla nods and steps aside.

"Cole, this is your house, too." She replies with a sigh. "You don't have to ask my permission. This is your bedroom just as much as it is mine. Your clothes, your stuff is all in here. I only prepared the other room just in case you felt uncomfortable sleeping in here with me." She explains, looking around the room, and I rub the back of my neck awkwardly.

"I know you probably don't want to hear this, but it doesn't feel like home to me," I tell her earnestly and once again see the sadness in her eyes. "I mean, not yet anyway," I add, and she nods.

"Yeah, I suppose it would feel strange to you, wouldn't it?" She utters, biting her lip with a shrug. "I'll let you shower." She whispers and walks further into the bedroom. I watch her for a couple of seconds while she slides the cupboard open and looks through it with a little frown on her face as if she were in deep thought.

I walk into the bathroom and breathe in that exotic smell again. It was passion fruit and coconut. Is that her shampoo? I toss a couple of painkillers in my mouth and swallow them.

That should take the edge off the pain for a couple of hours. I try and lift my shirt off, but every time I move, my ribs hurt like a bitch. "Ahh shit." I groan, exhaling as the doctor told me to.

"Cole, are you all right?" I hear Shayla ask from behind me. I bite my lip with a shake of my head.

"I can't." I groan, closing my eyes. "Would you mind helping me get undressed?" I ask, and she nods and moves over to me.

"Of course." I watch while she steps in front of me, her bottom lip between her teeth. "Lift your arms slowly," Shayla instructs, patiently waiting for me to lift my arms over my head. I hiss when I move, and a sharp pain makes me keel over.

"Ahh." I whimper, closing my eyes, and Shayla steadies me by placing her small hands on my shoulders.

"Careful baby," She whispers in my ear, helping me upright again. "Stay still." Shayla lifts my t-shirt carefully up and over my head. I open my eyes and watch her as she brushes her fingers over the bruises on my ribcage. Her eyes glaze over a little, and I see them well up. I inhale deeply, not because she hurt me but because her touch sent a tremor through me. Shayla jumps and pulls her hand back, lifting her eyes to mine. "I'm sorry." She breathes, looking at me apologetically, and I shake my head.

"You didn't hurt me. Your hands are a little cold." I assure her, and she nods, focussing her attention on unbuttoning my jeans and feebly tugs them down my legs. I step out of them, and she stands up again. Not even the slightest bit phased that I was standing butt naked in front of her. Why would she be phased? I'm her husband, after all. She's obviously seen me naked, but a tiny part of me was a little disappointed for some strange reason.

I watch her as she runs the shower for me and turns to look at me again. "If you need anything, just give me a shout." I nod and thank her before she walks out of the bathroom, leaving me to shower.

OVER THE NEXT couple of weeks, things went from bad to worse between Shayla and me. I was almost fully healed, my ribs only a dull ache. Our frustration with one another hit its peak. We were continually arguing and butting heads at home and work. I was yet to remember a thing about the last four years, and it was beginning to get on my nerves. I'm missing a huge chunk of my life, and I can't remember a single thing. There was one moment where I thought I remembered something, but it passed too quickly, so I wasn't sure if it was a dream or a memory.

Frankly, the longer I'm stuck living with Shayla, the more baffled I am about why I fell in love with her in the first place-- or even married her *twice*, for that matter.

She's so fucking stubborn; it's infuriating. For example, the other night, we sat in the living room listening to a couple of songs that seemingly held some special meaning to us. "Shayla, I do not remember any of these songs. This is pointless." I sigh, rubbing my forehead, and she rolls her eyes.

"Cole, you're not even trying if you'd just listen--"

"I am listening, Shayla!" I shout, agitated. "Do you think I'm sitting here for the fucking fun of it? I don't remember any of these stupid songs, all right!" I yell at her and get up. I storm off, leaving her sitting there watching me as I walk out of the house, slamming the door shut behind me.

I don't know how much more of this I can truthfully take. It's becoming unbearable living together. I can't even go someplace to talk to someone because everywhere I go, people talk about Shayla and how much I loved her. Josh, my parents, my employees. It's the same old spiel every damn time, and I'm sick of it. If I was happy before, I sure as shit am not now-- and neither is she.

Where was this great love of ours? Shouldn't I have remembered something about us by now? It's been almost three weeks, and I'm no closer to placing anything. People keep waffling on about how great Shayla is, but what about the four years of hard work I put into these projects and can't remember a single thing about any of them. I'm sat here in my office at home staring at the last project I was working on before my accident, and for the life of me, I can't figure any of it out. It's really beginning to grate me.

"Cole?" I look up and see Shayla in the doorway, watching me. "Why don't you take a break from work and let's go out for a bit?" She suggests, and I sigh, rubbing my hands over my face.

"I have too much work to do, Shayla," I reply, looking down at the files in front of me. Shayla walks over to me and leans against my desk, looking at me.

"Work can wait. Besides, you're getting nowhere just sitting there staring at it. You were already having trouble with this project before the accident. You'll figure it out. You always do." She assures me, and I lean back in my chair and look at her. "I want to take you someplace special to me."

I nod and bite my lip. I suppose a little break wouldn't hurt. "Okay." I agree, and she smiles.

Thirty minutes later, we walked along the river toward a crowded place with fairy lights, carts, food trucks, and music. "What is this place?" I ask her as we walk through the crowd, and she smiles up at me.

"Our favourite place." She says, lacing her fingers with mine. I look down at our hands and back at her. "Before we got divorced, you took me to play crazy golf, and we made a bet that night. If I won, you agreed to end our agreement to stay married early, and if you won, you got to kiss me whenever you wanted for a week." Shayla explains as we walk, and I smile a little.

"Who won?" I question, and she smiles, licking her lips.

"You did." I nod, smiling, and watch her as she leans over and hugs a little girl that comes running over to her.

"Shayla!"

"Hi Esme, how's my little princess?" She greets her and squeezes her nose gently. "I'm going to get something to eat with Uncle Cole real quick, and then I'm going to find you, and we're going to dance, okay?" Esme beams at her and nods. Esme lifts her chocolate-coloured orbs to me and smiles beautifully.

"Hi, Uncle Cole." She waves at me, and I feel my heart melt. I perch down in front of her and touch her little chin.

"Hi, Gorgeous girl." I smile when she hugs me and runs off toward a truck. I stand up and look at Shayla, who was watching me.

"What?" I ask, looking down at her, and she smiles a little.

"You called her Gorgeous girl." She states and I nod with a shrug. "That's what you call me." I frown, but before I had time to dwell on it, Shayla was pulling me through the crowd of people toward the cart Esme ran to.

"Princesa!" The beefy man inside the truck excitedly shouts when we walk over to the truck. "Hola Muchacho." He greets me. I blink and look at Shayla, who stood beaming at the man.

"Rico! Como estas, Guapo?" Shayla replies as he leans over, and they do a special handshake. I watch the two interact, and Shayla speaks to him in Spanish, and his face falls before he looks at me sullenly and back at Shayla, his hand on his mouth.

"I'm truly sorry to hear what you've suffered, brother. I'll be praying for you to heal and get your memory back promptly." He tells me, holding out his hand, and I nod shaking it. "Maybe my Shayla special will help jog your memory, huh Muchacho?" He grins at me, and I nod with a shrug and look at Shayla, confused, who giggles a little.

"Shayla special is a dish he prepares for me whenever I'm here. It's also your favourite." She explains, and I nod in understanding.

"I see," I utter and look around at the crowd of people everywhere. "So, you speak Spanish?" I ask, and she nods with a pretty smile. "You're just full of surprises, aren't you?"

Shayla chuckles and rubs her forehead. "You have no idea. So, anything seem familiar to you at all?" She questions, a little hopeful, but when I shake my head, she bites her lip and averts her gaze.

"Here you go, Guapa," Rico says, handing us the food. I reach for my wallet, and he shakes his head, waving it off. "You take good care of my girls, both of them." He tells me, gesturing to Shayla and the baby.

I nod and smile a little, "Of course." I tell him, and he winks at Shayla, and we start walking through the crowd of people again. I look at the food in my hand and sniff it. It actually smells quite nice. I eat a little and moan, closing my eyes at the explosion of flavours in my mouth. "Mm, wow. This is excellent. What is it?"

Shayla smiles, shaking her head, "It's paella." We eat our food, and she pulls me through to another cart. "So, I take it we're following the steps we did the first time we came here?" I ask, looking down at her, and she nods and looks at me. "Did I just stand around like a sap the whole time?"

Shayla sighs and hands me a giant triangle pastry. "No, you did not. You were a lot happier last time. You couldn't keep your hands off me."

She explains, dropping her gaze as we walk. "You would always find excuses to touch me, whether it was brushing your fingers through my hair or poking me or pinching my nose because you knew I hated it, and you got off on teasing and torturing me." I look over at her and bite my lip.

That sounds nothing like me.

"Shayla, I know this is all really hard on you. I wish I could remember something about us. I honestly do. I mean, it sounds like we had some great times together. But that Cole that you knew isn't me. I don't like public displays of affection. I get uncomfortable and clam up. It's not because I don't want to touch you and try and be close to you. I just..."

Shayla shakes her head, chewing her lip, "I get it, Cole, you're not the same man I fell in love with. He was passionate and didn't take himself so seriously. We had great chemistry, and we couldn't stay away from one another, like two magnets we'd constantly be drawn to each other." She explains with a heavy sigh while picking at her food. "I just don't understand how you can go from that Cole, who was affectionate and fiery, to this cold and frigid version. It's like you're two completely different people. It's just weird." She adds with a shrug as we walk over to a crowd of people dancing. Did she just refer to me as a robot?

I shake my head and open my mouth to say something, but a tall brunette suddenly pops up, takes her hand, and pulls her to the crowd of people dancing.

What the fuck?

Shayla laughs as he spins her around, and they start to dance together. I watch as she sways her hips to the rhythm of the song, and he holds her hips drawing her closer against him. I fist my hands at my side and clench my jaw tight as I watch them singing to one another and dancing passionately. Their foreheads pressed together, smiling, arms wrapped around one another.

Hell no.

I don't know what came over me, but I felt my gut clench tight, and I found myself walking through the crowd toward them. I curl my fingers around Shayla's wrist and yank her to me. I glare at the guy firmly, and he nods once, holding his hands up, and scampers off. I look down into her face, and Shayla looks up into my eyes, her lips parted, softly panting. We stand there, staring at one another. My eyes drift down to her soft lips before they meet her eyes again, and I suddenly have the most overwhelming urge to kiss her.

Chapter 5

SHAYLA

"So?" Aimee questions, looking at me, her blue eyes wide and hopeful. "Did it work?" I shrug and look around, gnawing on my bottom lip. "I mean the way he possessively pulled you away from Dante, from over here it looked like he was a little jealous?"

"It absolutely did. That was very Cole." Jo agrees, biting into her churro and chewing gingerly.

"Oh, girls, I don't know. I mean, the way he was looking at me for a very brief second, it felt like it used to." I explain, glancing over at Cole talking to Josh, a profoundly serious expression on his face.

The girls decided we should test and see if Cole would still get jealous if he saw another guy near me or touching me, and sure enough, he did react like I hoped he would when he saw Dante— my very good-looking, completely gay friend—dancing with me. I thought he would kiss me when he pulled me away from him, but he didn't. He asked who Dante was, and when I told him he was my friend, he went right back to his emotionless self again.

"That's fantastic, Shay. It means he still cares enough to get jealous of another man touching you. You need to keep pushing him into feeling these things, and eventually, he will start to realise that he does love you." Aimee tells me while I watch Cole sullenly. I miss him so much, and it kills me every time he looks at me, and I don't see that love in his eyes. He's so different, so cold, distant, and moody.

That's not the Cole I know. Where was the guy who would touch me and constantly want to be around me? Where did that passionate man go that would gaze deep into my eyes and tell me he wants me and would die if he didn't have me. Where was *he*?

"I really hope so, Aimes, because the way we're going now, I don't see us making it through this at all," I whisper woefully, and Aimee shakes her head.

"Shayla, babe, don't say that. You have to keep fighting for him. As much as it hurts, you can't give up." I shake my head and look at her with a sigh.

"You think I want to? Of course, I don't. I'm still in love with him, but he doesn't love me, or at least he doesn't remember that he does." I mutter, closing my eyes.

"If anyone is going to pull him through this, it's you, Shayla. You might have been wiped from his mind but, you're still etched in his heart. Every time you think about giving up, you remember that, okay?" Jo expresses, taking my face into her hands and looking at me. "Who knows, one day he might wake up and remember everything. You just have to be patient and hold onto the hope that he will remember. A love as strong as yours doesn't disappear overnight."

I nod and bite my lip, glancing over at him again. Cole was watching me. Our eyes meet, and I feel my heart race like it used to when we first met.

I can do this. I love him too much to lose him. Cole looks away and turns his attention back to Josh, and nods. I wonder what Josh was telling him. "Shayla?" I look down at Esme and smile at her. "Can we dance now?" She asks excitedly. I nod and take her hand. We walk over to the crowd dancing, and we start to dance together. Esme was Rico's five-year-old daughter. She's the sweetest thing. I laugh and spin her around while we sing and sway together. Aimee and Jo join us, and we all dance with her. I watch as Esme runs off toward Cole and Josh and pulls them to come and join us.

Josh scoops her up into his arms, and they walk over to us. Jo, Aimee, and Josh dance with Esme while Cole comes over to me.

"Dance with me?" I ask with a smile, and he hesitates for a moment but nods and steps closer to me. I take his hands and place them at my waist, and I rest my hands on his chest, and we sway together.

"You're an incredible dancer," Cole tells me as he snakes his arms around my waist, drawing me closer against him. I smile up at him and lick my lips enticingly, drawing his eyes from mine to my lips.

"So are you," I reply, wrapping my arms around his neck, and he smiles, pressing his forehead to mine while we dance together. Cole jumps when he feels the baby kick against his stomach and looks down.

"Was that...?" He trails off, his green eyes wide.

"Your baby girl? Yes, it was. It seems she's as excited to be dancing with Daddy as I am." I tell him sincerely, and he stares down at my stomach, and for the first time since his accident, he places his hand on my tummy. I smile when he looks into my eyes and bites his lip.

"I can see why this place is so special to us." He tells me, looking around as we sway together.

"It really is astounding."

"It sure is."

"What did we do after we danced last time?" I smile.

"I uh, made you try churros for the first time, and we sat on the banks by the river over there till closing time just talking and..."

"And...?" Cole presses, and I feel my face go all hot.

"Kissing," I finish, staring into his eyes while he nods wistfully

"Right, I was taking full advantage of the bet, I take it." He smirks, and I nod with a shrug.

"You sure were, but that one week following the bet was one of the best weeks we spent together. You broke down all the walls around my heart, and it was in that week that I realised I was in love with you." I confess, and Cole heaves a sigh and rubs his forehead, taking a step back from me when the song ends.

"I want to remember Shayla. Josh keeps saying if anyone has the power to pull me through this, it's you. Do you think maybe we can start over, like go back to the beginning and act like we just met?" He suggests, and I nod in response. "Maybe if I get to know you again as I did before, it may help jog my memory."

"Of course we can," I answer, and he smiles a little, nodding. "But on one condition," I add, and he looks at me questioningly.

"You need to relax a little and drop this whole awkward, robotic demeanour you've got going on. Don't overthink and hold yourself back. Even on the first day we met, you were confident and charming. Where is that guy?" I question, and he looks at me bewildered and frowns a little. "Cole, we never had an awkward moment ever, we were always comfortable around each other, so if you want this to work, you need to relax around me."

Cole clears his throat and rubs the back of his neck awkwardly. "All right, I can do that." He agrees, and I nod, smiling up at him.

"Great. Then..." I hold out my hand to Cole. "Hi, I'm Shayla." I introduce myself, and Cole looks at my hand and back at me with a smirk.

"Is this how we met the first time?" He questions his brows up in his hairline, and I chuckle and shake my head.

"Nope, the first time I accidentally backed up against your chest, and you said, 'Dance with me.' in my ear, and then you said, 'what's your name, sweetheart?'" I explain, and Cole nods, licking his lips.

"Oh, so..." I gasp when Cole takes my hand and spins me, so my back was pressed against his chest.

I close my eyes when his lips brush against the shell of my ear when he speaks into my ear. "Dance with me."

I smile and bite my lip. I tilt my head back and look up at him with a mischievous smile.

"Was that a demand or a request."

Cole's eyes narrow a little before he smirks, "I'm happy with either as long as you're dancing with me." He drawls while I smile up at him. "What's your name, sweetheart?"

"Shayla. Yours?" I ask, and he looks into my eyes and grins, showing his dimples exactly the way he did that night.

My heart starts to beat like crazy in my chest.

"Cole." He replies with a lick of his lips, eyes narrowing a little as he studies my face. "How about I take you out to dinner this week?"

I turn to face him and shake my head. "Dinner? No." Cole frowns a little, and I chuckle. "I don't do dinners. I'm all about adventures. I prefer doing something more fun where we can interact and get to know each other more rather than sit around in a restaurant making small talk." I explain, and Cole nods in understanding.

"Such as?"

I shrug and bite my lip, "That is for you to figure out, stud." Cole chuckles while he looks around, pursing his lips a little.

"Okay, we're obviously limited to what we can do." He drawls, looking down at my baby bump, and I shrug, nodding in response.

"I'm easily pleased. It doesn't have to be anything outlandish or lavish." I pull him through the crowd toward the churro cart. "You can start by buying me churros." I grin, and he laughs. I look over at Josh and the girls watching us while he was paying for the churros, and they all smile, nodding supportively.

I sigh and place my hand on my stomach, inwardly praying this whole thing works for all our sakes. Cole hands me the churros, and we walk over to the banks like we did last time and sit down. I fed him churros, and he--of course, loved them. He asked me questions about the night we met, and I told him about the day I showed up at his office as his assistant, at which he laughed hysterically. "That sounds like the plotline of a cliché romantic comedy film."

"Yeah, then you had the cheek to accuse me of stalking you when I didn't even know who you were in the first place," I tell him, sucking the caramel syrup and cinnamon sugar off my fingers. Cole reaches up and brushes his thumb over my bottom lip, eyes on mine while his thumb lingers for a second, and he blinks a couple of times, brows knitting together. "You okay?" I ask, and he nods.

"Yeah, you know when you're doing something, and you all of a sudden have a déjà vu." He expresses, perplexed, and I shift putting the churros down.

"Cole, this moment feels familiar because we've lived it before," I tell him with a smile, and he brushes his fingers along my jaw-- a distant look in his eyes, and I could see he was trying to recall something.

"What is it?"

Cole blinks and shakes his head before his hand drops from my jaw. "Nothing, I uh, I had a weird hallucination, I think."

I sit upright, "A hallucination? Of what?"

Cole frowns, looking at me, "You...standing in the rain looking up at me with so much... misery in your eyes." He whispers, and I take his hand in mine.

"Cole, you're starting to remember. That was the day I found out you were engaged to Sophie. We got back from presenting my design for the super hotel in Dubai. Do you recall our trip to Dubai?" I ask him, and he frowns, shaking his head.

"No. Only that moment with you standing in the pouring rain looking at me with such anguish in your eyes. That's all." Cole sighs, brushing his fingers through his hair, "Josh wasn't exaggerating when he said I put you through hell, was he?"

I sigh and shake my head. "No, he wasn't. I've been through a lot in my life, but that period with you was by far the most pain I have ever suffered in my life. You broke me, again and again. I walked out of your life twice, and you would come find me and bring me back, then something else would happen that would wreck me all over again." I explain, absent-mindedly brushing my thumb over his knuckles while I recall the pain I suffered.

"And you still loved me despite all the pain I put you through?" Cole questions reaching up and brushing his fingers through my hair as he used to. My heart aches gravely, and I close my eyes.

"I did, like crazy. I still do." I whisper, leaning into his touch. I open my eyes and look at him, watching me sadly. Cole pulls his hand back and closes his eyes briefly, swallowing hard.

"I know." He utters, looking everywhere but at me uneasily. "It's getting late, shall we go?" I nod, getting up to my feet. We walk back to the car and head back home.

LATER THAT NIGHT, I lay in bed, unable to sleep. I felt a little glimmer of hope that he was starting to remember. Maybe that means his memory is gradually coming back.

It was past three in the morning when I finally dozed off, only to jump awake when I heard a strangled cry from the room next door. I push the covers off and rush out of the bedroom to Cole's room next door.

I hurry into the bedroom and turn the lamp on beside his bed. Cole's eyes were squeezed shut, and he was vigorously shaking his head, whispering 'No' again and again. He's having a nightmare. I crawl up on the bed beside him and touch his face, pearls of cold sweat rolling down his face.

"Cole. Hey, it's okay, baby, wake up," I say, shaking him a little. "Cole." I jump when he suddenly shoots up with a gasp, panting, trying to catch his breath. His eyes dart around the room, disoriented. "You're okay. It's just a nightmare, baby. You're safe," I whisper soothingly, cupping his face with my hands. Cole looks at me and heaves a shaky breath of relief, and wraps his arms around me, hugging me tight, "Are you all right?" I ask, wrapping my arms around him and brushing my fingers through his damp hair and feel him nod slowly.

After a couple of seconds, Cole pulls back, and I run my fingers down his chest, where I felt his heart beating wildly against my hand. "Cole, your heart is racing," I whisper as he inhales and exhales, his chest rising and falling quickly. "What were you dreaming about?"

Cole shakes his head and looks at me, "I don't know. It was all in pieces. I can't...explain it. I just remember the fear... as I've never felt before. Flashing lights, voices, and constant beeping."

I stroke his jaw, and he presses his forehead to mine. "It's all right. It was just a dream. You're safe now." I comfort him, and he bites his lip, wincing a little. "Let me get you some water," I shift to get off the bed, but he grabs my hand, stopping me. I glance back at him and met his beseeching gaze.

Cole shakes his head, holding my gaze, "Stay with me?"

I nod.

"Of course." I pull the covers back and climb into bed with him. Cole shifts to the other side to give me some space to lay down facing one another. He looks so troubled and frightened it broke me so much. The nightmare must have been of the crash. Dr Bennet did say most patients that suffer trauma from accidents often block out the memories in fear of reliving them.

"Tell me something about you," Cole utters, looking at me. I bite my lip thoughtfully.

"Um, what do you want to know?" Cole shrugs, hugging his pillow.

"I need to understand why or how I fell in love with you." I watch him as his eyes search mine. "You make no sense to me at all."

I exhale deeply. "Cole, I can't tell you the reasons why you fell in love with me. Only you know the answer to that--or you did know the answer to that." I answer, chewing on my lip. "We spent six months together at work and home, so we got to know one another really well. We laughed, we fought, we bickered, we fooled around...a lot. Our attraction for one another and the chemistry we had, played an incredibly significant part in us falling in love."

Cole sighs, closing his eyes, "The harder I tried to resist you, the more I wanted you, and it was the same for you. We'd go to bed on separate sides of the bed and somehow wake up in each other's arms." I smile fondly. "You made me feel a type of way I'd never felt before," I whisper, closing my eyes recalling all the moments he would tease me relentlessly. "You would suck me into this sexual trance with the barest of touches, and you'd whisper things to me that would take my breath away and make me dizzy with desire." I open my eyes and watch Cole, his eyes closed, his lips parted.

"You even made me orgasm once without touching me."

Cole's eyes open, and he looks at me, astonished. "I did?" I nod, swallowing hard. "How?"

"This was on the day I moved into your apartment. As always, we were bickering. I called you an egomaniac, and you didn't like it. You were showing me the difference between arrogance and confidence." I smile, wetting my lips. "You had me on my back, with you on top of me, your leg in between mine pressing against me intimately," I explain, closing my eyes again while Cole watches me, lifting himself, so his head was resting in his hand, peering down into my face. "You asked me if I remembered what you said to me in the elevator in Vegas the night we met."

"What did I say?"

"I can't wait to taste you, baby," I whisper, looking up at him as he stares down into my face. His Adam's apple jumps in his throat when he swallows.

"And then what happened?" He questions, and I—by some means—plucked up the courage and lean up, gently push him onto his back. Cole lays back and looks up at me, watching me intently.

"Then you said..." I breathe, brushing my lips against the shell of his ear like he did mine. "What if I told you I can still remember just the way you taste and would give anything to taste you again..." I whisper in his ear. "Would you let me taste you, baby? Would you let me flick my tongue over your clit and suck it just a little?" I say with a breathy moan. Cole's breathing quickens when I run my tongue teasingly against the shell of his ear, and he instinctively pushes his thigh up against me.

"And then." He moans, biting his lip.

"And then you said..." I sigh, "What if I told you that I wish I could bury myself deep inside you right now, just to feel you clamp down on my dick as you come hard." I whisper, rocking my hips against his thigh the same way I did that day. "Would you want me to, baby?" I murmur in his ear, nipping faintly. Cole groans and rolls me over onto my back and looks down into my eyes. The hunger in his eyes stole the breath right out of my lungs. "What if I told you I was dying to kiss you right now..." I moan, pressing my forehead to his. "Would you let me, baby?" I whisper, brushing my thumb over his lips.

"Shayla." Cole moans, rocking against me, sweeping his tongue along my thumb, and sucking softly. I hiss, ghosting my lips over his.

"Cole," I whimper and arch up as he grinds himself against me, the friction sending shock waves through me. "You feel that ache deep inside you, baby?" I purr, trailing my lips along his jaw, and he bites his lip hard. "That heat that consumes you and makes your mind all hazy. That's not even a fraction of the passion and need we have for one another." I breathe, licking up his throat. "We make each other crazy." I moan, sucking the part of his neck I know drives him wild.

"Fuck," Cole growls, bucking his hips, rubbing himself against me harder, making me cry out. "What are you doing to me." He groans when I suck his pulse point.

"Giving you just a taste of our love."

Cole leans down to kiss me, but I stop him just as his lips push mine apart, and his tongue seeks out my own. "Ah, ah."

"Let me kiss you." He pleads hungrily, and I shake my head, despite dying to be kissed by him. I figure if I had any chance of getting him to remember us, he needs to recall how much he wanted and yearned for me first.

"You have to earn that pleasure." I moan, trailing my tongue along his bottom lip, and he groans throatily, leaning in to kiss me, but I pull back.

"Shayla, please..."

Chapter 6

COLE

"SIX WEEKS and eight days since my accident and I still haven't got my memory back."

Dr Bennet observes me and takes his glasses off. "Cole, I understand your frustration, son, but brain trauma isn't like any other physical illness or a broken bone. We can't just bring all your memories back with an operation. The brain is the most complex organ we possess, and it's very unpredictable. I am confident your memory will come back in time. The question is, do you want your memory to come back?"

I stare at Dr Bennet blankly for a couple of seconds. What kind of question is that? "Of course I do. I'm missing a huge chunk of my life. One day, I woke up with a wife and a baby on the way four years in the future. In a life that is unfamiliar to me. I've also been having some bizarre dreams lately."

"How so?"

I frown and shrug, "I don't know. It's all a jumbled mess in my head. Some nights it's Sophie, and other nights it's Shayla. I don't know if it's a memory or a dream. How do you even differentiate between them?" I ask, rubbing my forehead with a sigh. Dr Bennet leans forward, narrowing his brown eyes at me thoughtfully.

"Dreams are stored in our short-term memory, and it disappears after a little while. Our memories, however, are stored in our long-term memory, which you won't forget. Can you recall these dreams after you've had them?"

I lean forward and rub my eyes with my thumb and finger. "I don't know. My head is a literal mess. I don't know what feeling is real and what isn't any more. It's so aggravating." I say, rubbing my temples.

"Your CT scan came back perfect Cole, the swelling has completely subsided, so all you need now is time, don't force yourself, let your body do its thing, and hopefully, you'll soon start to remember." I nod and stand up. Dr Bennet walks me to the door and shakes my hand. "Don't forget what I told you. Sometimes our fear causes us to suppress certain things from our past, that could be the key to unlocking your memories." He explains and pats my shoulder with a kind smile.

"Thank you, Dr Bennet, for everything." I smile and walk out of his office when he nods in response.

My mind was in a haze as I walk mindlessly through the hospital corridor. "Tristan?" I stop dead in my tracks when I hear her voice. Sophie. I turn slowly and face her. I gaze into those familiar blue eyes and resist the urge to walk over and pull her into my arms.

"Soph?" I utter surprised to see her standing in front of me. She appears just as I remember her. Absolutely gorgeous, but there was a deep sadness in her eyes. "Hi."

"Hi Tristan," She responds a little hesitantly. "I heard about your accident. It was all over the news and papers. I wanted to come and see you, but I didn't think you would want to see me after everything that happened." She explains, and I frown a little. "I'm so glad you're okay. I've been so worried."

I nod and clear my throat, "I don't, uh, the accident caused some memory loss, so I don't remember anything that happened. Only what others have told me." I explain, and she frowns and takes a step toward me. I rake my eyes over her, a little confused. "Josh mentioned you were pregnant. Have you had the baby already?" I question and notice her eyes fill with tears. Sophie bites her lip, shaking her head.

"No, I lost the baby a couple of weeks after everything that happened between us. There were some complications with the pregnancy and the baby--he didn't..." She trails off with a shrug and wipes away the tears that gather in her eyes. "It was a stillbirth." She whispers, dropping her gaze.

I walk over and hug her. "I'm so sorry, Soph. I can't even begin to imagine how devastated you must feel." I whisper, and she sobs into my chest. I rub her back soothingly while she cries.

Sophie pulls back a little and stares up at me, her eyes swimming in tears. I reach up and brush her tears away and kiss her forehead. Some familiarity—finally. Her smell, the way her body felt pressed up against mine, it all felt so familiar to me.

"Shall we grab some lunch and catch up?" I suggest and she smiles, nodding.

"I'd like that." She replies with a little smile, and I nod, grinning back at her. We walked out of the hospital together and went to an Italian restaurant we both loved.

"So, you don't remember anything at all? Marrying Shayla, us getting back together?" She questions before taking a sip of her water as we eat our starters.

"Nope, the last thing I remember was being in a relationship with you. You remember that yacht party we went to, and we sneaked into the owner's bedroom and had sex in his bed?" I say, and she laughs.

"Of course, we almost got caught. That was like two months into our relationship. We couldn't get enough of one another." She expresses, smiling. Nodding, reaching over, I take her hand in mine and brush my thumb over her knuckles.

"That's one of the last memories I have before I woke up in a hospital to a life I don't even know, to a version of myself I don't even recognise," I explain, playing with her fingers.

"What about Shayla? Are you still with her? I did hear she was pregnant?" Sophie questions glancing down at our hands before she lifts her eyes to mine.

I sigh and bite my lip. "She's supposedly my wife, and she's having my baby. I keep being told that we have this fierce love, but I don't feel anything for her-- at least I don't think that I do. My life with her doesn't make any sense to me. From what I can tell, she seems like a great girl, and I..." I trail off, and my mind goes to that night we were in bed together. The way her body was rocking against me, the way she was touching and whispering things to me, her moans. I don't know what came over me, but it was intense. I'm attracted to her for sure--if my body's reaction to her was anything to go by.

"Tristan?" I snap out of my trance, focussing on Sophie again. "You were saying, and you..." She trails off, urging me to continue.

"I'm just overwhelmed at the moment with everything." I declare, pulling my hand back from hers and looking at the wedding band on my finger.

"I'm not surprised, Tristan. Shayla was never any good for you. She made you a completely different person. It's like she moulded you into being the type of man that would suit her. She messes with your head and manipulates you. She's also the reason we aren't together right now."

I lift my gaze to Sophie's and narrow my eyes. "Didn't you break up with me and start seeing another guy before I even met Shayla?" I ask, and a flash of surprise crosses her features. "Josh filled me in."

"Yes, I did break up with you, but only because you never made me your priority. You always put your work before me, before us, and you didn't make any time for me or in the three years we were together. We were drifting apart. I waited for you to commit, but you didn't, so I made a decision and left." She explains and leans forward, her eyes on mine.

"Tristan, I never stopped loving you. You were always the guy for me, just as I'm the girl for you. A part of you always knew we belonged together. That's the reason you divorced Shayla and got back together with me. And we were happy, till she came back into your life and started screwing with your head again. Maybe there's a reason you forgot about her, and you still remember me... you remember us. Perhaps this is fates way of telling you that you belong with me."

I rub my hands over my face and sigh deeply. My brain was fried.

Honest to God, I feel like I need a day off from my life. "I don't know, Sophie. Shayla's my wife, and I did marry her twice--there must be a reason. From what everyone keeps telling me and judging by the pictures, we seemed to have a happy life together before all this happened."

Sophie leans back in her seat and fixes me with a look I couldn't quite decipher. "The Tristan I know would never base his future on the words of other people. You always trusted your gut honey, what is it telling you?" She questions openly, and I avert my gaze to the window, to the river stretched out beside us. I truly didn't know what to feel any more. I feel like my mind and heart are at war with one another, and I don't know which one I should listen to.

"At this moment, it's telling me to rip my brain out of my head and throw it as far as I can in the river," I utter, irritated, and Sophie reaches out and takes my hand in hers. I glance over at her, and our eyes meet. We hold one another's gaze for a long moment, and I feel that familiar stir in my belly that I would get whenever she would look at me with those beautiful ocean blue orbs.

"Hey, listen, I don't know if you would want to, but do you remember Daniel?" She asks, and I nod, taking a sip of my water. "Well, he's throwing one of his infamous parties at the country club this Saturday. Do you want to come? I'm sure everyone would love to see you." She offers, and I wince, rubbing my neck.

"I'd love to spend more time with you, Soph, but I can't. It wouldn't be right to be out with you while I'm married to Shayla." I tell her sincerely, and Sophie's shoulders slump in disappointment before she nods.

"You're probably right. I mean, you would hang out with Shayla while you were engaged to me--all the time--actually, and I was fine with it." I watch her while she chews on her bottom lip gingerly while pushing her food around on her plate. "If she doesn't trust you to meet up with some old friends, then you've got more problems in your relationship than your lost memory, babe."

I massage my forehead and sigh, "I don't want to promise you anything, but I'll try, okay." I tell her, and she smiles and nods before she reaches over and takes my phone off the table. "What are you doing?" I ask, and she gives me a playful smile.

"I'm putting my number in your phone. I changed the last one." Sophie explains, typing away on my phone. I smile, shaking my head. "Call or text me whenever you want." I take my phone when she hands it back to me.

"I'll keep that in mind. I have to go now. Can I drop you back to your car?" I offer, gesturing to the waiter for the bill, he nods and hurries off. Sophie smiles beautifully, nodding, and after I pay the bill, we walk back to the car together. I drop her back off at her car at the hospital, and she turns to face me before she gets out.

"Thank you for lunch, and I hope this isn't the last time I see you, Tris. I really miss you." She declares, tucking her soft blonde hair behind her ear, her eyes on mine.

"It was wonderful seeing you, Soph. It's hard to explain, but at the moment, you're the only thing that's familiar to me between all this chaos in my mind." I confess, and she smiles warmly at me and takes her seatbelt off before she presses a kiss to my jaw, her soft full lips lingering for a couple of seconds. When she pulls back a little, our eyes meet, and she gazes at my lips longingly for a second-- and I wanted to pull her close and kiss her, but I couldn't. As she inched closer, something made me shrink away and clear my throat. "I better go. Shayla's probably wondering what's taking me so long."

A flicker of disappointment flashes across her features, and she lowers her gaze, licks her lips, and opens the door after looking back at me once more. "I hope I'll see you soon, Tristan." She states before she gets out of my car. I release a breath I hadn't realised I was holding and watch her as she walks off toward her car.

Jesus. What am I doing?

◊

I HAD this dreadful feeling in the pit of my stomach the whole drive back to the house. I couldn't tell if it was guilt or what. I kept wondering if I should tell Shayla that I ran into Sophie or if I should let it be.

It's our date tonight, and I don't want to ruin that for us. I walk into the house, and my eyes search for Shayla. Sure enough, she pops her head out of the kitchen, grinning with what I'm hoping is chocolate smeared over her cheek and forehead. "Please, tell me that's chocolate on your face." I chuckle as I walk toward the kitchen.

Shayla throws her head back and laughs. "I have a little over three months before you come home to me covered in shit, so you're safe for now, stud." She tells me with a grin and sucks the chocolate off her fingers with a satisfied moan.

I laugh and toss my keys on the side. "What are you doing?" I question, leaning on the island and watch her stirring melted chocolate in a saucepan on the stove.

"I'm making those gooey chocolate brownies you love." She answers, biting her bottom lip while tossing chunks of chocolate into the saucepan. "Do you want to help?"

I smile and nod, rolling up my sleeves as I walk toward her. "Sure, I'm warning you, though, I can't cook for shit. What do you need me to do?" I question, leaning over her shoulder to see the saucepan. Shayla lifts the wooden spoon and swipes some chocolate onto her finger, and holds it up to my lips.

"Taste that for me." She replies, lifting her jade green eyes to mine. I wrap my fingers around her wrist, bring her finger to my lips, my eyes on hers the entire time as I open my mouth and suck the chocolate off her finger. Shayla bites her lip, watching me, "Is it sweet enough?" She questions, her voice an octave over a breathy whisper, and I moan lowly.

"I can't tell," I burr, leaning closer, brushing my nose over hers. I guide Shay's finger toward the spoon and smother it in chocolate again, only this time, I smear it over her bottom lip, and she gasps. "Let me see," I whisper, licking the chocolate off her lip. Shayla's eyes slid shut, she moans quietly, and just as I'm about to suck her bottom lip to kiss her, the doorbell chimes, and we jump apart.

Unbelievable.

What a moment to get interrupted. Shayla's eyes snap open, and she peers up into mine, her disappointment clear as day as I'm sure mine was. "I'll get it." I sigh and begrudgingly move away from her and stroll over to answer the door. I pull it open and see a young guy with a clipboard and a giant cardboard box.

"Delivery for Mrs Hoult?" He states, gesturing to the box.

"Shay, did you order something?" I call out, and she walks from the kitchen toward us.

"No. I didn't order anything." She states, eyeing the box. "Where is it from?" The guy shrugs and holds out the clipboard to her.

"Uh, baby-world?" Shayla frowns a little and peers up at me questioningly. "It was ordered by a Mr Tristan Hoult?" I blink bewildered, and Shayla watches me just as confused.

"I didn't order anything," I mutter with a shrug, and Shayla scratches her forehead and takes the delivery note to read it.

"It's a crib. It was on pre-order." She lifts her eyes to mine. "You ordered it before the accident." She tells me, and I gape at her, surprised, unsure of what to say or do.

"I guess it was supposed to be a surprise?" I shrug unwittingly, and Shayla smiles and looks over at the guy who was watching us with a bored expression on his face.

"You can leave it in the foyer. Thank you." She smiles, signing the papers and handing them to the boy once he's done hauling it inside the house.

"Have a wonderful day." He smiles charmingly at Shayla, who smiles back sweetly, and his beady eyes linger on her a little too long for my liking. I push the door shut in his face, and Shayla blinks and stares up at me, puzzled.

"Well, that was rude," She utters, her brows fused a little while I glare back at her.

"Oh, I'm sorry, did I interrupt your little moment with the delivery guy?" I utter rather irritated, and she laughs, clearly amused.

"Cole, what are you talking about? What moment?" Shayla questions, placing her hands at her waist and looking at me expectantly, her brow arched.

I sigh and roll my eyes before I turn to walk off when her lips curl into a full-on grin. "Hold on, is the infamous Lord Hoult jealous of the delivery guy?" She questions tauntingly, reaching out and taking hold of my wrist, and pulling me back to her. I look down into her upturned face, and she gazes back at me adoringly.

"Jealous? No. I just thought it was rather disrespectful to be openly checking you out right in front of your husband." I tell her coolly, and Shayla's brows go up with intrigue.

"Cole..."

"What?"

"You're adorable." She coos with a chuckle, and I shake my head, trying desperately to fight the smile pulling at my lips.

"Bite me," I utter and walk away when she starts to laugh.

"Just say where baby." She croons after me with a snigger. I glance back at her before I jog upstairs to get changed for our date.

"That's cute. We're leaving in an hour. You might want to get ready for our date!" I remind her and hear her chuckle.

"An hour? I can get ready three times over stud muffin!" I smile as I walk into the bedroom. What is it with this girl? She makes my heart flutter in my chest.

AFTER I COME out of the shower, wrapping a towel lowly around my waist, I see Shayla walk into the bedroom. She stops when she sees me in just a towel wrapped loosely around my waist. Her eyes slowly skim over my wet torso, her head tilted to the side, a dreamy look in her eyes. I smirk and brush my fingers through my hair, deliberately flexing my muscles, and she bites her bottom lip.

I stroll over to her, and Shayla blinks, snapping out of her stupor, looking at me when I hold her chin, tilting her head back a little to gaze deeply into her eyes. "Like what you see, sweetheart?" I drawl huskily. Shayla licks her lips, clearing her throat.

"I mean..." She breathes, swallowing hard. "It's not a bad sight to walk into."

I smirk and lean in closer till our noses were touching. "Is that right?" I whisper, brushing the back of my fingers along her jaw. "You're not a bad sight yourself," I tell her, ghosting my lips over hers, and she sighs. Then, just as I'm about to kiss her, my phone starts to ring, causing us to pull apart once again.

Fucking hell! What's with the constant interruptions?

"You should get that." She sighs, pulling away and walking toward the bathroom. I exhale, shaking my head frustrated as I snatch up my phone and see it's my mother.

Thanks for cock blocking Mum. I toss the phone aside. I'll call her later.

Once Shayla was ready, which surprisingly only took her thirty minutes, we got into my Maserati and drove to the location for our date. It was a lovely evening. The sun was setting, and the sky was a beautiful mixture of orange and red. Shayla had her window down, eyes closed as the wind blows her dark hair back.

Leaning over, Shayla turns the music up, and she starts to sing along to a country song, looking at me with a smile on her face. "We're always gonna be best friends, baby." She sings, pointing at me.

"I see you and me, making babies..." She sings, rubbing her belly with a grin. "Flirtin' at eighty, living on love." I watch her and couldn't stop smiling, "Yeah, we're living on love, baby." She sings to me while leaning over and kissing my cheek, grinning adorably.

"You have interesting taste in music.

Shayla laughs, "I'll have you know, Lord Hoult, that after you met me and I introduced you to Caraoke, your taste in music improved vastly."

I frown. "Caraoke?"

"Yes, it's our thing. It's like Karaoke but in the car. I'll show you." I glance over at her while she scrolls through her song list and grins at me when a song starts thundering through the speakers.

"Chicago? Seriously?"

"If you leave me now..." She starts to sing to me with the goofiest grin on her face, and I laugh despite my best effort to keep a straight face.

This girl is crazy.

"You're crazy. You know that?"

"What?!" She shouts over the music, grinning.

"You're crazy!" I laugh while she giggles and forces me to sing along to the song with her.

"Where are you taking me?" She questions once the song was over.

"You're about to find out," I grin, making a turn, and she sits back in her seat and gasps, her eyes wide and vibrant.

"No way!" She chirps, turning her elated gaze to me. "Oh, Cole, you brought me to a drive-in cinema?" I gape at her worriedly when she gets all emotional.

"Did I do good? I'm confused. You seem upset?" I say in a flurry as I pull up in a bay, and she laughs a little.

"Are you kidding? I love it." She answers excitedly, placing her hand on her chest, her face glowing beautifully. "What are we watch—The Notebook?" She truly is easy to please.

I nod and take my seatbelt off, looking at her. "What? Why are you looking at me like that?" I ask warily when she stares at me wide-eyed

"The Notebook is my favourite film." She tells me, and I frown a little, watching her.

"Isn't it like every girl's favourite film?" I state, and she blinks a couple of times and sinks back in her seat, a little deflated. Oh, did she think I remembered and brought her because of that reason? Did I remember? I don't think I did.

"Yeah, it probably is." She forces a smile and jumps when a scrawny boy pokes his head through her window, asking for the tickets. I chuckle and hand them over to him, and he smiles sheepishly.

"I'll be back with your pre-ordered snacks," He tells us before he scurries away. Shayla takes her seatbelt off and scans her surroundings.

"I've always wanted to go to a drive-in cinema. It was actually on the list of things I wanted us to do while we were living together before." She tells me, and when I give her a confused glance, she smiles a little and scratches her temple. "Right, you don't remember."

"What was this list?"

"Uh, well, we made a promise that for the duration of our agreement, we do something the other person enjoys every weekend. You took me for a ride on Casper, and I took you to that place by the river. We went golfing, wine tasting..." She explains and laughs a little. "We went to fright night, which was pretty hilarious, actually."

"Fright night?" I intone, and she nods slowly.

"Yeah, it happens in October for Halloween. You go to the theme park at night and ride roller coasters and drink beer, go through haunted houses. There are these actors that would jump out and scare you." I watch her with a smile as she enthusiastically explains that we got so drunk on beer we both threw up. "That was such a fun night."

"It sounds like it," I reply and briefly wonder how this girl got me to do these things I would never dream of doing ever—riding roller coasters while drunk? Haunted houses? I would never be caught dead doing any of these things, so why did I do it with her?

"All right, here you go." Shayla smiles warmly at the boy who hands us our speaker and the snacks we've ordered. "Enjoy the film."

"Thank you." Shayla grins and takes a sip of her diet coke. "I'm so excited." She gushes, handing me the big bucket of popcorn and a mixture of sweets. "Got a little over-excited with the food, huh?" She teases me, and I laugh, eating the popcorn.

"I love my food," I defend, looking at the screen as the lights dim and the film begins

"Oh, I know." Shayla chuckles, chewing on some lacy sweet. We watch the film while enjoying our snacks until Shayla got too full up, and we couldn't stomach it any more. I glance over at Shayla throughout the film, watching the screen, her eyes all big and bright while watching Noah and Allie kissing. I'd love to know what she was thinking at that moment. Suddenly, her gaze turns to me, catching me in my stare, and she flushes a little. "What?" She utters with a smile, and I shake my head.

"Nothing, you were just so engrossed in the film. I was wondering what you were thinking about."

Shayla heaves a deep sigh, "I was thinking that we were a lot like Noah and Allie. Our love, our passion. We had that great love." She explains quietly, looking at the screen again. I reach over and brush my fingers through her hair, and she turns to look at me. I stare into her eyes, my fingers tangled in her hair. "I'm dying to kiss you," I whisper, gazing longingly at her lips, which she parts as mine inch closer to hers. "Let me taste you, sweetheart." I breathe, feathering my lips over hers lightly.

"Ok--" I don't even wait for her to finish. I press my lips to hers and kiss her. Shayla moans softly when our tongues glide over each other teasingly before I draw her mouth closer and deepen the kiss.

It felt so weird, a good weird, not like a first kiss at all. It's like my mouth was acting on its own as if it knew its way around her mouth. And fuck, she's a sensational kisser--the type that makes you eager for more the longer you kiss.

The film was long forgotten. We spent the rest of the duration heatedly kissing until the windows in the car steamed up completely, and we were utterly lost in one another.

Chapter 7

SHAYLA

IF SOMEONE TOLD me a year ago that I'd be living the life that I am now, I would have laughed in their faces.

Had they said to me that I would fall out of my mind in love with a man, who would lose his memory a couple of months into our blissfully happy marriage, and forget I ever existed, I would have told them to have their head checked.

Alas, that is my reality. I have to get my husband—who was already crazy about me— to fall back in love with me all over again, or at least make him remember that he did love me not too long ago.

So, here I am, kissing said husband who seems to have forgotten me but is kissing me like he's never stopped.

Completely in sync like we've always been. How can Cole say he doesn't remember me when he's kissing me with that same affection? The same urgency and need as he ever did.

He's even doing that slow teasing lick on my tongue that he knows makes me mewl softly into his mouth.

How does he know to do that if he doesn't remember any of it? Could it just be a habit, or was that something he did with all the girls he kissed?

I just don't understand.

"Mm, Cole, maybe we should stop," I suggest while he kisses down my throat.

Those nimble fingers were slowly inching under my shirt, drawing lazy circles around my nipples, over the thin material of my bra, causing them to perk up and tighten under his touch. "People can see us," I murmur when he nips at my ear.

"Let them." He groans languidly, his velvet tongue hot on my neck. I force myself to pull away from him, and he opens his eyes and looks at me with a sexy smirk.

"Uh-huh, then we end up in the tabloids. I can imagine the headline now—Tristan and wife Shayla get frisky in public." I drawl, and Cole chuckles, biting his lip, his emerald gaze on mine.

"How about I take you home, and we continue getting frisky there?" He suggests with a cocky grin, and I laugh.

"You expect me to put out on the first date? That only happens once, Lord Hoult." I state impishly, and Cole shifts in his seat and leans in close to my face.

"But we're married."

"That's just a word, Cole," I say, looking into his eyes. "Unless it's backed up with emotions, it holds no meaning," I tell him earnestly, and Cole looks over my face before he nods.

"I suppose you're right." He agrees, sitting back in his seat and rubbing his palms over his jean-clad thighs. "Shall we head back home?" He starts the car fumbling to turn on the air-con to clear up the windows that got all steamed up amidst our heated make-out session.

"It's only midnight. Are you up for some late-night hot chocolate?" I suggest, and he looks at me with a smile and nods.

"Sure. Got someplace in mind, I take it?" I nod enthusiastically and lean over, putting the address in his satellite navigation.

Let's go, stud." I grin at him, and Cole smiles before we drive away from the outdoor cinema. We drive to the café in silence, just the music playing from my playlist. I stare out of the window pensively while rubbing my stomach when the baby kicks restlessly.

"You okay?" I look over at Cole and nod with a smile.

"Yeah, she's kicking like crazy," I tell him, and he looks at my stomach before he looks at the road again. He always gets so awkward whenever I mention the baby. I stifle the wince when I feel a pinch in my heart. My Cole would have reached over and caressed my stomach and spoke to our baby to soothe her.

I wonder if *that* Cole will ever come back entirely.

A LITTLE WHILE LATER, we pull up outside the café in Islington. The girls and I would come to this café to drink hot chocolate during winter and eat waffles. They have the finest waffles in the city.

Cole holds the door open for me and smiles as I walk into the café. The smell of the freshly cooked waffles and coffee makes my mouth water instantly. I notice an empty booth in the back and take Cole's hand, pulling him to it. The café had a very vintage look to it, almost like you're sitting in your living room.

There was a bookshelf full of books at the back, a huge fireplace, comfortable sofas, and floor pillows. I adore it here. There were groups of friends, couples, and families around, which gave it a very homely ambiance. "Well, this is different," Cole utters, glancing around.

"Shayla, hi." I look up at Chloe, one of the owners. "It's been a while since you've been in here. Welcome back." She greets, smiling at me warmly.

"Hi Chlo, it's been too long. This is Cole, my husband. Honey, this is Chloe. She's one of the owners of this café." I introduce. Cole smiles, and they shake hands.

"Nice to meet you, Chloe, nice place you've got here. Very cosy." He tells her politely, and Chloe looks around with a delighted smile.

"Thanks, that's what we were going for. Kind of like a home away from home feel. A place where people can come and unwind for a little while, whether it be for a date or to work or just read a good book in peace." Cole nods, his green eyes darting around as he takes in his surroundings. "Usual for you, Shay?" Chloe questions, and I nod.

"Yes, please. Cole, would you like something different? They have great coffee here, too, if you're not in the mood for hot chocolate?"

Cole shakes his head and smiles, "No, I'll have the same as Shayla, thank you." Chloe nods and walks off, leaving us alone. "So, you come here quite often, then?"

I nod and smile when Cole reaches over and takes my hand in his. "I did. I haven't been in a while. The girls and I come here all the time in winter. We order some waffles and hot chocolates and sit by the fireplace over there and 'chillax' as Jo likes to say."

"I like it here," Cole utters, looking around with a little smile. "It feels like..."

"Home." I finish for him, and he looks at me for a drawn-out moment and finally nods.

"Home," Cole repeats, staring into my eyes. "I'm starting to see why I was so fascinated with you." He declares as I rest my head in my hand and observe him.

"You are?"

Cole nods, mimicking my action, and rests his head in his right hand while his left plays with my fingers. "I've never met anyone like you." I smile, holding his gaze. "I've said that to you before, haven't I?" He adds, his eyes narrowed, and I laugh a little, my cheeks aflame.

"Yes, many times. You said that the very first night we met." I answer, chewing on my lip. I drop my gaze from him to our hands, resting on top of the table.

"You're unquestionably different from the girls I'm used to being around. You're very kind, and you have this warmth about you." He explains, reaching up and brushing his fingers along my jaw. "I can't put into words what it does to me."

I close my eyes, "Like the first sip of a steaming cup of hot chocolate when you're freezing." I whisper with a smile and open my eyes to look at him again.

"Exactly," Cole whispers back, gazing into my eyes. "You fill my insides with a warmth I'm not really familiar with."

I couldn't contain the smile. Cole smiles back, and for a fleeting moment, we felt like us again, how we used to be.

"Sorry to disturb you guys," Chloe sheepishly utters while holding our drinks and waffle in a tray. "You were looking at one another so wonderfully I felt awful coming over here, but your order is getting cold." She apologizes, and I laugh, blushing profusely as we pull apart. Cole chuckles, observing me flush like a teenager.

"Thank you, Chloe. God, it smells so good." I moan, looking down at my white chocolate and Raffaello waffle with coconut whipped cream. Cole looks down at the waffle with wide eyes.

"Enjoy guys, if you need anything, give me a shout," Chloe states and walks off once we thank her.

"You're about to taste heaven, Lord Hoult." I tease, grinning while cutting into the waffle. I hold out a piece to his mouth, and he eats it. He chews slowly, his eyes closing with an audible moan.

"Oh, my God." I watch him as he tilts his head back, moaning, and I grin, eating a forkful myself.

"Mm, I forgot how good it tastes." I moan, licking the cream. Cole lifts his eyes to me, watching me as I suck the fork clean. He clears his throat, blinking a couple of times before he picks up his fork, and we eat the waffle while sniggering uncontrollably.

"Hey, hey, stay on your side," Cole grumbles, laughing and pushing my fork away with his when I reach over to steal a piece of chocolate off his side.

"But you've got the good chocolate." I giggle, pushing his fork away. Cole picks up the last chocolate with his fingers and holds it between his lips.

"Come and get it. I dare you." He snickers, teasingly goading while wagging his brows at me.

I laugh, "You think I won't." I retort when he leans in close, his eyes challenging. I lean closer, my eyes on his as I tilt my head to the side and take the chocolate from his lips. Cole seizes the opportunity and kisses me softly, sucking my bottom lip.

"Mhm, now that's heaven indeed." Moaning, Cole pulls back a little to look into my eyes.

"You're a bad man, Cole Hoult," I whisper against his lips, and he grins, cupping my face with his large hands and kisses me slow and deeply.

"And you love it." He groans gruffly, sucking my tongue sensually, making me quiver inwardly. We pull back from the kiss a couple of minutes later, minds hazy and breathless.

After we finish our waffle, we drink our hot chocolates with tiny marshmallows and whipped cream while we sit by the fire and talk for over an hour.

BY THE TIME we got back home, it was four in the morning.

"I had an amazing time tonight, thank you," I tell him sincerely as we walk toward our separate bedrooms.

Cole nods and looks at me with a smile, "Me too. Thank you for coming out with me." I smile and step closer to him, push myself up on my tiptoes before I drop a lingering kiss on his cheek.

"Good night Cole Hoult," I say once I pull back, and Cole nods, smiling, and leans down, taking my face into his hands and presses his lips to my cheek.

"Good night, Shayla Hoult," Cole whispers, pulling his head back a little, but not completely. My heart flutters wildly in my chest whenever he's close to me. I had every urge to pull him to our bedroom and beg for him to make love to me, but I couldn't. Not until I know he feels something for me. I don't want to be a meaningless hook-up to him. I won't.

I pull away from him before he kisses me, and I smile as I slip into my bedroom. "Go to sleep. We have to be up for work in like three hours."

Cole chuckles. "But I'm not tired." He leans against the door frame with a devilish smile. I fix him with a sultry gaze, and he leans in close again.

"We will be in the morning when we can't focus on our work," I answer, deliberately softening my tone as he stares at my lips avidly.

"Then we'll stay home." He whispers back, huskily, "I do own the company."

"You do, but you have work to catch up on and projects that need your attention. And I have meetings all afternoon with our investors." I remind him, and he sighs, closing his eyes.

"Fine, can I at least have one last kiss?" He murmurs, brushing his nose over mine, and I shake my head.

"You've filled your quota of kisses for the day." I smile, pulling away, and he groans.

"Does that mean I get a fresh quota to fill daily?" He tries with a hopeful smile, and I laugh.

"You're incorrigible. Go to bed." Cole chuckles, charmed and presses a kiss to my forehead before he straightens.

"Okay fine, I'm going, but don't be surprised if you wake up and find me in your bed." He grins sexily as he walks off toward his room. "I have a habit of sleepwalking."

"You do not, and I'm locking my door." I quip, watching him as he strolls to his room and stops just before he walks in and looks over at me.

"I'm not." Cole drawls with a wink. "Feel free to slip in if you get lonely." When I go red and roll my eyes mockingly, he chuckles.

"Good night Cole!" I sigh, exasperated, and close my door. I can hear him cackling to himself through the wall as I lean against the door with the biggest smile on my face—one I couldn't get rid of however hard I tried. I place my hand over my heart and bite my lip. That connection is still there.

As I had suspected, the following morning, we were both exhausted after only having three hours of sleep. I think I dozed off at my desk twice, unable to keep my eyes open.

Cole wasn't much better. Of course, he could drink coffee--so he was at least getting some aid to stay up, whereas I didn't have anything but some caffeine-free tea, which makes my stomach turn at the mere thought of it.

I don't know how we managed to get through the day, but we did.

On Friday night, we had Josh and Aimee over for dinner. I hadn't seen the girls in over a week, and I missed them terribly, but Jo was away with Sam meeting her parents.

"So, how are things between the two of you?" Aimee asks as we prepare the table for dinner. I smile and glance over at Cole, who was in the living room, watching a football match with Josh.

"We're getting there, I think. Our date was incredible...we felt like us again. Albeit, it's very hit-and-miss with him at the moment. One day he's all flirty and can't keep his hands to himself, then he goes all cold turkey and doesn't even talk or acknowledge me." I explain with a shrug as I mix the salad. "It's emotionally draining, you know?"

Aimee nods, picking up wine glasses off the glass rack. "I know, but I'm sure he's feeling the same. I can't even imagine the pressure he's under at the moment. It can't be easy for him, Shay."

I sigh and look over at Cole—texting someone on his phone. He's been on that phone all day.

Who the hell could he be texting all bloody day? I look over at Aimee when something on her hand catches my attention.

No way! I walk over to her, take her hand, and look at the diamond engagement ring on her finger, and she looks at me, her blue eyes startled before her lips curl into a smile. "Bish?" I whisper, looking at her, stunned. "Are you...?" Aimee grins with a nod. I scream and hug her.

"Oh, my God!" I squeal excitedly. Josh and Cole come running into the kitchen when they hear my screams.

"What? What?!" The boys shout, watching us hug and sob. I pull back and look at Josh, who was watching us, concerned. "You're engaged?!" I scream, and he presses his hand to his chest and smiles.

"Jesus, Shayla, you scared the crap out of us. Yes, we are. I asked Aimee last night, and she said yes." Josh confirms and opens his arms when I run over to hug him.

"Oh Josh, I'm so happy for you both." I cry, and he laughs, wiping my tears.

"Stop crying, then." He teases with a chuckle, and I move over to Aimee and hug her again. I look over at Cole, who was smiling cheekily.

"You knew, didn't you?" Cole nods, slapping Josh's back.

"He told me last week he was planning on proposing, so I helped him pick out the ring," Cole explains, squeezing Josh's shoulder proudly while he pulls Aimee into his arms and kissing her temple.

"Why didn't you tell me?" I ask with a pout, and he smiles, pointing at Josh.

"Blame him. He wanted it to be a surprise." Josh shrugs, defencelessly hiding behind a laughing Aimee.

"Please don't kill me. I knew you'd run and tell her straight away. You think I don't know what you girls are like?" Josh claims, pointing at Aimee and me.

"You're lucky I love you both. Does Jo know?" Aimee shakes her head.

"No, even though I wanted to call you as soon as he proposed, I wanted to tell you both face to face and see your reaction," Aimee answers, pulling me to her and hugging me again.

"We were going to tell you at dinner, but you ruined it when you saw the ring, Bish," Aimee explains, gazing lovingly at her fiancé. "Obviously, this goes without saying, but we want you two to be the best man and maid of honour."

I grin excitedly, "Of course, are you kidding me." I reply, hugging Aimee again and smile while Josh hugs Cole. This was so incredible. Imagine your husband's best friend marrying your best friend. I couldn't be happier for them.

We sit and eat our dinner. We toast to Josh and Aimee's fantastic news. While Aimee and I excitedly discuss her ideas for the wedding, Josh and Cole talk about work. I was listening to Aimee gush about the proposal when Cole's phone flashes on the table. I feel my heart sink to the pit of my stomach when a message pops up with 'Soph' and a red heart next to her name.

It can't be. Please, God, let my eyes be deceiving me.

I stare at the phone, motionless for a moment until I lift my gaze to Cole, who looks at the phone and then at me. That's who he's been texting all day. *Sophie*. Aimee and Josh exchange glances before they look back at Cole, and I stare at each other. I push my seat away from the table. "Excuse me," I whisper. Standing from the table, I walk toward the stairs.

"Shayla," Cole calls my name and pushes his chair back as I near the stairs. I feel his hand on my arm, and I yank it out of his hold. "Shayla, let me explain."

I look up at him, "Explain? There is no reason, nor an explanation feasible enough to justify your ex-fiancée texting you." I tell him and swallow the lump forming in my throat.

"I ran into her at the hospital a couple of days ago. I didn't go looking for her--she was just there." He tells me, and I brush my fingers through my hair. "She told me she lost her baby after everything that happened between us. She was upset and needed someone to talk to, so we had lunch, that's it." Cole explains, and my hand instinctively goes to my stomach as my gut clenches painfully at the thought of losing my baby.

"Why didn't you tell me, Cole? Why keep it from me?" I question and watch as he closes his eyes.

"I was going too, but then we had our date that night, and I didn't want to ruin that." Cole opens his eyes and looks at me again.

"Why is she texting you?"

Cole rubs his forehead and sighs, "I don't know."

I glare at him, "What the hell do you mean you don't know?!" I exclaim angrily, and he sighs.

"You've been texting her all-fucking day!"

"She's talking about some party tomorrow night; she wants me to go with her to see some of our old friends."

I stare up at him, tears burning the back of my eyes, "You said no, right?" I ask, and when I see the look of guilt on his face, I already had my answer. "You didn't." I take a step back, shaking my head.

"Oh my God. You were going to go. You were going to spin some bullshit to me and go off with her, weren't you?!" I shout.

"Shayla, it's not like that! It's not that big of a deal. It's just a party with some of our mutual friends." Cole clarifies, and I look over at Josh and Aimee, watching us utterly stunned.

"It's happening all over again," I whisper, placing my hand on my chest and looking pleadingly at Aimee, who glares at Cole.

"Shayla, nothing has happened," Cole says, taking hold of my arm and turning me to face him.

"YET!" I scream, shoving him away from me. "But it will. It always does. If you've started lying to me and texting her behind my back and arranging get-togethers, it's only a matter of time."

"Do you not trust me?!" He barks hotly, and I look up at him disbelieving.

"Trust?" I intone. "You want to talk about trust? Okay, tell me truthfully, hand on your heart. Did she try and kiss you? Or did you think about kissing her? Were you tempted, Cole?" I ask and hold my breath waiting for him to tell me to stop being stupid, that the thought didn't even cross his mind...but he didn't. He just stares back at me apologetically.

"Oh God." I exhale and turn my back to him.

Cole sighs and turns me to face him again. "Shayla, listen to me. You have no idea how much I wish I could remember all my moments with you. I'm trying, but it's so frustrating being told by everyone how much I loved you and having no recollection of it. I woke up one day seemingly four years in the future with a girl I've never seen in my life, telling me she's my wife and is pregnant with my baby." He explains, shoving his hand through his hair.

"In my mind, it's 2016, and I have a girlfriend named Sophie, who I was falling in love with." He tells me apologetically. "I can't imagine loving anyone but her."

I gasp, look up at him and shake my head slowly. "Cole, I'm trying to understand, but please, I'm begging you don't drag me through this whole Sophie mess again," I plead with him, and he shrugs. "I can't do this again."

"I love her."

"No, you don't! You love me, Cole!" I exclaim, looking up at him, tears spilling over my cheeks, and he just stares back at me blankly.

"No, I don't!" He shouts back. "I'm attracted to you, yes, but I don't love you, Shayla!"

"Yes, you do! I'm the one you want to be with, not her! Are you not listening to a fucking word everyone is telling you? You don't love Sophie; you hate her for lying to you and trying to trap you, Cole. You married me! I'm having your baby! ME!" I shout, shoving him away from me. "God damn it!"

"Cole, don't listen to Sophie," Josh tells him, and Cole glares at him.

"Stay out of this, Josh!" He growls hotly before he looks at me again. "I've tried, okay, I have, and I'm sorry, but I can't force myself to love you, Shayla. I can't."

"Cole, don't do this to me again," I whisper, shaking my head, tears streaming down my face while he looks at me ruefully and shrugs.

"I'm sorry, I am." He states, taking his ring off and hands it to me. I gasp and stare at it as he turns and walks to the door.

"Cole!" I call out, and he turns and looks at me. "You turn your back on me and walk out of that door, don't think for a god-damn second this baby and I will be here when your memory comes back," I tell him gravely, and he walks over to me and stares into my eyes.

"Don't fucking threaten me!" He shouts, glaring at me.

"It's not a threat. It's a fucking fact!" I scream at him.

"Suit yourself. I don't want you, and I don't want your baby!" Cole growls angrily, and I take a step back like an invisible force just shoved me.

"Then go, Cole!" I shout, pushing him back. "What are you waiting for?! Huh? GO!" I sob, throwing the ring at him. We stood glaring at one another furiously, and every step he took backward made my heart clench painfully. I release the agonizing breath I was holding when he turns his back and walks toward the door.

Aimee comes rushing over to me. I feel my heart beating in my ears.

"Cole, stop! What the fuck are you doing, bro?!" Josh shouts, pulling him back. "That's your fucking wife. She's carrying *your* baby."

I stare dazedly at the ground while everyone shouts around me, trying to catch my breath. I hiss and hold my stomach when I feel a sudden cramp. "Josh, let him go!" I shout, shaking my head when I see Josh following him to the door, trying to stop him from leaving.

"Shayla?" Aimee holds my arms and looks at me when I lean over. "What's wrong? Are you okay?" I cry out when I feel another sharp pain in my stomach.

"Ahhhh!"

"Josh?!" Aimee screams when my knees give away, and I collapse into her arms. Josh looks back and comes running over to us.

"Shayla, hey, what is it?" He questions in a flurry while I cry, holding my stomach.

"The baby..."

Chapter 8

COLE

"JOSH!" I halt before I walk out of the door and look back when I hear Aimee scream for him. Josh looks back, and we both watch as Shayla collapses into Aimee's arms, holding her abdomen. Josh lets go of my arm and runs over to her, falling to his knees beside her.

"Shayla, hey, what is it?" He asks, watching her concerned while she cries out in pain.

"The baby," She whimpers. "Something's wrong."

"Okay, don't panic, we're going to the hospital. Come here." Josh says, helping her up to her feet, and she hisses, clutching her stomach and shaking her head.

"Josh...." Aimee whispers, holding up her hand, her fingers covered in blood. "She's bleeding." Josh and Aimee both look over at me as I stood watching, utterly frozen.

Shayla's wide eyes stare down at the blood on Aimee's fingers and gasps. "No, no, no. NO!" She screams, crying hysterically while Aimee wraps her arms around Shayla to soothe her.

"What the fuck have you done..." Josh lifts his blue eyes to look at me. I couldn't move. I couldn't tear my eyes off Shayla.

"Josh, do something?!" Aimee shouts, trying to calm a hysterical Shayla down.

"What are you standing there for?! Help me get her into the fucking car!" Josh exclaims, and I rush over to her side. Shayla looks at me with such anguish—the memory I had of her recently flashes through my mind.

"NO! Get away from me!" she shouts, hitting my chest and pushing me.

"Shayla, hey, calm down. We're going to get you to the hospital," Josh tells her. "It's going to be okay. You're both going to be okay." He reassures her again and again, but Shayla shakes her head sobbing.

"I can't lose her too, I can't, I can't. Aimee...." She cries into Aimee's chest, who presses her lips to Shay's temple, rocking her, her own eyes swimming in tears.

"Shh, you're not going to. You're both going to be fine. You and Alaia are both going to be just fine, I promise you." Aimee lifts her eyes to look at me and shakes her head disappointedly. "You're going to be fine." She whispers, tearing her eyes away from me again. "Josh, let's go." I numbly watch as Josh picks her up into his arms and rushes her out of the house.

I go to follow her, but Aimee puts a hand on my chest, stopping me. "No! Don't you dare! You made your choice, and now you can fuck off to it! You don't deserve her! This is the last time you wreck her because of that good for nothing bitch, you hear me!" She bellows before she turns and runs out of the house when Josh calls for her.

I stand in the empty house, staring, stock-still at the door they all rushed out of.

What did I just do?

I glance around and down at the bloodstain on the white marble floor where Shayla was on the floor. My stomach clenches painfully. I pick up the wedding band that I took off and handed to her, which was lying on the floor.

"Ever Thine, Ever mine, Ever ours."

I fall to my knees, cradling my head in my hands.

"And I swear to you, in front of all our family and friends, that I will make each day we spend together better than the last. I'm so in love with you."

I wince, and when I close my eyes, I see Shayla's face smiling up at me.

"Oh God," I gasp, shaking my head.

I push myself back up on my feet, my knees shaking as I grab my keys and rush out of the house.

My head was hazy as I walk over to my car. My heart, hammering against my ribcage so hard, I could barely catch my breath. I somehow manage to drive to the hospital, my mind running amuck as I replay what just happened again and again.

My entire body is shaking apprehensively. If anything happens to either of them, I'll never forgive myself. I didn't intend for this to happen. I didn't.

I pull up at the hospital and run inside to the front desk. "Shayla Hoult, she was just brought in. She's uh...pregnant."

"Maternity ward, fourth floor." The nurse tells me, and I race through the corridors. My heart up in my throat as I take the steps two at a time till I got to the fourth floor. I rush over to the nurse's station, panting.

"Shayla Hoult. Where is she?" I ask in a flurry, and the nurse looks at me, startled.

"Relation?"

I hesitate and look at her, trying to catch my breath, "I'm her..." I drop my gaze to the floor, unable to finish my sentence.

"Sir?"

"Husband...I'm her husband," I whisper, and she nods in understanding.

"Your wife was brought in not too long ago with cramps and bleeding. She's being examined right now. If you would like to go to the waiting room on the left, the doctor will take you to her when they're done with the examination." She explains. I nod and walk toward the waiting room, where I see Josh anxiously pacing back and forth.

He stops pacing when he sees me standing at the door. "Josh is she..." Josh walks over to me, grabs me by the shirt, and slams me hard into the wall.

"Shut the fuck up." Josh snaps hotly. "What the fuck is wrong with you?! I have never in all the years of my friendship with you felt so fucking disgusted," Josh states, his eyes angrily glaring into mine. "You should have got a knife and plunged it straight into her heart and finished her off, man. You've fucking wrecked her good this time." He hisses furiously, letting go of me and stepping back. "I was envious of you, bro. You had it all. The beautiful wife who loved you, a baby on the way, you were so in love and happy." Josh declares, shaking his head. "And you threw it all away for what? Fucking Sophie? If she's all you want, why the fuck are you here, Cole?! Go on, fuck off to her. Get the fuck out of here!"

I shake my head and stare at the ground, unable to hold his gaze. "Josh. When I saw the state of her, my heart wouldn't..."

"Your heart what?! It hurt, did it?" Josh hisses through clenched teeth, grabbing me, he slams me hard against the wall again. "Imagine what she's feeling right now, you fucking prick!" He shouts, and I lift my gaze to his stormy ones.

"I don't know what the fuck happened to you in that accident, but this version of you is truly despicable. This isn't you, Cole. You woke up a different fucking person because my best mate would die before he ever thought about uttering those words to that girl in there. You were willing to die for her, Cole. When you found out she was dating me, you thought you lost her; you fucking flipped and wanted to die. That's how crazy you were about that girl in there. What the hell happened to you?"

My vision blurs, and I feel my chest constrict painfully. "I pray you don't get your memory back because if you do, you're going to want to die when you realise what you've fucked up," Josh utters icily and moves away from me. "She's never going to forgive you for this, especially if she loses..." He stops and exhales slowly, shaking his head. "Christ.."

"I don't know what came over me. I was angry and frustrated. I didn't think—"

"No, you fucking didn't. I told you how much you've hurt her in the past, and what do you do? You go and hurt her all over again! You better pray nothing happens to them because when Sam finds out what you've done, he's going to kill you and I'll be right there helping him." Josh angrily mutters as he continues to pace back and forth.

"Have the doctors said anything?" I ask, and Josh glares at me darkly.

"No! They rushed her straight in. Aimee's gone in with her because she was hysterical. It should be you in there with her!" He shakes his head irately.

I close my eyes. I did want to be in there, but how could I possibly face her after what I did. I'm the reason she's in there. I don't know what the hell came over me. I wince and rub my temples when I feel a sharp, penetrating pain in my head.

"Daddy will be back before you know it. I love you, baby girl."

Josh looks over at me and frowns when I groan and slide down the wall with my head in my hands. "Cole?"

"I love you, you silly girl."

I shake my head and rock back and forth, my heart racing in my chest like it was about to stop. I couldn't catch my breath. "Cole? Hey."

"I can't breathe...Josh...I can't..." I pant, wincing through the pain in my head.

"The fuck? Hey, can we get a doctor in here!" Josh shouts and looks at me worriedly. "Cole, your nose is bleeding. Jesus man, just breathe." He utters and looks up at the doctor, who comes rushing in.

"What's going on here?" The doctor perches in front of me and lifts my head.

"He says he can't breathe, and his nose just started bleeding," Josh explains and moves aside to give the doctor space.

"What's his name?"

"Cole," Josh answers, rubbing the back of his neck.

"Hey, Cole, I'm Doctor Davies. I need you to try and calm down and take some deep breaths for me, okay." I hear him say through the rapid thumping of my heart in my ears. He shines a torch in my eye, and I grimace when it sends a ripple of pain through my head.

"Stop, stop, it hurts. Fuck, it hurts." I pant through clenched teeth as I brace my head in my hands.

Shay's sobs echos in my head, and I groan.

"Cole, what hurts? I can't help you if you don't tell me what's wrong?" Dr Davies asks, pulling my hands away from my head while I pant, gasping for air.

"Ahhh God. My head..."

"Has he suffered any head injuries recently?" He asks Josh, who nods, watching me.

"He was in a plane crash and fractured his skull, which caused him to lose his memory. He can't remember the last four years."

"Right," Dr Davies looks at the nurse. "Call down and arrange an emergency CT scan." She nods and walks out of the room. "Cole, it sounds like you're having a panic attack. You're okay. I need you to focus on your breathing for me, okay?"

"A panic attack?" Josh inquires.

"Yes, it is very common for patients who suffer trauma to the head to have episodes of panic, especially if they're suffering from amnesia. The stabbing headaches and dizzy spells are all common signs, but I want to do a scan to make sure nothing was overlooked. Do you happen to know if he's had any form of therapy following the incident?"

Josh shakes his head with a shrug. "I'm not sure."

"PTSD often follows after a traumatic head injury. His Doctor would have recommended he speaks to someone. I'm going to assume that he hasn't. Cole, we're going to head down and have my colleague take a little look at your head, okay?" He explains, and I shake my head, rocking back and forth.

"No. I'm not leaving until I know they're okay." I pant, squeezing my eyes shut, willing the ache in my heart to stop squeezing the life out of me.

"His wife was brought in with cramps and bleeding," Josh answers him.

"You mean Shayla? I was just with her. Your wife is fine Cole, she and the baby are both going to be fine. We'll have to keep a close eye on them both the next few weeks." I open my eyes and look at him, and a slow breath of relief escapes me. "Too much stress can trigger off early labour, which is why she was cramping. She's still only twenty-nine weeks pregnant, so we need to keep the baby in for as long as possible so its respiratory system can develop and become stronger. We've given her some medication, which has stopped the labour for now. It's vital for her and the baby that she stays away from stress."

"What about the blood?" Josh asks, and Dr Davies looks at him.

"It happens in the third trimester. There's nothing to be concerned about. The walls are thinning in her womb as the baby grows and her body prepares for birth. We've done all the necessary checks, both Mum and baby are perfectly fine and healthy. As I said, you must keep her away from stress to avoid triggering early labour." He explains, and I rub my temples. "Now, let's have you checked out, okay?" I nod and allow him to help me up to my feet and hiss when another pain shoots through my skull.

"I'll come with you. I just need to tell Aimee." Josh says as I walk over to the wheelchair they brought in for me and sat before I lean over and curl my trembling fingers in my hair.

ONCE JOSH COMES BACK, they wheel me down to the neurology department. Doctor Bennet comes in as they prepare me for the scan. "Cole, what's happened, son?"

I lift my eyes to him and stare vacantly. "I feel like someone is driving a knife into my brain. Please make it stop. I can't take it. My head feels like it's about to implode."

"All right, let's take a look, and we can give you something for the pain." I nod and close my eyes, leaning forward. I feel another surge of panic when my chest gets all tight again.

"I want you to have my babies..."

"Cole, hey, take some deep breaths for me, son." Doctor Bennet instructs as he lays me down on the table. And I try, I do, but each breath I took hurt so fucking much. "Stay still for me, okay? It will be over in a couple of minutes." I hear him say as he walks out of the room, and the table starts to move until my head was inside the machine.

What was happening to me?

The machine's groans make my headache unpleasantly, and I feel sick to my stomach.

"All right, Cole, it's all done. You can get dressed." I hear Doctor Bennet's voice echo in the room as the table moves again. I stare up at the ceiling motionlessly.

"Jason, what is going on?!"

"Mayday, Mayday, Mayday, Gulfstream Golf 650 Echo Romeo. Engine failure, we are in an uncontrolled dive, descending at thirty-one thousand feet. We're declaring an emergency. We are heading to the nearest airport."

"Negative Gulfstream Golf 650 Echo Romeo. You're too far out to the nearest airport..."

"Sir, we're going to crash. Please go back to your seat, strap in tight, and brace for impact."

"Oh my god..."

I gasp and sit up breathless. "Cole, deep breath's son, slow deep breaths."

"What's happening," I whisper.

"Cole, talk to me, tell me what's going on?" Doctor Bennet asks, watching me.

I shake my head.

"I don't know. Everything is in pieces," I tell him and squeeze my eyes shut. "I keep getting these random moments flash in my mind for a second, and then it's gone again."

"Cole, it sounds like small pieces of memories are starting to come back. This is a wonderful thing."

"Why now?"

Dr Bennet rubs his forehead. "It's hard to say why, son. It could be a number of things that may trigger some memories into coming back. A particular smell, for example, a meaningful word you hear or even bouts of sudden stress." He clarifies.

I sigh, shaking my head, "I don't...I don't want to remember. Make it stop...please, make it stop!" I growl, my head in my hands, rocking back and forth.

"Cole, it's going to be okay—"

"No! It's not!" I lift my eyes to his, unshed tears blurring my vision, "The crash." I breathe, staring at the wall ahead. "I remember..."

"Tell me?"

"The distress call. The moment the pilot told me we were going to crash, and I should brace for impact. The terror in his eyes when he told me that. We were falling so fast. The smell of smoke filled the cabin, and I—I remember the moment just before hitting the ground, that split second before everything went dark. I had one thought—*Shayla*." I whisper, looking over at Josh, tears flowing down my face, and he shakes his head sullenly.

Dr Bennet sighs, "Cole. You must go and speak to a professional. Now you're starting to remember the accident, the panic attacks, the anxiety will only get worse, and you're already showing early signs of PTSD, which is very common in cases like yours. You have to open up and talk to someone and not shut your feelings off because you're scared of facing them. I know it may feel like it, son, but you're not alone. You have people around you that love you and want to support you."

"They don't understand. No one understands." I whisper, shaking my head. "They keep telling me over and over that I've changed and that I'm not myself-- only I don't know I've changed because, to me, I'm just me. It's just that my life doesn't seem like mine any more. I feel like I'm living in another person's body trying to figure out where I fit in their life." I explain woefully, rubbing my temples.

"I remember some things, but most of them I can't place the emotional connection to go with it. Other than the accident, I just can't, and I'm tired of letting people down, especially her."

I sob. "I can't stand to see the disappointment in her eyes every time she tells me she loves me, and I just stare at her blankly or when she talks about the baby and expects a reaction from me and gets nothing-- because I can't even remember the moment we conceived it." I cry and look at Josh, who was watching me.

"The last thing I ever wanted to do was hurt her, Josh, I swear.

I'm just trying to take each day as it comes and figure this shit out the best that I can."

"Why didn't you tell us any of this? You should have explained all of this to her instead of blowing up at her like that. Shay didn't deserve that, Cole." Josh sighs, walking over to me.

"Josh, I've tried, but no one understands what I'm going through, man. It's like me shoving a stranger into your life who is pregnant and saying here—this is your wife and your baby, love them." I explain, wiping away the tears that kept streaming down my face.

"It's just not that simple, and I've never felt so alone and alienated from my own life. No matter what I fucking do, whatever choice I make, someone will end up getting hurt because of me."

Josh shakes his head and walks over, and hugs me tight. "You're not alone, bro. I'm always here for you. You know that." I weep into his shoulder, finally letting out all the pent-up emotions I've been suppressing since the accident. "We're going to help you through this, all right." I nod silently and pull back from his embrace.

After Doctor Bennet examined my CT scan, he assured me everything was perfectly normal, and the headaches and nosebleeds are related to my amnesia. I would experience this on and off for a while. Well, that's simply great, just one more thing on top of everything else I have to deal with.

"Josh," I call out as we walk back up to the maternity ward where Shayla and Aimee were. Josh looks at me questioningly. "I need to see her and apologise."

Josh shakes his head swiftly. "Cole, no. That's not a good idea. You're the last person she wants to see or even needs to see for that matter." He declares ruefully, and I sigh wistfully, rubbing my forehead.

"I understand that, but I need to apologise for the things I said to her. She needs to know I'm sorry." I explain, and Josh exhales deeply.

"You two are going to be the death of me, I swear to god. Aimee is furious with you, and she will kill you before she lets you anywhere near Shayla." Josh sighs and pinches the bridge of his nose. "I'll steal her away, but make it quick, and if Aimee asks, I didn't help you, or she will castrate me. Understand?" I nod and hide around the corner when Josh walks into the room to get Aimee.

I wait anxiously until they both come out a couple of minutes later. Josh gestures me to go, and I slip into the room and close the door. Shayla opens her eyes and looks at me, her eyes rimmed red and puffy. She sucks in a sharp breath and closes her eyes again.

"Get out." She whispers, her voice quivering.

"Shayla—"

"Get out, Cole."

"Shayla, I'm sorry," I apologise, moving over to her, and she sobs, turning her head away from me.

"Oh, you're sorry? Okay, great." She bites her bottom lip. "I feel much better, thank you." She cries, wiping her tears with her fingers. "You can leave now."

I bite the inside of my cheek hard. "I never meant to hurt you, either of you. You have to know that." I express, moving closer to her, and she shakes her head, still avoiding looking at me. Shayla doesn't say anything, so I continue. "I was angry and frustrated, and I took it out on you. I know I shouldn't have. You didn't deserve any of that, Shayla, you've stood by me through all of this mess, and I just couldn't stand disappointing you any longer."

Shayla closes her eyes, "You did a hell of a job of not disappointing me, Cole. It no longer matters. You said what you said, and no amount of words or apologies will ever change that. I won't forgive you. You've made your choice, so you can go and live with it." She sniffles, wiping away her tears. "I no longer want you in my life. There's only one thing I care about, and that's my baby, who I almost lost today because of you. So, you can take your guilt and apologies and get lost because they're worthless to me." I reach for her hand, and she jerks it away as if my touch burned her. She wouldn't even look at me, and it killed me. "I'll pick up my things

from the house tomorrow, and I'll appreciate it if you weren't there."
She adds frostily.

"Shayla, please, you don't—"

Shayla sighs. "That house, our marriage, it all means nothing anymore." She cries and finally turns her gaze to me, and the pain she had in the depth of her eyes made me ache terribly.

"You asked me to marry you, and I said yes. You asked me to have your baby, and I got pregnant, only to have you scream in my face that you don't love me, nor want our baby or me, and I stood there, I watched you walk away to be with your ex-fiancé again." She sobs, shaking her head. "I've given you everything I am and all I have, so please, just go." She whimpers, dropping her gaze from mine and presses her lips together, "You've managed to do the impossible--you've made me hate you." She whispers woefully. "So, go back to the girl you stood there and said you couldn't imagine loving anyone else over and leave my baby and me in peace."

"Shayla, she's my baby—"

"Don't you dare! You don't get to say those words to me and come in here acting like you suddenly give a shit! She's mine, and one day when she asks me where her father is, I'm going to tell her that he died in a plane crash because he did. The man I love, the father of this baby, died that day in that accident." Shayla utters, lifting her distraught gaze to me again. "I don't even know you, and I don't want my baby to either. As far as I'm concerned, you can go to hell and take that bitch with you."

I stood still watching her and felt my heart snap and fall to my feet at her words.

"Shayla..."

"You know where the door is."

Chapter 9

SHAYLA

I STARE at the window to my right. I can see Cole in the reflection of the glass. He just stood there looking at me miserably. I can't simply put into words how devastated I feel right now because there are no words that could ever describe how I felt. I lay down and turn my back to him, sobbing.

"Shay,"

"Get out. I don't ever want to see you again." I utter brokenly and watch through the glass as he turns and walks to the door.

Cole stops suddenly and looks at me, "I swear to you in front of all our family and friends that I will make each day we spend together better than the last." I still when I hear him repeat his wedding vows. I turn my head and look back at him; he holds my gaze. "I'm truly sorry that I couldn't keep my promise to you," Cole whispers before he opens the door and walks out of the room.

I bury my face into my hands and weep.

He's starting to remember, and the fact he's putting us through this, knowing he made me a promise like that, kills me even more.

I was so scared that I would lose our baby, and I had to go through that scare without him. Granted, he was the cause of it, but I needed my Cole, the man I love telling me everything was going to be okay, that our little princess will be all right, but he wasn't there, and he never will be again.

I made a promise to God, if he keeps her safe until she's ready to be born, I will put all the love I have for Cole into my baby girl. I will love her enough for both of us. I will not let Cole and that bitch be the reason I lose my baby. I'm living for her and her alone from this day on.

My midwife wanted to keep me in for the night to ensure the medication they gave me to stop the early labour was working.

THE FOLLOWING DAY, Aimee, Jo, and I went back to mine and Cole's place while he was at work to pack up my things. I was worried he would have been there, but he wasn't. It broke me walking back into that house; we have so many memories tied to this home. I thought we would raise our family and grow old together in this house, but I guess I was wrong.

"You okay?" Jo inquires, hugging me from behind, resting her chin on my shoulder while she rubs my bump. I nod sadly and wipe away the endless tears that roll down my cheeks.

"It's just so hard to face that this is my life. We walked into this house so happy, and a couple of months later, I'm leaving more devastated and broken than I have ever been." I confess, looking at our photo above the fireplace. "I hate him."

"I wish that were true, babe, but we all know you're going to love that idiot forever. I just can't believe this is all happening." Aimee sighs, looking around the house glumly while shaking her head.

"You and me both," I whisper, staring at our wedding photo. The more I looked at it, the angrier I got. I walk to the kitchen, take out a kitchen knife from the block on the island, and stride over to the picture.

"Shay?" Jo mutters, watching me as I angrily rip the picture off the wall and drive the blade straight through Cole's face and drag it down.

"That's what you did to my heart!" I shout, stabbing the photo over and over again. "How could you do this to me! How?!" I wail, dropping the knife and tearing the picture apart with my hands. "I hate you! I HATE YOU!" I scream and fight Aimee off me when she tries to hug me. "NO!" I sob sorrowfully. I yank every photo of us hanging on the walls and tear them apart angrily. "I loved you more than anything!" I weep as I pick up a vase and hurl it against the wall where another picture of us smiling happily was hanging. "Go...go and be happy with her! I'm going to rip you out of my heart, just like you did to me! YOU'RE DEAD TO ME!" I scream, curling my fingers in my hair while sobbing.

I fall into Aimee's chest when she wraps her arms around me. "I hate him. I hate him!" My body shook with raspy sobs, my cries echoing in the walls of what was once our home. "My heart is shattered. How am I going to survive this?" I whimper while Aimee and Jo sit on the floor, holding me.

"You'll find the strength for your baby girl, the day you hold her in your arms for the first time you're going to love her so much she's going to piece your heart back together again slowly," Jo tells me, stroking my hair as I continue to cry.

"It hurts. He's ripped apart my heart and left me for dead. I wish more than anything that I could erase all my memories of him because I'm slowly and painfully dying Jo, I'm DYING!" I wail, holding my aching chest.

The girls cry with me while they watch me fall apart yet again.

"Shayla, I know this is hard, but you have to pull yourself together. This isn't good for you or the baby. Think about Alaia." Aimee says, brushing her fingers through my hair, and I shake my head.

I lift my gaze to look at her, "Aimee." I whimper.

Aimee nods in understanding, wiping away my tears, and presses her forehead to mine. "I know, babe, you're devastated, I know. " She sighs sadly. "Come on. You can't be here, Shay. Jo, get her out of here. I'll pack your things, okay?"

I nod and peer up at Jo, "I want my mum. Take me to my mum." I sniffle, and Jo nods, wiping away my tears with her fingers.

"Okay, come on." She helps me up as we walk to the door to leave the house. "Aimee, how are you going to get home?"

"I'll call Josh, don't worry about me. Take care of Shay." She contends, waving us off. Jo and I walk to the car. I get in and rest my head against the window.

Why does this keep happening to me? What have I done to deserve this? Am I such a horrible person? I've never hurt anyone in my life to be punished like this.

I just don't understand.

If I weren't pregnant, I don't know how I would have coped. The way I'm feeling right now, I would have swallowed a bottle of pills and ended it all because I can't take much more. I just can't--I have nothing left. Cole's wrecked me beyond repair. I just want this pain to stop. Every breath I take feels like it's choking the life out of me. And the more I think about him with *her,* happy, while I'm hurting, the more I feel like dying.

I wish I never met him. I wish I could rip out my heart and hurl it at him and scream, here, take it because it's worthless to me now. I feel the life being excruciatingly siphoned right out of me, and I can't bear it.

"Shay, we're here." I jerk out of my thoughts when Jo touches my leg to get my attention. I get out of the car and walk to the front door of my childhood home. I didn't have my keys, so I knock on the door and pray my mother was home. The door opens, and I watch the smile disappear off her face when she sees the state of me.

"Oh, honey, what's wrong?" She asks worriedly, taking my face in her hands and looking into my tear-filled eyes. I couldn't speak. I choke on a sob and throw myself into her arms, and she holds me tight. My mother looks at Jo standing behind me questioningly. Jo shrugs and shakes her head. "Come on, darling, let's go inside." She leads me inside to the living room. "Shayla, what's going on? You're scaring me." My mother questions when I lay my head in her lap, sobbing. "Jo? Is Cole okay? Did some-thing happen?"

Jo sits on the sofa next to my mother and looks down at me. "They broke up. It's all so complicated, but as you know, Cole doesn't remember that he loves Shayla. He still thinks he's in love with his ex-Sophie. So, he told Shayla he doesn't love her, that he loves Sophie, and left her." Jo explains, and my mother clamps her hand over her mouth and looks down at me, stunned.

"Oh, good heavens,"

"I lost him, Mum," I whimper. "I couldn't make him love me again. I couldn't."

My mother closes her eyes and strokes my head. "Oh, my sweet girl, he may not remember you now, but he will. The heart doesn't forget Shayla. That boy will wake up every day with that big void you left in his heart and wonder why he doesn't feel complete. I promise you, sweetheart, even if his mind doesn't remember you, his heart will lead him right back to you." She conveys, and I shake my head.

"It's too late." I sob weakly. "He stood there and screamed in my face that he doesn't want the baby or me. Cole left us...he left us like we meant nothing to him."

My mother tearfully shakes her head. "Oh baby, I know, I know how much it hurts to lose the man you love, but you're going to get through this, okay, you'll have your beautiful baby girl in your arms soon. You have to be strong for her. You don't need him; you have your family and your friends."

I shake my head and press my hand to my stomach. "I may not need him, but she will, Mum. What am I going to tell her? I can bury the pain deep in my heart and live with it, but how am I going to look her in the eyes one day and tell her that her father didn't want us, didn't want her. How, tell me, how am I going to tell her that?!" I sob wretchedly. "I know first-hand what it's like growing up without a father. I don't want that for her."

"Honey, her father is still very much alive. You do the best you can to fill that void, and one day, when she's old enough, you tell her who he is, and she can decide if she wants a relationship with him. We all know that Cole would have died before he ever left you and his baby. He was crazy about you both. I saw the love that boy had in his heart for you. It's not his fault, honey. Cole didn't wake up one morning and decide he doesn't love you or the baby. He lost his memory; he's just as innocent in all of this as you and this baby." She explains, looking down at me while combing her fingers through my hair.

I wince, "I know that, but I can't just stand by and watch him fall in love and live happily with another woman...especially *her*. I can't. Cole could have tried harder-- but he didn't. He chose the easy way out. He chose to be selfish and walked away from his family to be with her. That was his choice, memory loss or not. I can't forgive him for that, and I won't." I utter, sitting up and wiping away my tears. "I don't ever want to see his face again."

My mother turns to face me, "But you will, honey. Every time you look into your baby girl's face, you will see him, just like I see your father when I look at you." She explains, and I hang my head and cry.

"What am I going to do, Mum. I don't know if I'm going to survive this." My mother pulls me in for a hug and kisses my head.

"You will, baby, you'll find the strength, I promise you." She assures me, rubbing my back soothingly. "Shayla, I want you to move back home, and I can help you with the baby. You need to be around your family right now."

I shake my head and sigh, "I'm moving back in with the girls for now while I look for a place of my own and hopefully find a new job. Although, I don't know who will hire me when I'm so close to giving birth." I sigh tiredly, wiping away my tears.

"Shayla, Cole can—"

"No," I mutter firmly, closing my eyes. "I don't want a damn thing from him. I'm going to resign from my position at the company and erase him from my life for good. He's dead to me. I have some savings, so I'll be fine for a while."

My mother nods, "Okay, honey, I have a job now too, and so does your brother. You selflessly took care of us for years, and now it's our turn to take care of you and our baby. Don't worry about a thing."

"Aimee and I too. You don't have to move out, you can stay with the baby, and we can help you with her." Jo states, smiling at me sadly.

"Thank you. I need to figure something out soon before she comes. I'm not even ready for her, and she's due in twelve weeks." I sigh, defeated. "Cole and I were supposed to go and get everything she needed after he got back from his trip, but..."

"Then we will go and get everything she needs." My mother states, kissing my temple and rubbing my bump. I sigh, suddenly exhausted, and nod. "How about I make you and my granddaughter your favourite dish?" I shake my head.

"I'm not hungry. I just want to go home, shower, and sleep for a while," I answer, and she nods in understanding.

"Okay, but make sure you eat honey. I know food is the last thing on your mind, but the baby needs the nutrients to grow and be strong, especially the weeks leading up to the birth." My mother explains, and I nod. "Make sure she eats." She firmly tells Jo who nods in assurance.

"Of course. We'll take care of her, don't worry," Jo tells her. We left my mother's place and went back to my old apartment. Just walking into that place, I remembered all the breakdowns and memories of Cole and me, and it emotionally crippled me.

It felt strange being back in my old room. This wasn't my home anymore. My home was with Cole, in *our* house. As I lay on my bed, I remember the day we walked into the room we decided would be the baby's nursery.

"I think this would be perfect, it's right next to ours, and I will have them build an interconnecting door, so we can leave it open at night for easy access when you need to feed," Cole says in a flurry as he looks around the room. The excitement in his eyes at that moment made my love for him grow tenfold. "What?" He asks when he catches me watching him adoringly.

"I'm crazy about you, Cole Hoult." I declare lovingly, and he grins. Walking over to me, he wraps his arms around my waist and looks deeply into my eyes.

"Say it again, baby." He whispers, pressing his forehead to mine.

"I'm crazy about you," I tell him again, and he smiles, biting his lip.

"Oh baby, I'm even crazier about you...both of you." He affirms earnestly and kisses me slow and deep in that way that makes my head swim.

I close my eyes at the ache in my heart and sob into my pillow. How did we go from that to this? How? I want to scream until my lungs give out. I'm going to lose my mind. The more I think about him being with Sophie, holding her, and kissing her, the more it kills me.

At least the last time we broke up, I knew he was hurting just like I was, and I somehow found comfort in that. It was easier to breathe. But this time, knowing he doesn't care and is just getting on with his day drives me crazy. I need him to feel pain, I want him to hurt like I am, but he isn't.

I was in absolute agony, and I was angry, with him, with the situation, with the fate that let this happen to us. I have the sudden urge to walk into his office and throw everything I possibly can at him so that he can feel *something*. God, I hate him. I *hate* him.

I pull my phone out when I feel it vibrate in my back pocket. Josh was calling. I push the button and answer it. "Josh."

"Hey, pretty girl. You okay?"

I close my eyes and weep, "No." I hear Josh heave a deep sigh. "Josh, please tell me he's not gone to her, *please*."

"No, Shay, he hasn't. Cole's head is a mess. We just got to the house because he couldn't even focus on work. He's just trying to figure all of this out, but it's not making much sense to him. I've not seen him like this ever, Shay. He's just sitting on the floor, his head in his hands, staring sadly at the picture you ripped apart." Josh explains, and I cry. "Shayla, please stop crying. Think about the baby. The doctor said no stress, remember."

I shake my head, hugging my pillow. "It hurts, Josh. I feel like I'm about to lose my mind every time I remember those words he said to me. I don't want to believe that my Cole would ever say those things to me."

"He wouldn't." Josh sighs, "He's just not himself right now. Yesterday, he had a bit of a breakdown at the hospital and admitted he's really struggling with everything. I was furious with him for hurting you, but I get where he's coming from. Cole said he remembers things, but the emotional attachment to those moments isn't there. The only thing he remembers clearly is the accident. You should have seen the fear in his eyes when he was describing what happened." Josh explains, and I close my eyes. My heart clenches painfully, picturing him terrified in that flight. "Cole said the last thought he had just before they hit the ground...was you." I whimper into my hand.

"Oh, my God."

"Believe me when I tell you, he's not doing any of this to hurt you in any way. He just doesn't want to disappoint you anymore, Shayla."

"I know, but that doesn't make it hurt any less, Josh. I have no right to be angry with him because it's not his fault—but I am. I'm hurt, and I'm mad, and I don't know who else to blame. Who do I blame Josh, tell me? Do I blame God? Do I blame myself for not getting on that plane with him? Who do I blame? Tell me!" I cry into my pillow. "Tell me because I'm about to lose my mind."

"Shayla, no one is to blame. It was an unfortunate accident, babe. That's all." He sighs, and I jump when I hear a crash on his side. "Oh fuck, I have to go."

"Cole, stop!"

I sit up.

"What was that? Is that Aimee?"

Josh groans, "That's Cole turning over the dining table. I'll come and see you later, okay? He says before I hear him shout Coles name, followed by another crash, and then the line cuts off.

I stare at the phone for a couple of seconds. *God, please give me the strength to get through this.*

TWO WEEKS CRAWL ON BY, and the pain has yet to subside. There's a constant ache and heaviness in my chest that I can't seem to shake. I've not seen or spoken to Cole at all, nor did I have any desire to.

I force myself to go outside to get some air. I feared I'd lose what little sanity I have left if I kept myself hauled up inside. I went for an appointment with my midwife to check everything is okay with the baby, and thankfully she's perfect, growing nicely. Well, she would, the amount of food Jo and Aimee keep shoving down my throat.

On the thirteenth day, I got a visit from Cole's mother. I was surprised to see her standing at my door. "Hi, sweetheart."

"Hi," I reply and step aside to let her in. "Come on in." I close the door and walk to the living room. Elaine looks me over, a deep sadness in her honey-coloured orbs, as she takes a seat on the sofa beside me.

"I've wanted to come and see you for a while, but Tristan told me to give you space." I stare at my hand and ignore the pinch in my heart at the mention of his name. "How are you, sweetie?"

I lift my eyes and look at her. "As well as can be, given the circumstance," I reply, blinking away the tears that gather in my eyes. Elaine nods, reaching over, and takes my hand into hers.

"You're devastated, honey, I know. I'm devastated for you. Tony and I both are. I can't even begin to fathom what you're going through right now. Especially while being pregnant." She says forlornly and squeezes my hand gently. "I wish I could make sense of all of this, Shayla. I am absolutely beside myself that this has happened to you two when you were so happy together." Elaine expresses, tears rolling down her face. "When I found out what he said to you, I was heartbroken. I couldn't believe that my son, my Tristan, would ever say such a thing, especially to *you* of all people."

I stare down at my hands and shake my head. "Neither could I," I whisper, wiping away the tears with my fingers. "But he did. He chose Sophie over his baby and me."

"Shayla, he would never choose her over you honey, he's just not himself since the accident. He's still stuck in 2016 when he first met her. Right now, she's the only thing that makes sense to him. Even though he's married to you, emotionally, he's tied to her, and he said he feels like he's unfaithful to her." I close my eyes and sigh. "He's confused, and his feelings are all over the place. His head is a literal mess. I can see him sinking deeper and deeper into this depressive state, and I don't know how to help him. We've tried to be there for him, but he's shutting us out." Elaine cries, shaking her head.

"I tried to be there for him, I did, but he doesn't want me. Cole made it very clear when he took his ring off and handed it back to me," I tell her while twirling the ring on my finger. "I didn't give up on us. He did."

"I understand that sweetheart, and of course, you're angry and hurt. You have every right to be. Any woman in your position would be, but Shayla, I think you're giving up too easily. Tristan loves *you*, darling. Deep down, we both know you're the one he needs in his life, not that fiend Sophie. Are you really going to roll over and let her wreck everything you both fought so hard for?"

I pull my hand away from hers and look at her through my tears. "*Too easy?* Do you have any idea how much it hurt to stand there and have him scream in my face repeatedly that he doesn't love me? That he doesn't want me, or that he can't see himself loving anyone but her? How do you expect me to just brush that aside and stand by him like he never tore my heart right out of my chest and handed it to me? It's not like this is the first time either. Your son has destroyed me over and over again, and I forgave him--but not this time." I tell her. "I'm not his doormat, all I have left is my baby and my pride, and I plan on holding onto them both for dear life." I cry despairingly. "Cole chose a life without us, and that's a decision he's going to have to live with, whether his memory comes back or not."

Elaine reaches up and brushes my tears away with the back of her hand, "Shayla, he's lost without you. His life, his work, it's all slipping away from him, and he's drowning in it all. Tony is trying to help him, but you're the only one that knew the ins and outs of all these projects you were both working on. Word has gotten out about his amnesia, and investors are in a state of frenzy, and there's talk of them pulling out. I know it's incredibly selfish of me to even ask this of you, whether Tristan knows it or is too proud to admit that he needs you, but he does. Tristan has always been good at putting on a facade to hide his feelings, but I know my son, he's on a downward spiral, and he's lost the one person that's capable of pulling him out."

"I can't," I whisper, shaking my head. "It's just too hard to face him every day. I have to think about my mental state and my baby, first and foremost."

"Just think about it, okay? I'm hoping and praying the more Tristan sees you around, the more chance he's got of remembering you and how much he loves you and not that harpy Sophie." She voices, brushing my hair away from my face and tucking it behind my ear so that she could see my face.

"I'll think about it." I sigh.

"Very well. I also want you to know that even though Tristan doesn't..." She sighs and closes her eyes briefly. "Want to be any part of this baby's life, Tony and I do. We want to have a relationship with our granddaughter, and we want you to know that we're here for both of you emotionally and financially for whatever you need." Elaine expresses, and I nod, unable to hold back the sob any longer. "Oh honey, come here." Elaine hugs me tight while I weep into her chest.

"I wish I had the power to ease some of your grief." She cries, pulling my head up and wiping my tears away in a motherly manner. "You're the best thing to ever happen to my son, and you'll always be a part of our family no matter what, okay?" She states sincerely, and I nod. "Please think about what I said." She adds, rubbing my stomach before she stands up. I see her to the door, and we hug once more before she leaves.

I close the door and press myself against it. While everyone is asking me to save him—I'm wondering who's going to save me.

Chapter 10

COLE

"Mr Hoult?"

I blink and look back when I hear someone knock and enter my office. I was lost in thought, standing at the floor-to-ceiling window staring at the bleak city before me. "Yes, Jessica?"

"I'm sorry, I did knock, but..."

"It's okay. What do you need?" I sigh, looking back at her, and she shifts uneasily, chewing on her bottom lip.

"The investors are here, and they're asking to speak to Shayla. I don't know what to tell them. They seem pretty upset." Jess informs me, and I sigh, pinching the bridge of my nose.

"Take them into the conference room and offer them refreshments. I'll be there in a few minutes," I instruct her, and she nods, leaving my office. I look out of the window again and wonder what the hell I'm going to tell these people.

It seems Shayla has built quite a rapport with the investors to the projects we were working on that they're demanding to speak to her and no one else. I've lost a major account already this week because we couldn't agree on costs and materials for the new mall in Madrid. Evidently, I hadn't realised just how much I entrust on Shayla around here, especially on these projects that we started together.

I vaguely hear my door opening and closing and the sound of heels clicking on the marble floor.

"I'll be there in a minute Jessica." I snap, agitated, not even bothering to look back.

"Cole." I whip my head around when I hear her voice so fast I'm sure I gave myself whiplash. I thought I was hearing things again, but I wasn't. She was there, standing in my office, eyes cast down to her feet. I turn and face her fully and take a couple of steps closer.

"Shayla?" I utter surprised, and she finally lifts her eyes to look at me.

"Do you have a minute to talk?" She asks her voice soft. I nod and walk across the room to stand closer to her. I don't know why she was here, but I was thankful. I didn't think I would see her again.

"Would you like to sit?" I offer, and she shakes her head, averting her gaze, looking everywhere, but at me. I caught the tears that were glistening in her eyes before she looked away.

"No, I—"

"Oh, Shayla! Thank God you're here. Blake Bryant is here, and he is pissed." Jess explains, walking into my office in a flurry. I glare at her hard when she just barges in, interrupting us. Shayla looks over at Jess and nods.

"Uh, okay. Please tell him I'll be there in a second." Shayla instructs her, and Jess nods before she rushes off out of the office.

"We'll talk after," Shayla walks out of the office. I observe her as she walks away until she disappears from my sight before I follow her to the conference room.

"Mr. Bryant, I'm so sorry to keep you waiting." Shayla greets politely as she walks over and shakes his hand. Blake Bryant stands when he sees Shayla and the deep scowl he had on his face softens to a frown. "I've been off work sick for a week, but I'm back now."

She is?

Blake's brows shoot up as they take a seat. "Oh, I'm sorry to hear that. Nothing serious, I hope?" He replies, and Shayla smiles, shaking her head.

"Thankfully, nothing some rest and comfort food couldn't fix." She retorts with a pretty smile, and Blake smiles back at her with a nod. I greet him and shake his hand before I take the seat beside Shayla as she opens the files, and they dive straight into talking about work.

I silently observe as Shayla speaks softly, professionally. She leans forward, flicking through the paperwork, and Blake, much like myself, listens avidly to every word she says, his eyes flickering to her mouth every so often while she speaks and stops to lick her lips.

"Mr Bryant, if you're not happy with the budget that we've set for this project. Cole and I will review and work on cutting back on some costs," Shayla explains, and Blake leans back in his chair and gazes at her with a flirtatious smile.

"Shayla, I've told you a thousand times, please, call me Blake." He chastises her playfully, and Shayla smiles a little and nods, tucking a strand of her hair behind her ear delicately. "You promised me, remember?"

"Right, of course, I'm sorry. Blake, how do you feel about the budget? Are you happy with it, or would you like us to look into it some more?" She inquires, and Blake shakes his head.

"I'm happy with it. I'm running late for another meeting, but I can swing by this week sometime, and we can work on the contract and get it all signed and sealed?" Blake suggests and glances over at me and then back at Shayla again. Surprised he even remembered I was sitting there—what a knobhead.

"Sounds good to me."

"Excellent. We'll do it over lunch. There's this great restaurant I know you'll love." Blake suggests while rising to his feet, and Shayla looks at him surprised but nods, standing as well.

They shake hands while I get up, and he shakes my hand too. I stare at him soberly and give his hand a firm squeeze. Blake's ocean blue eyes flitter down to our hands and back up at me again, his lips quirk ever so slightly before we let go, and he walks out after one last lingering glance at Shayla.

Is this moron flirting with her right in front of me?

I stare at Shayla, who gathers her papers and slides them into the file again. Her green eyes flicker up to mine, and she blinks. "What are you looking at?" She grumbles, irked, and I blink, surprised by her sudden icy demeanour.

"Nothing. I'm just surprised you're here, that's all. Do you want to go and have that talk?" I question, and she nods curtly before walking out of the conference room. I follow her to my office and close the door. "What did you want to talk about?"

Shayla sighs, looking down at her feet for a long moment, seemingly gathering her thoughts before looking at me again. "It took a lot for me to come here and face you again after everything that happened. Your mother came to see me, and she told me that you're struggling with the accounts for the projects we were working on together." Shayla explains swiftly, and I roll my eyes, shaking my head. Great. Thank you, Mum. "I'm here for the job and the job only--at least until the baby is born, then you're on your own. I don't want anything to do with you. As far as we're concerned, it's done, and the less I see of you, the better."

I look at her wordlessly for a long moment and sigh when she doesn't even bother looking at me. "Of course."

"Great. What happened with Saris Corp?"

"They walked."

"Why?" She questions with a frown, and I shrug.

"We couldn't reach an agreement on the budget, and they demanded naming rights," I reply, shoving my hands in my pockets and look at her steadily.

"What did you offer them?"

"Ten percent," I answer and watch as she rolls her eyes and shakes her head slowly.

"Cole, Saris is one of our biggest investors. They won't agree to anything below twenty-five percent. You negotiated this." She states, then sighs. "You no longer remember that. Jesus, okay, I'll call and speak to Peter to see if we can win their account back."

I nod, "Great." I utter, rubbing the back of my neck rather awkwardly. Our eyes meet, and she glares at me angrily, trying her best to mask the despair in her green eyes as she stares into mine. I sigh heavily. "Shayla, I'm sorry."

"Don't." She hisses frostily. "I don't want to hear it. You have less than twelve weeks to get your shit together with these projects, then I'm out of *here* and your *life* for good." She grimly states before she turns and walks out of my office.

I exhale deeply and close my eyes. Fucking great. It was one thing not having her around and hating me, but having her in my face daily spewing venom and glaring daggers at me is just the cherry on top of the cake.

I'm not used to seeing this angry side to her. I know she's still hurting, and it must have taken everything for her to come back here and face me after I wrecked her.

I remember hearing her sobbing on the phone to Josh two weeks ago.

I was having a shitty day at work, couldn't focus on anything, and my head was hurting again, so I had Josh bring me home. A tiny part of me hoped I would catch Shayla when she was packing, but she wasn't there. It was just Aimee. I walk into the living room and saw the photo of Shayla and me that we had above our fireplace was on the floor ripped to bits. I sink to the ground and stare at the torn-up pieces of what used to be our wedding photo. Christ, what have I done to her? She must really despise me to shred our picture.

"Shay, please stop crying. Think about the baby. The doctor said no stress, remember." I hear Josh say. He was on the phone with her. I get up and move over to where he was in the kitchen. "He wouldn't." Josh sighs, rubbing his forehead as he paces back and forth, "He's just not himself right now. Yesterday, he had a bit of a breakdown at the hospital and admitted he's really struggling with everything. I was furious with him for hurting you, but I get where he's coming from. Cole said he remembers things, but the emotional attachment to those moments isn't there. The only thing he remembers clearly is the accident. You should have seen the fear in his eyes when he was describing what happened, Shay." Josh explains, and I sigh, pressing my forehead against the wall.

"He said the last thought he had just before they hit the ground...was you." I wince when I get a sudden flash of my last moment before we hit the ground. I walk over to Josh, and he looks at me questioningly when I gesture for him to put her on speaker, and he does.

"Believe me when I tell you, he's not doing any of this to hurt you in any way. He just doesn't want to disappoint you anymore, Shayla."

Shayla sniffles on the other end, "I know, but that doesn't make it hurt any less, Josh. I have no right to be angry with him because it's not his fault, but I am. I'm hurt, and I'm mad, and I don't know who else to blame. Who do I blame Josh, tell me? Do I blame God? Do I blame myself for not getting on that plane with him? Who do I blame? Tell me!" She sobs, so utterly broken. "Tell me because I'm about to lose my mind." I bite my lip hard. Something deep inside my gut stung at the devastation in her voice.

Josh looks at me and shrugs helplessly as she weeps on the phone. I turn to walk out of the kitchen, and my foot hits the chair on the glass dining table, a sudden surge of anger erupts inside of me, and I furiously lift the table and turn it over in a rage and watch as it shatters. I couldn't comprehend all these foreign feelings inside me, and it felt like I was slowly drowning in my own emotions.

I was mad at myself for breaking her, and if I could take back those words I said to her, I would in a heartbeat. I pick up the chair and hurl it at the wall and watch as it hits the floor in pieces. "Cole, stop!" I hear Aimee shout as I reach for another chair, but Josh pulls me back and looks at me.

"Cole, hey, stop. It's okay, it's okay, bro." He urges, taking hold of my arms and looking at me as I pant furiously, staring at the ground.

"It's not," I whisper, shaking my head. "I broke her man. I did that to her. She's a wreck because of me! And I still can't feel anything! I don't feel a fucking thing, Josh!" I shout angrily, hitting my head. "Why can't I remember her, huh? Why?!" I growl stormily.

Josh sighs and squeezes my shoulder, "I don't know Cole, but it will come, brother. Shayla was the love of your life. In time, I'm confident you will remember her."

"And if I don't? Then what? I've got so many people telling me different things, and I'm so tired of trying to make sense of my feelings.

When I look at Shayla, I get a feeling of deep sorrow, and my gut hurts like never before, but when I look at Sophie, I feel..."

Josh frowns, "You feel what?"

I sigh, rubbing my forehead. "I don't know. I don't know what I feel. A big part of me wants to be with Sophie because it's easy, and it makes sense to me, but something deep down inside..." I place my hand over my heart and sigh. "Something, somewhere, just doesn't feel right," I explain, closing my eyes.

"Cole, you need to give yourself time. I think you need to focus on yourself for a while and try to sort through your own feelings before you jump into another relationship, whether it's Sophie you want or Shayla. You need to fix *you*." Aimee tells me, and I look over at her. She was right.

I *do* need to fix myself first.

"You're right," I agree, nodding. "I do." I sigh, rubbing the back of my neck tiredly.

It's been weeks, and my head is still a mess.

I've started therapy, and that's helping me piece some things together in my head. Sylwia—the therapist I've been seeing, told me that the gut-wrenching sadness I feel over Shayla was likely my guilt over not remembering and hurting her. She explained that I need to stop feeling like I'm obligated to give people an explanation for the way I feel because I don't. She told me they would never understand what it's like to be me or be in my situation, and I need to stop torturing myself trying to please everyone.

I have to be *me*--whoever that may be and not the version everyone expects me to be. "You'll find yourself again, Cole, it's going to take time, but you will," Sylwia assures me, and I had no other choice but to hold onto the hope that I will because living with the chaos in my mind at the moment is proving more difficult than I ever imagined.

THE FOLLOWING week I was sat in my office with Shayla working on the Dubai project. It was the end of the day, and the office was near enough empty. I keep telling myself to keep my head down and focus on work, but my eyes drift up to her face, and I find myself watching her. I study her face closely while she concentrates on her sketch.

Her long, soft, brown hair is swept to one side, a strand fell in front of her face, and my fingers are itching to reach out and brush it back so that I could examine her pretty face more clearly. Eyes cast down, and she's gingerly biting her bottom lip while she works, her green eyes narrowing every so often when she focuses on something in particular. We have music playing in the background to drown out the silence while we work.

I force myself to look at the work in front of me, but I glance up at Shayla when she stills for a moment and looks at her phone, where I believe an Arabic song starts playing. A faraway look in her eyes. She blinks away the tears that gather in her eyes.

I look away just as she turns her gaze to look at me and pretend to work. I could **sense** her eyes on me, and I so desperately wanted to look at her.

Fuck it.

I lift my gaze slowly, and our eyes lock. There was something about her gaze that caused my breath to hitch up in my throat. I couldn't look away. I was, in all honesty, spellbound. I stare deeply into her eyes, and that warmth spreads through me again.

What is that? I can't even tell you what made me do what I did next —it's like my body just took over, and I reach over, brushing my thumb along her jaw, and her eyes close at my touch, tears spill over her cheeks. I brush away them away and close my eyes when I get a sudden flash of Shayla and me, it was very brief, but she was looking at me the same way she was just before.

"Shayla, I think I'm in love with you."

I wince and shake my head when my head pains suddenly. I draw back and press my fingers to my temples and groan. "Cole?"

"I don't know when or how, but I love you, Shayla...so much."

"Cole, are you okay?" I distantly hear Shayla ask through the thumping in my head. I feel her fingers curl around my wrist as I squeeze my eyes shut tight, and I **see** her gazing up at me beautifully, her eyes alight, full of such emotion it made me ache someplace deep in my core.

I press my forehead to hers. "Tell me you love me, baby," I whisper and open my eyes. Shayla looks at me, her green eyes wide and searching my own.

Chapter 11

SHAYLA

"Tell me you love me, baby," I stare at Cole motionless when he presses his forehead to mine and whispers *those* words to me. I fought the tears that were threatening to fall when he slowly opens his eyes and looks at me.

"What?" I whisper, watching him as he gazes at me, his eyes searching mine for something. He said the words, but the look in his eyes wasn't the same as that night. The love wasn't there, and it pained me deeply that he remembers the night he told me he loves me for the first time, but there's no emotion behind his words. Cole pulls back and looks at me, bewildered.

"Uh, was that a... memory of ours?" He questions, and I nod silently, stepping away from him. Cole stands and takes hold of my arm and pulls me back to him again. I look up at him questioningly.

"Fill in the blanks. Please?" He says pleadingly, and I blink, my eyes already welling up.

I shake my head.

"I can't," I answer, and he looks at me beseechingly. "You can't ask that of me, Cole. You can't ask me to relive that moment while you're looking at me like you don't even know me. I can't." I take a step away from him, but he tightens his hold on me and draws me closer, looking down into my face.

Cole presses his forehead to mine, his eyes shut.

"Tell me you love me, baby," Cole whispers again. My heart aches, and I wince when those very words scald me from the inside out.

I close my eyes, "I love you, Cole," I whisper back, unable to stop the tears that flow down my face before I pull away and hurry out of his office. I run into the bathroom and press myself against the door, sobbing quietly into my hand.

What the hell is he trying to do to me?

I move over to the sink and stare at myself in the mirror for a moment. "He doesn't love you, Shayla. Stop holding on and let go. That's not Cole. He's gone." I run the water and splash some cold water on my face. After I get a grip on my emotions, I walk out of the bathroom to my office, where I pick up my jacket and bag, so I could get out of there before he catches me again.

"Well, I'll be damned. I didn't expect to see *you* here again." I still and close my eyes when I hear her voice behind me. I suck in a deep breath before I turn and face her.

"Right back at you, *Sophie*." I hiss, glaring at her hard as she walks into my office with a rather smug look on her face. "I would ask what you're doing here, but I honestly don't care," I sigh, looking for my keys in my purse.

"I'm here to see my *boyfriend*." She replies, tossing her blonde hair over her shoulder.

The term *boyfriend* made my insides clench tight.

"Of course you are," I tell her with an exasperated roll of my eyes. "Well, don't let me keep you. You know where his office is," I add, gesturing to the door. Sophie smirks, her icy blue eyes rake over me, and stop at my stomach. I see the sadness in her eyes and figured she must be reliving the moment she lost her baby.

I instinctively place my hand on my tummy and look at her. As much as I hate her, I sympathize with her situation. A mother losing her baby is tough for anyone. I sigh and walk past her out of my office.

"You know, Shayla, I thought you were a prideful woman. I'm curious as to why you're still here, buzzing around Tristan after he *left* you?" I stop walking, close my eyes to control the rage, and bite my lip before I turn to face her again.

I laugh bitterly and take a step toward her. "You want to talk to me about pride, Sophie? *You?* I know Cole has forgotten, but did you happen to forget that he left your deceitful arse in your wedding dress and came looking for me?" I sneer, shaking my head. "Not that it's any of your business, but I am proud and fiercely loyal to my job and my clients," I tell her and let my eyes rake over her. "Not that I'd expect you to know a damn thing about loyalty. I'm not here for Cole. I'm here for my job and my future." I utter scathingly and turn to leave again.

"But he left you too, though, didn't he, Shayla? He left you for *me*. Tristan didn't want you or your baby. Guess you're not that special after all. He forgot all about you like you never existed to him, but he still remembers me. Tristan still remembers the love we had for one another." She retorts taciturnly, and I force myself to smile and take a step closer to her as I look her firmly in the eyes.

"God, you really are pathetic. He left you *by choice* Sophie," I reply, "Cole didn't leave me—he suffered a traumatic head injury and lost his memory--that wasn't his choice. Only you would use this as an advantage to worm your way back into his life again, which doesn't surprise me one bit, given the lies you've told him to keep your hooks in him. But guess what, you can have him." I tell her and lick my lips. "You know, I honestly feel sorry for you."

"*You* feel sorry for *me?*" Sophie laughs bitingly, and I smile, nodding in response. "Oh, this I have to hear." She grins, crossing her arms over her chest and watching me expectantly.

"I do because I will eventually get over him, but you're on limited time, babe. You will go to bed with him every night, and every morning you will wake up terrified, wondering if that will be the day he will remember that he absolutely despises you and drops you like he did last time." I tell her with a smirk. "You will live in my shadow every single moment you're with him, just like before. He's already starting to remember things, so I suggest you get in there and enjoy what little time you have with him, sweetie." I declare with a shake of my head.

"Well then, I'll be sure to erase every single memory he has of you when I'm fucking his brains out and getting pregnant while you're home playing mummy to your brat." She utters grimly, and I fist my hand tightly at my side. I had the strongest urge to slap the bitch, but I wouldn't dream of putting my baby in harm's way.

"Listen to me, you delusional bitch. I'd watch myself if I were you because I *can* and *will* take Cole back from you whenever I feel like it, and you better believe I will do it just to spite you." I hiss snidely, narrowing my eyes at her.

"Every second of every day, you'll wonder if he's really where he says he is or if he's balls deep inside *me* somewhere in this office... or in our bed." I grin and wink at her. "Sooner or later, Cole will remember, despite your best effort to keep us apart. His mind may have forgotten, but his heart will always remember me and the love we had. Remember that, when you're sitting all alone, crying over your pathetic attempts to manipulate him." I smirk and walk off toward the elevator. "Adiós puta!"

Shove that in your pipe and smoke it, you crazy bitch!

I feel so much better after that. It was high time I put that skank in her place. Oh, if I weren't pregnant, I would have rearranged her face ten times over by now.

"You DID WHAT?!" Aimee shouts, her blue eyes wide like saucers as she shoves popcorn in her mouth and chews excitedly like you do when you're watching a fascinating part in a film. "Tell me again...tell me again. I need to hear this word for word...*slowly.*"

I sigh with a smile shaking my head as I pull my hair up in a messy bun. After I got home, I told the girls about my exchange with the witch. "I am not explaining it all over again. I basically put her in her place and told her if she keeps pissing me off, I'll steal Cole back from her just out of spite."

"Yes! That is my bitch right there!" Aimee exclaims, excitedly throwing her popcorn in the air, and it falls around her. "Oh, damn." She utters, looking at the mess she made.

Jo and I laugh and throw the popcorn at her. "That was a long-time coming, Shay, and we're proud of you, baby girl." Jo praises me with a hug, and I smile, sighing.

"Heck yes, it was. Who the fuck does she think she is? Prissy little bitch. Can I beat her *for you*, please?" Aimee asks, giving me the puppy eyes and pressing her hands together like a child.

I laugh and shake my head. "As much as I would love to see that, no, you can't because we are not going to stoop to her level. I honestly cannot see what a guy like Cole saw in her for the life of me. She's rotten, and how he can't see that, I just...it baffles me." I explain, leaning back against the sofa and rub my stomach when I feel the baby move. "Steering away from the subject, we really need to build that crib we bought before she comes."

"No time like the present. I'm sure we can figure it out. We are three intelligent women, after all." Jo says, helping me off the sofa, and we all walk to my bedroom and stare at the cardboard box and then at each other.

"Josh?" Aimee mutters, turning her blue eyes to look at me, and I nod with a sheepish smile.

"Good call." Jo nods, lifting the box, and jumps back when it falls flat on the floor, almost crushing her foot. "Huh. I forgot how heavy that was."

"Honey, there's an emergency!" Aimee shouts hysterically down the phone to Josh, who immediately panics.

"Emergency?! What? Is the baby coming? It's not time yet!" He shouts, and we all hear a crash, which I assume was him falling over something. We all laugh and hear Josh curse on the other end.

"Anyone would think he's the father." Aimee chuckles, amused, looking at me.

"Awe, but this is good practice for when you do get pregnant," I tease and hear Josh sigh.

"Aimee, for God's sake, stop joking around. I literally fell over trying to put my jeans on, thinking the baby was coming." He grumbles, and we all laugh.

"Dang, that would have been a hell of a sight, baby." She mocks him with a grin, and Josh mutters incoherently to himself. "We need your sexy man muscles."

"We?" Josh intones bemused, and Aimee snickers.

"Yes, we, as a collective." She utters and winks at me. "You see, Shayla hasn't got any action in a very long time, and her prego hormones are running wild, so I told her she could borrow you for the night for some fun time? What do ya say?" I gape at her and slap her arm while she presses her finger to her nose, giggling.

"What?" Josh mutters deadpan, and Aimee covers her mouth to smother her laugh while Jo and I giggle hysterically. "Are you high? What are you girls smoking over there."

"Is that a no, then?" She asks, grinning.

"Of course, it's a no! Jesus Christ, Aimee!" He sputters, and we all laugh. "Oh, you're taking the piss. I'm hanging up!"

"No, wait!" Aimee laughs, "I'm sorry, baby, I was only teasing you. We do really need your help, though. We're attempting to put the baby's crib together, and we don't have a scooby-doo where to begin."

Josh sighs, "Okay, I'll be over in a bit."

"That's my man. Bring a pizza. I love you, bye!" She says in a flurry and hangs up. I chuckle and shake my head at her in disbelief.

"How that boy puts up with you, I will never know," I declare, sitting on my bed, and she grins toothily and wags her brows at me.

"I'm a dynamite in bed, baby." She states cheekily, and I laugh.

"We know!" Jo and I say together with a shudder.

"We share a wall." I remind her, and she nods, rather proud of herself.

"Hey, I'm not the only one, you're lucky you've missed the few times Jo and your bro were going at it." She declares, thrusting her hips to illustrate her point. "I thought they we're going to go through the wall,"

"No!" I shout, covering my ears, and Jo throws a pillow at Aimee while she cackles. My phone rings with an unknown number, and I pick it up and answer it.

"Hello?"

"Shayla, hey, it's Blake." I hear someone say on the other end and frown. When I don't say anything, he continues. "Bryant?"

"Oh!" I gasp when I finally realise who it was. "Blake, I'm sorry, you're the last person I was expecting to call me. How did you get my number?" I question and hear him chortle on the other end.

"I'm a very resourceful man," Blake states, and I knit my brows. Why was he calling me at this time? "Listen, I know you're probably wondering why I'm calling you out of office hours, but I wanted to invite you to join me for lunch tomorrow?" I look at the girls who are watching me inquisitively.

"Lunch? Tomorrow?" I repeat and scratch my head. "Sure, we can have lunch." I agree and shrug when Aimee gives me her signature 'what the fuck' look.

"Excellent, I'll pick you up from the office, around one 'o clock? This is my personal number. Save it." Blake replies, and I nod.

"Uh, okay, I'll see you then," I hang up, staring at the phone dumb-founded. I jump when Jo hits my leg to get my attention.

"Explain...." She drawls, her brown eyes peering at me curiously.

"Who the hell is Blake, and more importantly, is he hot?" Aimee questions and I set my phone aside and shrug.

"Blake Bryant is an investor for one of our projects, and yes, he's a very handsome man," I explain with a sigh, and they nod slowly, still looking at me expectantly. "What?"

"What do you mean, what? Why is he asking you out?" Jo questions, her brows drawn together.

I roll my eyes, "He's not. It's a business lunch to go through the contract for the project, that's all." I clarify, and Aimee doesn't seem convinced.

"He went out of his way to find your *personal* number to call you, out of office hours to invite you for a business lunch?" She drawls sardonically, and I nod and shrug. Aimee looks at Jo, and they shake their heads. "It's definitely a lunch date." Aimee snorts.

"What does he look like?" Jo questions, intrigued, and I shrug indifferently.

"I don't know, tall, dark hair, blue eyes," I explain, chewing on my lip. "Oh, actually, he follows me on LinkedIn," I suddenly remember and pick up my phone again. I load up the app and search his name before I hand it to the girls. "That's him."

"Yowza!" Aimee exclaims, her blue eyes wide as she stares at the phone. "Oh, sweet lord, is that a face made to be sat on or what."

"Let me see," Jo says, taking the phone, and her mouth drops open. "Holy crap, Shay. He's hot!"

I roll my eyes and snatch my phone back off of them. "You two are ridiculous. It's business. I'm not dating him, for God's sake. I'm married *and* pregnant." I utter, laying back on my bed and rub my bump. Aimee giggles a little, looking at me. "What?"

"You know it sends him a notification that you checked his profile." She states. I sit up and gape at them while they laugh at me as I turn five different shades of pink. I throw my pillow at Aimee, who falls over on the floor, cackling.

"Why didn't you tell me that before?!" I complain, irked, throwing my stuffed bear at her, and she shrugs, still laughing.

"It only just occurred to me."

"Oh my God, how embarrassing, now he's going to think I'm interested in him!" I groan and fall back on my bed, covering my face with my hands. The doorbell rings and Aimee gets up and dashes off to answer it. I'm actually thoroughly humiliated; how am I going to face him tomorrow? I could throttle Aimee.

Shortly after, Josh came over with a pizza for us, and we tackled building the crib together.

"Josh, I'm sure that's back to front," I advise him, looking at the instructions and the typical man that he is, of course, doesn't accept that he is wrong until he steps back all proud of himself and the crib collapses. "I did—"

"Don't you dare say I told you so." He utters, scowling at me and then at the pieces of wood on the floor.

"You're doing great, baby." Aimee praises, chewing her slice of pizza. Josh looks at her and shakes his head before he sits back on the floor, attempting to rebuild it again.

I sit back, watching him, and sigh deeply before I turn my gaze and stare out of the window. "You okay, bish?" Jo asks, and I nod.

"She called him her boyfriend. I guess that means they're officially together." I admit shaking my head forlornly. Jo scoots over to me and wraps her arm around me, and I lay my head on her chest. Josh looks over and frowns.

"She was probably trying to hurt you, Shay. Don't pay no mind to her." Josh says, picking up another piece of wood for the crib.

"She was at the office after hours, Josh. They're spending time together." I glance down at the ring on my finger. "He's moving on with her, and I'm here in agony, crying like a fucking mug, doing all the shit on my own that we should have been doing together to prepare for our baby." I shake my head, angrily wiping away the tears.

"You're not on your own, Shay. You have us." Aimee assures, and Josh nods in agreement.

"I know, and I love you all so much, but it's not the same," I admit. "It wasn't supposed to be like this. In a matter of weeks, I'm going to have this tiny person who will rely on me for everything, and I'm terrified I'm going to screw it all up." I sob.

"Shayla, you're going to be an amazing mum," Jo says and watches while I shake my head, getting up off the bed.

"I can't. I'm sorry, I need some air." I walk out of the room. I stand out on the terrace and inhale deeply, filling my flaming lungs with air.

Josh and the girls have been my absolute rock lately, and I appreciate them and so much, but these moments, us getting the nursery ready for the baby was supposed to be mine and Cole's moments together. Now, I have to figure out how the hell I'm going to be a single parent on top of everything else. Like everything else in my life, I'll do this on my own too. Even if it kills me, I'll love my baby enough for the both of us. She'll never know that her father ripped the very soul right out of me and left me for dead like we never meant a damn to one another.

~

THE FOLLOWING day I was sitting in my office going over the contract before Blake arrived to pick me up for our lunch. I was avoiding Cole like the plague after what happened the night before.

I tried my best to push it out of my mind, but every time I saw him walking toward my office, my heart would race, only for him to walk past it. I wondered what happened between him and Sophie after I left. The more I tried to convince myself I didn't care, the more it was bugging me, so much so that I couldn't focus on a damn thing on this contract. "Shay?"

I look up when I hear my name and see Cole standing at the door. *Oh shit.* "Yes?"

"Can we talk for a second?"

I sigh, "If it's about work, yes, we can. If it's not, then no." I tell him, dropping my pen, and he exhales.

"Shayla—" Cole interjects, but my intercom goes off, interrupting whatever he was going to say. He scowls at it.

"Mrs Hoult, Mr Bryant is here and waiting for you in the lobby." Jenny, the receptionist at the front desk, informs me.

"Thank you, Jenny, please tell him I'll be right down," I respond and gather up the papers for the contract.

"Why is Blake waiting for you? Are you going somewhere?" Cole questions and I nod, avoiding his gaze.

"Yes, he's taking me to lunch." I slide my phone in my bag before I walk to the door, but Cole blocks my way. I lift my gaze up to him, and he stares back at me gravely.

"Why?" He asks, narrowing his green eyes at me.

"To eat food, Cole, why else do people go to lunch?" I retort, trying to sidestep him, but he moves in front of me again. "Cole, get out of my way. He's waiting." I glare up at him, and he glares right back.

"I don't care. Let him wait. Why is he taking you to lunch when we have a perfectly good conference room where you can discuss work matters?" Cole queries, his dark brows knitted together tightly.

I sigh and close my eyes momentarily, "Maybe he doesn't want it to be so formal. How am I supposed to know?" I utter, growing agitated, and try to brush past him, but he blocks me off again. "Get out of my way, Cole." I hiss through clenched teeth, and he glares at me, his jaw set tight.

"I don't like him."

"That's your problem. Excuse me." I say and push past him. I look back at him as I wait for the elevator. Cole looks over at me and shakes his head before he storms out of my office toward his own. What right does he have to question me when he was hauled up in his office with Sophie doing god only knows what last night?

Unbelievable.

I push Cole Hoult out of my mind, or I try to for the duration of my lunch with Blake. "The contract looks great, Shayla," Blake says, smiling warmly as he picks up the pen and signs every page I marked for him. "Now that we're done with work matters, let's eat because I'm absolutely famished." He smiles, picking up his menu as I slide the contract into my bag. "They have the best lasagne here,"

I look at him and smile politely while picking up my menu, I skim over the items, and nothing catches my attention, so I decided to go with his recommendation. "Actually, lasagne sounds great," I tell him. Blake beams at me and calls the waiter over to place our orders. Once the waiter walks away, he turns his attention to me and licks his lips, his azure eyes searching mine.

"You're wondering why I've invited you to lunch when we could have done this at the office, aren't you?" He enquires, and I smile and nod a little.

"Actually, I am."

Blake leans forward, smiling. He laces his fingers on top of the table and looks at them for a long moment before lifting his eyes to mine. "I know this is going to sound really odd, but that day we had that meeting, I noticed a deep sadness in your eyes; even right now, you're trying your best to mask it, but I saw and still do see so much misery in your eyes." He states and smiles faintly, dropping his gaze from mine.

"I recognise that look all too well because that was the look I had in my eyes not too long ago." I frown, waiting for him to continue. "I lost my wife, Demi, a year ago. She died during childbirth." He explains, biting his lip thoughtfully.

"Oh, Blake, I'm so sorry," I gasp, reaching over and place my hand on his in an attempt to console him. Blake nods dolefully and covers my hand with his.

"It was honestly the worst year of my life, and if it wasn't for my daughter Elle, I don't know if I would have survived." Blake declares, looking at me again. "I heard about Tristan's unfortunate accident, and obviously, I knew you before, and I sensed a lot of animosity between the two of you."

I take a breath, pulling my hand away from his, and scratch my forehead, "Uh, that's because we broke up." I admit looking around the restaurant, suddenly feeling very uncomfortable.

"I figured as much," Blake nods in understanding, leaning back in his chair. "Look, Shayla, I remember how alone I felt after I lost Demi. I don't want you to get the wrong impression of me because my intentions aren't wrongful, I promise you. I think having someone in your life who understands what you're going through, who is also a single parent, will be good for you." He explains, and I shift in my seat.

"I'm sorry. I'm a little confused. What are you saying, Blake?"

Blake chuckles a little and rubs his forehead, "I'm saying I'd like us to be friends. If you ever need any advice on baby stuff or just to talk even. It can be very overwhelming as a new parent, especially if you're doing it alone, as I did."

I sigh, relieved. I thought he was asking me out for a minute. That would have been awkward.

"That's really kind of you to offer Blake, and as much as I'd like to be friends with you, I don't think it's wise for professional reasons."

Blake shakes his head, "Don't worry, I'm mature and grown enough to keep my personal and business life separate, I promise you." He chuckles a little. "I'm not asking you out or anything, don't worry. Once you have the baby, maybe we can go out for coffee sometimes, or you can join me in the parent-toddler classes. They are accommodating, and you're going to need all the support you can get, trust me." He goes on to explain as our food arrives and we eat. I listen as he tells me all about his struggles as a single parent, and I'm not going to lie, I was terrified. Blake advised me to sign up for Lamaze classes, which I had no clue about. It truthfully hit me hard how unprepared I was for this baby.

"Oh God, that's a lot of information to take in over lunch," I utter, setting my fork down, feeling extremely thunderstruck. Blake smiles at me and reaches over, squeezing my hand supportively.

"Hey, come on, you're going to boss this. If you need any advice about anything, just call me, and I'll help where I can, all right?" Blake assures me sweetly as I stare at him, feeling more lost than I ever have in my life.

As I sat there listening to him while internally freaking out, all I could think was—damn you, *Tristan Cole Hoult.*

Chapter 12

COLE

TWO WEEKS LATER.

"WHAT ARE YOU DOING?" I jump out of my skin, look back and see Josh standing behind me as I watch Shayla grinning at a basket of some sort and flowers she's just received. "Are you spying on Shayla?"

I rub the back of my neck and shake my head. "What? No." I utter, glancing over at her again, and Josh chuckles.

"Right, so you're hiding behind the wall looking into her office...why?" I sigh, relenting.

"Fine, maybe I was spying...a little," I sigh, looking at him before I turn my gaze over to her, opening a book and skimming through it. "Who sent her those, and what the hell is that basket?"

"Uh, it appears that it's a nappy basket. It's filled with blankets and booties and clothes for the baby." Josh explains, looking over at her with a smile. "She said it's a gift from Blake Bryant."

I grind my teeth. Every hair on my body goes up when I hear that man's name, and my gut twists. "Why? Why is he sending my wife gifts?"

Josh's brows furrow and he looks at me, surprised. "Your *wife?* Weren't you out on a dinner date with Sophie the other night?" I turn to look at him.

"It wasn't a date." I grate irritated. "And I wouldn't have gone if she wasn't out with that knobhead." Josh sighs, shaking his head.

129

"Cole, you made your choice, bro. You chose Sophie. Now you need to stick by your decision and let Shayla get on with her life. You have absolutely no right to be angry with her when you're the one that walked out on her and your baby." Josh explains, and he has a point, but I couldn't help the annoyance gnawing away deep inside me. "She's trying to move on, and Blake seems to be good for her. Look at her. She's finally smiling again like she used to."

I scowl. "Good for her? What kind of man pursues a woman who is still married and pregnant?" I ask, observing Shayla as she speaks to someone on the phone.

"What kind of man leaves his wife and baby to be with his ex?" Josh throws back at me, and I glower at him hard.

"The kind that lost his memory. I didn't leave because I woke up one morning and felt like a change. I don't remember her. It wasn't by choice." I argue, and Josh shakes his head with an exasperated sigh.

"Yes, it was. I get that you're going through some shit, man, I do, but you could have made the right choice--the honourable choice and stuck it out with Shayla and your baby—but you didn't. And now, you get to stand by and watch another man make her happy and live the life *you* once had with her." Josh tells me and looks over at Shayla again.

"Even if it's over for you and Shay, and you truly want to be with Sophie, how are you going to let some other man hold *your* baby girl in his arms?" I close my eyes and imagine Blake holding my baby, and I couldn't ignore the pull at my heart. "The first man she sees should be you, bro."

"You think I don't know that or think about it every single day? I'm scared, Josh," I admit sullenly. "I'm scared I'll look at her and not love her or see her as my own, and more than anything, I'm terrified of Shay's reaction to that. I don't want to hurt her more than I already have."

"Cole, that's not possible. That's your flesh and blood." Josh assures me while squeezing my shoulder. "You told me after you found out she was pregnant that you hoped it was a little girl so you would have another mini-Shayla." I sigh, and for a fleeting moment, I picture a little girl with long shiny brown hair, dark green eyes, and a beautiful smile running toward me.

I glance over at Shayla and nod. Josh was right. I have to push past my fears and anxiety and be there for my baby despite everything happening between Shayla and me. Yes, I was scared shitless, but I need to do what's right. "You're right. I'm that baby's father, and I need to man up and take responsibility for her." I slap Josh on the back. "I'm going to go and talk to her," I say, and Josh watches me bewildered as I walk toward Shayla's office.

"Shayla?" I call out, pushing the door open and walking into her office, her head snaps up from her tablet, and she looks at me with a little frown.

"Yes?"

"Can we go someplace and talk?" I quickly ask before I lose my nerve. Shayla leans back into her chair, regarding me curiously.

"Why can't we talk here?" She asks, dropping her pen while staring up at me. I exhale and walk over to her desk.

"Because I don't want the whole office overhearing our conversation. You know, it's personal." Shayla leans forward and rubs her forehead with a groan.

"Cole, we don't have anything personal to discuss, and I'm honestly not in the mood." She expresses tiredly, picking up her pen and looking down at her tablet.

"Is there anything more personal than our baby?" Shayla's eyes snap up to mine, and she glares at me hard.

"Our baby?" Shayla scoffs, shaking her head. "You lost the right to call her yours when you said you didn't want her." She hisses hotly, and I place my hands on her desk and lean closer, so I could look into her eyes.

"Shayla, can you please be a little understanding and try to acknowledge and empathise with what I've been going through the last four weeks?" I argue, and she shakes her head and places her own hands on her desk. She stands up and leans in, glowering at me.

"Are you fucking kidding me, Cole? I stood by you through everything, and I was willing to keep supporting you, but YOU walked out on

US, not the other way around." She declares angrily, and I hold her gaze as she continues to scowl at me

"This isn't about you and me, Shayla. It's about what's right for our baby." I retort, and she blinks at me and shakes her head before she sinks into her chair, rubbing her head.

"Now? Our baby's best interest has only just now occurred to you?" She questions, looking up at me. "Why now, Cole? What? Did you suddenly wake up this morning ready to be a father? I don't understand what you're trying to do here?" She utters and starts to cough.

I frown and look her over as she continues coughing. "Are you okay?" I question, and she sips some water and exhales slowly.

"No, I am not okay. You're pissing me off." Shayla groans, closing her eyes. I look over her face a notice she was a little pale as she sips her water. "Stop staring at me. I'm fine. It's just a little cold,"

I reach out and touch her cheek, but she slaps my hand away. "Get your hands off me." She sputters, rubbing her temples.

"Shay, you're burning up," I say, touching her forehead again, she sighs, closing her eyes, but shrinks away from my touch, and I notice she's shivering.

"I'm fine."

"You're not fine. How long have you been feeling like this?" I ask, moving around her desk and kneel in front of her.

"Cole, I'm fine," She insists, pulling her face away when I reach out to touch her. "I woke up with a little cold. I'll live."

I scowl at her and roll my eyes. "Shayla, you're pregnant, and you've got a fever. I'm taking you home. Come on." I tell her, and she shakes her head stubbornly and starts to cough again.

"I can go. I don't need you to baby me." Shayla grumbles, getting up to her feet; she staggers a little, so I reach out and steady her.

"Yes, of course, you can. Stop being difficult. I'm taking you. Are the girls home?" I help her put her jacket on.

"No, Jo is with Sam, and Aimee is with family." She sighs and winces, rubbing her head. "I'm a big girl. I don't need a babysitter." I watch her as she presses her forehead to my chest. "Ow."

I rub her arms and bury my nose into her hair--she feels hot to the touch. I can feel the heat radiating off her head. "All right, come on, we're going home." I wrap my arm around her shoulders, and she nestles into me as we walk toward the elevator.

"Can you walk? Do you want me to carry you?" I ask, looking down at her, and she shakes her head. I can feel her shivering in my arms, and she can barely stand up straight. As the elevator hits the underground car park, I lift her into my arms and walk to my car. "Gerald, get the door," I tell my driver, who runs around the car and opens the back door, and helps me get Shayla in the back seat.

"Sir? Is Shayla okay? Are we going to the hospital?" Gerald questions in a flurry, looking at Shayla, concerned.

I shake my head as I climb in next to her and pull her into my arms. "No, the hospital will take too long to see her. I'll get a doctor to come home and check her over," I tell him as he gets in the driver's seat and he drives out of the car park. I press my lips against her forehead, her fever seems to be getting worse, and she feels clammy. Shayla coughs again and groans, burying her face into my chest.

"Cole..." she groans. "I don't feel good."

"I know, sweetheart. I know you don't, but you're going to be okay, I promise," I assure her brushing my fingers through her hair while I dial our family doctor's number. "Doctor Giles, I need you to come over to the address I'm going to send you. My wife is sick, and she's pregnant."

"Okay, what are her symptoms?"

I glance down at Shayla, "She's burning up, coughing, headache. She can barely stand." I tell him. "Please hurry."

"I'm on my way, Mr Hoult. How far along is she in the pregnancy?" I shake my head.

"I don't know, like thirty-two weeks, I think."

"Okay, we need to get her temperature down because a high fever this late in the pregnancy can cause complications and be harmful to the baby." Dr Giles informs me, and I close my eyes. Oh God.

"What do I do?" I ask in a panic looking down at her, trembling in my arms.

"You need to get her in a lukewarm bath or shower, not cold because that could increase her internal body temperature. I'll be with you in twenty minutes." I nod and hang up.

"Gerald, hurry up," I sigh, looking down at Shayla. I wrap my arms around her, and she groans. "We're nearly home, sweetheart," I murmur, kissing her head. The usual ten-minute drive home felt like ten years to me at that moment. I was worried sick something would happen to her and the baby.

"Cole. I'm...so cold." She breathes, snuggling into me further while she trembles incessantly, her teeth clattering. I felt so fucking helpless. I didn't know if I should wrap her up or take some layers off.

"I know, baby, I'm going to take care of you, and you're going to feel better real soon," I whisper while stroking her head. We finally arrive at the house, and Gerald helps me get her out of the car. He rushes to open the front door as I carry her inside and upstairs to the bathroom. "Gerald, let the doctor in when he arrives!" I shout and hear him reply with a 'yes sir' as I carry Shayla into the bathroom.

I look around frantically and kick the toilet seat shut before I sit her down on it gently. I ensure she was steady before I reach over and turn the shower on, adjusting the water, my eyes on Shayla. Once the water was lukewarm, I move over to her and take her shirt off before I lift her into my arms, and we step into the shower together. Shayla hisses when the water hits her body, and she clings to me.

"It's...cold." She gasps, her teeth chattering. I press my forehead to her head and hold her frail body against me. "Cole..." She gasps, coughing. "I'm freezing."

"We need to get your temperature down baby, just hold on to me," I tell her while brushing her hair out of her face.

"Mr Hoult?" I hear Doctor Giles call out to me.

"In here!" I answer and see him pop his head around the door, probably to check if we were decent before he enters. "You can get her out now. Can you wrap her up and lay her down on the bed?" He instructs me, and I nod, turning the water off.

"Would you pass me that towel from under the sink," I request and take it when he hands it to me. I wrap it around Shayla, and we step out of the shower. I scoop her up into my arms, walk her to the bedroom, and gently lay her down on the bed. I brush her hair out of her face, and she opens her eyes and looks at me, still shivering uncontrollably.

"Cole."

"I'm right here," I answer, kissing her temple. "The doctor is here. He's going to examine you. You're going to feel better real soon, okay." I tell her, and she barely nods.

"Shayla. I need to check your temperature and have a quick listen to your chest." Doctor Giles informs her, and she nods coughing again.

"How long have you had this cough?"

"Last night." She whispers.

"Okay, you're running a remarkably high fever Shayla, and your chest is all congested. Are you feeling any aches and pain? Headache?" Shayla nods.

"Everything hurts." She complains, coughing.

"Is she going to be okay? What's wrong with her?" I question, and he nods.

"She's got a viral infection. It's nothing that won't clear up in a few days. I'll give her some paracetamol through an I.V. That will bring her temperature down quicker, and then you can give it to her orally every four hours. Because she's pregnant, we can't give her medication, so her body will have to fight the virus on its own, and the paracetamol will ease some of her aches and pains." He explains, pulling her eyelids open and checking her pupils. "You'll need to get her out of these wet clothes, and I can put the drip on for her." He adds, looking at me, and I nod. I watch Dr Giles as he leaves the room so that I can undress her.

I lift Shayla up gently, remove her bra, and toss it aside before taking her skirt off along with her underwear. Shayla hisses when the cool air hits her damp skin. I dress her in a pair of my boxers and one of my t-shirts. "You can come in Doctor, she's decent," I inform him, and he comes in a second later and proceeds to put the drip on her hand. I look down at her pale face and brush my fingers through her damp hair.

"You're going to feel better real soon, sweetheart," I whisper, kissing her forehead.

"She needs plenty of fluids for the next couple of days. If her condition doesn't improve or her temperature doesn't drop, you must take her to the hospital immediately." I look down at Shayla and nod in response. "The drip should take about ten minutes. Am I okay to hang around?"

"Of course, thank you so much for coming out so quickly. I was honestly worried sick something was wrong with her or the baby." I declare uneasily, looking down at her, and he smiles.

"No problem at all. A man's first and most important priority is always his family." Doctor Giles states, his smile warm and paternal. "She's fortunate to have a husband who loves her as much as you do."

I stare at Doctor Giles for a long moment before I look at Shayla. Love? Was that *love,* though? His words had me questioning quite a bit in my head the rest of the night. Once the drip was finished, Dr Giles handed me the prescription for some tablets for Shayla to take before he left. I sent Gerald out to get the medicine. I couldn't bear the thought of leaving her side for a second.

I LET her sleep for a couple of hours, only waking her up to drink some water. Around ten 'o clock, her phone was ringing in her purse. It was Aimee. "Hey, Aimee," I answer it.

"Cole?" comes her surprised reply. "Shay's with *you?*"

"Yes, she's with me," I tell her. "She's sick. I brought her to our house, so she's not alone at your place."

"What do you mean she's sick? What's wrong with her? Is she okay?"

I rub my forehead, "Doctor said she's got a viral infection, he's given her medication, and she's asleep right now."

"Why didn't you call me? I'm coming over."

I shake my head. "She'll be out for the rest of the night. I'm keeping an eye on her, don't worry. I'll let you know how she's feeling tomorrow." I reassure her, and she sighs.

"Okay, call me if you need anything." I nod, looking over at Shayla when she coughs.

"I will." I hang up and move over to sit on the bed beside her. I touch her forehead and frown when I notice she's sweating. I pick up the cold compress and press it against her forehead. Shayla gasps a little against the coldness of the compress against her warm skin.

"Cole.." She whispers, opening her eyes a little to peer up at me.

"I'm right here, sweetheart," I whisper back, brushing my fingers through her hair as I press the cloth to her neck.

"It's hot." She groans, closing her eyes and pushing the covers off, but I stop her.

"I know you are, but the doctor said you need to sweat out the fever so you can feel better. You have to stay covered up." I inform her, and she sighs when I press the cool compress to her face.

I wait for her to fall asleep again before I move off the bed, but she wraps her hand around my wrist and looks up at me pleadingly. "Don't go." She whispers, closing her eyes again. "Don't leave me."

I set the compress on the side and lay down beside her. "I'm right here. I'm not going anywhere," I reassure her while I comb my fingers through her hair. Shayla shifts closer and lays her head on my chest, nestling herself into me further. I wrap my arm around her, pulling her closer, and I press my lips to her forehead.

"Mm, I love you, love of my life," Shayla whispers with a breathy sigh. I still at her words and close my eyes, biting the inside of my cheek hard.

I press my nose into her hair, inhaling her scent. "I love you too, sweetheart," I declare, and her lips quirk ever so slightly.

"Say it again, baby." Shayla moans while nuzzling my neck. I couldn't contain my smile.

"I *love* you, Gorgeous girl," I affirm, kissing her nose affectionately, and she smiles, content, before she drifts off to sleep. I don't know what made me say those words to her, but it felt—right. It didn't feel forced or fabricated, which left me somewhat bewildered. I thought I was just telling her what she needed to hear in an attempt to comfort her while she's sick, but what if, deep down, I actually meant it?

I feel the baby's movements against my hip, and I look down at her stomach. Shayla did mention before that she gets active late at night. I press my hand against her tummy and feel the baby move under my touch. She kicks, and Shayla jumps a little, stirring in her sleep, her hand covers mine, and she dozes off again. I felt that all-consuming warmth engulf me again. I don't know why or how, but I felt at peace for the first time in a long time, so I allowed myself to soak up that feeling for as long as possible before she wakes up and remembers she hates me.

I KEPT STIRRING out of sleep throughout the night when I heard Shayla cough or whenever she started to shiver in my arms. I had to wake her up in the middle of the night to take her tablets to reduce her temperature when she started to burn up again.

The sun was coming up by the time her fever dropped, and I finally allowed myself to doze off and get a couple of hours sleep. Shayla's stirring rouses me from my slumber. I peel my eyes open and look down at her. She groans and rubs her head before she opens her eyes entirely and looks at me, confused. "Cole?" She croaks, her voice raspy from a night spent coughing.

I lift my head and look at her. "Hey, you okay?" I reach up to touch her face to check she's not running a fever. Shayla closes her eyes and licks her lips.

"Ow, my head." She groans, covering her face with her hands, "How did I get here?"

I lean on my elbow and look down at her. "I brought you. You were sick, and I didn't want to leave you by yourself. Are you feeling okay?"

Shayla shakes her head, coughing. She winces a little and rubs her chest with a groan. "No, I feel like death."

"The doctor said you caught a viral infection," I inform her, and she sighs, closing her eyes for a second.

"Great." She drawls groggily and opens her eyes to look at me again. "Did you take care of me all night?"

I nod, and she blinks, chewing on her lip gingerly. "Of course I did. I wasn't going to leave you all alone when you're sick. You couldn't even stand on your own."

"You didn't have to do that, Cole. I would have been fine." Shayla states, clearing her throat a little. "But thank you."

I smile at her a little, and she looks at me for a long moment. "I'd be a pretty shitty husband if I didn't take care of my wife when she's sick." Shayla sighs tiredly, shaking her head. "Do you recall anything from last night?"

Shayla coughs, shaking her head again. "No, the last thing I remember was arguing with you in my office about the baby."

I nod and sit up, cracking my neck with a groan. "You were pretty out of it, so I'm not surprised,"

Shayla frowns alarmed. "Oh god, I didn't do anything stupid, did I?" I smile, and my eyes linger on hers for a couple of seconds before I shake my head, rubbing the back of my neck.

"No, as I said, you were out of it, so you slept most of the night," I assure her and get out of bed. "Do you need anything?"

Shayla sits up and holds her head. "No, I have to pee." She pushes the covers off her body and looks down at herself and then at me. "Why am I in your clothes?"

"Oh, uh, you were running a high fever, so the doctor told me to get you under a lukewarm shower to help cool you down. Your clothes got wet, so I had to get you into some dry clothes."

Shayla winces and closes her eyes, her cheeks aflame. "Wow, okay."

I bite back the urge to smile when she gets all flustered. "What? You're not...embarrassed, are you?" I tease her a little, and she looks at me with a frown.

"Of course I am," She grumbles, wrapping her arms around herself. "I can't believe you saw me naked and in such a state."

I chuckle, licking my lips, "Shayla, you've got nothing to be embarrassed about. I've seen you naked before, remember? Besides, I was a little too worried about *you* actually to stand there and admire your naked body." Shayla groans, rubbing her forehead before she gets out of bed and staggers a little. I place my hands at her waist to steady her while she lays her hands on my bare chest. Those jade eyes slowly flitter and lock with mine. I raise my hand and brush a loose strand of her hair away from her face.

"You shouldn't get too close, or you'll get sick too." She speaks quietly, her eyes never leaving mine.

I smile, pressing my forehead to hers, "Good. I hope I do. Then you can stay and take care of me." I state while my thumb strokes her jaw. Shayla's eyes close when I brush my nose over hers softly.

"Cole, what are you doing..."

"I don't know." I breathe, my lips inching closer to hers.

Chapter 13

SHAYLA

PULL AWAY, Shay! Don't get sucked in again. Pull. Away. What are you doing, you stupid girl?!

Thankfully, I start coughing uncontrollably and take a step back from Cole. My head was swimming, half from being so close to him and the other from this stupid virus that has my head thumping like someone was bashing it in with a cleaver.

I avoid looking at Cole and brush past him to walk to the bathroom.

What is wrong with me? Why have I got no might when it comes to this man? One-touch, and I melt, ready and willing to let him do whatever he wants with me.

It's borderline pathetic. And I don't get him either. What the hell is he doing? I'm honestly getting real fed up with asking myself that question and trying to figure him out. He says he doesn't want this baby or me and wants to be with Sophie, then he goes off in a rage when another man shows any interest in me, and now he suddenly wants the baby and is trying to kiss me? Did he wake up from the coma with a split personality, or is he just trying to drive me insane?

After I empty my bladder, I look at myself in the mirror as I wash my hands. I look like absolute shit, pale face, eyes rimmed red, my hair was a mess, and on top of all that, I felt sticky and gross. I have to get out of here, and I needed a shower desperately. I walk out of the bathroom with a drawn-out sigh and see Cole lying back on the bed, staring up at the ceiling.

It's so upsetting that my initial instinct when I see him is to walk over and straddle him like I used to. Cole would smile up at me; those gorgeous green eyes lit up with so much love it would make my heart soar.

"What are you smiling prettily about over there?" I blink, snapping out of my thoughts, and mentally slap myself over the back of the head for staring at him like some lusty loser.

"Uh, nothing." I lie and quickly avert my gaze. Cole chuckles and gets up, walking over to me. I crane my neck to look up at him while he towers over me.

"You're a terrible liar. Anyone ever told you that?" He drawls gruffly, staring deeply into my eyes, just like he used to before. I feel my defences slip away from me again. "You were staring at me and smiling. You were thinking about something to do with us, weren't you?" Cole goads, and I cough, shaking my head.

"It doesn't matter," I utter, trying to move away, but he catches my arm and draws me closer to him.

"It matters to me. Tell me?"

"Why does it matter to you, Cole? It's not like you'll remember, right?" I pull my arm from his hold. Cole licks his lips, and his eyes narrow a little while he continues to watch me intently.

"It matters because it's *you*. It matters because I want to know what I did before that made you smile at me the way you just did." Cole declares earnestly, and I sigh, closing my eyes.

"You want to know, fine, I was thinking how sad it was that my first instinct when I saw you lying on the bed was to crawl on top of you and have you look up at me lovingly and smile as you used to." I lift my eyes to his and bite back the tears that were burning the back of my eyelids. "You didn't have to do a lot to make me smile, Cole. Just having you look at me was enough," I add, not bothering to wait for a reaction before I brush past him and scan the room for my clothes.

"What are you doing, Shayla?" Cole asks, watching me pick up my shirt and skirt.

"I'm getting dressed. I can't go home like this, can I?" I utter, looking for my underwear. I still can't believe he saw me naked while I was in that state.

"You're not going anywhere, not until you're better." I look over at him with a frown.

"I feel much better. I can rest and recover at home, in my own bed." I hear Cole sigh before he moves over to me.

"Shayla, you are home, and this is your bed." He states, turning me to face him. I groan and rub my head a little when I feel it ache suddenly.

"No, it's not." I insist. "It *was* our home, and that *was* our bed, but it's not anymore, just like there is no us anymore. I don't belong in this house, and I don't belong in your life, Cole." I explain as we stare at each other. "Thank you for taking care of me, but this doesn't change anything between us."

Cole's jaw clenches as he looks into my eyes, "What about our baby?"

I exhale slowly and pinch the bridge of my nose. "Cole, you made your choice. You chose a life without us. You can't just up and change your mind like you didn't say those things to me. You can't just fix what you've broken inside of me with a simple apology--that's not how it works!"

Cole takes hold of my shoulders and draws me closer to him while his eyes search mine. "Then tell me what I have to do, Shayla? I want to be a part of my daughter's life. You can't keep my own child from me. I know what I said, and I regret it deeply, believe me, but I want this baby, I want our baby girl."

I shrug out of his hold, " Stop. It's too late Cole, the damage is done, and it's not even about you. I would rather die than let Sophie anywhere near my baby." Cole frowns, watching me as I back away from him.

"What are you saying? The only way I get to have my own daughter in my life is if I stop seeing Sophie?" I shake my head and brush my fingers agitatedly through my hair.

"She's vile and toxic, and I don't want my baby around her, especially not after what she said to me the other day." Cole's frown deepens, and he takes a step toward me.

"What day? What did she say?" He inquires, and I bite my lip and avert my gaze to look at anything but him. I can feel the rage burning deep in my gut, and I'm struggling to keep it buried.

"It doesn't matter--"

"Will you stop fucking saying that!" Cole shouts hotly. "What did she say to you?"

"She said she was going to erase what little memories you have of me while she fucks your brains out and gets pregnant while I'm at home taking care of my brat!" I reply stormily, and Cole looks at me, stunned.

"What? I can't believe she would ever say such a thing." Cole shakes his head, and I roll my eyes in annoyance.

"Of course, you wouldn't believe it," I state dryly. "I know you want to believe she's this great girl Cole, but she's not. You know what, I'm going to let you figure this one out for yourself because sooner or later, her true colours will come out." I inform him while searching around the room for my bra. "She's ready and willing to give you a baby if you're so eager to be a Dad. By all means, go right ahead and knock yourself out. Just leave my baby and me alone," I state further, picking up my bra off the back of the chair while Cole watches me, a deep scowl on his face.

"I don't want a fucking baby with her!" Cole retorts, and I look back at him. "I want my baby with you!"

"You should have thought about that before you walked out on us then, shouldn't you!" I exclaimed, throwing my clothes at him angrily. Cole looks down at the pile of clothes and kicks them away while he stares at me angrily. "Just because you helped make her doesn't make you her dad, any idiot can make a baby, Cole, but a father's responsibilities aren't just when the baby is born. It starts the moment that baby drops into the mothers' womb! You were either in this or not, and you chose not to be."

Cole shoves his fingers through his hair agitatedly, "You're seriously holding a decision I made after suffering a traumatic head injury against me? I wasn't thinking straight Shayla, how many times do I have to keep telling you that before you get it?!" Cole growls, looking down into my face, his usual green eyes dark and stormy.

"I don't know, Cole, maybe when it finally stops hurting! Though you might be waiting a fucking while!" I scream, shoving him away from me as he steps closer.

"Don't push me, Shayla!" He barks, glaring at me darkly.

"Or what?!" I hiss, glaring right back. "What are you going to do, Cole?" I provoke as we stare at one another heatedly, our chest rising and falling with every furious breath we took. Cole takes two large steps, and before my brain could acknowledge what was happening, his mouth was on mine, hot and hard. I groan when he parts my lips with his and swipes his tongue against mine, eliciting a lusty moan from me.

Oh, boy, it's been a while since I've was kissed—or even touched for that matter; add raging pregnancy hormones to that mix, and you can see why it was extremely difficult to convince my sexed-up, angry brain to put a stop to what was happening.

We kissed like two hungry animals, attacking one another. It took a good couple of minutes, but my senses come rushing back to me, I shove Cole off me, and he groans, looking at me insatiably. "What the hell do you think you're doing! You don't get to kiss me anymore." I pant, and he looks at me, a dark glint in his eyes.

"Oh no?" He smirks. "Watch me." With a growl, he presses me up against the wall, his mouth on mine, kissing me hungrily. I moan again, my arms snake around his neck as I kiss him back just as eagerly, my sickness no longer a thought in my mind. Cole moans while his fingers sneak under his oversized shirt I was wearing and cups my now enlarged and heavy breast in one hand, his fingers tweaking and tugging at my tight and hardened nipple. I whimper, arching up, pushing my breasts further into his touch, and he groans, sucking my tongue, making me dizzy. I couldn't tell if it was my fever or what, but I felt real hot and clammy, though my whole body was quivering.

"Cole, stop., stop." I pant, pulling back from the kiss. "I can't," I close my eyes, pressing my head back against the wall. Cole brushes his lips on my forehead and frowns.

"Your fever is back. Come on." Cole says between breaths, scooping me into his arms as I cough hysterically. My chest felt like it was on fire.

"What are you doing?" I croak as he carries me to the en suite bathroom.

"You need to cool down," Cole tells me, sitting me down on the stone counter by the sink before he picks up a bottle of pills, takes two out, pops them into my mouth, and hands me a water bottle. "Swallow those." He instructs, and as I take the pills, he walks over to the walk-in shower and runs the water before moving over to me again, a serious look on his handsome face. "We need to take these off." I shake my head and wrap my arms around myself, already feeling cold. I didn't want to freeze. It felt like every hair on my body was on end, and it hurt.

"I'm cold," I whine, and Cole sighs.

"I know, but you have to cool down. The doctor said running a high fever can harm the baby." I instantly unwrap my arms and allow him to lift the shirt up and over my head. I hiss and close my eyes, quivering when the cool air hits my naked body. I felt exposed, and despite feeling so cold, I felt my cheeks go red under his gaze.

"Stop looking at me like that." I scold him and cover myself up with my arms, and his lips quirk a little. "I can shower on my own, so, you can go—hey, put me down," I complain when he lifts me into his arms, and we both step into the shower. I whimper when the barely warm water hits my flesh. "Oh...my God, Cole, it's...cold...it's cold." I shiver visibly and sink into his arms, searching for some warmth.

"I know, I know, sweetheart, just a couple of minutes more." He reassures, wrapping his strong arms around me as I cling to him. "I'm not letting you go anywhere like this. You're staying here till you're fully recovered." Cole murmurs against my temples, and I sigh, not even having the energy to argue with him.

"Okay, okay, please, Cole, I'm so c-cold." I plead and feel Cole's lips press against my forehead before the water cuts off, and we're stepping out of the shower again.

～

A COUPLE OF HOURS LATER, Cole had me hauled up in bed and was currently trying to force-feed me some vile-looking vegetable noodle soup. "I don't want it." I croak with a grimace, and I turn my face away.

"Shayla, my mother said it's good for you and the baby. You have to drink a little, come on." Cole insists, and I wrinkle my nose in distaste but open my mouth and begrudgingly eat the soup. It didn't taste as bad as it smelt, but I still wasn't impressed.

Cole stayed by my side the entire time until I was feeling better. We watched films in bed; he even read me a book and played a song on his guitar. Save for our bickering, we almost felt like us again-- the old us back when we first met, and everything was a lot less complicated.

"Can I give you a lift home?" Cole offers the following day while I walk out of the bathroom. I shake my head and hold up my phone.

"Aimee is on her way," I reply with a shrug and force a smile on my face. "Thank you again for taking care of me." Cole nods, rubbing the back of his neck awkwardly with a smile.

"Of course. I'm glad you're feeling better. I guess I'll see you at the office tomorrow?" I nod, chewing on my bottom lip while he stares at me intently.

"Yeah." I look down at the clothes I was currently wearing. I was in his oversized grey hoodie, which was long enough to look like a dress on me even in my pregnant state. I had a pair of black Armani boxers on underneath. "I'll wash and return these," I tell him, and he chuckles, his eyes rake over me slowly.

"Nah, you keep it. Looks better on you anyway." He drawls with a lazy smile. I look at him for a couple of seconds before I drop my gaze and nod, my cheeks aflame. I have to be more careful and guarded around him because if I let him get close to me again, I know I won't be able to fight my feelings, and I don't have another heartbreak left in me. I just don't.

"Thank you. It is amazingly comfortable. I might have to live in this for the rest of my pregnancy." I reply with a chuckle. Cole grins, taking a step closer to me, and I feel my heart jump up to my throat. A reaction that is becoming quite normal whenever he gets close to me.

Thankfully, my phone starts to ring, and I look down at it and see Blake's name flashing across the screen. Cole stares at my phone, the flirty smile from before now replaced with a deep scowl. He lifts his gaze to mine and licks his lips.

"What's the deal with you and Blake Bryant?" He questions, his tone tight. I silence the call and shrug, looking everywhere but at him. "Look at me," Cole demands, taking hold of my jaw and turning my face so that I could face him.

"It's none of your business, Cole," I utter, pulling my face out of his hold. "Do you see me questioning you about your relationship with Sophie? No, because it's no longer my business what you do."

"Relationship?" He intones, staring into my eyes. "You're in a relationship with him?"

I sigh and turn to walk to the door, but he grabs my arm and pulls me back. "Answer me!"

"I don't owe you a god-damn explanation about my love life, just like you don't owe me one about yours." I hiss angrily, and Cole shakes his head. His icy stare sends a chill through me.

"You're still my wife!" He grits through his clenched teeth as he draws me closer to him.

"On paper!" I retort hotly. "I'm only your wife when it fucking suits you, but I stopped being your wife the moment you took your ring off and handed it to me, Cole!"

"This ring?!" Cole argues, holding his hand up and showing me his wedding band. I look at it and then at him.

"What? Am I supposed to be impressed that you decided to put it back on again *after* you wrecked me?" I ask sceptically. "It's just a piece of metal now. It means nothing, just like this marriage." I turn to walk to the door, but he pulls me back to him again, his chest pressed up against my back.

"Shayla, I'm getting real tired of explaining myself to you again and again. I can't make it better if you don't give me a chance or tell me how to fix it?" He speaks lowly in my ear, and I close my eyes for a moment to compose myself before I turn and face him.

"You can't *fix it*, Cole." I look up at him. "You can't fix the damage you've done to me. If you genuinely want to make it better, let me be and stop trying to hold onto something that's already lost." I tell him sincerely, and his green eyes search mine, and he shakes his head. "What do you want, Cole? Tell me? You want me to be alone and to watch you live your life happy with Sophie? What about me? Don't I deserve to be happy?" I ask him pleadingly as the tears I promised myself I would not shed roll down my cheeks. "I'm tired," I whisper, gazing into his eyes.

Cole reaches out to touch my face, but I step away, "Shayla—"

"The answer to your question is yes. I *am* in a relationship with him. And I'm happy, okay. Blake makes me happy." I lie and pray that he doesn't see right through it. Cole's shoulders slump, his jaw set tight as he watches me turn and walk out of the door. I force myself to look ahead and not look back as I get into Aimee's car.

"You okay?" She asks, concerned, and I nod.

"Drive," I utter, turning my gaze to look at Cole standing in the doorway watching me, his whole posture stiff. Our eyes remain locked on one another till the very last second as we drove away. I close my eyes and sigh. "Fuck."

"Did you?" I look at Aimee, who was watching me wide-eyed as she drives. "You slept with him, didn't you? I knew I shouldn't have left you alone with him."

I shake my head and groan. "No. I just did something idiotic."

Aimee frowns, "Talk, bish, I'm dying here."

I lean forward and rake my fingers through my hair with a frustrated growl, "I just told Cole I'm in a relationship with Blake." Aimee slams her foot on the brake and gapes at me, surprised as I scream and place my hands on the dash. "Aimee, what the hell are you doing?!" I ask, placing my hand on my rapidly beating heart.

"When the fuck did you start a relationship with Blake?" She asks as cars honk their horns at us.

I exhale and look at her, "I haven't! Can you drive, please?" I demand, and Aimee shakes her head and starts to drive while muttering under her breath. "I lied, okay! He was just pushing and pushing, and I just...I lied and said I was dating Blake to get him to finally back off."

"Shayla, why would you do that? You've just given him even more reason to pursue Sophie. You've practically gift-wrapped him and dropped him in her fucking lap for the taking." Aimee scolds me, and I sigh, staring out the window. "What was his reaction?"

"He was pissed, of course. Heaven forbid I try and be happy. I don't understand, Aimee!" I exclaim, hitting my hands against the dashboard. "I don't understand what he wants from me! Why did he kiss me? Why did he spend the last three days taking care of me when he said he doesn't want me? Why is he doing all of this? I don't understand." I cry, burying my face into my hands. "I'm going to lose my mind!"

"Oh Shay, I wish I knew, babe. It sounds like he's just as confused as you are."

"I'm not confused about what I want, Aimee!" I shout, perturbed, wiping away my tears. "It's always been Cole for me, and it always will be. Cole's always been the confused one throughout our whole relationship. He just fucks with my head, he did then, and he still does now, and like the idiot that I am, I fall for his shit every time. What is wrong with me?" I shake my head sobbing. "I'm tired of feeling like this, Aimes. I just wanted him to feel something, just a little of the pain he's put me through. Maybe then he will understand what I'm going through inside." Aimee sighs and reaches over; taking my hand in hers, she squeezes supportively.

"I'm a horrible person, aren't I? I just put Blake in a shitty situation for my gain." I weep, and Aimee shakes her head.

"No, babe, you're not a horrible person. You would never do anything to hurt someone intentionally. But then again, maybe this is a good thing; he will either realise that deep down he does love you, or he will finally leave you alone to move on." She explains as I press my head against the window and close my eyes.

"Either way, it doesn't matter anymore. However hard I try, how much ever I still love him, I can't forgive him, Aimee." I sigh, wiping away my tears. "He's broken too much inside me for that. I have to think about myself and this baby first, so there's only one thing left for us to do at this point."

Aimee frowns, glancing at me curiously before she looks at the road again, "What's that?"

"Get a divorce."

Chapter 14

COLE

"COLE, for the love of God, man, slow down," I hear Josh groan as he holds the punching bag while I put my fist through it furiously. "You're going to hurt yourself."

I ignore him and continue to plough my fist into the bag as hard as I could. My arms were aching, and my lungs burned, but I didn't stop. "She's in a relationship with him," I mutter sourly, even saying those words left a bad taste in my mouth. "She *can't* be in a relationship with him!" I growl, driving my fist into the bag hard. I feel the skin on my knuckles split in the gloves, but it didn't phase me.

Josh frowns, watching me, wincing every time I hit the bag, and it hit his chest, "Why can't she be?"

I stop and glare at him, "Because she can't!" I gripe irately, and Josh sighs with a roll of his eyes.

"Well, it seems she is, bro." He states calmly. "What did you think was going to happen? You think she was going to wait around for you to get your head out of your arse forever?"

"Of course not! But I didn't expect this for fucksake." I pant, holding the bag and pressing my forehead against it while I try and catch my breath.

"Cole, even I'm confused with what you want, mate," Josh says, stepping away from the bag and placing his hands at his hips. "I'm not even surprised in the slightest that Shayla wants to move on because your indecisiveness is driving me crazy, let alone her. Just let her go, man. She's been through enough."

"You think I haven't tried." I hiss, glaring at him hard. "I don't know what the hell this girl has done to me man, because I can't stop thinking about her. I can't focus on anything when she's not around. And when she is, I just have this uncontrollable urge to touch her and hold her and fuck—I want to kiss her till I can't breathe." I explain and punch the bag hard. "For the life of me, I can't fucking leave her alone. What the fuck is wrong with me?" I utter, panting. Josh narrows his eyes while he observes me.

"Sounds to me like your arse is right back to where you were when you first met her. You've gone and gotten yourself tangled up in her love web all over again, bro." Josh smirks with a shake of his head. "This is what we've been trying to tell you. If you just stuck it out with her, things wouldn't have gotten this messy," Josh explains, and I sigh, staring at the floor. "Now it's too late, Cole. She won't forgive you. Shayla deserves to be happy. Just let her be now, bro."

"I can't! I fucking love her!" I exclaim angrily, punching the bag hard while everyone in the gym stops and looks at us.

"Oh-kay." Josh frowns, gesturing with his arm so people can get back to their business and not gawk at us. I stood there panting, staring at the bag swinging in front of me.

"I love her," I whisper and look at Josh, who was watching me, his blue eyes wide. "I'm in love with her."

"Halle-fucking-lujah!" Josh exclaims, throwing his hands in the air excitedly. "Yes! You do love her! He's back, ladies and gentlemen!" He hollers at the men and women in the gym who watch us puzzled. Josh grabs my face and kisses my forehead, and then winces and wipes the sweat off his mouth, heaving. "Oh gross, I did not think that through."

I stood there, speechless. Of course, it all makes sense to me now why I've never been able to leave her alone, why she's always on my mind. The reason I kissed her the other day and why I feel that burn deep in my gut when I see her with that knobhead, Blake. Wow. I'm in love with her— I've *been* in love with her this whole fucking time! It was never Sophie. The love I had in my heart was for Shayla. It was always Shayla. *Oh fuck.* I bite the strap to my glove and pull the velcro so I can take my gloves off.

I grab Josh by the shirt and look at him, "Call Aimee and find out where she is. I need to talk to her."

"Whoa, hold it there, bud. First, you need to be a thousand percent sure this is what you want because if you fuck her about again, I will put you in a chokehold and kill you." Josh threatens gravely, and I roll my eyes and let go of his shirt. "What about all your feelings for Sophie?"

"Fuck Sophie, I was just projecting, man. I had all these feelings inside me, and I thought it was for Sophie because Shayla didn't exist to me—but it wasn't. While I was at that dinner with Sophie, I still wasn't happy, not as happy as I was at home taking care of Shayla. That fucking warmth that spreads inside me when I'm with her, it's love, it's *her* love!"

"Yes!" Josh claps his hand, grinning. "Yeah, it fucking is. Ahh, welcome back bro!" Josh pulls me in, and we hug. "If you've remembered that you're in love with her, your memories will come back again soon too, I just know it." He says, pulling back and looking at me excitedly.

"Yeah, but she hates me," I utter, suddenly remembering all the agony I caused her. I feel my stomach drop when I recall the last time I saw her, the pain in her eyes, the tears.

"Cole, it's Shayla. She could never hate you, not really," Josh assures me, and I sigh deeply. God, I sincerely hope that's true.

"I need to talk to her...tonight. It's late. She should be home now, right?" I ask, and Josh shrugs and takes his phone out.

"Let's find out." He sighs and dials Aimee's number, and waits for her to answer. "Hi baby, are you home?" He questions and looks at me with a frown as he listens to what Aimee says. "Oh, you're still at work. Is Shay at home?" I watch his facial expressions closely. His frown deepens. "Oh, really? What is that? Huh, she is?"

"Josh!" I hiss, gesturing for him to hurry up. He widens his eyes and presses his finger to his lips, silencing me.

"Okay, call me when you get home. I love you too." He smiles and frowns when I glare at him before he hangs up and scratches his fore-head. "She's not home. She's gone to some lamazee class or whatever."

I frown, "A *what* class?"

"Lamazee, I don't know man, Aimee said it a class where pregnant women go to prepare for the birth or some shit," Josh utters with a shrug, and I sigh. I should be with her doing all these things. God, I'm such an idiot.

"Well, where is it? I told her I wanted to be a part of the baby's life, and she's still fighting me on it. She's so fucking stubborn." I groan, shoving my hand through my hair in frustration, and Josh shrugs, nodding in agreement.

"It's why you love her, my man," Josh chuckles as he picks up his gym bag.

"It's truly bizarre because usually, you know the reasons why you love someone, right?" I utter, and Josh nods, watching me. "I can't remember the reasons why I love her. I just know that I do, isn't that strange?" I explain, looking down at my split knuckles, which were bleeding a little. "If she asks me why I love her, I wouldn't be able to give her an answer," I add as we walk out of the gym together.

"It will come, brother, and if it doesn't, you'll soon realise the reasons for yourself because she's a great girl with a lot of qualities any man would fall head over heels for," Josh tells me, and I nod. I can see that—she was different for sure. Maybe that's one of the reasons. "Aimee sent me the address to this place Shay is at. You wanna go check it out?"

"Yeah, let's go. I don't think I can wait all weekend to speak to her." I tell him as we get into his Mercedes-AMG. "I just hope she hears me out." I sigh, pulling my seatbelt on. I was feeling nervous—

actually, I was terrified she would tell me to go fuck myself—which she has every right to do after everything that's happened. I gaze out of the window, trying to figure out what I'm going to say to her. Do I just run over to her and tell her I love her? Or do I break it to her gently? Ah, fuck, now I'm all in my head.

"Cole!" I jump and look at Josh with a scowl. "This is the place." Josh gestures to the building in front of us. It seems like those studios you would use for dance or yoga. I nod, and we get out of the car and walk toward the building. "Do you have a plan? You're not just going to ambush her, are you?" Josh questions warily, and I rub my hands over my face with a sigh.

"I don't know. I honestly don't know what I'm going to say to her. I'll just—"

"Oh...*shit*." Josh halts and puts his hand out, stopping me, his blue eyes wide as he stares ahead. I frown and follow his gaze and feel my gut twist agonizingly as I stood frozen, watching Blake kiss Shayla. *My* Shayla. I felt like a bucket of boiling water was thrown over me. Hot rage erupted inside me, and I take a step to go and beat the living crap out of him, but Josh jumps in front of me, keeping me back as I fight in his hold. "Whoa. Whoa, easy Cole, don't, don't man! She'll hate you even more if you do this. Stop!" Josh shouts, pushing me back as I try to storm over to them. "Come on. Come on, Cole. Let's go get a drink, bro." He utters, pulling my arm so we could go back to the car, but I had yet to look away—I couldn't look away. Blake had his arms around her, his fingers in her hair, kissing the lips that I was kissing a few days ago. It feels like someone was squeezing the life out of my heart. I pull my arm out of Josh's grasp and try to walk over to them again, but he grabs me and stops me. "Cole, stop, listen to me, you do this, you will lose her for good. Any chance you have of winning her back will be lost, you hear me?"

"I already have." I breathe numbly as I watch them walk away hand in hand. "I've lost them both."

Josh sighs, shaking his head, looking over at Shayla, who was laughing as she gets into Blakes car while he holds the door open for her, "No. You haven't. Those are still your girls. Shayla might be angry with you, but deep down, she loves *you*, Cole. You know this too. You're the guy for her. If you want her, you're going to have to be prepared to fight for her, brother."

"I was about to, but you stopped me, you dickhead!" I shout angrily and shove him. Josh rolls his eyes, exasperated, and shakes his head.

"Not literally with your fists, you idiot!" He shouts, shoving me back. "Figuratively, you win her back and remind her that you're the guy she loves, *not* him."

"How the fuck am I going to do that?!" I bellow, stormily kicking the tire of the car I was standing next to.

"The same way you did it last time."

I stop pacing and look at Josh irritably, "I don't remember how I did it last time, do I?! Fuck! I've royally screwed this all up!" I punch the wall.

"Cole, listen to me. You and Shayla have this outstanding connection. Even if you've lost your memory, that chemistry is still there. You need to tap into that connection you both share and listen to your heart... she's locked away in there bro, the rest will surely follow." Josh states, placing his hand on my shoulder. I look at him and heave a sigh.

"I really hope you're right, Josh," I sigh as he guides me back to his car.

"Well, you've got a hell of a battle on your hands, my brother, because I know Shayla, and she is not going to forgive you easily this time, especially if she's got another man. One of the things you loved about her— she's fiercely loyal." Josh expresses and looks over at my face when I wince and chuckles. "Let's go get you some drinks, huh?" I nod with a groan. Josh and I went to a bar nearby and had a couple of drinks while discussing how I would attempt to win Shayla back.

"What if she's really into this guy? She said he makes her happy. Am I selfish? I'm being selfish, aren't I?" I mutter sourly, staring into my glass of scotch.

"Hey, all is fair in love and war, right? That's your wife, bro. You have every right to fight for your wife, especially if there are love and a baby involved. If I were you, I would flirt the fucking pants off her. Don't be brash or annoyed when she pushes back because she will. Believe me. Just do what Cole Hoult does best, break down her barriers slowly, and remind her that deep down, you're still you and make her want you. Shayla is still holding out for the old you. The man she fell in love with, if he shows up, she won't be able to fight you off for long." Josh explains, and I nod slowly, letting his words sink in.

"I can't believe she took that dickhead with her to the baby classes. I'm the father, I should be there with her, but no, she chooses some fucking stranger over me." I utter acidly as I knock back my drink and wince when it burns my insides.

"She's not without her reasons, Cole. You want them both back. You need to be understanding to her side of things. End of the day, whether you meant it or not— you fucked up, not her."

Don't I know it.

THE FOLLOWING DAY, I made sure to look my best. If I was going to win Shayla back, she needs to know I've got my shit together. I wore my royal blue Hugo Boss suit with a crisp white shirt and blue tie. Hair styled, aftershave on, I felt better already. Shayla Hoult— prepare your heart because I'm coming for you. I slide my shades on and leave for the office.

"Good morning, Mr Hoult." Jenny, the receptionist, greets me as I walk through the lobby toward the elevators.

I smile charmingly and nod, "Good morning Jenny." I greet back and push the button to the elevator as I check my emails—invitations to various New Year's Eve galas. I'll pass. I've still got Christmas to get through, and the baby will be here by then. That reminds me, what am I going to get Shayla and the baby? Christmas is in six weeks. I make a mental note to plan something special for them.

"Good Morning, Mr Hoult." Jess greets me waiting by the elevators as she does every morning with my schedule in her hand. Shayla really has trained her well. I smirk at that.

"Morning, Jess." I greet her as I walk to my office with her hot on my tail. I glance at Shay's office as I pass by and see she's not in there. "Shayla not in yet?" I question, and Jess shakes her head.

"Not yet, Mr Hoult." She replies, looking at her tablet. "You both have an early meeting with all the head architects, so she should be here shortly. Also..." She adds with a smile and hands me a brown envelope. "This came for her this morning. It's from the university. It might be her degree. I thought you would like to be the one to give it to her." I smile and nod, looking at the envelope in my hand.

"Thank you, Jess. Let's go through my schedule." I sip my coffee, and I sit back and listen as she goes through my day.

"Miss Sophie has called a couple of times for you. She has arranged lunch for the two of you at your usual spot at one o'clock." I frown as I type on my laptop.

"Cancel it. She is no longer welcome at this office. Understood?" I reply, not bothering to look at her as I type an email.

"Yes, Mr Hoult. I'll alert the concierge," Jess answers before she gets up and walks out of my office. I pick up my phone and see a good morning message from Sophie. I delete the message and block her number before I delete it from my phonebook. I don't know who the hell she thinks she is, talking to Shayla in such a repulsive manner and plotting to get pregnant like she didn't lose a baby a couple of months ago. She truly is as delusional as Shayla says if she thinks I'm stupid enough to fall for that trap. I look down at the wedding band on my finger and brush my thumb over it.

"Do you have any idea the hell you've put me through? You need some serious mental help! I can't believe I ever fucking loved you! You make me sick."

I frown and close my eyes when I get a brief flash of Sophie and I arguing before it disappears. That must have been the moment Josh was telling me about it, the moment I found out she was lying to me. There's no emotion behind the memory again, but it was clear I was livid. I can't believe how wrong I was about her. How could I have been so damn blind?

I sigh and shake off the annoyance that I was suddenly feeling and focus on the positive. I'm starting to remember things more and more, which is a blessing with or without emotions.

While I force my brain to focus on work, Jess notifies me it's time for our meeting. I felt a nervous pull in my stomach at seeing Shayla again. I didn't know how I would feel seeing her after I saw her kissing Blake, but I don't have the luxury to dwell on that at the moment. It was a minor setback. That's all.

I gather my papers and walk through the office to the conference room. I walk in, and my eyes zero in on Shayla instantly. She's staring down at the table, her mind off far away someplace, it seems. I wonder what she's thinking about. She lifts her eyes and looks at me, straightening in her seat. I, of course, didn't miss the look of surprise that flashes in her green eyes as she watches me walk past her to take my seat at the table beside her.

"Shall we start?" I ask, looking her directly in the eyes, and she blinks and nods.

"Sure, go ahead." She replies, her brows fused together while she eyes me warily. I start the meeting, talk through all the projects and where we currently stand with each one.

"Shayla and I are currently working on the hotel in Dubai and the Mall in Madrid, so Adrian and Emily, I expect the both of you to pick up the slack and familiarise yourselves with this project because you will be taking over the account once the baby is born. As you all are aware, our baby is due in the next couple of weeks, so I don't want Shayla unnecessarily stressing leading up to birth." I assert and look at Shayla, who looks at me surprised. "Can you spend some time with Adrian and Emma to catch them up?" I ask her, and she nods, looking at the two in question with a smile.

"Of course." Shayla agrees, leaning back against her chair, and I nod, closing the file in front of me.

"Do any of you have any questions before I end the meeting?" I ask, looking at my watch briefly and glancing around the room; everyone shakes their heads. "Shay, do you have anything to add, sweetheart?" I question, looking at her pointedly, and she blinks and shakes her head slowly.

"No, you've covered everything." She replies, her eyes narrowing slightly, and I nod, looking around the room before I stand up.

"Excellent. Have a great day, everyone. Shayla, can I please see you in my office?" I utter, and she frowns a little but nods, watching me as I walk out of the conference room.

I turn and face her as she walks into my office, looking at me expectantly. God, she's beautiful. I couldn't tell if it was just me or what, but she's glowing like an angel in that red dress she's wearing. For a woman who is eight months pregnant, her bump isn't that big. It's about the size of a basketball, cute and round. She looks damn good. Then again, she always does. "Cole? What did you want to see me about?"

I blink and snap out of my thoughts when I hear her call my name. "Oh, right," I pick up the envelope off my desk and walk over, handing it to her. Shayla looks at it and then looks at me before she opens the envelope, pulls the diploma out, and gasps. "Congratulations."

"Oh my God," She whispers, looking over her diploma, her eyes filling with tears. "I can't believe it. I mean, I knew it was coming but to actually have it, it doesn't seem real."

I couldn't contain my excitement for her. I grin proudly. "It is real. You did it, Shay, you worked hard and never gave up on your dreams, and the result is right there in your hands." I tell her, reaching up and brushing her tears away. Shayla looks up into my eyes as I stroke her jaw. "You should be proud of yourself," She smiles, and her whole face lights up.

"Actually, we did it. You probably don't remember, but I couldn't have done it without you, Cole. You were honestly so supportive and helpful. You stayed up late nights helping me with assignments, and when I was ready to give up, you wouldn't let me. You always reminded me who I am and kept me on track." Shayla says with a sigh. "No matter what has happened between us, I want you to know that I'm grateful to you and all the opportunities you and Cult Designs have provided me."

I smile and brush my fingers through her hair, my eyes on hers. "I can't think of a single person more deserving than you. I'm so proud of you, sweetheart." I declare earnestly before I drop a gentle kiss on her forehead. Shayla smiles, closing her eyes for a second before they open, and she looks up at me while I draw back a little.

"Thank you," She whispers, holding my gaze steadily. I trail my thumb along her jaw, drawing gentle lazy circles as I gaze into her beautiful jade eyes. "Cole, there's something I really want to talk to you about. Can we talk later?"

"We can talk now. I'm free for the next hour before my conference call," I suggest and notice the sudden apprehension in her eyes. "What is it?"

Shayla closes her eyes and heaves a sigh, "There's no easy way for me to say this— in fact, I never thought I would have had to, but..." She drops her gaze and bites her lip. "I want a divorce."

I stare at her, unblinking for a while. Did I just fucking hear her right? My heart drops to the deepest core of my stomach. "You want a...*what* now?" I sputter, dumbfounded as I look at her. Shayla finally lifts her gaze to mine.

"Cole, this wasn't an easy decision for me. I thought long and hard, and this is what's best." She explains sullenly, averting her gaze again to the envelope in her hands.

I scoff, watching her, "Best for who, Shayla? You and Blake?" Her green eyes snap up to mine, and she frowns, shaking her head.

"No, Cole, best for the both of *us*. What do our problems have to do with Blake?" She questions, dropping the envelope in her hands on my desk and placing them on her hips while she glowers at me.

"Oh, I don't know, maybe you want to be able to kiss him more freely without feeling guilty, although you didn't seem all that guilty last night." I retort dryly, and she frowns.

"How did you— were you following me?" Shayla crosses her arms over her chest.

"No, I wasn't following you! I was coming to tell you— you know what, it doesn't even matter why I was there. The fact is, I saw you kissing him, and suddenly now you want a divorce? What the fuck Shay?!"

"My decision has nothing to do with Blake and everything to do with us, Cole! This isn't something I decided on a whim overnight. It just doesn't feel right anymore." She states with a shrug, and I shake my head.

"No."

Shayla scowls, "What do you mean, no?"

I take hold of her arms and pull her close to me. "No. I'm not divorcing you." I declare sternly while I stare into her eyes. Shayla shakes her head, and before she could say another word, I cup her face in my hands and press my lips to hers. Shayla squeaks, surprised at first but kisses me back for a very brief second before she pulls back and blinks up at me, then slowly looks down at the ground.

"Oh god." She whispers.

I frown and look down at the puddle of water on the floor. "Did you just—"

"My water broke."

My frown deepens as I look at her, perplexed. "What does that mean?"

Shayla's eyes go wide, and she shakes her head. "It means she's coming." I gape at her and take a step back.

"Now?" I look around frantically, "She's coming now, like right now?!" I shout, panicked, and Shayla shakes her head slowly. She visibly pales. "I still have four weeks. She's early. It's too soon. She can't come yet!"

I pace the office, "Okay, okay, we should go to the hospital, right?" I utter, and she looks at me motionless. This is where you need to be the strong one and comfort her, Cole. Get your shit together! I exhale and walk over to her; I take her face into my hands and look into her fear-filled eyes. "Hey, listen to me, it's going to be okay, it's going to be fine," I assure her, and she blinks and looks at me, her eyes swimming in tears.

"Oh God, what if she's not. It's too soon." Shayla cries, and I shake my head and kiss her forehead.

"No, baby, no, don't think like that. Our baby is fine. She's just ready to come out and meet us, that's all. She's probably sick of hearing us bickering." I joke, and Shayla laughs sadly. "Let's go. We can call your doctor on the way," I tell her, and she nods as we walk out of my office toward the elevator. "Are you okay? Do you need me to carry you?" I ask worriedly, and she shakes her head.

"No, I'm okay. I can walk." She sighs, closing her eyes. "Oh God, I'm so scared." I watch her pressing herself up against the wall. "Cole, I'm not ready to have this baby yet."

I step in front of her and rub her arms while we wait for the elevator. "Sweetheart, stressing yourself out right now isn't good for you or the baby. You are the strongest, most courageous woman I know. Now, I know you're scared, and so am I, but you got this, and I'm going to be right there by your side the whole time, okay?" I reassure her, and she nods while I dry her tears.

TEN MINUTES LATER, we are on our way to the hospital. Shayla called Janet, her midwife, who told her not to panic and come in right away. I look over at Shayla, who winces a little while she inhales and exhales slowly. "You okay, sweetheart?" Shayla shakes her head, closing her eyes.

"I'm getting contractions." She whispers, rubbing her stomach. I bite my lip, feeling so utterly useless. What the hell do I do? I'm trying so hard not to panic and stay calm for her, but I am freaking the fuck out inside. "I need to call my mum and the girls. The hospital bag, my medical file, it's all at home." Shayla explains, taking out her phone but stops when she gets another contraction. "Cole, please hurry."

"We're almost there, baby, just a little bit longer." I drive faster, and each time I hear Shayla whimper in pain, my insides clench tight. We finally get to the hospital, and they take her in right away and hook her up to a CTG machine that measures the baby's heart rate and her contractions. I take hold of Shayla's hand as the midwife examines her.

"Okay, Shayla, you're about six centimetres dilated already. This little princess is very eager to come out and meet you both." Janet says with a warm smile. "I know you're worried because she's a little early, but everything looks good. She's happy and healthy as far as we can tell, so you don't worry. You just focus on your delivery and nothing else." Shayla heaves a sigh and nods, resting her head back on the pillow.

"Ahh, shit," She hisses, squeezing my hand as she breathes through her contraction. "Where is Aimee with my mum? Can you call her?" She cries, and I nod; taking out my phone, I dial Aimee's number, and she answers right away.

"Cole, did we miss it?" Is she here?!" Aimee shrieks down the phone, and I wince, pulling the phone away before she bursts my eardrum.

"No, not yet. Shay's asking where you are?" I ask and hear Shay's mother in the background.

"Cole, how is my baby? Is she okay?" Sara asks, and I look at Shayla, who was breathing heavily through another contraction.

"She's okay for now, but she needs you here. Just hurry. The midwife said the baby is eager to come out," I inform them while I kiss Shayla's hand.

"We're literally ten minutes away. See you in a bit." Aimee hangs up, and I set the phone on the side and focus on Shayla. I feel so powerless. What can I do other than offer her my hand to hold while she's in agony? An hour later, her contractions were more severe and closer together, which meant the baby was ready to come out, and I was ready to pass the fuck out. Luckily, Shay's mother was there with us, and she was doing great at keeping Shayla calm. Josh, Aimee, Jo, Sam, and my parents were all outside in the waiting room.

"You're doing great, baby. Just keep breathing. It's going to be over real soon," I whisper to her as she sobs.

"Ahhh! It hurts so much. This is all your fault! You did this to me, you stupid, selfish knobhead! I hate you!" She growls at me, and I look at Sara wide-eyed, who shakes her head smiling.

"She doesn't mean that, darling. It's just labour talk." She assures me while she presses a cool compress to Shayla's flushed face.

"I wouldn't be so sure," I mutter more to myself and shake my head when Sara gives me a confused glance.

"All right, Shayla. It's time to start pushing." Janet tells her as she snaps on her gloves and mask. Shayla and I exchange glances, and she nods, tightening her fingers around mine. "On the next contraction, I need you to take a deep breath and push for ten seconds. Okay?"

"Okay." Shayla pants and sucks in a deep breath before she pushes hard. "Ahhhhh God, I am never having sex again!" She cries, falling back on the bed, panting. Sara and the midwife both laugh a little while I look at them, horrified.

"If I had a penny for every time I heard that, I'd be on a beach in Bali right now instead of up in your hooch, honey." Janet jokes, and Shayla cries, shaking her head.

"I can't do this! I can't. It hurts so much." She sobs weakly, and I kiss her sweaty forehead. "Just leave her in there!"

"She can't stay in there, sweetheart. You can do this. You're so close baby, it's almost over, just a little bit longer, and our baby will be here. Our little Alaia Mae will be in your arms. You can do this, baby, come on." I urge her on, and she nods and pushes again, and again, and again until she lets out a shrill scream when the baby's head crowns. I watch in horror and astonishment as the baby's head sticks out of her vagina. My eyes fill with tears, "Oh my God, she's got so much hair." I tell Shayla, and she opens her eyes, panting, and looks at me.

"Really?"

I laugh a little, nodding, and move over to her side again. I kiss her forehead. "She's almost here—our baby is almost here. Come on, baby, one last push, you got this." I whisper, taking her hand, and she sucks in a deep breath and pushes one last time before she groans and collapses back on the bed, panting.

"Here she is. Oh, hello, princess." Janet welcomes her with a little laugh. I watch, stunned as she lays the baby on Shay's stomach, who sobs uncontrollably, looking down at her.

"Oh my God, she's here," I whisper, looking down at my baby girl. I'm a father. Alaia starts to cry, and the midwife takes her away to check her over, make sure she was healthy.

"Welcome to the world of motherhood, my sweet girl." Sara cries, kissing Shayla's hand, who continues to sob. "You did so well, my darling."

"Is she okay?" Shayla asks me, and I nod, looking over at her while they clean her up. I smile and kiss her head again and again.

"She's perfect, Shayla." I whisper, wiping away her tears while she continues to cry, "She's absolutely perfect."

"All right, mama meet your little angel," Janet announces, handing a now clean and dressed-up Alaia to her mother. I watch Shayla's face as she looks down at our baby in her arms. I wanted to remember that moment forever. There was such love in her eyes. It absolutely stole the air right out of my lungs.

"I'll go and tell the rest that she's here and give you three some time alone. Sara says, kissing Shayla's head before she leaves the room.

"Hi, Alaia," Shayla whispers, tears streaming down her cheeks. "Oh, you really are perfect." She cries, brushing her finger over her head of soft dark hair.

"Just like her mother," I whisper, lifting my gaze to Shayla, who looks up at me through eyes filled with tears and so much emotion.

"And her father." She whispers back, and I smile. Leaning in, I press my lips to hers, kissing her softly. We pull back and look down at our baby girl, and suddenly nothing else but this beautiful little human being mattered.

"Welcome to the world, Alaia Mae Hoult," Shayla whispers as we gaze lovingly down at her.

Chapter 15

SHAYLA

THE WORDS LOVE at first sight didn't mean much of anything to me until I laid my eyes on my daughter. *My daughter.* I have a *daughter.* How crazy is that? A couple of hours ago, she was inside me, and now she's out and sleeping peacefully beside me.

It was just like everyone said to me, she will heal all the broken pieces inside of you, and she has. The moment I held her, and she opened up those beautiful green eyes, my heart was captivated. There really is nothing more important to me than her. After her birth, we had to spend a week in hospital because she was born preterm, and the paediatricians wanted to keep an eye on her; however, she was absolutely perfect. She's feeding well and gaining weight by the day. All her tests have come back clear, which meant we finally get to take her home.

I jump awake when I hear Alaia fussing and see Cole was holding her against his chest, rubbing her back softly. He's obsessed with her. You wouldn't think this was the same man that said he didn't want her a couple of months ago. It almost felt like the old Cole.

The excitement and love he had in his eyes for her made my heart swell. Cole's been by our side every day, and the nurses had to literally kick him out so he would go home and rest at night. It's been overwhelming, to say the least. As thrilled as I am he's bonding with Alaia, things are still very much up in the air between us, and I think neither

168

one of us wants to bring anything up in fear we will burst this blissful bubble of ignorance we're living in.

Now more than ever, I want to remove any unnecessary drama out of my life and focus on raising my daughter in a happy and healthy environment. That is all I want, and the sooner Cole and I get a divorce, the sooner we can both move on and focus on making Alaia our top priority. I lay back and watch Cole as he cradles Alaia in his arms, singing to her quietly. "Is she hungry?" I ask, and Cole looks at me with a smile.

"I think she might be," He chuckles, looking down at her when she whines. "She's on the hunt for boobs."

I smile, sitting up and wince when I feel how full my breasts were. "Oh yeah, it's definitely feeding time." Cole hands Alaia to me and sits at the end of the bed while I feed her. That first moment she latches on hurts like hell, and I wince as she suckles hungrily.

"Are you hungry? Do you need me to get you anything?" Cole asks considerately, rubbing my ankle, and I shake my head, watching Alaia while she feeds. She blinks, looking up at me.

"No, I'm good, thank you." I smile at him. "I honestly can't wait to get out of here and take her home already." I sigh, brushing my finger over her soft cheek.

"Shay, I want you to come back home," Cole says, and I look at him, surprised.

"Cole, I already told you, that's not my home anymore," I reply, and Cole shifts and sits closer to Alaia and me.

"That will always be your home Shayla, both of yours." He claims, looking down at Alaia. "I know things are complicated between us, but we have Alaia to think about, and she needs us both right now," Cole explains, taking my hand in his and kissing my knuckles.

"You're right. Alaia is the only thing that matters to me right now, Cole. I'm going to put all my energy into providing a happy home for her, not one where her parents are at each other's throats all the time—which you know will be the case with us," I tell him earnestly and lift Alaia so I could wind her.

"Shayla, whether you like it or not, we're a family now, and the best thing for Alaia is for her parents to be together under the same roof." I sigh and switch breasts when she lets out a gassy burp.

"Not necessarily," I shake my head, glancing down at Alaia before I look at Cole again. "I can't just forgive and forget everything that's happened between us, Cole. Just because we have a baby together doesn't automatically fix everything that is broken between us. Everything has changed, and if we really want what's best for our daughter, we need to let go of the past and move on and be the best possible parents we can be for her." I explain and see the disappointment in Cole's eyes as he looks at me.

"I'm not giving up on us, Shayla." He solemnly states while reaching over and brushing his fingers along my jaw. "I love you."

I close my eyes and sigh, "No, you don't. You're only saying that because you think it's what I want to hear, but it's too late for that now." I utter, pulling my face away from his touch.

"Shayla, look at me." Cole takes my face into his hands and turns my head so that I could look at him. "I'm in love with you. I've always been in love with you. All those feelings I had inside of me, I thought it was for Sophie because I didn't know you and I didn't know where to place all those feelings, but the love I've had in my heart all along was for *you*. I know it's taken me a while to figure it out, but it's true, and I don't care how long it takes or what it takes. I'm going to prove it to you." He declares, gazing into my eyes. "Just give us a chance, please."

"I have Cole. We're all out of chances. You might not remember, but I still do. I still remember all the chances I gave us and ended up more broken than before, and I don't have another heartbreak left in me. I just don't." I explain with a sigh. It's not that I didn't want to believe that he does love me, but it's just not the same anymore. He's not the same. The way he looks at me isn't the same. It's like he's saying the words, but the emotions in his eyes aren't there. I'm still holding out for my Cole to show up, I want my Cole back, and this just isn't him.

"Shayla—"

I shake my head and lift Alaia onto my chest while I rub her back gently. "Can we please not talk about this now." I request, and Cole sighs, standing up when the young female doctor walks in.

"Hi Shayla."

I smile and nod, "Hi."

"I have your discharge papers here. You guys are free to go." She smiles, handing the papers to Cole, who nods. "Your midwife will come and visit you at home for the next couple of weeks to keep track of Alaia's weight and check-ups."

"Oh, okay, thank you so much," I say with a smile. "I can't wait to go home and shower." I hold Alaia out to Cole, who takes her from me, dropping a kiss on her head before he lays her in the little bed beside mine.

"Ah, nothing like being home in your own space," The doctor says with a warm smile as she looks over Alaia. "Just remember to sleep when she's sleeping. You need plenty of rest. Keep in mind your body is still recovering. Lucky for you, it seems Daddy here is already hands-on." She teases with a wink, and I look at Cole smiling proudly.

"Anything for my girls." He expresses lovingly, dropping a lingering kiss on my temple. I look up at him when he pulls back a little, his gaze on mine.

"Congratulations again. She's truly an angel." The doctor says before she leaves us alone.

"Thank god, I can't wait to get out of here," I utter, pushing the covers off me and hiss when I feel a dull ache between my legs.

"You okay?" Cole questions, concerned, moving closer to me. I nod and hold my hands out to him.

"Yeah, it's just a little uncomfortable. Can you help me up?" Cole nods and takes my hands gently, helping me off the bed. "You know, I was thinking last night how weird this all must feel for you."

Cole looks questioningly at me, "How do you mean?"

I chuckle a little awkwardly as I take my clothes out of the hospital bag, "Well, you obviously don't remember us sleeping together, but you witnessed me giving birth to your child that you don't remember conceiving. You've handled it all quite well, considering."

171

Cole shakes his head with a little laugh, "Yeah, I'm not going to lie, I was freaking out. It's all been a little overwhelming, if I'm honest, and I probably won't forget seeing her head right there...." He trails off, shaking his head. "As magical as it was watching you give life, I was equally horrified and have never felt so useless in my life."

I sit on the edge of the bed and look at him. "Thank you for being there, I know it probably feels strange, but you've been so great with us both this week," I state, looking down at Alaia, peacefully asleep.

Cole smiles affectionately down at his daughter, "My greatest fear was holding her and not feeling that connection or love, but I am honestly so besotted with her, Shay." Cole admits and looks at me. "With both of you." I drop my gaze with a heavy sigh.

AFTER DRESSING myself and getting Alaia ready and strapped in her car seat, we finally leave the hospital and head back to the apartment, much to Coles dismay.

"Aww, here's my princess." Aimee coo's when we walk into the apartment. She takes the car seat from Cole and sets it on the sofa. "Welcome home, baby girl." Josh, Aimee, and Jo all gather around the baby as I watch them. Not even a week old and she's already so loved by so many people.

"Hey, I'm home too." I voice put out, and the girls look over at me and wave before cooing over Alaia again.

I hadn't noticed I was crying until Cole lifts my head and brushes my tears away. "Hey, what's wrong?"

I shake my head, "Nothing, I'm just feeling overly emotional again." I tell him, and he smiles and pulls me close hugging me. I lay my head on his chest and sigh, closing my eyes as he holds me tight. "I better go shower and get some rest while she's asleep. Can you keep an eye on her while I shower? I won't be long." I ask him, and he nods with a handsome smile.

"Of course, go ahead."

I glance over at Alaia in Aimee's arms before I nod and walk to the bathroom to shower. I was feeling utterly drained. It's been a hell of a week, and I honestly couldn't wait for some peace so I could rest. Unfortunately, that wasn't about to happen anytime soon because Cole's parents and my mother came to visit the baby.

I must have dozed off while everyone was clucking over the baby because I jump awake when I feel myself being lifted off the sofa. I blink up at Cole tiredly and lay my head on his chest as he carries me to my bedroom. "Shh, go back to sleep, sweetheart." I hear him whisper before he kisses my forehead while he lays me down on the bed.

"The baby.." I sigh, trying to sit up, but he pushes me down again with a smile.

"We've got her. She's sound asleep. You're exhausted Shay, get some rest." Cole insists, brushing his fingers through my hair, and I sigh, closing my eyes.

"Okay, just for a little bit." I sigh before I drift off to sleep again. I stir from my sleep when I feel someone shaking me. I peel my eyes open and see Alaia's face wide awake in front of mine.

"I'm hungry, Mama." I hear a squeaky voice and laugh tiredly and look at Cole grinning rather pleased with himself for making me laugh.

"You're such a dork," I utter and push myself up with a yawn and take Alaia from him. It was dark out. "How long was I asleep?"

"Not long, like two hours." He tells me, laying back on the bed, watching me feeding our daughter. "Everyone left like a half-hour ago."

I groan, closing my eyes, "Two hours? It felt like five minutes. Oh god, I can't believe I fell asleep while we had guests over."

Cole smiles, "Shay, they understand you've just had a baby. Of course, you're going to be tired, sweetheart."

"I am. I honestly can't keep my eyes open. I'm so tired... and hungry." I yawn, and Cole leans over, brushing his fingers over my calf.

"What do you want to eat?" Cole asks, peering up at me with those startlingly gorgeous green eyes. I chew on my bottom lip thoughtfully and shrug. "Pizza? Chinese? Thai?"

I smile, licking my lips. "Mm, I can't eat anything too spicy because

I'm breastfeeding. Chinese sounds good." Cole nods and takes his phone out.

"Chow Mein?" I nod gratefully, lifting Alaia so I can wind her. Cole looks at her face and smiles adoringly at her. "You want some Chow Mein too, my princess?" He coo's leaning close and kisses her nose softly. "She's got your nose. I love that."

I chuckle and look at her, "How can you tell? She's still so small."

Cole grins, reaching over, and he tweaks my nose lovingly. "I can tell." He laughs amused when I slap his hand away with a scowl.

"Stop."

After putting the baby to sleep in her bassinet, Cole and I ate our food and talked for a while before we fell asleep. This was our routine for a couple of weeks. He'd spend some nights with Alaia and me at my apartment so he could spend some time with her. This wasn't good for me because my emotions were piling up on top of one another. My head and heart were battling one another for rationality, and I'm wedged in the middle, wondering what the hell I'm supposed to do.

Last night, while we were lying in bed, things got a little hot and heavy, and if I weren't post-partum, we would have, without a doubt, lost control and had sex.

Since Alaia was born, I've been sleeping with a night light on so I could see her while she's in her crib. After we got into bed, Cole and I lay on our sides, facing one another. God, this man makes my heart run wild with just one look. Cole watches me intently, those brilliant green eyes of his leisurely flitter over my face. His fingers reach over and brush my hair away from my face, gently tucking it behind my ear. My eyes slid shut when his fingers stroke my jaw and brush down the side of my neck, his thumb caressing my pulse point, which causes my heart rate to spike under his touch. When I open my eyes, Cole was nearer, so close, that I'm almost intimately pressed against him. The intoxicating smell of his aftershave surrounds me, and the heat radiating off his body had my stomach twisting with anticipation.

Cole's fingers trailing over the bare skin of my shoulder raised goose-bumps all over my body. "I had a vision the other day, and I can't stop thinking about it. I couldn't tell if it was a dream or a memory of ours." Cole speaks quietly, his eyes on mine.

I watch him closely, and my mouth suddenly goes bone dry. "What was it?"

Cole licks his lips before he speaks, "We were in my old apartment, in the kitchen. You were sitting on the island eating ice cream, and I..."

"Smeared it all over my body and licked it off." I finish, and his eyes flash with desire, and he stares at me so raptly I forget to breathe. "It wasn't a dream. That was a couple of months into us living together." I explain quietly, and Cole blinks, biting down on his lip.

"I wanted you. I wanted you more than I've ever wanted anything in my life. The memory was very brief, but the passion and need, it was so..." Cole swallows hard, staring at my lips.

"Intense," I whisper, and he nods, silently shifting closer to me till our foreheads were pressed together.

"Did we have sex that night?" I shake my head.

"No, but we would have had the fire alarm not gone off and interrupted us," I tell him, and he smiles a little.

"So when did we?" He questions, raking his fingertips over my collarbone. A shiver thrums through me when he ghosts his lips over mine.

"Um, at your parent's place after our post-wedding party, your mother insisted on throwing us," I explain and gasp a little when Cole's thumb brushes over my hardened nipple over the material of my vest top.

"I love the sounds you make when I touch you," Cole admits gruffly, pinching my nipple and rolling it between his fingers. "I want to hear my name on those gorgeous lips when I make you come for me."

I bite my lip hard and sigh when Cole presses an open-mouthed kiss on my neck and sucks teasingly, eliciting a breathy moan from me. "Cole, we can't.."

"Why can't we, baby?" Cole groans, nipping at my ear. "Don't fight me, sweetheart. Let me make you feel good." I whimper when his fingers slide into my shorts, and he brushes his fingers through my moist cleft.

"Oh baby, you're so fucking wet." Cole moans, stroking my clit with slow, steady circles. I rock my hips, mewling while he caresses me. "Don't hold back, come on, baby, show me what my touch does to you."

"Cole." I moan, curling my fingers in his hair when he kisses down my throat. "Please.."

"I'd give everything right now to have you riding my tongue, fucking my mouth till you're damn near weeping with pleasure." Cole expresses hungrily, his finger stroking me languorously toward my climax. I lose my bearings and arch up when I hit that enchanting peak just before I go over.

"Oh god, yes, Cole. I'm going to..."

"Come, baby, I've got you. Come for me. Shayla." I cry out when Cole presses down on my clit and takes me over. I shudder, and my body pulses with every wave of pleasure as it crashes over me.

"Uhh, Cole...Cole, yess." I moan, biting down on my lip to stop from screaming and waking everyone. Cole watches me avidly while he continues to caress me through my climax.

"Fuck Shay, I want you." Cole burrs, brushing his lips over mine. "You're making me fucking crazy." Our lips part, and just as his tongue glides over mine Alaia starts to cry, interrupting us. My eyes snap open, and I look up at him breathless while he stares down into my flushed face desirously.

"I should uh..." Cole nods and draws away from me as I slip out of bed, my knees still quivering while I walk over to the crib. Cole falls back on the bed with a sigh and stares up at the ceiling.

∼

"So, what is the deal with you two now?" Jo asks me quietly as she takes a bite out of her slice of pizza.

I sigh and look over at Cole, talking with Josh. "I don't know. He keeps saying he wants us to be a family and that he loves me, but I..." I trail off thoughtfully.

"You're scared he's only saying that because of the baby," Aimee finishes for me and I nod, closing my eyes. "Have you mentioned the divorce to him again?"

I shake my head and look at her. "No, he keeps changing the subject whenever I try to bring it up. He's refusing to give up on us, even though there hasn't been an us for months now. It's just not the same anymore."

Jo frowns, "Does that mean you don't love him anymore?"

"Of course I do, but my heart still wants the old Cole, and I know he's not coming back," I utter miserably while picking at my slice of pizza. "There are these moments where I feel like he's back to himself again, but then he'll look at me impassively, and it hits me all over again that he's never going to look at me the way I'm yearning for him too ever again," I explain, lifting my gaze to look over at him.

"What about last night?" I look at Aimee questioningly, and she grins, wagging her brows. "Thin walls Shay."

I feel my cheeks burn with embarrassment. "You heard that? I thought I was quiet." Aimee and Jo both giggle.

"Quiet? Whatever he was doing to you in there had you mewling like a porn star." Aimee sniggers. "And I thought Josh was good at the dirty talk...boy, the things he was saying to you even had me hot and bothered." I gape at Aimee, and she laughs.

"Jesus, what did have a glass pressed to the wall?" I ask, affronted, and Aimee laughs, shaking her head.

"Fuck no. I think you both got lost in the heat of the moment and forgot other people actually live here too."

"Shay, ignore this little nympho," Jo says, throwing a breadstick at Aimee. "This is a really good thing. You guys still share that special connection and sexual attraction for one another despite everything. This is how it all started for you both, remember?"

"Girls, I don't know. I'm just so confused." I sigh tiredly.

"He's stepped into the father role pretty well. He's great with Alaia." Jo states and I nod.

"Yeah, he is. I always knew he would be a great Dad." I agree, averting my gaze when he looks over at me, catching me watching him.

Everything seems ten times more complicated between us now, and ignoring the elephant in the room is making things worse.

THREE WEEKS GO by rather quickly, and Alaia is now a month old on her original due date. She's growing nicely and is now the size she would have been had she been born full term. So essentially, she's the size of a new-born instead of a month-old baby. It's all very confusing, and it took a while to wrap my head around it when the midwife explained it to me.

I just finished feeding and changing her when I hear a rather abrupt knock at the front door. Aimee and Jo are both at work, and it was the middle of the afternoon. I lay Alaia in her crib before I walk over and answer the door to a livid Cole.

"What the fuck is this, Shay?" He hisses, holding up an envelope in his hand. I sigh and watch as he storms into the apartment, and I close the door before I lean on it. "You've filed for divorce?"

I sigh and drop my gaze, "I told you I want a divorce. Cole, receiving the papers shouldn't have been that big of a surprise." I tell him, and he shakes his head, glaring at me.

"I thought we already worked past this divorce nonsense?" Cole questions angrily, and I rake my fingers through my hair. "We were getting on fine. Where the fuck did this come from all of a sudden?"

"We didn't work past anything, Cole. We just ignored it like we do everything else. This marriage is over; you know this as well as I do. What's the point in dragging it out?" I argue.

"Our daughter?! Is there a bigger reason than that, Shayla?" Cole states hotly while taking a step toward me.

"She will still be our daughter, whether we're married or not, Cole. Stop using Alaia as an excuse to hold onto this marriage. The best thing we can do for her is part ways before things get ugly between us." I explain, looking up at him.

"I'm not divorcing you," Cole states, staring into my eyes as he rips up the papers. "I love you, Shayla, and I'm not giving up on us. You can keep sending me these papers, but I'll just keep tearing them up."

"You love me, Cole? Prove it." I sigh, gazing up at him. "Look at me like you used to, right now, let me feel your love, make me believe it," I add pleadingly and search his eyes when he looks at me. My shoulders slump when I see nothing but bewilderment in his gaze. "You can't love me because you don't know me," I utter before I step away from him. "I know you truly want to believe that you love me, Cole, but what I hear from your mouth and what I see in your eyes tell me two completely different things."

Cole takes hold of my arms and draws me against him, cupping my face in his large hands, he whispers, "How can I know you when you won't let me get close to you?" I watch him tightly as he presses his forehead to mine. "How am I supposed to show you that I love you if you won't let me?"

"Cole..." I breathe, closing my eyes when I feel his lips trailing along my jaw.

"Let me love you, baby." Cole whispers, ghosting his lips over mine, his fingers tangled in my hair. Cole's lips brush mine apart, and just as our mouths were about to fuse, Alaia's cry makes us jump apart.

"I better go check on her," I utter, stepping away from him. Cole nods, watching me as I walk to my bedroom and pick up Alaia. He walks over to us and leans close, dropping a kiss on Alaia's head, all the while his eyes staring into mine.

"Don't break up our family, Shay," Cole whispers pleadingly. "We can make this work. I know we can."

"We've never been a family, Cole," I reply, looking at him steadily. "I'm tired of being married to a ghost. My husband is gone, and it doesn't look like he's ever coming back."

Cole licks his lips with a shake of his head, "Shayla, you're not married to a ghost. I'm right here." He tells me, frustration evident in his tone. "Why are you so reluctant on giving us a chance, babe?"

"Because you hurt me one too many times, Cole. I've given you plenty of chances, and in the end, I end up more wrecked and devastated than before. We've tried, it's just not working. It shouldn't be this hard to be together. I won't survive another heartbreak. I just won't."

"Shayla, I would never—"

"Stop." I shake my head and sigh. "I've heard those words one too many times, and it's always a damn lie because you do, Cole. One way or another, I end up getting hurt, and I'm done with it." I explain, looking down at the baby when she starts fussing. "I don't want to argue with you anymore Cole, we're going to be in each other's lives for a long time because of Alaia, so I want to do the right thing by her and have a good friendship with her Dad."

"Friendship? I don't want to be your *friend* Shay." Cole contends with a scowl.

"That's all I have to offer, Cole." I retort, and Cole stood stunned, looking at me morosely for a moment before he shakes his head and walks out of the bedroom. I close my eyes and let the tears flow when I hear the front door slam shut a couple of seconds later.

After that day, things between Cole and I went from bad to worse, especially when he got the notice for our divorce hearing. As you can imagine, it was dragging on between the solicitors because Cole was refusing to give me a divorce. So, here we were three weeks later standing before a judge— as luck would have it, the same judge that divorced us before.

"Didn't I divorce you two already?" He questions, looking at Cole then at me. "You're the young lady that refused a settlement before, am I right?"

I nod, "Yes, your honour."

"So, you got married again?" He probes, and we both nod in response. "And in Vegas. Drunken mistake again?" I shake my head while Cole rolls his eyes. "Right, let's see here. Mrs Hoult, you want a divorce on the grounds of irreconcilable differences." The judge states and Cole scoffs audibly, shaking his head. "Mr Hoult, may I ask why you are refusing to divorce your wife?"

Cole looks over at me. "Because I love her." He states pointedly before he looks at the judge again. "I love my wife and my daughter very much and want to work on this marriage, but she's too stubborn to see that."

"This has nothing to do with me being stubborn." I retort, annoyed while glaring at him. "I already told you my reasons a hundred times, Cole. I'm tired of repeating myself."

"You're tired of repeating yourself?! I'm tired of apologising to you." Cole chides irritably as he sits back in his seat again.

"Then stop apologising, Cole, because it's not making a difference, is it?" I utter, leaning back in my seat and averting my gaze.

"I'm starting to see the irreconcilable differences." The judge mumbles sardonically as he looks through the paperwork on his desk.

"Irreconcilable difference, my arse," Cole grumbles, tapping his finger on the desk in front of him.

"Oh no? What would you call it then?" I hiss, annoyed, watching him as he leans over, his angry gaze penetrating my own.

"Cowardice." Cole grits through clenched teeth.

"Excuse me?" I hiss hotly, standing up from my seat.

"You heard me." Cole throws back, rising from his seat also as we glower at one another furiously.

"You walked out on me when I was pregnant, and I'm the coward?!" I shout furiously, and the judge looks back and forth from me to Cole while we argue.

"I wasn't in the right state of mind! Your honour, I lost my memory after I was involved in a plane crash and forgot who she was. She's holding something I did while I was in a state of amnesia against me. Is that fair? Please tell me?" Cole asks, looking at the judge, who turns his eyes to me. "I told her I love her, but she refuses to believe me."

"How can I? When you're looking at me like I'm just a stranger to you. Words are meaningless without the emotion, which is something you lack, Cole!"

Cole slams his hand down on the table angrily. "You won't let me within two feet of you! What is it going to take Shayla, what more do I have to do for you to believe that I'm crazy about you!"

"Enough!" The judge shouts, hitting his mallet on the table. "I think

I've heard enough here." He states, shaking his head, looking at me first, then Cole. "I've seen a lot of couples come through this courtroom to dissolve their marriages, but this is the first time in my thirty years as a judge, seeing a couple who love each other this fiercely so eager to walk away from one another for a second time. I granted your divorce last time even though I saw the love you both had for one another in your eyes. You both chose to get married again, and it's truly unfortunate what happened to you, Mr Hoult, but marriage is not a game." He expresses gravely and looks at me.

"Do the vows for better for worse, in sickness and in health mean nothing to you? I hear enough blame to go around for both of you. It's abundantly clear mistakes have been made, but are those mistakes worth throwing away a marriage for, especially when you both love one another enough to fight with this much passion?" He questions, and Cole looks over me. Our eyes meet across the room, and I hold his gaze for a touch too long before I stare at the wall ahead. "I'm not granting your divorce." My eyes snap to the judge first, then to Cole, who smiles.

"What? But your hon—" I try to interject, and he holds his hand up.

"You two seem to believe that marriage is all fun and games, and at the first sign of trouble, you're quick to walk away—well, I'm saving you both from making another mistake. You will stay married, and on top of that, I'm ordering you to see a marriage councillor once a week to talk through your issues. I see separate addresses on the papers filed. You will move back in together and work on your marriage for six months—"

I gape at him, "Six months?!" I shriek wide-eyed, and the judge crosses his arms over his chest and glares at me. "Your honour, with all due respect, I can't live with him for six months. We'll kill each other." I state pleadingly.

"Looks like you're stuck with me, sweetheart," Cole utters smugly, leaning back into his chair.

"Like *hell*, I'm living with you." I hiss irately, and the judge hits his mallet on the desk again to silence us.

"It's a court order, young lady, you will live together, and your marriage councillor will report back to the court whether you are both attending and your progress. If you refuse to cooperate, I will have no other choice but to get child services involved to take a closer look at your relationship and what effect it's having on your child." Cole and I exchange concerned glances, and I sink back into my seat. "If after the six months is up and you both still want a divorce, I will grant it, but not before you work on this marriage and at least try and keep your family together. Am I making myself clear?"

"Yes, your honour." Cole and I say together.

"Excellent, now go on and face your issues because no one can fix them but the two of you." He says before he hits his mallet on the desk again. "Adjourned."

Cole and I living together for another six months?

Oh Christ, not again.

Chapter 16

COLE

─────── ❈ ───────

"WHAT DO YOU THINK?"

Shayla looks at the wall and wrinkles her nose in distaste. "I am not loving it."

I frown and look at the wall and then at her. "You said pink." I remind her, and she lifts her jade gaze to mine and narrows her eyes.

"I thought it would look cute, but now that I see it, I hate it." She utters with a shrug of her shoulders.

I exhale and frown thoughtfully. "Okay," I bite my lip and look at her again. "I'm thinking, yellow?" I suggest, and she tilts her head to the side and looks around the nursery, and nods.

"Yellow might work. It will definitely brighten up the room." She sighs, glancing down at the baby monitor to check on Alaia before she looks at the wall again. "Maybe we can do a feature wall with her name in the middle."

I nod again and look at Shayla. It's been two days since she and Alaia have moved back into our home. Shay's been pissed about having to come back, but day by day, I'm hoping her anger will simmer, and we can finally start working on our problems. I couldn't be happier to have them both under the same roof as me, where they belong. Shayla's refusing to sleep in the same room as me, which is as I expected anyway. I was in no rush for that, and I'm confident it would come when she's ready. We have our first court order counselling session later today— if

184

we ever finish decorating this nursery, that is. "I like that idea. Let's do that."

Shayla smiles, nodding, and walks over to the tin of paint and pops it open. For the life of me, I didn't understand why she wouldn't let me get the decorators in to have it done, but I didn't argue and just let her do what made her happy. If it meant we get to spend some one-on-one time together, I'd paint the entire bloody house with her. I kneel and watch her as she stirs the paint before she tips some of it out into the tray. "It's a nice yellow, not too bright. What do you think?" She questions, looking at me. I smile and pick up my brush and dab it in the paint.

"Let me see." I hum and swipe the brush over her forehead with a little paint and grin. "Looks real good." I chuckle amusedly while she looks at me wide-eyed.

Her brow goes up, and she picks up her mini roller and rolls it down my nose with a satisfied smirk. "Yellow is not your colour, Lord Hoult," Shayla mutters and picks up the pink brush and swipes that on my cheek before I can catch her wrist and move my face. "Pink looks good on you, though."

"Oh, really?" I grab her face and rub mine over hers, smearing the paint all over her pretty face while she squeals, trying to push me off.

"Stop it. Cole! Oh, you're so dead." Shayla laughs, trying to paint my face with her brush, and topples over, landing on top of me. Laughing, I grab hold of her wrists and look up into her eyes while she holds my gaze, her smile slowly fading when my eyes lower to her lips before they meet her stunning eyes again.

"Oh my!" We jump back when we hear Shay's mother's voice in the doorway. "I'm sorry, kids, I heard shouting," Sara utters, flushing a deep red and averting her gaze. Shayla scrambles off me and clears her throat.

"We were just trying to decide on colours." She lamely explains as I sit up and nod sheepishly.

"That we were." I grin at her charmingly, "I think we decided on yellow?" Shayla nods, rubbing her paint-stained forehead.

"Uh-huh, yes, yellow is a good choice." She mumbles and looks at her mother, watching us, amusement evident in her eyes. "Did you check on Alaia?"

Sara nods, "Yes, she's asleep. I'll leave you two to...carry on with painting." She says with a smile and winks at me before she walks out of the nursery. Shayla looks at me when I chuckle while getting up to my feet.

"It's not funny, Cole," She complains, hitting my shoulder while clearly fighting the urge to smile herself.

"It's a little funny. The look on her face when she saw us on top of each other was priceless," I say, pulling a strand of her hair covered in paint off her face. Shayla slaps my hand away with a mock glare. "Ow, someone's feisty today." I tease, and she looks me over, slowly narrowing her eyes.

"I'm feisty always...you just don't happen to remember, Cole Hoult." She tells me proudly and jumps away when I swipe my brush on her nose.

"I'm looking forward to finding out Shayla Hoult." I drawl, taking a step closer while staring into her eyes. I groan when she jams her roller into my stomach and steps away.

"Paint Cole, *paint*." Shayla urges me as she starts rolling the paint on the wall. I laugh and follow her and begin painting the walls. While painting, we exchange flirty glances and touches as we pass by one another. I'll break her soon. I just know it. How long can she resist me?

I watch her as she paints the wall opposite to mine, we had music playing from a Bluetooth speaker, and she was swaying her hips as she paints. I observed her every movement avidly, fighting off the compelling urge to wrap my arms around her from behind and bury my face into her neck. She'd probably kick me if I tried.

"I think we're done," I hear her sigh while looking around the room. I walk over to her and sling my arm around her shoulder as we admire our handy work.

"This does look better than the pink— it makes the room look fresher," I voice, looking around, and she nods in agreement.

"Sure does. Jo is really artsy, so I'll ask her to do the feature wall for us." Shayla explains, and I nod.

"That's awesome. You know, I never asked, what do the girls do for work?" I question, curious as I watch Shayla drop the roller in her hand in the tray.

"Uh, Aimee is a web designer, she's crazy creative if you ever want to change up our website, and Jo works with Autistic kids." She explains, and I nod, watching her.

"That doesn't surprise me about Jo. It makes sense how patient she is with Sam; now I see why," I rub my neck, following her out of the nursery. Shayla smiles and looks at me as she walks to the bathroom.

"Jo is a saint. Honestly, she's the calmest person I know. I just pray my idiot brother doesn't hurt her." Shay sighs, unclipping the straps to her overalls.

"I think he's rather smitten with her," I tell her as I unclip my own overall and poke her side playfully. "Just like you are with me." Shayla jumps and slaps my hand away with a nervous laugh, her cheeks going rosy.

"Keep wishing, Hoult." Shayla mumbles, placing her hands on my chest and pushing me out of the bathroom. "I need to shower, get out." She huffs, looking up at me when I hold the door open with my hand and gaze down at her.

"Want some company?" I suggest wagging my brows at her, and she looks at me startled as I lean in close to her face. "I can scrub you down..." I whisper, brushing my nose over hers. Shayla licks her lips and smiles playfully.

"I mean, it has been a very long time since I've been *scrubbed*." She breathes, reaching up and trailing her fingers down my throat.

"That makes two of us, sweetheart," I groan, pressing my forehead to hers. I can't remember the last time I had sex actually, I know it's been a hell of a long time if my achy balls were any indication. "When was the last time I gave you a good...scrubbing? Other than that little moment in your bed a few weeks ago, that is."

Shayla's cheeks go beet red, and I chuckle when she looks at me with wide eyes. "I am not answering that. Get out." She incoherently mutters as she shoves me away from the door and slams it shut in my face.

"That long then?" I tease, pressing my face against the door with a grin. "I know you want me, Shayla." I sing to her.

"Shut up, Cole!" I hear her complain on the other side of the door before she runs the shower. I laugh, shaking my head, and leave her to shower in peace while I go and check on Alaia.

I look down into her crib where she was lying awake, staring up at the colourful mobile. "Hi Princess, did you have a good nap." I coo, and she looks up at me, kicking her little legs. "Oh my goodness, Daddy is going to eat your little feet, yes I am. I can't pick you up, baby. Your mummy will kill me if I get paint all over you." I pout, and she fusses and lets out a little cry. "I know, you're getting hungry, aren't you." I rock her crib, and she stops fussing and blinks up at me, all innocent and beautiful. "Don't look at me like that. I don't have boobies. I can't feed you." I look back when I hear footsteps behind me and see Shayla walk out of the bathroom wrapped in a towel.

"Is she up already?" Shayla asks, drying her hair with a towel, and I nod, looking at Alaia fussing when I stop rocking her crib.

"She sure is. She's trying to eat her mittens," I say, pulling Alaia's hand away from her mouth. "I better go shower and let you feed her before we're late for our first marriage counselling." Shayla nods and watches me as I walk past her and into the ensuite bathroom while taking off my shirt.

An hour later, we were sitting on the sofa in the marriage councillor's office rather awkwardly. Natalie McNeil, the marriage councillor was supposed to be the best in the business, so I was intrigued, to say the least, to see what her input would be to our situation. "So, why don't we start from the beginning. Shayla, why don't you tell me how you and Cole met?"

Shayla looks at me and sighs before she looks at Natalie, "We met in a club called Luxe, I was out celebrating a new job with my two best friends, and he came up to me and demanded I dance with him...I agreed, and we spend a good while dancing." Shayla explains, looking down at her hands, laced together in her lap while she spoke. "The next morning, we woke up in Vegas hungover and married."

Natalie nods while writing in her notepad. "What stopped you both from getting a divorce right away? Why did you stay married?"

Shayla sighs, "Uh, Cole asked for my help. His family was arranging his marriage to a girl he didn't want to marry. It was his grandfather's dying wish to see him married before he signed over his shares to the family business." I watch her closely as she speaks, a distant look in her eyes as she harks back to the time we first met.

"Why did you decide to help him?"

"I don't know, he seemed desperate and genuinely helpless, and I didn't agree with him being forced into a marriage with a girl he didn't love." Natalie nods and pushes her black slim framed glasses up her nose.

"Do you remember the moment you first realised you were falling in love with Cole?" Shayla remains silent for a while and turns her gaze to me before she looks ahead again.

"Yes, it was on the trip to Nice that Cole surprised me with. We were, um... making love under a waterfall." She explains, her cheeks aflame.

"You want me... you're going to have to earn me."

I blink a couple of times while watching Shayla as she speaks softly.

"Oh, sweetheart, I have earned you. I've waited four agonizing months to have you. Please don't torture me anymore."

Wait a minute. I remember that. My mind wanders off while Shayla and Natalie converse. I remember the clear blue water, the coolness of the stream as it hit us while we stood under it. I remember peeling off her bikini before I lay her out on the rock, and we... "Cole?" I jump out of my thoughts and look at Natalie, a little startled.

"Hm?"

"Does any of what Shayla is saying seem familiar to you?" I turn my gaze to Shayla and look into her eyes.

"You wore a white bikini. I remember...watching you as you stood under the waterfall, your head thrown back, smiling beautifully while the water washes over you." I say with a smile, and Shayla watches me, astonished, her green eyes searching mine.

Natalie smiles, "That's marvellous, Cole. I am confident the more you both discuss old memories you've shared together, the more it will jog your memory into remembering them." She voices while Shayla and I continue to look at one another. That's the first memory of us I could place with the emotions attached. I could feel my nerves, the excitement I felt being so close to her.

"Shayla, it's understandable that you're apprehensive about opening up to Cole again after he's hurt you countless times. It's only natural for you to want to protect yourself from going through the same things again, but I want you to stop focussing on the bad and remember all the good things that made you fall in love with him in the first place." Natalie states with a smile as she watches Shayla turn her gaze to look at me.

"I need you both to communicate more. Don't be afraid to bring up the past and relive it all over again. Sometimes you'll find it brings us closer and makes our relationships stronger, and as you just witnessed, it can also trigger things for Cole." Natalie expresses. "I want you to start over, go back to the basics, and date. I want you *both* to remember just how much you still want one another, so I'm forbidding you both from any sexual contact till our next session." Shayla and I gape at her in response. "Exactly the reaction I was hoping for." She chuckles at the look on our faces. "That's all we have time for today, but I'm looking forward to hearing all about how your date goes in the next session."

"Thank you, Dr McNeil," Shayla says, standing up and shaking her hand. I do the same, and we leave her office in silence. I sneak a look at Shayla, who seems to be lost in thought as we walk back to the car.

"What are you thinking about?" I ask, unlocking the car as we walk over to it. Shayla shakes her head with a deep sigh.

"Nothing really, just trying to process everything she said." She replies with a little shrug as she looks ahead, avoiding my gaze. I smile and take her hand in mine as we reach the car and spin her around so she could face me. Shayla gasps when her body is pressed to mine, her fingers splayed out on my chest as I back her up against the passenger side door.

"Cole, what are you doing?" She questions breathily as she glances around warily before she cranes her neck to look up at me. I brush my thumb along her jaw gently while I look into her eyes.

"Reminiscing." I drawl hoarsely as I press myself against her more intimately. "That little flashback I had of us in Nice has got me feeling some type of way." I moan, looking at her lips hungrily when she licks them. "Stop torturing me, baby."

Shayla's eyes light up, and she bites her bottom lip, "You heard the therapist, sexual contact is forbidden. You're breaking the rules, and it's not even been five minutes."

I groan, dipping my head and nuzzling her neck, "Sometimes you have to break the rules, sweetheart." I murmur, brushing my lips against the shell of her ear. Shayla gasps, her fingers fisting my shirt when I nip at her ear lightly.

"Cole, *shit*, we can't." She moans, tilting her head back while I drag my lips down the length of her throat. I inhale her scent, and it makes me dizzy. Suddenly I'm hit with so many emotions all at once I didn't know which one to focus on. My stomach was twitching with anticipation every time I hear her quiet moan.

"Ahem!" I pull my head back and look at the elderly couple watching us, both with entirely different expressions on their faces. The man was smiling widely while the lady was scowling, clearly mortified while she drags her husband away. I press my lips together to smother the laughter as I watch them walk away, muttering among themselves. Shayla had her face buried into my chest, giggling hysterically.

"Oh, my God." She laughs, shaking her head, her face so red it resembled an overcooked lobster. "That was embarrassing."

I groan, smiling, "Why are we constantly interrupted at the perfect moment?" Shayla shrugs and looks at me, smiling.

"Because we're doing something we're not supposed to." She states and pushes me back a little before she gets into the passenger seat. "Now behave yourself." She adds before she closes the door with a mischievous grin.

I felt rather antsy around Shayla, and it was now harder to keep my hands to myself— especially after Natalie told us we couldn't have any sexual contact. I know it's childish, I'm a grown man, but if someone tells me I can't have something...I want it that much more. I'm sure I'm not alone with this. I was already yearning for Shayla like crazy, and now she's suddenly off-limits to me—it makes me want her ten times more.

So, here we are, a couple of days into the 'no sexual contact' agreement, sitting on opposite ends of the sofa watching a movie that neither of us is paying any attention to while Alaia is asleep in her crib upstairs. I'm trying so hard to behave, I really am, but she's deliberately goading me by walking around in tight little shorts and a crop top with no bra—I mean *fuck,* she just looks enticing right now. I feel my cock strain against the thick material of my jeans, and I groan inwardly. I let my eyes wander over to Shayla while she watches the film— or rather pretends to watch it. We both stare at the screen during a love scene. I gulp and shift in my seat when the two characters start to have sex rather explicitly. Shayla and I look at one another before we look at the screen again.

I gulp.

"What is this movie?" I ask, clearing my throat, unable to look away as the male character goes down on the female.

"Aimee suggested we watch it." She breathes, watching wide-eyed, her lips parted. "Shall we... turn it...off?" I look at Shayla and we both nod in unison. I pick up the remote and turn the tv off. We sat there unsure of what to do for a second before Shayla clears her throat and looks at me, her face flushed. "Maybe we should go to bed." She states and chuckles a little when I look at her, surprised. "Separately...to sleep." She adds, and I bite my lip, forcing myself not to stare at her hard nipples.

"Sleep?" I hum, narrowing my eyes at her. "It's eight 'o clock," I say with a smile, and she looks at the clock on the wall and sighs. "Why don't we just *talk*? Our therapist said we should communicate, right?" I suggest shifting to sit closer to her, and she watches me warily.

"Talk?" She intones her green eyes, looking over my face as I shift nearer to her. "About what?"

I shrug and lick my lips slowly while I stare into her eyes. "Something fun." I drawl, letting my eyes linger on her lips before I lift them to her eyes again.

Shayla smiles a little and looks down when she feels my fingers brush along her thigh lightly. "Define fun?" She sighs, biting her bottom lip and lifting her quizzical gaze to mine.

I smile lazily and hold her gaze, "The kind that barely requires any words...or clothes." I whisper as my fingers leisurely inch closer to the elastic of her shorts. Shayla exhales a little when my fingers brush against the lace of her underwear.

"Are you suggesting we speak the language of love?" She whispers, and I grin, leaning in closer so I could brush my lips along her jaw.

"Precisely." I groan, gradually pushing aside her underwear and dragging my finger through her soaking slit. *Fuck.* Shayla gasps, her eyes closing when my finger brushes her bundle of nerves. "I'm dying to taste you, baby." I breathe, pinching her clit gently, and she whimpers, rocking her hips. "I just *know* I won't be able to get enough." I burr hoarsely whilst I watch her glowing face.

"Cole, we can't." Shayla moans, rocking her hips, rubbing herself against my fingers while I lick up her throat. "Uhh, God."

"You've got the taste of heaven between your legs," I groan as I nip at her ear gently. "And baby, I'm burning to drown in it." I moan, sinking my finger into her, and she cries out, her entire body quakes in my arms.

"Cole..."

"*Christ*, Shayla."

Chapter 17

SHAYLA

OH BOY.

It feels good to be touched, *especially* by him. I know I shouldn't let him get this close to me because it's too soon, and our therapist has put a ban on any sexual contact, but *damn*, everything he is doing, every single word coming from those gorgeous lips, is driving me wild. I feel like I've gone back in time to when we were first getting to know one another. I believe that is the purpose of this little experiment. Hold on a minute. I'm still angry with him. Oh, but the way his lips feel on my neck is reason enough to forgive him.

No Shayla! This is why you get hurt. You give in to him too quickly— make him work for it!

While Cole's sticky fingers were slowly tugging my shorts down, his lips hot on my neck, sucking my pulse point, I couldn't think straight for the life of me. Thank god, the doorbell rings, and my eyes snap open at the same time as Cole's head pops up from my neck. "Ignore it." He groans, burying his face into my neck again.

"Cole, we can't ignore it," I sigh, pushing him off and pull my shorts back up where he'd slid them down my thighs. Cole growls in frustration and looks up at me, his eyes all big and pleading. "Stop looking at me like that." I slap his hands away when he tries to pull me close to him and pull his t-shirt on as I wasn't wearing a whole lot.

"Who the hell is here at this time?" Cole whines, his brows fused tightly while he looks up at me from his position on the sofa. I shrug and walk to the door to answer it. I pull it open and see Aimee and Josh grinning from ear to ear.

"Jesus, took you long enough," Aimee mumbles, walking in followed by a sheepish Josh who shrugs when Cole throws a dirty glance his way.

"Please, *do* come in," Cole utters dryly as Josh walks over to the sofa, and they fist bump. I close the door and look over at Aimee, who was holding a binder in her arms.

"What is that?"

Aimee looks at the binder and then at me. "Last-minute wedding stuff I really need my maid of honours opinion on?" I laugh and nod as I guide her to the coffee table. "Where's princess Laia? I miss my little bubba."

I look down at the baby monitor and see she's wide-awake, kicking about in her crib. "You're in luck. She's up. Come on, it's time for a feed anyway," I say, dragging Aimee upstairs to my bedroom. I turn the monitor off before I look down at Alaia. "Hi munchkin, look who's here to see you." I coo, lifting her and kiss her head before I hand her over to a beaming Aimee while she cradles her in her arms.

"It's only been a week, but I really miss you guys being at home with us," Aimee says, looking down at the baby before she looks at me. "How are you finding it being back here? Did we interrupt something before?" She asks with a guilty grin.

I feel my cheeks go hot when I remember the things Cole and I were doing before we got interrupted. "Yes, but I'm thankful because I'm not ready to be physical with him just yet, and we're not even supposed to be having any sexual contact as per our marriage counsellor," I explain with a frustrated sigh.

Aimee chuckles while rocking Alaia in her arms, "Really? I bet Cole is super thrilled about that."

"It's so hard being around him and not feel things, and now we're supposed to start over, date each other, go back to the basics. I feel like our relationship keeps going around and around in a big fat circle." I explain, taking Alaia when she starts fussing. "A part of me is thrilled to be reliving all the excitement and sexual tension, but at the same time, it's bringing back so many memories that I would rather not remember," I add, watching Alaia as she starts to feed.

"Shayla, I know you're scared of getting hurt again, but you've suffered through the worst, and maybe now you're at the point where you two can finally be happy again," Aimee states, rubbing Alaia's foot as she feeds. "You still love him, don't you?"

I close my eyes and sigh deeply, "Of course I do. I'm crazy about him, but I miss the way we used to be. It's still not the same, and maybe I need to accept that things won't ever be the same between us because he's different now." I answer, brushing my thumb over the baby's cheek, and she sighs while she looks up at me with her startling green eyes.

"Has Blake called you?" I look at Aimee and nod. "He came looking for you at the apartment the other day. He was worried when you didn't pick up his calls." She adds, and I lift Alaia to burp her.

"I know, I feel shitty about the way I left things with him. He's such a good guy, but I don't want to drag him through all this mess with Cole and me. Blake helped me out that night at the Lamaze class when you warned me about Cole, and he didn't have to play along with the stupid lie I told and kiss me, but he did."

Aimee sighs, "Josh said Cole was livid when he saw the two of you kissing, and had he not stopped him, he would have probably beaten him to an inch of his life."

I roll my eyes and groan. "Which is why I'm steering clear. Besides, Cole and I have to work on our marriage for the next six months, or we could risk child services getting involved, and I will not risk losing my baby for anyone." I explain, looking down at Alaia sleeping in my arms. After I put her down to sleep Aimee and I discussed the wedding details she needed help with. I couldn't believe she was getting married in less than six weeks.

"I can't believe how much our lives have changed in less than two years." Aimee sighs, laying her head on my shoulder.

"I know, it's crazy, it feels just like yesterday I moved in with you two knuckleheads, now look at us. I have a baby and a husband who doesn't even know who the hell I am. You're getting married. Jo is about to move in with my brother." I explain, and Aimee laughs heartily.

"Oh, baby girl, like the sands through an hourglass..."

"These are the days of our lives." We sing dramatically together and burst out laughing. Once we were done with the wedding talk, I turn the baby monitor back on, and we go back downstairs to the boys who were playing video games.

"And just like that, I kicked your arse...again." Cole grins, dropping the remote and falling back against the sofa in triumph.

"I let you win, bro," Josh grumbles, tossing the remote at him, and Cole laughs, rolling his eyes dramatically.

"Yeah, yeah, you're a sore loser. You've always been a sore loser, my friend." Cole states, catching my hand and pulling me down into his lap when Aimee settles into Josh's arms in the love seat.

"We need to discuss the Bachelor and Bachelorette parties," I declare, giving Aimee a pointed look, and she grins. "And let's not forget the no nookie rule you two put on Cole and me weeks before our wedding. Oh, it's payback time, bish." Aimee and Josh both groan while I cackle with laughter. "However, Aimee, you were right, it made our wedding night incredibly special, and I think you should apply that rule to yourselves also," I advise with a chuckle, and Josh throws me a dirty glare, shaking his head slowly. "It will be my greatest pleasure to keep you two apart as maid of honour."

"I hate you," Josh complains, and I grin toothily back at him. Aimee goes to kiss him, and I throw a cushion at them just before their lips met, and they pull away, glowering at me.

"Ah, ah, not on my watch." I tut, and Cole laughs when Josh flips me off and goes to kiss Aimee again, but I throw another cushion at them, and he glowers at me.

"Cole, control your woman."

"Welcome to my world, bro." Cole drawls, nuzzling my neck while his hand rubs and squeezes my thigh. "I'm married, and I still can't get any." He groans, pouting when I pull away, and looks into my eyes. "I'm going to get that kiss, Mrs Hoult."

"Keep dreaming Mr Hoult," I whisper back as he stares longingly at my lips before I get off his lap and pull Aimee off Josh, who tries slapping me away while I pry her out of his lap. "You'll thank me later." I sing as I pull her to the kitchen to get some drinks for us.

"I knew that idea would come back and bite me in the arse one day," Aimee complains, pulling her golden hair up into a messy bun.

"Listen, Cole and I have to go out on a date this week, and I was wondering if you and Josh will come too? I'm thinking of winter wonderland?" I suggest, and Aimee frowns, leaning on the island in the kitchen.

"Sure, but shouldn't you be alone? Isn't that the whole point of the dating thing?" She questions curiously, resting her head in her hand as she watches me open a bottle of wine.

"Yes, but there's also a lot of pressure and sexual tension between us, which I think having you and Josh with us will ease some of the strain, you know?" I explain, handing her a glass of white wine, and she nods.

"Yeah, count us in. I love Christmas time. It's such a magical time of year." Aimee sighs with a smile but frowns when I look at her blankly. "What? It is."

"Since when have you loved Christmas? You're our holiday grinch, remember?" I state with a grin, and she slaps my arm.

"Yes, because I was all alone year after year. You try and make merry when you're horny and alone during the holiday season." I laugh, shaking my head as we walk out of the kitchen back toward the boys.

"Why must all your woes begin and end with your vagina?" I question, amused, and she bumps her hip with mine as we walk.

"Because she's the fucking star of my show bitch." I laugh, shaking my head. She's honestly impossible.

～

Two DAYS LATER, on Saturday morning, I woke up early while Cole and Alaia were sleeping and went out to get Christmas supplies to decorate our house. As it's Alaia's first Christmas and our first as a family, I wanted it to be special. I had Gerald help me haul in the twelve-foot Douglas fir Christmas tree in the huge bay window in our living room.

"What is all this?" I hear Cole chuckle as he walks into the living room, holding our daughter in his arms and a grin on his handsome face.

"It's our first Christmas!" I chirp excitedly, gesturing to all the decorations. "And we are going to do it right, Lord Hoult." Cole walks over to me, smiling as he looks up at the large Christmas tree in our living room.

"Wow, that's a lot of stuff. We only ever had a professionally decorated tree growing up in the foyer of the house." Cole states, rubbing Alaia's back as he looks at me, his green eyes alight with excitement.

I frown, "You did celebrate Christmas growing up, right?" I ask, and Cole nods with a smile.

"Yeah, we did, but it was all very traditional and proper." He chuckles when my face falls, and I frown.

"So...*boring?*" I utter dryly, and he laughs with a shrug. "Wow, okay. I'm going to show you the Shay way of doing Christmas, Cole Hoult." I say and push a button, and All I want for Christmas starts playing loudly through the speakers. Cole laughs when I plop a Christmas hat on his head and a mini one on Alaia's head. "Oh my goodness, don't you two just look adorable." I coo, kissing Alaia's hand, and she smiles back at me.

"Wait," Cole mumbles, picking up a hat and putting one on my head before he grins, nodding. "Stunning." He adds charmingly while looking into my eyes. We lay Alaia in her bouncer beside us while we decorate the tree together while singing along to the Christmas songs. Cole grabs me and wraps me up in tinsel and laughs when I throw baubles at him, and he bats them away.

"I'm thinking we can have a lot of fun with this tinsel." Cole drawls sexily, wrapping the tinsel around my neck and tugging me closer to him.

"Mm, I may be inclined to agree," I smile up at him playfully as he leans in to kiss me. "But we can't," I add, pulling his hat over his eyes and duck under his arm, jumping away when he tries to catch me. With a groan, he crawls over to Alaia, watching us, those gorgeous green eyes all big while she gazes at all the colours around her.

"Princess, what am I going to do with your naughty mummy, hm?" Cole questions, picking her up and kissing her cheek. "She won't kiss me, so I'll give you my kisses instead. Kiss Daddy, and let's make her jealous." He grins, brushing his nose over hers, and Alaia giggles. I watch them as I hang baubles on the tree. "You like that?" Cole chuckles when she smiles adoringly at him. "You really are like your mummy, aren't you? You're just the cutest, happiest girl ever." He laughs, kissing her nose. I love watching them together. It's truthfully the most beautiful feeling in the world and fills my heart with such love, watching the way Cole's eyes light up when he looks at her. Cole catches me watching them, and he holds my gaze and gestures me over to them. "Come here, sweetheart." I hang the bauble I had in my hand on the tree and walk over to them. Cole pulls me down on the floor with them and wraps his arm around me, pulling me close.

I look into his eyes as he gazes into mine, "All I want for Christmas is *you*." He whispers, brushing his fingers through my hair. I close my eyes when he presses his lips to my forehead.

God, I love him so damn much.

"Just for Christmas?" I ask with a teasing smile, and he grins, shaking his head.

"I don't know. I may keep you a little longer; we'll see." Cole groans, laughing when I elbowed him lightly in the ribs.

"I hate you." I sigh cheerfully, laying my head on his shoulder and looking at Alaia, who coos at us.

"Liar." Cole grins, tilting my head and pressing his lips to my jaw, deliberately missing my lips.

LATER THAT NIGHT, Aimee, Josh, Cole, and I walked through winter wonderland together on our 'date'. Alaia was at home with her two grandmothers, who were excited to be babysitting her. The weather was freezing as it usually is in December in London. It was so magical; every-thing was lit up beautifully, Christmas music playing as couples and families get together to soak up the enchantment of Christmas.

"God, I love Christmas." I sigh excitedly, looking around feeling like a kid again. I watch Cole as he looks around in amazement. "Don't tell me you've never come to Winter wonderland?" I ask, astounded, and he shakes his head, looking at me.

"Neither have I." Josh pipes up, wrapping an arm around Aimee, who grins and nestles into him. Aimee and I look at one another and smile.

"Well, Aimee, Jo, and I come religiously every year. It's one of our favourite traditions. Be prepared to have your socks blown off, boys." I tease. Cole laughs while lacing his fingers with mine, and he pulls me close.

"Mm, sounds promising." Cole drawls, wagging his brows sugges-tively, a sinful glint in his eyes.

I feel my cheeks flush under his gaze. "You have a one-track mind Cole Hoult," I utter impishly, and he grins, gazing into my eyes.

"Only with anything and everything that involves you, baby." Cole drawls playfully, leaning in to kiss me, but I pull back, and he groans. "Kiss me, baby. My lips are cold."

"You have to earn that pleasure," I quip and pull him along to the roasted chestnut stand. We all buy hot chestnuts and walk to the Ferris wheel. I peel the chestnut and feed it to Cole, who, surprise, surprise, has never had roasted chestnuts before.

"Ow hot, hot!" Josh grumbles and spits it out, fanning his mouth while Aimee laughs hysterically. "I don't know why you're laughing. If anything happens to this tongue, you're the one missing out, baby—Ow!" Josh laughs, rubbing his arm when Aimee punches him, her blue eyes wide. "Look how pleasantly Shayla is feeding her man, and I'm over here getting abused," Josh complains, pointing at us while I feed Cole chestnuts, who beams, chewing happily, and wraps his arms around me.

"That's because there is no other like her, and she's mine." Cole burrs, looking down into my face.

I raise my brow at him, intrigued. "Yours? How very presumptuous of you." I scold him mockingly, and he smiles, feigning innocence.

"Oh, really?" I watch as he bites his lip and trails his thumb along my jaw gently while staring into my eyes. "Are you saying you're *not* mine?"

I shrug indifferently, all the while fighting the urge to smile when he narrows his eyes at me. "This is only our first date. It's a little early to be making stakes, isn't it?" Cole's lips curl into a gorgeous smile, and he shakes his head, eyes never leaving mine.

"I married you the day I met you. I made my claim on you back then." Cole tells me while he slowly walks me back as the queue moves. "I asked you to be mine forever, and you agreed, did you not?"

I lick my lips, smiling, and resist the urge to roll my eyes when he smirks. "I might not remember every detail, but I just know you stole my heart that very first day, Shayla Hart." He lovingly expresses as I look up into his eyes. "I love the person I am when I'm with you. If having more than one lifetime was possible, I know I would find you and love you with every single one, sweetheart." Cole declares sweetly, and I feel my heart quake at his words. For the first time in months, I see a glimmer of that love I was searching for in his eyes.

"Cole," I whisper, closing my eyes as he leans in to kiss me.

"Hey! Kiss in your own time, move with the queue—"

"Shhhh!" Aimee shushes the obnoxious man behind them, complaining that we were slowing down the queue. "Don't interrupt the big romantic kiss, you moron." She scolds him and turns to look at us as Cole brushes his lips over mine, kissing me slow and deeply. I moan and kiss him back just as fervidly.

Aimee sighs, watching us, and hits Josh's arm. "Why don't you ever say romantic shit like that to me?" She pouts while Josh rubs his arm, scowling.

"Ow! Could it be because you keep hitting me?" Josh complains, laughing when she sulks, crossing her arms over her chest. "Come here, my tough cookie." He grins, wrapping his arms around her from behind. "I may be bruised from all your punches and slaps, but I'll gladly take each one and be beaten black and blue than spend one day without you in my life, baby."

"Aww, babe." Aimee coos bashfully and turns so he could kiss her. The date honestly turned out better than I could have ever imagined. Cole and I spent the entire Ferris ride kissing passionately without a care in the world. We still had a long way to go—but I was excited to see a glimmer of *my* Cole, however small.

Chapter 18

COLE

"SHAYLA, get your sexy butt back here!" I shout, laughing as I chase her to the ice slides.

"No!" She laughs, running up the steps. I catch up with her at the top and pull her back to me before kissing her lovingly.

"Oi, move it, you two." Aimee pants nudging past us as she and Josh slide down the ice slide together. "Woohoo!" Aimee exclaims as she slides down in Josh's lap.

"Come on," I sit and pull Shayla into my lap before we go sliding down together and tumble over once we reach the bottom. I groan when Shayla lands on top of me, laughing hysterically.

"My bum is frozen, but that is so worth it." She giggles as I look up at her grinning.

"Oh baby, I've got a thousand different ways I would love to warm your bum up," I croon and spank her shapely behind while she gasps and scrambles off me, her cheeks bright pink.

"Cole, there are kids around." She chuckles, slapping my hands away when I reach for her. "No groping on the first date." She scolds me playfully and tries to walk off, but I wrap my arms around her waist and lift her into my arms.

"Yo, love birds, let's go get some hot chocolate. My fucking arse is frozen!" Aimee calls out to us as she jumps up on Josh's back. "Giddy up, baby."

"You guys go ahead. We'll catch up," I call back, looking at Shayla, who frowns a little watching Aimee and Josh go off toward the hot chocolate stand. I set Shay back on her feet before I take her hand into mine and pull her toward the haunted house. I needed some alone time with her, not that I'm not having fun with Aimee and Josh, but it was supposed to be our date to reconnect.

"Oh!" Shayla jumps, startled when a clown jumps out at her. We laugh as we carry on walking through the house, and either a scary object or actor dressed as some scary character jumps out, frightening the shit out of us. I find a dark corner and pull Shayla into it before I press her up against the wall. "What are you doing?" She gasps, looking up at me perplexed.

I grin, pressing my forehead to hers, "Warming up." I murmur, ghosting my lips over hers, and just as I'm about to kiss her, she ducks away laughing and runs off further into the house. She really wasn't making this easy at all. I groan and follow her until I come into one of those mirror maze rooms. I see her standing there, biting her lip, looking at me all seductively while she gestures me to her with her finger.

"You want that kiss. You're going to have to come and get it, stud." Shayla purrs, smiling teasingly. I walk over to her and stop when I hit a mirror. I place my hand on it, and she laughs. "Turn around." I spin around and see three of her.

"Oh, come on..." I groan and walk over to the middle and hit a mirror again, and she grins, pressing herself against it, looking into my eyes. "Stop tormenting me, baby." I moan, looking at her lips as she licks them slowly, and then she disappears.

"Psst." I turn and see her behind me, her green eyes alight with such love it made me ache deeply. "Come here."

"You better be real." I groan as I walk over and hit another mirror, and she shakes her head. "Oh, baby, I'm going to ruin those lips when I get my hands on you," I warn her playfully, and she grins, shrugging her shoulders.

"You'll have to catch me first, Lord Hoult." Shayla hums sensually, unzipping her jacket a little and pressing her breasts against the glass, giving me a clear view of her cleavage.

"You're a bad, bad girl Shayla Hoult," I growl, lifting my eyes from her beautiful breasts and staring heatedly into her eyes.

"Come and get it, baby." I take a step away and look around and see her leaning against a pillar. I walk over to her but hit another mirror. Goddamn it! There were like ten of her, and I couldn't figure out which one is real and which one wasn't.

"Shayla, I'm about to start smashing my way through these mirrors." I chuckle, frustrated, and she laughs again.

"How does it feel, Cole? Just when you think you have something you so desperately want and you're just a touch away from having it all, it turns out to be nothing but an illusion. Frustrating, isn't it?" She drawls, smiling, but it doesn't quite reach her eyes. I feel like she's trying to teach me a lesson here. "That frustration you feel right now is how I felt throughout our entire relationship until we got married." I sigh, licking my lips as I watch her walk around. "I'm constantly living in fear, waiting to hit that metaphorical mirror and discover that this whole thing is just yet another illusion."

I walk up to her and hit another mirror and sigh, "It's not an illusion Shayla, I love you, and I'm going to keep loving you today, tomorrow, and every other day after that until I die."

"You promised me that before, too, and look what happened."

I place my hand on the glass when she steps closer and look into her eyes. "I found my way back to you, though, didn't I?" I state, looking into her worry-filled eyes, and, at that moment, I wanted nothing more than to touch her. "I lost my memory, but my heart sill found its way back to you because you're the one Shayla, you always will be. I know it's hard right now, but I'm willing to do whatever it takes and go as slow as you want until you trust me again, sweetheart." I declare, looking at her pleadingly. "Please come out and let me hold you." I watch as she disappears from the mirror and turn when I see her standing behind me.

I walk over and pull Shayla into my arms before I curl my fingers at the nape of her neck, kissing her slow and deliberately until my lungs ran out of oxygen. We pull back from the kiss, eyes closed and panting, filling our deprived lungs with much-needed air. "I love you, light of my life," I whisper, and Shayla's eyes snap open, and she looks up at me astounded.

"How did you..." Shayla whispers, gazing up at me questioningly, her eyes probing mine. I smile, holding her gaze, my fingers tangled in her hair. "You remembered?" I nod slowly, and she smiles, her green eyes glistening with tears. "Oh, Cole..." She whimpers, wrapping her arms around my neck, hugging me. I circle my arms around her waist, hold her tight against me, and bury my face into her neck. "I love you, love of my life." She whispers, and I grin.

"Come on," I take her hand, and we walk out of the haunted house and meet up with Aimee and Josh, who already had a table and our drinks waiting for us. Shayla was currently on the phone with our mothers checking up on the baby for the fifth time. I miss Alaia terribly, but it must be even harder for Shayla as a mother to be away from her. Shayla comes back and sits beside me on the table with a sigh. "Alaia, okay?" I ask, and she nods, smiling, rubbing her hands together to warm them up.

"Yeah, she's fine. Mum just fed her, and she's sleeping." She sighs with a smile when I wrap my fingers around hers and blow on them to warm them up, my eyes on hers. "Are you hungry? They have the best fries and wings here?" She suggests smiling beautifully, and I nod.

"Sounds good," Shayla looks at Josh and Aimee, who also nod before she pulls me to the stand to order the food. While we stand in the queue waiting to order, I notice Shayla is shivering, so I wrap my arms around her, pulling her into my arms, and she nestles into me with a moan while I press my nose into her hair.

Once the food was ordered and arrived, we ate with some delicious German beer and walked around for a little while longer. Josh and I won the girls some cute stuffed animals.

"Shay! Look, Michael Bublé tribute act is singing his hits songs!" Aimee shouts excitedly, and the girls drag us over to the huge crowd of people gathered listening and singing along to Michael Bublé's songs.

This was by far one of the best dates I have ever been on. I don't know how she does it, but she just keeps surprising me. I've never been to places like these because I never found anything remotely interesting about them until now, until her. Shayla has this beautiful aura that sucks you in, and the things you would typically find mundane suddenly seem like the most exciting things ever. The singer starts to play Sway by Michael Bublé and tells everyone to start dancing. So, we do, in the middle of winter wonderland, in the freezing cold, we dance. I spin Shayla and pull her into me, and she laughs. All the ballroom dancing lessons my mother made me take finally pay off when I guide Shayla through the moves, and she follows my steps.

"Wait. You can Tango?" She questions as I spin her out and tug her back into my arms. I gaze into her eyes and brush my nose over hers, grinning wickedly.

"Yes, I most certainly can, Tango," I tell her with a smirk and spin her around so her back is pressed against my chest. I brush my lips against the shell of her ear as I speak lowly to her while I trail my fingers under her shirt. "In more ways than one." I burr, nipping at her ear, and she moans, closing her eyes.

I tighten my grip on her hips and spin her around to face me again, and she gasps. "You're just every woman's dream, aren't you?" She whispers as I walk her back slowly.

"Am I now?" I drawl, holding her gaze steadily as we move together. Shayla smiles, nodding. "Care to elaborate?" I add, pressing my forehead to hers, smiling cockily.

"Well, you can dance, you can sing and play the guitar," She states, looking up at me. "You're incredibly smart and accomplished."

I smirk, licking my lips. "Keep going..."

"You're an amazing kisser, every girl's fantasy in bed..." I grin and lower my gaze to her lips as we dance.

Shayla gasps when I spin and dip her down. "That's all?" I ask, looking into her eyes, and she laughs, her cheeks flushed.

"And you're just so very humble, not at all arrogant." I laugh and press a kiss to her lips before I pull her up again.

"Tango is a lot more fun with fewer clothes on," I whisper, brushing my lips over hers before I suck her bottom lip gently. "I would just love to teach you in more depth."

"Where do I sign up?" Shayla grins, pressing herself up against me. I stroke her jaw with my thumb gently.

"Right here," I whisper, drawing her mouth to mine for a feverish kiss. Shayla moans, parting her lips for me when I lick along her bottom lip, silently requesting access to deepen the kiss further. We kiss heatedly, moaning into each other's mouths for a good couple of minutes until Aimee and Josh interrupt us.

"Uh, excuse me, where did you two learn to dance like that?" Aimee questions her brows up in her hairline. Shayla laughs and looks up at me.

"That was all, Cole. I only know the basics, but he seems to be a pro." She states proudly, and I shrug, dismissing the compliment.

"Hardly, I haven't danced like that in years. My mother forced me to take ballroom dancing growing up. I hated it and quit the very first chance I got." I clarify as we continue to walk through the park.

"That's a shame because you're excellent," Shayla says, glancing up at me, and I wink at her before I draw her close to me and kiss her temple. "This has honestly been such a great date."

"It really has." Aimee agrees as she snuggles into Josh.

"Absolutely. Thank you so much for inviting us to tag along on your date. It's probably been one of the best dates we have been on in a while." Josh points out, and Aimee nods, smiling.

"Are you kidding? Thank you for agreeing to come along. Next time we can arrange something and invite Jo and Sam along too. I miss hanging out with all of you." Shayla sighs, and I nod in agreement. An hour later, we finally get back home. As fun as the date was, I was looking forward to some time alone with my girls. We got home just after ten 'o clock, and having been out in the cold since six—we were freezing.

"Hi kids, how was your date?" Sara asks, looking up from the book she was reading on the sofa.

"It was great." Shayla sighs, looking over at me with a smile while taking her jacket and scarf off. "Where's Elaine?" She asks, looking around.

"I'm right here." My mother chirps, walking back with two glasses of wine in her hand and hands one to Shay's mother. "So, what did you guys do?" She questions her honey-coloured orbs looking at us both excitedly.

"I took Cole to winter wonderland." Shayla beams, walking over to the bassinet to look at Alaia, who was fast asleep.

"Oh? How lovely, did you like it, honey?" My mother asks, and I nod, taking my jacket off.

"I really did. It was all very magical; you and Dad should go some-day." I suggest, and my mother shrugs, waving her hand.

"Oh, that's for young kids like you. We're too old for places like that now. We'd stick out like a sore thumb." She chuckles into her wine. Shayla looks at me and smiles, shaking her head. Yeah, I couldn't see my mother going to winter wonderland either. She's just not into that type of thing.

"Well, it's getting late. We should probably head out?" My mother suggests giving Sara a knowing look, who nods and chuckles.

"Oh heavens, it sure is late. Sam would be wondering where I am." Sara says, getting up from the sofa.

"Oh no, you guys can stay over if you want. It's late. You shouldn't drive, especially since you've been drinking." Shayla states and they both wave her off.

"Oh, nonsense. We've had two glasses of wine. I'm perfectly fine to drive, and I'll take Sara home. It's on my way anyway." My mother says, kissing me on the cheek before she hugs Shayla.

"Oh, okay, well, thank you for watching Alaia. We appreciate you both very much." Shayla expresses, hugging her mum, who says they're happy to watch Alaia whenever we needed. We walk them to the door and wave as they walk to my mother's range rover. We wait for them to drive off before I close the door and back Shayla up against it; she looks up at me with those jade eyes that penetrate straight through to my soul every time she looks at me.

"Alone at last..." I utter, gathering her arms up over her head.

"Cole, we're not supposed to have sex." Shayla breathes when I trail my free hand down her side and slide them under her shirt till I feel her warm skin. Shayla gasps when my cold fingers touch her soft skin, and she quivers visibly.

"I know, but..." I hoarsely drawl as I lower my head, brushing my lips along her throat. I stop at her collarbone, sucking her pulse point until she moans, biting her bottom lip while she arches her body up. "Let me explore your body, just a little baby." I groan as I peel her shirt up slowly before I tie it around her wrists, binding them together while Shayla looks up at me, her green eyes staring into mine fiercely.

"I'm sure this is against the rules." She whispers as I stare at her beautifully soft, plump lips, which she licks provokingly.

"Fuck the rules." I hiss when she rocks her hips against mine, deliberately brushing herself against my throbbing erection. I grind myself against her, and we both moan audibly. "Feel that, sweetheart? That's what you do to me." I groan, ghosting my lips over hers. "I lay in bed night after night, staring at that fucking wall between us, picturing all the things I would do to your beautiful body if you were next to me," I whisper, biting her bottom lip and tugging it lightly. Shayla's breathing quickens, and she tightens her fingers around mine. "Do you want to know what I think about baby?"

Her eyes close, and she swallows hard, "Yes."

I can feel her body trembling with anticipation, so I lift her into my arms and press her against the wall beside the door. Shayla's legs wrap around my waist, and she rocks herself against my erection again, eliciting another drawn-out guttural moan from me. "First, I think about kissing these beautiful lips. Like this..." I sigh lustily as I drop a soft kiss on her lips before I part them and kiss her hungrily, sucking her tongue into my mouth, earning a whimper. I pull back from the kiss, leaving her breathless, panting to catch her breath. "And then I wrap my hand around my rock-hard cock and imagine biting and teasing your hard nipples." I groan, kissing down her throat to the path between her engorged breasts. I swiftly unclip the clasp from behind and slide the bra up her arms as I flick my tongue over a hardened nipple, and she arches up, biting her lip, and lets out a breathy moan. "And you moan for me just like that," I whisper gruffly while tugging her nipple between my teeth.

"Uhh, Cole," Shayla moans, pressing her forehead against her arm I still had pinned up over her head.

"I stroke myself slow and steady as I picture myself kissing every inch of your body, baby." I moan, rubbing my erection against her. Shayla cries out, rocking herself against my rigid length, her body trembles with every urgent thrust of her hips. "And then I stroke harder when I picture pushing your legs apart and licking slowly between your folds, my tongue savouring your sensational taste, and my God baby, do you taste good." I moan, unbuttoning her jeans and sliding my fingers into her now soaked panties as I drag my finger up through her slit.

Shayla moans patently, pressing her forehead to mine when my finger brushes against her clit. "Oh baby, I want to watch you come wildly for me," I whisper, kissing her softly as I rub her clit in slow lazy circles, and she mewls sensually as she grinds herself against my fingers, demanding more contact. "Fuck." I groan, sinking a finger deep inside her, and my head spins when she clamps down around my fingers. "You're so fucking tight," I growl lowly as I slide my fingers out and thrust them into her again and again while my thumb strokes her clit, bringing her closer to her climax. "That's it, Gorgeous, let me see you come apart for me, come all over my fingers, sweetheart."

Shayla's body stiffens, and she pants, "Oh Cole, uhh baby, fuck, I'm coming, I'm coming!" She cries out, rocking her hips as she quakes in my arms. I moan, kissing her hard and deep when I feel her walls flutter around my fingers as she orgasms. "Oh my god..." She breathes, pressing her forehead to mine.

"I want you so fucking bad," I growl, sliding my fingers out of her. Shayla watches me breathlessly as I lift my fingers to my lips and suck them clean. My eyes roll to the back of my head when my tastebuds explode at the second-hand taste of her. This girl is going to be the death of me. I have never wanted anyone the way I want her. She's driving me fucking bat shit crazy.

"Cole," She pants, biting her bottom lip. I open my eyes and meet her glowing gaze.

"Yes baby."

"Make me yours." I stare into her eyes for a long moment, my heart up in my throat. She's said those words to me before. I had a very vivid dream of her saying those words to me before we made love.

"You've said that to me before," I whisper, holding her gaze, and Shayla nods, her lips curling into a breath-taking smile. "Do I say anything back?" Shayla shakes her head.

"No. You just look at me like you just did, smile, and kiss me before you completely turn my world upside down."

I smile, pressing my forehead to hers. "Oh baby, I'm going to make you mine again and again all through the night." I declare before I draw her mouth to mine, kissing her slow and deliberate.

And I kept that promise. Once we got Alaia down for the night, we spent *hours* making love, and it hit me once again how crazy I am about this girl. Sex with her wasn't just *sex*— it's no wonder I was so obsessed with her. Shayla's something else, something out of this world, and I want to spend every second of everyday drowning in her love.

Chapter 19

SHAYLA

So, Cole and I had sex.

Come to think of it, simply saying 'we had sex' doesn't do it justice—no, we made love—for hours, tirelessly, to a point where we were both soaked in sweat, with our heart beating wildly against one another's chests. After almost seven months, I couldn't keep it together anymore. I wanted him—and I wanted him bad.

I woke up early the next morning, wrapped up in his burly arms. I can't begin to explain how good it felt to wake up in his embrace again. Granted, we have many issues to work through still, but I think we are on the right path, and I'm praying and hoping that this was it for us. I've still got my guard up just in case, and just because we slept together doesn't mean our problems are automatically fixed.

We've got a long way to go before we get back to how we used to be. I hear Alaia cooing away happily in her crib, and I break away from Cole's hold and pull his shirt on before I pick up Alaia and walk back to the bed. "Shall we wake up, Daddy?" I whisper as I crawl up on the bed and lay her beside Cole. I lay on my side and watch as she reaches for Cole's nose with her little fingers. He stirs and peels his eyes open and lazily grins when he sees his daughter. He groans and wraps his arm around her, kissing her cheeks.

"Oh, my goodness, if this isn't one of the best ways to wake up, I don't know what is." He mumbles, his voice gruff from sleep. Cole reaches over and laces our fingers, his emerald gaze on mine. "Morning, sweetheart." He whispers, brushing his thumb along my knuckles.

I smile, holding his gaze, "Morning." Cole rolls onto his back and picks up Alaia laying her on her stomach on his bare chest, and he pulls me against him. I look at him, and he smiles at me lovingly before he presses his lips to mine softly.

"How did you sleep?" He asks with a knowing smile making me blush ten different shades of pink.

"Like a baby. You?" Cole smirks and nods, kissing my temple.

"Best sleep I've had in a very long time." He replies earnestly and turns his gaze to Alaia, watching us both with those beautiful big eyes of hers. "And how did you sleep, my little angel?" Cole pokes her sides gently, and she smiles at him, her little nose crinkling. "Did you sleep well too?" I smile, laying my head on his shoulder and watching our daughter make cooing noises trying to talk back to him. If I could start my day like this every morning, I would be a delighted woman. I'm so in love with them both. It's insane. Alaia begins to fuss, which usually means she's hungry and in need of a change.

"Oh no, come on, grumpy, let's change and feed you," I say, picking her up off Cole's chest and kissing her soft cheeks before I lay her down on the bed and change her. Alaia absolutely hates being changed and screams bloody murder every time I change her. "All right, baby, shhh shh mummy's almost done." I shush her while I dress her in her pink and white daddy loves me, baby grow.

I pick her up and look at her, and she stops crying, her bottom lip poking out while tears trail down her cheeks. "Oh princess, it breaks my heart when she cries like that," Cole pouts, wiping away her tears with his fingers. "She cries like you," Cole states looking at me. I scowl at him.

"Are you saying I cry like a baby?" I question, put out, and Cole laughs, shaking his head.

"No, sweetheart, I meant when you cry, it's heartfelt and hard to watch." Cole rectifies, quickly kissing my shoulder while I feed Alaia. I fight the urge to smile and nudge him away when he tries to nuzzle my neck. "Is my queen upset with me?" He mumbles, nipping at my ear gently, making me sigh.

"Maybe a little," I grumble, biting my lip, trying desperately to resist the urge to moan when he massages my shoulders.

"Forgive me yet?" He burrs huskily in my ear, and I shake my head smiling.

"No, it's going to take more than a little massage to get back into my good books, Lord Hoult," I say teasingly and lift Alaia so I can wind her. Cole looks at Alaia's face and smiles before he kisses her forehead.

"Say the word baby, and I'll worship the ground you walk on," Cole whirrs kissing along my neck but groans when I elbow him in the ribs gently. "No? Okay." He falls back on the bed with a huff.

"We've got our next session in a few days, and I don't even know how we're going to tell Natalie that we had sex," I sigh, getting up from the bed and laying Alaia down next to Cole.

"Who says we have to tell her?" Cole asks, rolling over onto his side, smiling at Alaia, making cute little noises while kicking her little legs.

I give him a skeptical look as I pull my hair up into a messy bun. "You think she's not going to take one look at us and know that we had sex?"

Cole laughs, shrugging, "Of course we're going to have sex. When you put a sex ban on two people who already have this intense sexual tension between them, what did she think would happen?" He states matter-of-factly and regards me thoughtfully for a moment. "Do you regret it?"

I shake my head, "No. Of course I don't. I just don't want us to get all caught up in sex and brush aside all of our problems." I sigh, looking at him. "Because that's what we do, sex alone isn't going to fix us, Cole."

Cole sits up and leans back against the headboard of the bed, "I know that, sweetheart, and I told you I was willing to go as slow as you want, and that still is the case." I sigh and nod, chewing my lip gingerly while he watches me intently.

"Okay, good, because I don't want to fuck this up again," I voice my thoughts sincerely, and he nods, holding his hand out to me. I crawl up on the bed and take his offered hand. Cole pulls me, so I was straddling him, his large hands resting on my waist.

"We won't, baby." I place my hands on his chest while he looks up at me dotingly. "I know what I want, and it's you, Shayla." I close my eyes and nod when he cups my face into his hands. "I'm crazy about you." Cole declares, kissing me softly.

"I'm crazy about you too," I admit curling my fingers at his wrists as he draws me in for a longer, deeper kiss that left me breathless.

Reluctantly, Cole had to leave us and go to the office to get some work done. It was almost Christmas, and the office would shut on the 23rd till the 2nd of January for the holiday season. While he was away at work, I was planning Christmas Day festivities. We decided we'd do it at our place with everyone we love, and on New Year's Eve, we would celebrate at a swanky Gala Cole's parents throw every year.

Alaia and I went out Christmas shopping hunting for the perfect gift for Cole, but what do you get someone who already has two of everything? It was so frustrating trying to find something special for him. "This is impossible." I sigh, defeated as I push Alaia in her stroller, and Jo looks at me with a smile. I called her having a meltdown on the phone, and she came to help me find a gift for him.

"Shay, he's going to love whatever you get for him, babe." Jo tries to persuade me, and I shake my head with a groan.

"No, it has to be special. It's our first official Christmas together as a family," I utter with a heavy sigh and look at Alaia in her stroller. "You're not very helpful either." I smile when she grins at me, showing her gums.

Jo chuckles, "My God, she's just so beautiful!" She chirps, reaching over and squeezing Alaia's cheeks gently. "Oh, I'm going to eat you up, you adorable little munchkin."

"Jo, you can eat her later. Please focus on the task at hand." I whimper, burying my face in my hands.

"I don't know, Shay, maybe get him something to do with the baby? He's a new Daddy, maybe go with a gift with that mind?" She suggests, and I look at Alaia thoughtfully. That's not a bad idea, but what can I get him? "You've already given him the greatest gift in the world," Jo adds, smiling as she picks up the baby and kisses her forehead. I wasn't going to get much out of her anymore. She's got the baby fever bad, and whenever she's around Alaia, she can't focus on anything else. Not that I blame her, she is pretty darn cute.

"Shayla?" I look up from my cup of coffee and see Blake standing before me dressed sharply as always.

"Blake? Hi." I stand, and we hug rather awkwardly. "What are you doing here?" I ask, genuinely surprised

"Christmas shopping." He answers with a small smile and shrug holding up some bags he had in his hands.

"Wow, I'm impressed. I thought a busy guy like yourself would have had his many assistants to do the shopping for him," I reply, only half-joking, and he laughs, clearly amused.

"It seems you still have a lot to learn about me, Shayla. I'm all about Christmas. It's my favourite time of the year." He explains with a charming grin and looks at Alaia in Jo's arms. "Oh wow, is this her?" I nod, and he smiles, setting his bags down. "May I?" He gestures, asking permission to hold her. I exchange a quick look with Jo and nod with a polite smile. Blake expertly takes Alaia from Jo and smiles, looking down at her. "Shayla, she's gorgeous."

I smile, rubbing my nape awkwardly, "Thank you." I take a sip of my coffee and watch as he rocks her in his arms, smiling rather handsomely. "How's Elle?" I question, pulling his attention from Alaia, and he grins at the mention of his own daughter.

"She's great." Blake beams, looking down at Alaia again. "Enjoy these moments because they don't stay this little for long." He sighs, handing her back to Jo, and he looks at me.

"Tell me about it. She's changing every day." I sigh, smiling dotingly at my daughter.

"They do that, at the blink of an eye, she'll be crawling, then walking and talking, and you'll wonder where the time has gone," Blake explains, catching my eye and smiling handsomely. "Listen, Elle and I have that parent-toddler class tomorrow afternoon if you want to join us. It's honestly so great for her development, and the parents there are supportive too. I know first-hand how overwhelming and daunting being a new parent can be."

I nod and shrug, "Sounds great. It might be nice to be around people who are experiencing the same things I am."

Blake smiles, nodding. "I'll text you the details later, then?"

I nod, taking Alaia from Jo when she starts to cry and lay her back in her stroller. "Sure, uh, I better go. It's her feeding time. It was nice seeing you, and I'm so sorry for disappearing on you like that. New mum life as you know it can get hectic." I say apologetically, and Blake shakes his head, waving his hand mindlessly.

"Don't be silly. I get it." He grins and hugs me again, holding on for a little longer this time. "I look forward to catching up with you tomorrow," Blake adds once he pulls away. "I better go finish my Christmas shopping. I have a meeting to get back to."

"Of course. I'll see you tomorrow." I wave, and he nods before he walks off. Blake glances back at me once more before he disappears out of sight. I look at Jo, who was watching me with her big russet eyes. "What?"

"What are you doing?" She mutters, her brows fused together. "How do you think Cole is going to react when he finds out you're meeting up with Blake?"

I sigh, rubbing my forehead, "I'm going to a parent-toddler class that he happens to be at. I work with the guy. I can't avoid him forever; we're going to have to see each other occasionally. Cole's just going to have to trust me and deal with it."

Jo shakes her head and gets up from her seat. "You're inviting trouble, Shayla. You and Cole have only just gotten back into a good place. Do you want to risk that for a play date with a guy you've kissed and who is very clearly interested in you?"

I shake my head as we walk together through the mall, "Blake isn't interested in me Jo, he's just a nice guy who wants to help out a friend. That is all." I reassure her as I look at the window displays at a store.

"Mark my words, Blake is trouble, and nothing good is going to come from this." Jo states, clearly concerned, and I sigh. Was she right? Was I just inviting more trouble into my life? Blake was clear he wasn't interested in me like that and only offered to be there as a friend. I'm not hiding anything from Cole, I'll tell him about the playdate, and if he's got an issue, we can deal with it like adults.

"You worry too much, Jo Jo," I utter with a smile, and she rolls her eyes smiling when I poke her. "Can we please focus on finding a gift for my baby daddy?" I joke, and Jo snorts with laughter.

"Fine, you little heifer. Let's go." I laugh affronted at the nickname, and she grins, hugging me when I flip her off.

"Let's go, bitch." I chuckle, and we continue our hunt for the perfect gift for Lord Tristan Cole Hoult. Later that evening, after dinner, Cole suggested watching a movie after putting Alaia down for the night. I honestly don't know why we pretend like we're going to watch these movies because ninety-nine percent of the time, the film is long forgotten, and we end up having some type of sex on the sofa or, at the very least, a heated make-out session. I won't give in to him tonight, though. Just because we slept together doesn't mean we're back together or that I forgive him...*completely*

"You pick the movie, and I'll make the popcorn," I call out as I heated the pan and dump a generous amount of sugar in before I add the popcorn kernels. I gasp when Cole suddenly wraps his arms around my waist and kisses my neck. My knees go weak instantly, and I moan, sinking into him. "Is this you behaving?" I ask breathily when he sucks my pulse point.

"Mhm," Cole groans, nipping at my ear gently. "I just can't keep my hands off you." I close my eyes and moan when his fingers tweak and pinch my nipples. *Goddamn it, get it together, Shayla!* The first couple of popping was missed entirely by us. We were too engrossed in one another until it was too late, and it was raining hot popcorn all over the place.

I gasp and try desperately to cover the top, but the hot popcorn kept burning my arm. "Oh my God, don't just stand there, grab that bowl and catch them!" I chuckle and hit Cole with a cloth when he laughs hysterically. We run around trying to catch some in the bowls in our hands. One hit Cole on the nose, and he drops his plastic bowl, which I then step into and go tumbling over, pulling Cole with me, who was trying to catch me before I hit the floor. Needless to say, we fell over in a heap of arms and legs. Cole lands on top of me, both of us laughing while it rains popcorn over us. Just another day at the Hoult residence. I look up at Cole and pull a piece of popcorn out of his hair as he gazes down into my eyes. "This is all your fault."

He laughs, "Me?"

"Yes, you! You had to come in with your irresistible lips and sexy hands and distract me. Well, this is what you get." I huff, pulling popcorn out from between my breasts.

"Oh, really? You think my lips are irresistible?" Cole questions, intrigued, grinning from ear to ear. I let my eyes drift down to his lips and bite my own.

"I mean..." I sigh longingly, looking at his full lips. "They're all right. I've definitely seen better." I tease.

Cole's brows go up to his hairline, "Is that right? And who might I ask is this person whose lips you find more irresistible than mine?"

"Mine," I whisper cockily and grin when he laughs deeply. "If only I could kiss myself, I'd have a grand old time, I think." I laugh when Cole pokes my sides chuckling.

"It surely is a shame you can't, baby, because you kiss so fucking good. Lucky for me, you can't kiss yourself, and you still need me. Now, show me what these perfect lips can do." He smiles, leaning down and brushing his lips over mine. I pull away before he could kiss me, and he blinks down at me.

"And what makes you think you get to kiss these lips whenever you want, Hoult?" I question, raising a brow daringly, and he gives me a devious smirk. One that silently informs me he's up to no good.

"Nah-uh. Don't you look at me like that. Cole..." I warn him grinning, and he lifts my arms above my head before he kisses me hard and hungry. After a very long, extremely heated make-out session on the floor in the middle of our kitchen, I managed to put a stop to it before we got carried away and had sex again, which is where things were heading. So much for not giving into him. God, I'm so weak when it comes to him.

Cole watches me as we clean up the mess the popcorn made all over the kitchen. Maybe this was a good time to bring up the whole playdate with Blake tomorrow. "So, Alaia and I are going to a parent and toddler class tomorrow," I say hesitatingly while sweeping the floor, and Cole smiles and leans against the island in the middle of the kitchen.

"Yeah?"

I nod and chew on my bottom lip, "Blake goes there too. He's actually the one that told me about it." I watch the smile disappear from his face, and a deep scowl takes its place.

"Come again?" He utters agitation evident in his tone as he steps closer to me. "When did you see Blake?"

"Today. I ran into him at the mall when I was shopping. He told me about this parent-toddler class and said it would be good for Alaia and me if we attended and invited me to go." I explain and observe Cole pace back and forth.

"You're not going."

I scowl up at him, "Excuse me? You cannot tell me where I can and cannot go. I'm a fucking grown woman." I hiss hotly, and Cole glares at me.

"You're not going!" He shouts angrily, stepping closer to me.

"Don't fucking yell at me! I'm trying to communicate and be honest with you here, Cole. What the hell is your problem?!" I shout back angrily.

"What's my problem?" He mutters acidly while rubbing his chin with a bitter laugh. "My wife is telling me she's going on a fucking play date with a guy she was sucking faces with a couple of months ago, and you've got the cheek to stand there and ask me what MY problem is?"

"Jesus Christ, Cole, he's just a friend, and that kiss meant nothing!" I explain, and he shakes his head, biting his bottom lip.

"It sure as shit didn't look like nothing to me, Shayla! It looked like you were both fucking enjoying it from where I was standing." He vents hotly as he glowers at me. I rake my fingers through my hair and close my eyes.

"It's just a class for new parents and their babies. You're acting like I'm going on a date with the guy. You do realise I'm going to have to see him eventually Cole. We work together—

he's one of our biggest investors."

"I don't give a shit who the fuck he is, Shayla. You're not going to see him. End of!"

"No, it's not the end of anything. Do you not trust me?" I question, taking hold of his arm and looking up at him expectantly. Cole looks at me silently for a painfully long moment. "You don't, do you?" I let go of his arm and take a couple of steps back. "Well, that's rich coming from you. I've never given you a reason not to trust me, Cole."

"How the fuck am I supposed to trust you when you're standing there arguing with me about going off and seeing a guy you were in a relationship with and fucking kissing not that long ago? Would you trust me if I told you I was going off to dinner with Sophie?"

"That's different!" I shout.

"How?!" He retorts back irately.

"You can't compare Sophie to Blake, Cole! He's just a friend, that's all. We have no interest in one another like that. He's only offering to support me as a new parent because he understands how difficult and scary it is to be a new parent." I explain, backing away from him as he takes a step toward me.

"I'm a new parent too! If you want support or you're struggling, why didn't you come to me? If it's support you need, I will arrange the best instructor money can buy for you. You don't fucking need him!"

I groan and shake my head. "It's not about that, Cole! It's not about him at all. It's about being around other women who are going through the same things I am. I didn't come to you because you don't understand."

"Oh, but fucking Blake does?! What did he suddenly sprout a fucking vagina that I wasn't aware of?" He snaps irritably. "Jesus, you know what, it seems you've already made up your damn mind, so arguing is just fucking futile at this point," Cole adds, walking out of the kitchen.

"Cole, where the hell are you going?!" I ask, following him and watch as he grabs his keys and storms off toward the door.

"Out!" Cole grits through clenched teeth. "Maybe I'll go pay Sophie a fucking visit!" He throws back irately before he slams the door shut. I stood staring at the door, motionlessly.

Did he seriously just say that to me?

Chapter 20

COLE

I SIGH DEEPLY for the millionth time as I stare down into my glass, swirling the amber liquid of my scotch while my mind runs amuck.

It's been over three hours since I stormed out of the house. I wandered around aimlessly till I found a bar, and well, here I am, nursing my fourth glass of scotch. Was I being an idiot and irrationally jealous over absolutely nothing? I don't think so.

Why is she so fucking eager to see that dickhead anyway? How can she say they were just friends when I fucking saw them kissing? That was more than friends for sure. I'm not a fucking idiot. I see the way he looks at her, and I'm supposed to just be okay with them spending time together? No. Fuck that. We're finally on the right track, things were good between us, and she goes and pulls this shit.

Maybe she's trying to sabotage us because deep down, she wants him and not me? They were seeing each other before she was forced into living with me. Perhaps pushing this wasn't the way to go. Could she be biding her time till the six months is up, and she's going to take Alaia and be with that idiot and divorce me? Oh God, the mere thought of it made my heart clench terribly.

I knock my scotch back and wince when it burns my insides on the way down. I drop a couple of bills on the bar and walk out back to my car. My head was a mess again. I didn't know what to think or what to believe anymore. I just know I love her, and I'm petrified of losing her. I told her I would visit Sophie just to piss her off. That was a shitty thing to do on my part after everything we've been through. I didn't think about the repercussions of my final words before I walked out.

I really hope she's at home and didn't think I would *actually* go and see Sophie and leave again. *Oh, Cole, you're such a moron.*

I drive home in a panic; my heart was beating up in my throat until I walked into the house and saw her sitting on the sofa reading. I heave a sigh of relief inwardly. Shayla's eyes lift from the book she was reading, and she looks at me. Just seeing her riled up the anger I felt before I stormed out. I keep picturing that arsehole kissing her, and I fist my hands at my side before I turn and walk upstairs without a word. Maybe steering clear of each other for a few days might do us some good.

I check in on Alaia, who was still asleep in her crib, before going to my bedroom and running the shower. A nice, long, steamy hot shower should help ease some of this annoyance I had brewing inside of me. You'd think the four double scotch's I had would have helped take the edge off, but it did nothing. I just added tipsy to the long list of things I was currently feeling.

I step out of the shower and wrap the towel loosely around my waist, rubbing the back of my stiff neck as I walk out of the ensuite bathroom. I hear a knock at the door and stare at it for a moment. For a fleeting second, I thought about ignoring it and letting her think I was asleep, but I was intrigued to see what she has to say. I walk over to the door and open it. Shayla looks me over, a little startled. She obviously didn't expect to see me half naked and dripping wet. I lift my arm and rest it against the doorframe as I watch her with my eyes narrowed.

"Can we talk?" Shayla finally voices, her tone soft, barely an octave over a whisper. I remove my arm and step aside, wordlessly inviting her in. I watch her closely as she walks into the bedroom, chewing her bottom lip a little. She turns and faces me with an audible sigh, her green eyes rake over me again, and I see a spark of desire ignite in the depth of her eyes. I bite back the smile and cross my arms over my chest, waiting for her to start talking. "Do you want to get dressed first?"

I shake my head and continue to stare at her intently. "No. You want to talk, so talk."

Come on, baby, just apologise so I can kiss you already.

Shayla sighs, closing her eyes briefly before she looks at me again. "Where were you? You've been gone for hours?"

I shrug my shoulder, "Out." I reply in a blasé manner, and she narrows her eyes at me. "I'm a big boy. I don't have to inform you of my whereabouts." I gripe coolly, and Shayla glares at me.

"You weren't with Josh." She states, and I shake my head slowly.

"I wasn't." I sigh, licking my lips. "Why don't you ask me what you really want to know, Shayla?" I add, taking a step toward her. Shayla watches me closely, her eyes skim over my body, looking for any sort of mark that will confirm her suspicions. She thinks I went out and screwed another woman—no, she thinks I went out and screwed Sophie.

"Who were you with, Cole?" She snaps impatiently. I clench my jaw, rubbing it gingerly before I comb my fingers through my wet hair and avert my gaze from her stormy one. Let her stew for a little bit.

"Does it matter?" I ask indifferently, and Shayla places her hands on her hips, her brows fused together snugly as she waits for me to continue.

"Yes, it matters."

"Why? I can't tell you who you can spend your time with, so I assumed the same would apply to me, no?" I reply coldly and walk around her. Shayla turns, watching me as I tug off my towel and hang it over my neck. "Was that all?" I casually ask as if I wasn't standing in front of her naked. Shayla stares at me, her lips parted, green eyes wide, radiating a mixture of annoyance and longing.

Shayla clears her throat and shakes her head a little before regarding me curiously again. She takes a step toward me, gazing up into my eyes. "Answer me."

I stare at her. "I will when you ask me a question worthy of an answer." I retort gruffly, and her eyes narrow to slits. I can feel the tension thickening between us, that electric pull flares up deep inside me as we glower at one another. She's feeling it too, I can tell. The way she's breathing slow and shallow, the way her soft lips are parted, and that fierce look in her eyes— we're going to either fuck hard or a very heated argument is about to erupt.

"You want to play?" She hisses, stepping up to me, nodding her head. "Fine."

I smirk at her darkly and lick my lips. "Playing is what I do best, baby." I drawl, staring into her eyes. I take her chin between my thumb and forefinger and tilt her head up till our lips are a breath apart. "But you already know that."

Shayla pulls her face away from mine and glowers at me. "You're avoiding the question, Cole."

I shake my head and bite my lip. "You've not asked me one yet, Shayla." I throwback with a one-shoulder shrug. "Ask me."

"Were you with Sophie?" She spits her name as if it were poison, and I resist the urge to smile. Maybe I was a little drunker than I initially anticipated.

I purse my lips and step closer to her, the scent of her shampoo surrounds me instantly, and I want nothing more than to bury my nose in her hair so that I can fill my lungs with that intoxicating scent. "And if I were?"

She shoves me away from her, shaking her head in disbelief as she watches me closely. "I don't believe you." I see the tears gathering in her eyes already, and it broke me. "Tell me you didn't?"

I sigh and shake my head. "You really have no faith in me at all, do you?" I ask, not bothering to mask the hurt in my voice. "I was alone drinking at a bar. I am capable of spending time on my own."

Shayla closes her eyes and sighs heavily. "When you said, I thought—"

"Thought I would go and have sex with Sophie because we had a stupid argument? Is that really what you think of me? That I would cheat on you out of spite? *Really* Shayla?" I question incredulously as I look down into her upturned face. "I would never do that, and it fucking kills me that you would ever believe I could do that to you. Even when I walked out on you, I still stayed faithful to you, but you didn't. I didn't touch Sophie, but you kissed him, Shayla. So, you don't get to stand there and act all hurt like I've done you wrong because I haven't."

Shayla blinks, and tears roll down her cheeks. "That kiss meant nothing, Cole." She replies, dropping her gaze from mine. "The whole thing was staged. I was trying to get you to believe that I was moving on so you would leave Alaia and me alone. Aimee told me you were on your way to the class. I saw you coming through the window, and I asked Blake to kiss me so you would think I was dating him and give up on us." She explains, and I watch her as she lifts her watery gaze to mine again. "I was never dating Blake. He was just playing along with a lie I told you."

I lift my gaze to the ceiling and sigh, shaking my head. "Why the fuck would you do that, Shayla?"

Because I was scared!" She shouts, looking at me helplessly. "I was terrified that you would somehow worm your way back into my life again, and I wouldn't have the strength to keep you out. And I was right because look at us. We hurt each other, Cole; this is what we do. We have no trust for one another, and without it, we just won't work." She tells me her voice was quivering with emotion.

"So, what are you saying? You just want to give up on us?" I question, grasping her arms and looking down at her.

"I don't know, but it's clear we jumped into this thing too quickly and without caution," Shayla admits pulling away from me. I let my arms fall by my sides as I watch her turn her back to me.

"No, that's bullshit!" I shout, turning her to face me again. "We were fine. We were happy and getting along perfectly fine." I cup her face and lift her gaze to mine. "Shayla, I love you. What is it going to take for you to believe that?" I ask, gazing into her eyes, and she sighs, closing her eyes.

"I do believe you. I do."

I frown, looking at her questioningly, "Then what's the problem? Is it me? Am I doing something wrong? I don't understand?" I question, perplexed, and she looks at me sullenly. "Do you not want to be with me?"

"Of course, I do." She sighs, watching me, but I see the lingering shadow of uncertainty in her eyes.

"Then what?" I ask frustratedly. "You don't believe we're going to make it, do you?" I utter deflated, letting my hands fall from where they were clutching her arms. "That's why you're reluctant to let me in because you don't see us working it out past the six months," I whisper, and she drops her gaze to the ground. I was right. She doesn't see us having a future together. I yank the towel off my shoulders and wrap it around my waist again before I turn my back to her. "I get it."

"Cole—"

"Nah, I get it," I mutter, shaking my head. "After all, you didn't want this, right? I pushed you into this by not agreeing to a divorce." I rub my neck and grimace, closing my eyes. "We'll just stick it out for the next five months for Laia's sake, and if you still want to divorce, then I'll sign the papers, and you can be free of me and move on with whoever you want." I force myself to say even though my heart was breaking one piece at a time.

"Cole, it's not—"

"You don't owe me an explanation, Shayla. I've said all I have to say, and you know where I stand." I bite the inside of my cheek hard. "If you don't mind, I'd like to go to bed now." I throw over my shoulder coldly, not wanting to face her anymore. I hear her sniffle before I feel her hand on my bare back, followed by her forehead.

"Cole..." She whispers, her voice quivering, and I close my eyes tightly. I stay silent and still, fighting every fibre in my body to not turn around and wrap my arms around her tight and kiss her. She evidently needs time, and I need to respect that and not push her or pressure her into being with me.

Our relationship is clearly still very broken. I just wish I knew what she wanted from me or how I could fix it, but I don't, and it's irritating me. When I say nothing, she finally steps away, and a moment later, I hear my bedroom door click shut. I sink onto the bed and bury my head in my hands. What the fuck is happening? This morning I woke up so happy, *we* were happy, and now everything has fallen into pieces all over again. I'm praying that we find a way to fix us because I can't see my life without her.

~

THE NEXT COUPLE OF DAYS, I buried myself in work. I woke up early, went for a run before the girls were up, showered, and went to work.

I spent most of my day at the office, working late so I wouldn't have to go home and see her. I was butt hurt and felt like I'd been rejected, and I wasn't even sure if that were the case—but that's how it felt. We haven't spoken in days, and I miss her like crazy and Alaia too. Friday evening was the last day of work, and the office was closing for the holiday season until after the new year.

I sat in the office all alone, drinking the day before Christmas Eve when I should be home with my family. I stare at the diamond bracelet I got for Shayla for Christmas sitting in the Cartier box. I had them design it, especially for her, with Alaia's name written in diamonds.

I wipe away the tear that rolls down my cheek and shake my head glumly. What the fuck am I supposed to do for the next two weeks without work? I was looking forward to it before, but now I'm dreading it. How am I supposed to stay in that house with her and pretend to be fine when I'm not? Everyone is coming over Christmas Day, and they're bound to pick up on the tension between us.

Do we just put on a show for them and fake our happiness? I can't fucking do that. Bollocks to the lot of it. I look at the time on my phone and see it's gone past nine. I finish off the glass of scotch and force myself to leave the office and head home. I could stay at my old apartment and avoid seeing her one more night, but what good would that fucking do.

Did I mention that I was starting to remember more and more of my life with Shayla? Yeah, that's just making my emotions a million times worse because every time I remember something new, it breaks me that much more. I remembered our honeymoon the other day while I was running. I got flashbacks of us making love on a white sandy beach, laughing endlessly, and getting drunk on cocktails and making love all over again. I want that happiness again. I want to be us again, but I don't fucking know how to make it happen. I'm terrified I'm going to lose them.

When I got home, I noticed Shayla was in the kitchen, so I set her present under the Christmas tree and made a beeline to the stairs. "Cole?" I stop when I hear her call my name.

"Yeah?"

"Are you hungry?" I hear her ask. I was hungry, I hadn't eaten much of anything in days, but I shake my head.

"No, I'm not." I force out and turn to walk upstairs again.

"Cole," Shayla calls out again, and I close my eyes.

"Shayla, I'm not hungry." I sigh. "I have a headache. I just want to see Alaia and go to bed."

"Cole, please don't be like this," She cries quietly. I press my molars together and blink away the tears that gather in my own eyes at the broken tone of her voice.

"Like what?" I ask evenly, looking at the ground. I know if I take one look at her, especially when she's crying like this, my emotions will come apart at the seams, and I'll fall apart. Shayla takes my hand and forces me to turn and face her. I keep my eyes cast down.

"You're being cold and distant. You won't even look at me." She states, reaching to lift my gaze to her, but I turn my head, looking at the wall beside her head instead. "Cole, please..." She sobs feebly. "Please, look at me." *Fuck*. Don't do it. Shayla brushes her soft fingers along my jaw, and I meet her teary gaze, and my chest constricts agonizingly. She's so fucking beautiful. "We haven't seen you in days. Why are you being like this?" She questions, her eyes searching mine.

"I'm not being like anything, Shayla. I've been busy with work." I lie, pulling her hand from my face and taking a step back.

"You're lying," Shayla whispers, tears spilling down her face. "You're avoiding us by using work as an excuse. I get you're angry with me but at least spend some time with your daughter. She misses you." Shayla sniffles, dropping her gaze.

"I'm not angry with anyone Shayla." Another lie. I was angry with myself more than anything. "I'm just giving you some space."

Shayla frowns, "Space?" She intones hastily. "You're not giving me space, Cole. You're full-on freezing me out. How are we supposed to work on us if you're avoiding coming home and seeing me? Or even talking to me? If anything, this is making things worse between us."

I sigh, biting my lip hard. "You think I don't know that? I don't know what else to do!" I shout irritatedly.

"Talk to me!"

"About what?!"

"I don't know, but anything is better than this, Cole!" She cries, her bottom lip quivering. "I miss you."

"I miss you too, but I'm lost trying to figure you out, Shayla. I don't know what you want from me. I don't know what I have to do, so I figured leaving you alone was the best bet." I admit in defeat with a shrug.

"Well, you're an idiot." Shayla sighs, wiping away her tears with her fingers. "Cole, we were friends first and foremost. Please don't freeze me out like this."

I scowl at her, "You want to be friends?"

Shayla rubs her head and exhales, "No. I don't know. I just *hate* this." I watch her, and when she looks at me, I shrug, shaking my head. "Come and have dinner with me?" She pleads, taking my hand in hers, and I sigh, closing my eyes.

"I'm not hungry." I press, and she looks at me all sad and teary-eyed, and I relent. "Fine." I let her drag me to the dining table. She's made my favourite pasta dish, and my stomach defies me and groans at the delicious smell of her cooking. I take my jacket off, and we sit at the table rather awkwardly, just looking at one another. I break the eye contact first, pick up the fork, and start to eat. I lift my gaze and catch her watching me. "Why are you looking at me like that?"

Shayla smiles sadly and shakes her head. "Nothing, just an old memory is all."

"What memory?" I inquire, taking a sip of the white wine she poured for us both. Shayla takes a sip of her own wine and bites her bottom lip.

"I just remembered the first time we cooked this dish together at your old apartment. I was teaching you how to cook, and we sat out on the terrace, eating and talking..."

I frown, listening to her as she speaks, and my mind recalls the moment she was talking about. *"...I was really drunk, and I just remember thinking God, his eyes are so beautiful, and I really want to stick my tongue in his dimple."*

"I'm intrigued. I need to know how it feels to have your tongue in my dimple. Do it!" I blink and smile a little.

"Get over here, and tongue fuck my dimple," I mumble and lift my gaze to Shayla, whose smile slowly fades, and she looks at me wide-eyed.

"You remember that?" Shayla whispers, leaning forward a little, and I nod.

"I do. I also remember how desperately I wanted to kiss you, and you let me." I utter, leaning forward, also getting lost in her beautiful sea-green eyes. "And then you lied and said it would be the last kiss I would get," I add, letting my gaze flicker down to her lips before I meet her eyes again. "You were a terrible liar then, too."

Shayla bites her bottom lip a little, "I'm glad you're starting to remember." She voices, resting her head in her hand while she watches me curiously.

"I'm not," I sigh, reaching up and brushing a strand of her hair away from her face. "Because it reminds me of what we've lost." Shayla looks at me despondently.

"If I had known what it would cost us, I would have done everything in my power to stop you from getting on that plane." She whispers forlornly. "I should never have let you go, or I should have gone with you when you asked me."

I shake my head and wince when I get sudden flashes of the crash. "I'm thankful you didn't. We're all alive and well, and that's all that matters to me. We have our beautiful daughter, everything else I'm hoping we can get back in time, and if we can't—then it was never really meant to be." Shayla frowns a little, closing her eyes.

"Don't say that." She whispers despairingly, her eyes watering when she opens them again.

"Do you still love me?" I question, gazing into her eyes. "The way you used to?" Shayla nods, her eyes overflowing with emotion. "Then we still have a chance, right?"

"Right." She sighs, lowering her gaze to our hands that somehow found their way to each other. I brush my thumb over her fingers gently, and she licks her soft pink lips thoughtfully. I'd give anything to be able to read her mind right now. We spent the rest of our 'dinner' murmuring to one another while we drank the bottle of wine. It almost felt like the old days again. I helped her clean up the kitchen, and it was gone midnight by the time we got upstairs. "Thank you for having dinner with me." Shayla smiles warmly, tucking her hair delicately behind her ear.

"Thank you for forcing me. It was nice. It felt a little like old times." I reply with a shrug, and she smiles, nodding in response.

"It sure was." I look over her face as she sighs. "And this is where we say good night," Shayla adds with a pretty smile, and I nod sheepishly, sliding my hands in the pockets of my trousers. Oh God, I just want to kiss her until my lungs give out. We agreed to go slow, but I know we're both thinking the same thing.

"Good night, Shayla Hart." I drawl as I used to, and her lips curl into a grin as she holds my gaze steadily.

"Good night, Cole Hoult." She replies and, after a beat, slowly turns and walks into her bedroom. I look back at her as I walk to my own bedroom, and she keeps her eyes on mine until her door closes. I walk into my bedroom and close my door before I lean on it and lay my head back with a thump and groan in frustration.

I feel like a lusty teenager falling in love again for the first time.

Chapter 21

SHAYLA

CHRISTMAS EVE.

ON THE EVE OF CHRISTMAS, I was looking forward to sitting at home, curled up on the sofa with my daughter and Cole, watching a Christmas movie. That was my tradition every year growing up. My mother, father, Sam, and I would get into fluffy PJs with a steaming cup of cocoa and watch Christmas movies. That tradition got scrapped as soon as I moved in with my two alcoholic best friends. Now, we spend our Christmas eve at a bar.

"Is this really necessary?" I grumble with a pout as I dress Alaia.

"Yes!" Aimee and Jo both shout in unison, causing Alaia to start. I glare at them when she starts to cry.

"Oh no, princess, we're sowwie." Aimee coos picking her up into her arms and cuddling her. Aimee lifts her and pouts when tears roll down her cheeks. "How is she this cute, please?"

I smile and sigh. "Have you seen her *father?*"

"What about him?" Says the man himself as he walks into the bedroom...*topless.* I look back at him as he slides the wardrobe open to get a shirt. Admiring the bulging muscles flexing in his back, as do the girls— shamelessly—might I add.

"Uh, we were just saying that Alaia is really cute," Aimee mumbles and winces when I smack her arm for checking out my husband. She mouths, 'Damn,' and I roll my eyes smiling. Engaged to be married, and she's still got her mind in the gutter.

"Of course she is. Just take a look at her mother." Cole smiles, pulling a white button-down shirt on and glancing at me.

"Huh, weird. Shay just said the same but about you." Jo sniggers and I watch as Cole walks over to Alaia in Aimee's hold and kisses her nose.

"Nah, she's a mini-Shay for sure." Cole smiles warmly at me before he walks out of the bedroom to join the boys in the living room again. I fall back on the bed with a groan.

"Okay, what the hell is going on with you two?" Aimee questions, handing the baby to Jo, who happily takes her while I groan and awkwardly rub my forehead. I've been dreading this question simply because I don't even know the answer.

I lean over and look at the door to make sure he's gone. "I don't know." I sigh, looking at the girls again. "Everything's all over the place with us at the moment."

"What does that mean, Shayla?" Aimee frowns, laying on her stomach and peering up at me, her blue eyes narrowed a little. "Last we knew, you two were happy again. What's changed suddenly?"

"We've got too many issues to work through, and trust is pretty much non-existent between us at this time, so we've taken a couple of steps back and decided to take it slow," I explain, pinching the bridge of my nose.

"You two are giving me anxiety about marriage. I'm really second-guessing this whole marriage thing the more I see you two like this." Aimee sighs sullenly. "It shouldn't be this fucking hard. You love each other. You're married, and you have a baby; just be happy."

I frown. "Not how it works, Aimes. We were happy, happier than ever, but things haven't been the same after his accident. *He's* not been the same, and neither have I. I just feel like he's putting too much pressure on himself to remember us, and he's forcing himself to act how he thinks I need him to. Does that make sense?"

"You feel like he's not being genuine with you." Jo nods, bouncing Alaia while she looks at me.

"I think he's just trying to find himself, and he's a little confused. Especially now, his memory is coming back."

"It is?" Aimee sits up on her knees excitedly. "Shayla, that's amazing!"

I smile, nodding. "I know, he's starting to remember things more and more, and it's exciting but frightening all the same."

Jo frowns. "Why is it frightening? This is a really good thing, Shayla. It's what you've been waiting and hoping for."

I shake my head and sigh, looking at Alaia. "I don't know, everything that's happened to me, to us, I'm scared to be happy because I feel like if I let myself feel any sort of happiness, something will come along, and it will wreck us all over again" I explain despairingly. Aimee reaches out and takes my hand in hers.

"Shayla, you can't live your life in fear of being happy, babe. I think you've reached your limit of bad luck. You've suffered the worst. What else could possibly—"

I hold my hand up and stop her. "Stop. Please don't say that. My anxiety is running wild in my head, don't add superstition to the mix." I sigh, rubbing my forehead. "I don't think my heart can take it."

Aimee and Jo both look at me sadly. "How long do you think he will keep chasing you and waiting before he gives up himself, Shayla?" Jo says, and I shrug.

"I can't help the way I feel, Jo. I wish there were a switch that I could flip and not be scared, but I can't. Keeping him at a distance is the only way I can think to protect myself, and that probably seems selfish and stupid to those on the outside, but to me, it's the only logical thing to do." I close my eyes. "I've lost so much in my life. I lost my Dad. And after almost losing him completely and then almost losing Alaia, I've come too close to having nothing, girls, and that scares me so much." I cry defenselessly, and Aimee wraps her arms around me. "I'm just too broken, and I don't know how not to be."

"Oh babe, we get it. Of course, you're scared, but in time it's all going to be okay, I promise you." Aimee assures me as I cry silently into her chest. Aimee lifts my head and wipes my tears away. "Now go get yourself dressed up and pretty, and let's go out and have some well-deserved fun." I nod, and we all hug before I go to my walk-in closet and get ready for this night out.

Alaia was staying home with my in-laws, who jumped at the chance to watch her while we go out. I honestly didn't want to leave her and go out, but the girls insist, so I figured I would agree to go for a couple of hours. I wear a silver sequin dress, and the girls curl my hair and do my make-up for me. "You look fierce, darling." Aimee drawls with an exaggerated British accent.

"Cole is going to lose his mind, baby girl." Jo grins, spinning me around.

"No! I want him to find it, not lose it more!" I quip, and the girls laugh. I pull my black stilettos on while they refresh their makeup. Aimee was wearing a red jumpsuit with her hair pulled up into a high ponytail with a pair of nude open-toe heels. Jo was in a black mini dress with a plunging neckline, her shoulder-length mousy brown hair straightened. My girls were hot.

"Shall we, ladies?" Aimee smiles, holding up her phone. We pose for a couple of photos before we head down to the boys.

"Jo, grab Alaia. I need to find my bag." I call out, and Jo shouts, 'Got her' while I reach up and pull out my black clutch. I can already hear my mother-in-law's voice talking to Alaia. I walk out of the bedroom and make my way downstairs. The girls were already by their men, and my mother-in-law was the first to see me, then Cole, who had his back to me, turns his head and does a double-take when he sees me coming down the stairs. His Adam's apple jumps up in his throat. I felt giddy under his gaze, his eyes skim over me slowly, and he walks to me, taking my hand as I come down the final three steps.

"You look..." I gaze up at him, waiting for him to finish his sentence, but he shakes his head. I didn't need any more words. The look in his eyes was enough for me.

"Thank you." I hold his gaze for a few seconds and avert my gaze to the girls who were grinning excitedly. I remind my mother-in-law about

Alaia's feeding times, and she waves us off. I kiss her head, and Cole does the same before he practically drags me out of the house.

"Do you think we should stay?" I ask, looking back at the house, and Cole shakes his head. "It's Christmas Eve. I don't want to leave her." I pout.

"Shay, she's fine, and my parents are thrilled to have some time with her. Staying home with her is great, but we need some adult time." Cole places his hand at the small of my back. "Besides, you look too damn good to be sitting around the house." He murmurs in my ear, making me flush.

"Right back at you," I purr, looking up at him through my lashes, and he smiles handsomely. Cole guides me to the limo the boys had arranged. As soon as we got in, the champagne was flowing. Thank god I pumped enough milk for Alaia for the next two days because I'm going to be dumping quite a bit over the next twenty-four hours.

I sip my champagne and glance at Cole, who was looking at me. "You look like the night we first met. Your dress was different, but everything else is the same." He speaks quietly to me, and I smile into my glass.

"You remember what I look like the night we met?" I question, and he nods, smiling a little.

"I do. I had a flash as you were coming down the stairs. I don't know how it's possible, but you're even more beautiful than the night we met." Cole whispers in my ear, making me blush profusely. I smile and turn my head so that I could look into his eyes. "What do you say we relive that night all over again?" He murmurs, holding my gaze, and I frown.

"Cole, I'm not going to Vegas and marrying you *again*." Cole chuckles, shaking his head.

"Maybe not all of it then." I smile. "How about we forget all our problems for one night and meet all over again." He redresses, and I watch him warily.

"You want to role play and pretend like we just met? Haven't we done this before?" I question, and he nods, licking his lips. "Is this a ploy to get laid?" I ask, and he grins handsomely, displaying those dimples that make me swoon.

"Not unless you want it to be." I laugh before I sip my champagne.

"You better bring your best game then Hoult. My standards have gone up since that night." I tease, and he laughs this time.

"A couple of porn star martinis will fix that little problem." Cole jests and groans when I elbow his ribs, and we snicker. I glance over at the girls—Jo was whispering and making eyes at my brother, who was stroking her leg, completely enthralled with her. Aimee and Josh weren't much better. Josh was for sure talking dirty to her because she's giving him the 'fuck me' eyes I've seen many, many times before. It was nice seeing everyone so happy and secure in their relationships. I crave that more than anything. A couple more flutes of champagne, some heavy flirting, and we had arrived at the rooftop bar. I was surprised to see how crowded it was on Christmas Eve.

We pile out of the limo and walk straight through. Josh and Cole clearly knew the bouncers because he greets them as we go through to the elevator. "This place is nice," I voice as soon as we walk out of the elevator. It was a 360 view of London. Hence the name 'Club 360'. The view was gorgeous, reminded me of Coles old place.

We make our way over to the VIP lounge. The atmosphere was lit— people were dancing, drinking, and having a great time. A waiter comes over and takes our drinks order. Cole orders himself a brandy and me a Porn star martini. I smile when he winks at me. The girls order the same as me, and after a couple more, I was dragged onto the dance floor. Jo, Aimee, and I were dancing, and I pull them closer. "Girls, Cole wants us to pretend like we're meeting for the first time. He wants us to relieve the night we first met." I say, and they look at me wide-eyed.

"What like get married *again*?!" Aimee shrieks, and I laugh, shaking my head.

"Are we going Vegas again?!" Jo chirps excitedly, and I roll my eyes.

"No, Jesus! Minus the marriage part." I explain and glance over and see him watching me as he sips his drink, nodding while Josh speaks to him. My stomach does a nervous flip-flop.

"But with all the hot sex part!" Aimee cheers, and I flush and hit her. "Do it! Fuck it. I might do it with Josh too. Let's all act like we're meeting them for the first time. How exciting."

"You don't think it's weird?" I ask them, and they shake their heads.

"No bish, it's just innocent fun," Jo assures, smiling. "Let go, Shay, have some fun, babe."

"I second that." Aimee agrees, and we all clink our glasses. All right, it looks like we're doing this. I do as the girls suggest and let go. After a couple more drinks, I had a nice buzz going. I still when I feel a solid chest pressed up against my back. I feel that familiar warmth spread through me when I feel Cole's breath against my ear.

"Hi." he drawls, placing his large hands at my waist. I lift my eyes to look back at him and smile.

"Hi back," I reply as we start swaying to the upbeat music that was playing. Cole spins me around, so I was facing him. He dips his head, and his lips brush against the shell of my ear as he speaks in that deep tone that makes my nether regions ache.

"What's your name, sweetheart?" He asks, and I feel butterflies take flight in my stomach.

"Shayla. Yours?" I answer, lifting my gaze to look into his endless green eyes. Cole wraps his arms around my waist and draws me closer until I'm pressed up against him.

"Cole." He grins wickedly, showing off his dimples, and I return his smile. "Single?"

I laugh and nod. "Last time I checked. You?"

Cole nods, pressing his forehead to mine. "Hopefully not after tonight."

"Do you feed that line to all the girls?" I ask bashfully, and Cole licks his lips slowly and narrows his eyes a little.

"Only five-foot-six brunettes with beautiful green eyes and killer smiles." I laugh and snake my arms around his neck.

"That's very specific."

Cole nods, brushing his fingers down my bare spine as we dance. "I like what I like, and you tick all the boxes, sweetheart." I bite my lip and tilt my head back when he kisses along my jaw.

"Lucky for you, I'm a sucker for very tall bad boys with sexy dimples." Cole smiles against my jaw, and his arms tighten around my waist.

"If you're lucky, I'll let you tongue fuck one later." I throw my head back and laugh, and Cole chuckles, taking the opportunity, he kisses my neck. "You hungry?"

"Starving." I moan, turning my gaze up to him, and he smiles charmingly and brushes his slender fingers through my wavy hair.

"How about we go someplace to get something to eat?" I smile and nod. Cole takes my hand into his, and he says something to Josh, who nods with a grin and gives him a thumbs up. I wave to Aimee, and she blows me a kiss with a wink and mouths 'Have fun' before Cole pulls me out of the bar.

"So, where are we going?" I ask when we step into the elevator. Cole looks at me and grins.

"Someplace you'll love." He laces his fingers with mine and pulls me to the limo waiting outside. We climb in. Cole looks at me and smiles handsomely. He reaches up and brushes his fingers through my hair. "You're something special, Shayla Hart."

I smile and press my lips together, lowering my gaze to his mouth before I meet his eyes again. "How can you possibly tell? You just met me."

Cole exhales slowly, and his eyes wander over my face. "Call it an intuition."

"How very perceptive of you, Mr Cole," I utter, brushing my index finger down the side of his face. Cole's eyes close at my touch, and he grins when I trace the outline of his dimple. Despite my best efforts not to, I find myself leaning in closer as he stares at my lips, slowly inching closer. However, just as my eyes slide shut and our lips are about to touch, the car rolls to a stop, and we pull back. I look around and see we're at a drive-through Mcdonalds. I smile as Cole rolls the window down and orders my favourites. Chicken tenders, a box of nuggets, large fries, and a banana milkshake. We drive around and wait for our food. "I haven't had Mcdonalds in so long."

Cole grins, "I know. It's one of your go-to places when you're drunk. You've got me hooked on it too."

I laugh, "I remember the first time I insisted we go to Mcdonalds. You thought I was crazy to want to eat processed junk." I remind him and take the bag of food from him and set it in my lap while he pays.

"Yes, you were rather appalled that I'd never been to a McDonald's." Cole laughs as I eat a fry.

"Of course I was! Who hasn't been to a McDonald's ever in their life? That's just sad." I utter, feeding him a chicken nugget, and he takes a bite.

"I wasn't allowed to eat stuff like this growing up. I was very cautious with my nutrition and what I ate and would put in my body before you came into my life. You're a bad influence, Shayla Hoult." He smiles, squinting his eyes at me playfully.

I laugh and bite into a chicken tender. "Life is too short to worry about such trivial things."

Cole laughs, shaking his head. "Yeah, let's make it shorter by eating deep-fried junk food that will inevitably clog up your arteries."

"Don't be such a Debbie Downer. I would prefer to die suddenly without any form of regrets than to spend my last moments in my death bed, pondering about all the things I wish I had done but missed out on because I was too worried about dying." I sigh, holding up a fry to his lips. "We're all going to die sooner or later, Cole. Life is what you make of it after all, right?" Cole takes a bite of the fry and nods.

"Mm, live in the moment, you say?"

"And seize every opportunity." I match his grin when we toast our nuggets and laugh. We spent the hour eating our food, drinking more champagne, talking, and laughing our arses off while driving around the city. While we were driving over Tower Bridge, I push the sunroof open and clambered up. It was freezing, but I didn't care. I lift my gaze when I see the snow falling. It never snows in December in London. "Cole, get up here. It's snowing!"

Cole climbs up beside me and looks around in wonder. It was coming down hard and setting, everything slowly turning white. It was beautiful. Cole wraps his arms around my waist and kisses my jaw when I close my eyes. "Merry Christmas, baby," Cole whispers in my ear, and I smile and look up at him.

"Merry Christmas, baby," I reply, and Cole dips his head and kisses me softly on the lips, his thumb stroking my jaw. I pull back and look up at him. "Let's go home," I whisper, and he smiles handsomely and nods. Cole pulls me back in the limo and closes the sunroof.

"You're freezing." He mumbles, brushing a snowflake off my cheek with his slender fingers. I shake my head and brush away the snowflakes caught in his hair. I was shivering, but weirdly I wasn't cold. It must have been all the alcohol.

"I'm not," I answer, looking over his face. Cole takes my cold fingers and presses them against his lips.

"I want to take you somewhere before we go home. Is that okay?" Cole questions, looking into my eyes, and I nod silently. I lay my head on his chest, and he wraps his arms around me, pressing his lips to my forehead. We stay like that, completely wrapped up comfortably in each other's embrace until the car rolls to a stop twenty minutes later.

～

COLE PULLS me out of the car, and I peer up at the building in front of me, then I look at Cole, who was smiling up at it.

"Cole, why are we here?" I inquire, puzzled, and he sighs, licking his full lips before he turns his eyes to look at me.

"We're revisiting old memories, remember?" He laces his fingers with mine and pulls me to his old apartment complex.

"Didn't you sell this place?" I ask while we walk into the building toward the elevator. I was hit with so many memories, good and bad, as we step into the elevator together.

"I didn't have the heart too. This place is very special to me; *to us,* I couldn't bear the thought of anyone else living here." Cole answers and turns to face me. "Every corner of the apartment has memories of you and me. I've been coming here quite a lot recently, and it's been helping me remember things about us." I smile, and he brushes my hair away from my face gently.

"That night we first met, my initial thought was to bring you here, but somehow we got derailed and ended up in Vegas." He smiles cheekily and pulls me out of the elevator, and we walk down the corridor to our old apartment. "So, we're doing it the right way this time." He holds his hand out to me after he pushes the code to the door. "The way it would have been." I slide my hand into his without hesitation, and Cole smiles and pulls me into the apartment.

My stomach was tying itself into knots, almost as if it's the first time we're sleeping together. That's the beautiful thing about Cole, no matter how many times we kiss or make love, he knows just how to excite me— not only in a sexual way, but he ignites my soul and makes my heart soar. "We don't have to do anything. I just wanted to be here...with you."

I set my clutch on the table by the door and step closer to him. Cole watches me intently heedfully. "Is that what would have happened that night if we did come here? Nothing?" I inquire, and he smiles. I glance down at our entwined fingers caressing and look at him again.

"Dance with me," Cole whispers and kisses my knuckles while I look at him, taken aback.

"There's no music," I look around the dark apartment, and he grins, taking my hand, he leads me to the living room. I watch as he walks over to the giant gas fireplace and turns it on.

The fire instantly illuminates the room. Cole disappears, and I slip my shoes off and sigh in relief. Damned things were killing my feet. I move closer to the fireplace and watch the flames. I smile when the music starts playing from the speakers in the house, and a moment later, I feel Cole's fingertips skim down my bare arms. He drops a kiss on my shoulder before he turns me to face him. Without my heels, I felt so small against him. Cole envelopes his arms around my waist, pulling me up against him.

I curl my fingers at the nape of his neck and rest the other on his chest as we slowly sway together to a cover of the classic, 'I want to know what love is.'

I couldn't help but wonder what might have happened had we ended up here instead of Vegas. Would we have eventually fallen in love again without the conflicts of our little 'arrangement'? Either way, he would have still been my boss. Whether we got married or not, Cole was always destined to be in my life. "What are you thinking about?" Cole asks, pressing his forehead to mine.

I peek up at him and bite into my lip a little. "Just wondering what would have happened if we did end up here instead of Vegas."

Cole smiles, "Huh..."

Chapter 22

COLE

Christmas Day.

It feels like I've gone back in time to when we met—having Shayla in my arms, where she belongs, dancing slowly in our living room—wrapped up in one another like we were the only two people in the world. Before the accident, before everything got all messed up—when nothing mattered but the two of us.

I gaze into her eyes, unable to look away. The love she has in her eyes for me leaves me powerless. I love the way she looks at me. I want to lose myself with her. I reach up and brush her hair away from her face before I let my fingers caress her jaw.

Shayla leans into my touch, her eyes closed. I dip my head and brush a kiss on her soft lips, which she responds to with a breathy moan, parting her lips for me to deepen the kiss.

We kiss slow and sensually, neither of us in any rush. It doesn't matter how many times I've kissed her or how many times I've had her. Every time with her feels like the first time to me. I suppose that's the power of her love. She makes me nervous in ways I can't explain.

We didn't make it to the bedroom. After we leisurely undress one another, lips still welded. I lay Shayla down on the rug in front of the fireplace and crawl over her. I look down at her, and she curls her fingers at the nape of my neck and draws me down for another soul-baring kiss. I pull back a little and gaze down at her while I press myself at her entrance. Shayla gasps when I push inside her gradually. She opens those olive eyes, watching me affectionately, and I hold her gaze as I glide deeper into her, inch by inch filling her up whilst she moans.

My eyes close, and I sigh when Shayla's fingers stroke my face lightly. Her legs wrap around my waist, and she draws me closer. I kiss her fingers and avidly watch as she trails them down my throat and presses them to my chest, just above my rapidly pounding heart. I brush my lips over hers, kissing her ardently as I thrust into her slow and steadily.

Our fingers entwine as we move, rocking together. I kiss down her throat, and she arches up, panting, her fingers tightening around mine as I feather kisses along her chest. I press my lips over her heart and close my eyes when I feel it thrashing against my lips. Lifting my gaze to hers slowly, Shayla pulls my head up and kisses me before she rolls me onto my back.

We make love for hours till our bodies were moist with sweat, spent and breathless. It was like a box had unhitched in my mind. While we made love, everything came rushing back to me. I lay my head on Shayla's chest, rising and falling, her heart beating in my ear while she runs her fingers through my sweat-dampened hair.

I remember everything.

After my breathing had calmed, I rolled onto my back and had Shayla sprawled on top of me. She was glowing, and I honestly couldn't get enough of her. I comb my fingers through her hair as we lay together in comfortable silence. Music playing softly in the background, the fire's crackling beside us, and our breathing was the only sounds that were needed at that moment as our bodies quieted. Shayla sighs contently, her head resting on my chest while she watches the snow falling outside. I kiss her forehead; she smiles tiredly and lifts her forest green eyes to mine.

"Hey you," I whisper, sweeping my nose over hers gently.

"Hi," She smiles and kisses me.

"It's been so long since I've felt like this," I admit, and she looks at me questioningly. "Like myself," I add.

Shayla smiles, resting her chin on my chest, and gazes at me tenderly. "I know. This is the first time since your accident that I've seen the Cole I fell in love with."

I nod and smile, "It's taken a while, but he's back, baby, and I'm not going anywhere ever again." I promise her, and she smiles, her eyes watering.

"You promise?"

"I swear." I declare, wiping away the tears that fall from her eyes. "Somethings are still a little fuzzy, but I remember everything," I tell her, and she looks at me curiously, lifting her head off my chest. "While we were making love, it felt like our entire relationship flashed before my eyes. I finally remember Shay. All the missing pieces, things that didn't make sense to me, all fell into place." I explain, and Shayla leans up on her elbow and looks down at me.

"You really remember?" She asks eagerly, and I nod.

"I remember." I grin. "Ask me anything." Shayla looks at me, her brows fuse a little, and she looks thoughtful.

"While we were making love in Nice, I did something, and it's been our special—" I kiss my fingers and press it over her heart, and she gasps, tears spilling down her flushed cheeks. She sits up and looks at me. "Our wedding night, you made a promise to me, and I told you I would hold you to it. What was the promise?"

I smile and lean up, gazing deeply into her eyes. "You're a Goddess, baby. I'm going to worship you till my very last breath." I repeat, and she covers her mouth with her hand while she looks at me with her eyes pooled with tears.

"Oh, Cole, you do remember." She cries, cupping my face in her small hands and kissing me. I wrap my arms around her, holding the back of her head while I kiss her back thoroughly as I lay down and pull her down on top of me. We continue to kiss passionately. After we make love once more, we leave the apartment and head back to our home. It was gone four in the morning when we sneak in, trying to be quiet. I had Shayla pressed up against the wall, kissing her hungrily when the lights come on suddenly. Shayla and I blink, allowing our eyes to adjust to the light and look at my parents standing at the top of the stairs watching us.

I clear my throat and step away from Shayla, smiling sheepishly. "Do you two have any idea what time it is?" My father scolds us, and we press our lips together to keep from laughing. I felt like a teenager who got busted by his parents sneaking a girl into the house.

"It's Christmas day, and I want to see my baby girl," I tell my parents as I take Shayla's hand and pull her up the stairs.

"Tristan, she's sleeping." My mother says, and I pick Shayla up and throw her over my shoulder as I carry her to our bedroom.

She laughs a little, "Cole's memory is back." She tells my parents, grinning. I hear my mother gasp and my Dad chuckling.

"Well, you can't just say that and leave!" My mother shrieks excitedly.

"Go to bed, mother! It's a Christmas miracle!" I shout, elated as I walk into our bedroom and set Shayla back down on her feet. I walk over to the crib and see my beautiful daughter asleep. Shayla closes the door to our bedroom and walks over.

"Shall we make another one?" I say when Shayla comes up beside me and looks down at her. I pull the blanket up to cover her.

"Another one?" Shayla sputters dumbfounded while she looks up at me, horrified. "Cole, she's only two months old."

"So?"

Shayla scowls at me. "So? It's easy for you to say, you get to do all the fun parts of making a baby." She quietly utters as she slips out of her dress. I observe her as I sit on the bed and gasp, feigning utter shock.

"Only me?" I grab her wrist and pull her to me. "Are you really going to stand there and tell me you didn't enjoy every second of making her?" I question, looking up at her keenly while she stands between my legs. Shayla grins, biting her lip when I kiss the valley between her breasts. "It seems I'm not the only one who has lost their memory around here. You need some serious reminding just how much fun you had making our baby." I groan, peeling her underwear down her shapely legs.

Shayla laughs and cups my face in her hand, and looks into my eyes. "I remember perfectly fine; thank you very much. Do you know what else I remember? The pain of pushing her out of me." I wince, and she nods, kissing me chastely before she pulls away. "You'll have to wait until she's at least two years old before we have another."

"Two?" I pout and look over at Alaia. I'll knock her up way before then for sure. She wanted to wait a year after getting married to have Alaia, and I got her pregnant on our honeymoon. I grin, remembering the night we conceived her. By the time we got to bed, it was almost five in the morning, and we were both beat. We had a busy Christmas Day planned.

I WOKE up the next morning alone in bed. I stretch and smile before I get up. The smell of food and the distinct sound of music coming from downstairs made me smile, so I pull on a pair of pyjama bottoms, and I walk into the bathroom to wash my face and brush my teeth before I make my way downstairs.

I hear laughter.

I see my Dad sitting on the sofa in the living room, smiling while he's watching something. I walk to the kitchen and stop in the doorway, unable to contain the grin on my face. I see Shayla, my mother, and Shayla's mother in the kitchen. They were all cooking, preparing the Christmas dinner. That's not what got me grinning like an idiot, though. It was watching them dance while they cook. Sara—Shayla's mother teaching my mother how to dance, and my mother was actually doing it and having fun. I've never seen my mother dance ever. She's always so prim and proper.

I watch my wife dancing with our baby in her arms, who was smiling. It brought tears of joy to my eyes, watching them together so happy. I'm a lucky man. I can see where Shayla got her dancing from; her mother was an excellent dancer. "That's some sight, huh?" I turn and look at my Dad, watching the women dancing joyfully together. I nod and look at my girls again. "The best thing you ever did was bringing that girl into our lives, son." He says, watching my mother lovingly.

I sigh longingly and smile. "Oh, I know. Even if I fail at everything for the rest of my life, they will always be the one thing I did right." I declare, and he smiles proudly and slaps my back. "What do you say we go and join our girls?" I grin, and my father nods as we walk into the kitchen.

"Hey! Is this a girl's party only, or are men allowed too?" My Dad asks, walking over to my mother, who beams at him and goes beet red. I walk over to Shayla, who beams up at me as I approach her.

"Good morning, love of my life." She greets me.

"Morning, light of my life," I murmur, kissing her soft lips. I pull back and look at Alaia. "Good morning to you too, Princesa." I chuckle when she smiles at me, and I kiss her cheek. I wrap my arm around Shayla, and we dance together, swaying to the music. "I remember this song. It's the one you were dancing with Josh to at the place with the street food." I murmur in her ear, and she laughs, nodding. "You were going to make me kill a man that night, you little minx." I chuckle when Shayla turns and faces me.

"Serves you right. You should have picked me from the beginning then, shouldn't you." I chuckle and kiss her.

"You're making me loco, bebé," I growl in her ear, and she flushes swaying to the song. "Think I can steal you away for a little bit?" I ask, twitching my brows at her, and she widens her eyes and shakes her head.

"No bebé, I have too much to do before dinner." I pout, and she peers up at me lovingly. "Why don't you take your daughter and spend some time with her while we cook. You can have me all to yourself later." She suggests looking at Alaia, who places her hand on my face.

I smile and kiss Alaia's fingers and press them over Shayla's heart, and she melts. "Stop. That's the sweetest thing ever. What are you doing to me." She pouts a little, and I grin, kissing her softly.

"Merry Christmas!" We all jump when Aimee suddenly

appears and exclaims excitedly. "Hold on. You guys are having a party without me?!" She walks into the kitchen with Josh, followed by Jo and Sam. Thus, began the best Christmas Day I have ever had. I look around the kitchen; everyone was so cheerful, dancing together, cooking, and laughing. There was so much love in the room, and it was all because of one person—Shayla Hart.

She has brought so much love into my life and the lives of the people I love most. I turn my gaze to hers, and she does the same, smiling up at me beautifully. "I'm so in love with you," I declare, pressing my forehead to hers, and she smiles, biting her bottom lip.

"Say it again, baby." She whispers.

"I'm so in love with you, baby."

Shayla smiles, holding my gaze. "I'm so in love with you, bebé." While others were dancing around us in the middle of our kitchen, we stood there kissing and whispering to one another until, of course, in true Shayla and Cole fashion Sam drags her away from me, and they start dancing with their mother. I made a mental note to take them all to that place by the river after the new year.

I dance with my daughter, who beams at me just like her mother, and I fall in love over again.

How did I get so damn fortunate?

After all the dancing was done, the girls kicked us, boys, out of the kitchen while busy preparing the food. I sat on the living room floor, Alaia in my arms with Josh, Sam, and my Dad watching the grinch.

"I can't believe you got your memory back bro, that's fucking amazing," Josh says cheerfully, and we fist bump.

"We're thrilled to have you back, brother. Shayla's been beside herself; it's nice to see her so happy again." Sam says, glancing over at his baby sister, laughing hysterically at something Aimee was telling her. "Jo and I have some news also." He says, and I look up at him intrigued, and he looks at Alaia smiling.

"She's pregnant," I say, grinning, and he nods, gleaming.

"She told me last night. I'm over the fucking moon. I can't wait to marry her." Sam gushes while looking over at her. "I asked her to marry me, and she yes." Josh and I gape at him, and he chuckles.

"Sam, congrats man. I'm so thrilled for you both." I grin, and we hug. "I'm going to be an uncle." I chirp excitedly.

"Sam, I'm thrilled for you, man. Jo is a hell of a girl." Josh congratulates him, smiling at Aimee when she blows him a kiss, and Sam nods, glancing over at Jo.

"They all are." I sigh, watching my beautiful wife. "We're the luckiest men on the fucking planet to land such amazing women."

"I'll drink to that," Sam declares, and we all clink our eggnogs.

"I'm going to remind you boys of this day when you're twenty-five years into marriage, with your receding hairlines while you grumble about why you ever got married." My Dad pipes up behind me with a chuckle making us all laugh.

An hour later, we were all sat around the dinner table, and my Dad was about to carve the turkey. As the eldest Shayla requested, he does the honours. "Before I carve the turkey and we start enjoying the delicious food set out before us, I just want to say a big thank you to Shayla." My Dad says, turning his gaze to her. Shayla looks at him, taken aback, a blush forming on her cheeks already.

"Believe it or not, our Christmas was always very traditional. It was always Elaine, Cole, and myself enjoying a meal prepared by our chefs. Until you came into our lives, it never dawned on us how grey and stale our lives had become. You brought colour into our lives, and you reminded us of the importance and power of love. It was a rocky start for many reasons, but my wife and I want to thank you for filling our hearts and our lives with so much love." I look at Shayla, and she smiles tearfully at my Dad. I press a kiss to her temple, and she closes her eyes.

"And Sara, thank you for raising such a wonderful daughter and agreeing to share her with us." Sara smiles, nodding gratefully while wiping away tears that had rolled down her cheeks.

"Thank you, that means everything to me." Sara cries, placing her hand on her chest and looking at Shayla, who smiles tenderly at her.

"Why am I crying on Christmas Day?" Aimee grumbles, sobbing, making everyone laugh. "Mr H, you're killing me! We're supposed to be eating, drinking, and making merry! Gosh!"

My Dad laughs. "Fair enough. Merry Christmas, everyone." He says, holding up his glass of mulled wine, and we all follow, holding up our glasses. "Let's eat." While he carves the turkey, and everyone starts chatting among themselves, I turn to Shayla, who looks at me.

"Thank you for choosing to love me," I tell her, and she smiles.

"Thank you for loving me back." I kiss her softly and jump back when a brussels sprout hits my head. I scowl and see Josh and Aimee giggling. I glare at them playfully and throw it back at them. Shayla laughs, shaking her head, and we join the rest enjoying our Christmas dinner.

Our home was full of laughter, love, and joy. It's all I could ever wish for—well, a couple more kids, of course, but that will come.

After dinner, we opened gifts. I hand Shayla hers, and she opens it with a smile and looks at me and then back at the bracelet. "Oh baby, I love it." She kisses me, and I help her put the bracelet on her wrist.

She hands me my gift, and I open it and pull out the Platinum Versace dog tag. She turns it over, and I see that it's engraved with a family tree starting with Shayla and my name at the top, then there was a branch with Alaia's name and a couple of empty ones. At the very bottom, it had the words 'Ever ours' engraved. "You can add the names as our family grows."

I stare at her in awe, and she smiles adoringly at me. "How did I get so lucky to find you." I sigh, pulling her to me and kissing her. "Thank you, baby. I'll be wearing this for the rest of my life." And I did.

She grins, "Merry Christmas, baby."

"Merry Christmas, Sweetheart,"

Chapter 23

SHAYLA

"ALL RIGHT, girls, are you ready to see the wedding dress?" I hear Aimee's excited voice behind the grey satin curtain. Jo and I exchange looks and smile before we answer her.

"Yes!" We chirp at the same time and watch as the curtain is drawn back, revealing an angelic Aimee in her beautiful lace wedding gown.

Jo and I gasp, our eyes instantly pooling with tears. "Oh, Aimes, you look beautiful." I cry emotionally, and she starts welling up.

"You look gorgeous, babe." Jo agrees, watching her in awe.

"Do you think Josh will like it?" Aimee asks, looking down at herself before looking at us again. We both nod enthusiastically, dabbing away the tears with tissues.

"Like it? He's going to lose his shit when he sees you in that." I assure her, and she bites her lip.

"He's going to be bawling like a baby when he sees you, Aimes." We walk over to her, and the three of us embrace.

"Can you believe it's only a week till the wedding? We still have so much to do, and I'm freaking out a little bit." Aimee admits a worried look on her face. I shake my head.

"Hey, no need to freak out. We have time. That's why you have your maid of honours. Jo and I will take care of everything. You focus on your vows and no stress, or you'll sprout a pimple before your big day." I tease, and she looks at me open-mouthed, touching her face instinctively.

Jo sniggers at the horrified look on Aimee's face. "She's joking, Aimee. Relax, girl, we've got you," Jo says, reassuring her, and Aimee's shoulders visibly relax.

Aimee sighs and takes a sip of the champagne flute I hand her. "Okay, I feel a little better." I grin and take a drink from my glass of champagne. "Your dresses look great." She smiles, looking at our turquoise bridesmaid dresses. We chose mermaid style dresses; the top half was a beautiful lace and off the shoulder, and the skirt had a high slit at the front with a small tail at the back.

As I watch my two best friends, I couldn't believe how much our lives had changed. Jo is having a baby and marrying my brother. Aimee is getting married to one of my dearest friends. Dare I say everything was perfect.

Cole and I have been blissfully happy. Since he's gotten his memory back, things have been amazing, and I finally feel like I got my husband back. I still have that niggle of fear gnawing at me, but I'm learning to ignore it and focus on the positive. After the final dress rehearsal, the girls and I have brunch and discuss the final wedding details and what needs to be done.

Cole, Josh, and Sam soon joined us after the fitting for their suits was done. Cole was sitting opposite me talking to the boys, laughing, and I couldn't help but admire him a little. I'm a lucky girl. He is one beautiful man, and he's all mine. Cole catches me looking at him and holds my gaze, smiling amply at me. He picks up his phone, smirking while he types. A moment later, my phone pings, and I see his name appear on my screen.

Bebé:
If you keep looking at me like that, baby, I'm going to haul you to the bathroom and do sinful things to you.

I grin and look at him seductively while I discreetly type a text back to him, biting my bottom lip as he watches me.

Me:

I think you should, stud. I'm wet and aching just looking at you.

I send the text back to him and watch him closely as he picks up his phone and reads it; his eyes go wide, and they flicker up and lock with mine. Cole swallows hard and shifts in his seat, and looks around before he gestures toward the bathroom with his eyes, smirking wickedly at me.

I feel my stomach flutter with excitement. I excuse myself and tell the girls I need to use the toilet before I walk in the bathroom's direction. I look back at Cole once more before I open the door and walk into the bathroom. Luckily, it was quite spacious and clean. I wait anxiously, and my heart jumps when I hear a knock at the door. I unlock the door, and Cole sneaks in, locking it behind him.

I look up at him when he turns to face me. Cole grabs my wrist, yanks me to him, and kisses me hard. I moan and kiss him back hungrily, sucking his tongue when it sneaks into my mouth.

Cole growls throatily; his large hands grab my bum, and he squeezes it hard, grinding himself against me as he backs me up against the wall. "You're going to be the death of me, baby." He groans, hiking up my denim skirt while I unbutton his jeans and push them down. Cole lifts me into his arms, and I wrap my legs around his waist.

"I can't get enough of you, baby." I moan lustily when he slides hard and thick inside me. Cole hisses, burying himself deep inside me before he captures my lips with his, drawing me in for another hungry kiss.

"Oh sweetheart, me either." Cole rasps, thrusting into me hard and deep, making me whimper into his mouth. "You drive me crazy. I feel like a fucking horny teenager around you. I'm addicted to your pussy, baby." He moans huskily, sucking my bottom lip as he pounds into me harder with each thrust. I cry out, gyrating my hips against his, meeting his thrusts until I feel that familiar stir deep in my belly. Cole is literally every girl's fantasy when it comes to sex. I love it when it's gentle and loving, but the way he fucks is just something else. He's dominating, hot and dirty, and it thrills me. I moan audibly when he sinks his teeth into my neck and sucks hard while he thrusts up and pulls my hips down roughly.

"Ohh, baby, yes, you're going to make me come." I whimper, and he grunts, thrusting harder, his tongue hot on my throat.

"Come for me, baby, milk my cock." He burrs deeply before he bruises my lips with a firm kiss. My head spins, and I pant breathlessly before I cry out, shuddering in his arms as I climax, rocking against him. Cole follows me over with a guttural growl. I feel him throb and pulse inside me while he comes.

"Ahh fuck, fuck, Shay," He hisses between pants against my lips. I press my forehead to his, and he grins, kissing me softly before he pulls back and looks at me.

I match his grin, "You fuck so good." I moan, and he chuckles, pushing his hips into mine, making me groan.

"I'm going to fuck you raw later," Cole promises, dropping a chaste kiss to my lips before he slides out of me and sets me down on the floor again. We get cleaned up, and he kisses me once more before he slips out of the bathroom. I wait a couple of minutes, fixing myself up before I walk out and join them at the table. Cole looks at me, and we smile at each other and go back to talking to our friends and eating our brunch. Luckily, no one noticed we were gone.

THE WEEK LEADING up to the wedding was hectic. Jo and I were running around trying to get the last-minute things Aimee needed to be done before the big day. We also had the Bachelor/Bachelorette parties two days before the wedding. Aimee wanted to do a joint one, so we all went together with our partners and a few of our other friends and got stinking drunk. It was a memorable night for sure. I had to practically rip Aimee and Josh away from one another most of the night. They were worse than Cole and me before we got married. They were ready to have sex on the dance floor in the middle of the club if Cole and I didn't stop them. The night before the wedding, I spent the night with the girls, and Cole was with the boys.

We all needed a night to relax and refresh after the heavy drinking the night before. I had Alaia with me, not wanting to leave her two nights in a row at my mum's, not that she minded, but I miss her and can't be away from her for too long. We spent the night talking, eating, drinking margaritas, and reminiscing about our time living together.

"This is all your fault. You started all of this with your whirlwind romance with Cole." Aimee laughs, throwing a chip at me, and I grin, throwing one back at her. "Now, look at us. I'm getting married. Jo's knocked up. You're married and have a baby. And it's all because of you, Bish,"

I chuckle and cuddle Alaia, who was sitting in my lap. "I know, it's crazy, but we're all happy, right?" I ask, and both girls nod, elated.

"Very happy." Jo sighs, placing her hand on her tiny bump.

"It's your turn next; you'll be Mrs Hart." I tease Jo, and she smiles coyly, reddening.

"We're not in any rush; I'm just looking forward to meeting our baby." Jo smiles, looking at Alaia. "I can't wait to be a mummy."

"You're going to be amazing. The way you are with Laia, you'll be a natural JoJo." I assure her, and she smiles, nodding.

"How are things with you and Cole?" Aimee questions curiously, rolling onto her stomach on the floor and looking at me.

I couldn't fight the shit-eating grin that was plastered on my face at the mention of his name. "We're amazing." I sigh longingly. "We're going through this phase at the moment where we can't get enough of each other. We're all over one another constantly. It's just..." I visibly quiver, and both girls watch me grinning widely.

"Bitch please, phase my arse. You two have been like that from the get-go. I've never seen or had the kind of sexual chemistry you two share in my life. I'm fucking envious." Aimee mutters, shaking her head and grins. "I'll be sitting next to you two, and the tension even makes me fucking randy." She explains with a chuckle. Jo and I laugh out loud.

Aimee suddenly sits up crossed-legged. "Like that day we went to brunch after the dress fitting, and you disappeared to the 'toilet' and Cole had to make a 'phone call'— you totally fucked in the bathroom, didn't you? You little nympho." She laughs, making me blush a deep red.

"Aimee!" I laugh, covering Alaia's ears. "Baby in the room."

Aimee cackles and takes Alaia from me, and lifts her into the air. "Can you say, nympho? Tell your mother she's a nympho. She's a dirty little minx!" She laughs when Alaia giggles at her. "See, your daughter agrees. I bet you see it all, don't you, your dads' hairy arse in the air every night." I roll on the floor, laughing with Jo.

"His arse is not hairy; thank you very much. It's smooth and firm." I defend, laughing, wiping away the tears that roll down my face. "If anyone has a hairy arse, it's Sam." I giggle, pointing at Jo, who gapes at me.

"No fucking way!" Aimee cackles, and Jo shakes her head-turning beet red.

"Shayla, shut up!" She mutters, throwing a cushion at me. "His bum isn't that hairy. I think it's cute."

Aimee pulls a horrified face and looks at Jo. "Oh God, I bet you play with his bum fluff, don't you?" She states, and I howl with laughter.

"I do not!" Jo insists, laughing. "I like my men with hair."

Aimee smirks, "In all the wrong places, babe. He should use some of the hair on his arse and put it on his head. Heaven knows he's probably got enough."

Jo throws her head back and laughs. "Oh my God, why am I friends with you two bitches!"

"Because we're fucking ah-mazing." Aimee states, and I nod in agreement from my position on the floor. I lean up and load up our song 'Pina colada song' on the Bluetooth player, and we all laugh. "Oh my God, yes! I was tired of my lady. We've been together too long. Like a worn-out recording of a favourite song."

Aimee sings along, dancing and points at Jo.

"So, while she lay there sleeping, I read the paper in bed." Jo sings along, shaking her shoulders, and points at me.

"And in the personal columns, there was this letter I read..." I sing, getting up to my feet and pulling Jo up with me.

"If you like pina colada's and getting caught in the rain!" We all sing together, dancing around the living room as we used to. I miss the good old days so much. I had a fantastic time with these girls. I record us singing and dancing and sent it to Cole.

I get a video back of them drinking beer and playing PlayStation—followed by a text.

Bebé:

Can I join your party instead? These idiots are doing my head in.

Me:

No-can-do, honey. We have a ton of cocktails and a drunken pillow fight to follow shortly. You'll be bored.

Bebé:

The fuck, I will! I love a good pillow fight, or have you forgotten about the ones we had in our old apartment when you first moved in?

Me:

How could I forget? It was the best time of my life.
I miss you. Have fun.

Bebé:

I miss you more. Dream of me, Gorgeous girl.

I scowl when my phone is plucked from my hand and tossed aside by Aimee. "Stop texting your sexy husband! No men tonight!" She scolds me and pulls me to dance with them.

THE NEXT MORNING, we were up bright and early. Jo was the only sober one, not being able to drink because of the pregnancy, while

Aimee and I were hanging after one too many cocktails. We had hair and makeup going on in my old bedroom. Champagne was flowing while we got ready for Aimee and Josh's big day. Aimee was a nervous wreck, and it was adorable. It took us all four hours to get prepared. The cars were waiting to take us to the church. Aimee's mother— Lorraine, joined us in the morning, and her father came to pick her up to accompany her to the church as he was walking her down the aisle. Alaia was picked up by my mother early on so that I could focus on Aimee.

"You look stunning." I smile, fixing her veil before she walks in. "This is it. You ready to marry your man?" She lets out a nervous breath and nods. We hug, and I take my place with Jo, ready to walk down the aisle. Jo goes first, and I follow. When Cole sees me walking toward them, he grins, his eyes never leaving mine until I take my place opposite him. His eyes rake over me and meet mine again. He was dressed in a tuxedo looking mouth-watering as always, as he stood beside Josh, who was fidgeting nervously.

"You're beautiful." He mouths to me, and I smile and wink at him. We turn and face the front as Aimee walks down the aisle with her dad. I watch Josh's reaction when he sees her in her wedding gown.

He turns to Cole, his eyes swimming in tears. "Oh, fuck." He whispers, exhaling, and Cole smiles, squeezing his shoulder supportively. I feel myself getting emotional already. They're such a beautiful couple, and I was so happy they found one another. I cry throughout the entire ceremony while they declare their love for one another. I smile at Cole when I catch him watching me lovingly. I get flashes of our wedding day, and I know he does too because his eyes water as he looks at me. Cole hands Josh his ring, and I give Aimee hers, and they repeat after the minister sliding the rings on one another's fingers.

"...I pronounce you husband and wife. You may kiss your bride." The minister declares, and Josh pulls Aimee to him, and he kisses her passionately while everyone stands and applauds, cheering. Once they pull back from the kiss, they gaze lovingly at one another. Josh turns to face Cole, and they hug while Aimee turns to Jo and me. "Congratulations!" We hug tightly, sobbing. I pull back and brush her tears away.

"I'm so happy for you, Aimes. I love you so much." I cry, and she returns my smiles with a tearful one.

"I love you more." She cries, hugging me again. "Thank you for everything,"

I smile, and we pull apart. "Always," I promise and watch her hug Jo next.

"I hope every day is as happy as this one for the rest of your lives, babe. I love you bitch." Jo cries, and Aimee smiles.

"I love you more bitch. I'm going to miss living with you." She cries when they pull apart.

"Oi, you two, stop making my bride cry," Josh complains playfully, coming up behind Aimee. I smile and wrap my arms around him tightly.

"Come here you." Josh grins and hugs me just as tight. "Look after her and make her happy. I love you, but if you break her heart, I will kill you." I sniffle, and he chuckles, nodding before he kisses my forehead and wipes away my tears.

"Thank you for bringing her into my life. I'm grateful to you, and I love you, sis." Josh affirms and hugs me again.

"I love you too, bro."

"Ahem, can I have my wife back now, please?" Cole grumbles with a playful scowl, and Josh pulls away laughing. "Your wife is over there, dickhead." He adds with a laugh and slaps his back. They fist bump, and Josh goes over to his bride. Cole pulls me into his arms. "Hi, Gorgeous girl." He greets me, pressing his forehead to mine.

"Hi, Stud." I greet back and close my eyes when he tilts my head up and brushes a kiss to my waiting lips. "As sexy as you look, I can't wait to take this tuxedo off you later," I whisper, and he grins roguishly.

"I was thinking the same about that dress. While you were walking down that aisle, I got flashes of our wedding day, and I saw you in your wedding dress, and my stomach got all fluttery."

"So did I. While they were saying their vows, I remembered ours, and I couldn't stop crying," I admit leaning into his touch, smiling, and Cole brushes away my tears before he kisses me softly.

"I would marry you over and over again, baby." He states charmingly, making me laugh.

"So, would I, but I think twice is enough. Let's just focus on *staying married* this time." I tease, and he laughs.

"That's easy because I'm never letting you go anywhere...*ever.*" I grin and brush my nose over his affectionately.

"Good, because I'm not going anywhere...*ever.*" Cole kisses my jaw, and we pull apart when my mother brings us Alaia, who smiles when she sees us.

"Oh my God, if this isn't the most beautiful baby in the world," Cole says, taking her into his arms. Alaia wore a flower girl dress with similar colours and designs to ours, but hers was with a tutu and had a big bow and feathers on the back. I found a matching headband with a bow and feathers, which finished the dress off perfectly. "What is this dress? Oh, my goodness. My heart can't take it. Are you both trying to kill me?" Cole coos pressing a kiss to Alaia's bow-clad head.

"She looks beautiful, don't you, baby girl," I say, smiling at her, and she giggles at me. Once we were done with the photos, we make our way to the venue, where the reception is held. Aimee and Josh chose to have a marquee reception rather than an indoor hall or a hotel. Which I thought was a fantastic idea. It was January, and it was still cold out, but inside it was beautiful. Twinkling lights and the décor, along with the white and blue flowers, were terrific. I watch Josh and Aimee while they have their first dance, and I couldn't contain my tears again. I was a mess.

And then came the speeches, which I was dreading more than anything. After Cole delivered his speech as best man, it was my turn.

I exhale and stand up, taking the microphone from Cole, who winks at me. "Hi friends and family, I'm Shayla, one of the Maid of honours. Aimee and I go way back; I'm talking secondary school. We've known each other since we were like twelve years old. I never had a biological sister, and God himself must have known how desperately I wanted a sister, and he gave me two. No offence Sam, I love you dearly." I tease, looking at my big brother, who laughs, shaking his head. I met Aimee and Jo back in our school years, and we quickly became more than friends, we became sisters, and we've been inseparable since. Aimee is the type of friend every girl needs in her life. She was there for me during the darkest times in my life and stood by me through it all tirelessly." I say, tears streaming down my face, and I look at her.

"We made a pact that no matter where we are in life, we will always be in each other's lives, and I'm so happy that I get to stand here on your wedding day and tell all your family and friends how much you mean to me," I tell her, and she looks up at me, tears rolling down her cheeks. "I'm fortunate and thankful that two of my best friends found one another and fell in love. I wish you both a long, healthy, and happy life together. To Aimee and Josh!" I weep into the mic, holding up my glass of champagne, and everyone toasts to them before they applaud. Aimee and Josh stand and both hug me.

"Thank you, babe, that was so beautiful. We love you so much." Aimee cries, wiping away my tears.

"That was a beautiful speech, Shay," Josh says, drying his tears. "I'm so glad you got drunk and married my idiot best friend."

"Hey!" Cole interjects affronted, and we laugh. "Bastard." Cole chuckles, shaking his head as I take my seat beside him. "That really was a beautiful speech, baby. I'm proud of you." He murmurs in my ear, brushing a kiss to my temple.

***

After dinner, the party was in full swing. My feet were aching from all the dancing.

"Baby, I'm going to go and change Alaia," I inform Cole, who was talking with Sam and looks up at me.

"Do you want me to come with you?" He offers, and I shake my head, leaning over to kiss him.

"No, it's fine. I'll only be a few minutes," I assure him, and he smiles, watching me as I grab Alaia's bag and go on a hunt for the bathroom, which was in the main building. Once I find it, I lay her down on the changing unit, and she starts to fuss while I change her. "I know, baby, you're not comfortable in that dress, are you." I utter, taking it off her and dressing her in her onesie instead. "Is that better?" I smile, kissing her feet, and she smiles up at me. I pick her up and kiss her forehead. "Come on, baby girl, let's go back to Daddy." I push the door and walk out of the bathroom and look around the corridor. Which way was it back to the Marquee? After getting lost, I finally step outside and smile at Alaia, kissing her fingers when she touches my face. I gasp, surprised when I feel someone wrap their arms around me from behind. I relax, thinking it was Cole, until something is pressed to my face, covering my mouth and nose. I tighten my hold on Alaia and struggle against whoever was holding me. I try to scream, but it comes out muffled.

My heart was thumping hard in my ears, and I feel my knees wobble until they give way and everything around me fades to darkness.

Chapter 24

COLE

"COLE, I'm telling you, it was the right move for the whole team. He's one of the best players they've had in years." Sam states, taking a sip of his scotch while he talks passionately about a football player transfer.

I shake my head and chuckle. "If you say so, bro, they need more than the likes of him if they're going to win the championship this season," I tell him earnestly, and Sam shakes his head. I look around the room, my eyes searching for Shayla, but I can't see her anywhere. She's been gone for over half-hour. "I'm going to go look for Shayla; she's been gone a while," I say, and Sam nods, giving me the thumbs up. I wander around the marquee looking for her, but she wasn't in there. "Mum, have you seen Shayla and Alaia?" I ask her mother, and she looks up at me.

"She went to change the baby, but that was a while ago. Isn't she back yet?" She asks, and I shake my head, scanning the room again.

"I haven't seen her if she is," I reply, and she frowns worriedly.

"She's got to be around here somewhere. Maybe she's with the girls?"

"Maybe, let me go check. If you see her, tell her I'm looking for her." Sara nods, her eyes sweeping the room. I sigh and see Jo and Aimee dancing but no Shayla.

"Cole, come dance. Where the hell is Shayla?" Aimee asks, looking around, and I frown.

"I came to ask you, have either of you seen her?" I question, and they

269

both shake their heads. "She went to the bathroom to change the baby, but that was like over half an hour ago," I tell them worriedly, and Aimee looks around the room.

"She's around here somewhere. Maybe she's feeding Alaia? Do you want us to check the bathroom?" She asks, and I shake my head.

"No, it's fine. You're probably right; she's likely found someplace quiet to feed the baby. I'll go check." I say and leave them to dance while I step out of the marquee. It was dark out, and there weren't many people around. I follow the signs to the bathroom and push the door open and see it was empty. Where the hell has she disappeared to? I'm starting to feel anxious, and I don't like it. I check every single room in the main building, and there was no sign of her.

I run outside and stop when I see a shoe by a plant pot. I pick it up and look at it. That was Shayla's shoe. I was there when she picked it out. Why is she running around with only one shoe? What the fuck is going on? Something's wrong—I can feel it. I hurry back to the marquee and sweep the room, looking for her. I see Josh talking to one of his cousins and walk over to him. I pull him to me.

"Have you seen Shayla?" I ask him, and he frowns, shaking his head.

"Not recently. Why? Is something wrong?" Josh questions when he notices the worried look on my face. I hold up her shoe.

"I can't find her or Alaia anywhere, and I found this outside," I tell him. "Why would she be running around with one shoe, Josh?" I ask fretfully, and Aimee walks over to us.

"Oh, did you find her? Why are you holding her shoe? Did the dopey tart break her heel?" Aimee chuckles, and her smile falters when she notices the look on both mine and her husband's faces. "What's going on, Cole? Josh?"

"Aimee, I can't find her or Alaia anywhere. I found her shoe outside." I tell her, holding up Shayla's shoe, and Aimee frowns, looking at the shoe and back at me.

"Cole, she's got to be around here somewhere. Where is she going to go?" She replies, trying to reassure me, but I shake my head.

"No, something is wrong. I can feel it." I sigh, closing my eyes. I look around the room again, gnawing my lip. My hands were starting to shake, and my heart was racing fretfully.

"Don't panic. We'll find her, bro. She's around here. She must be." Josh utters, scanning the room. "Come on, let's get Sam and go look for her."

I shake my head, rubbing my neck. "No, no, Josh, it's your wedding day, man. You stay. I'll keep looking."

"Cole, don't be daft. We'll cover more ground if we split up. Come on." He says, pulling my arm.

"Jo and I will look in the bathroom again," Aimee tells me, and I nod, following Josh. He was talking to Sam already, who was scowling.

"What do you mean you can't find her?" Sam utters, looking around the room, then at me. "Where the fuck is she going to go? She's got to be here." Sam murmurs, rubbing his head.

"Let's go look around," Josh urges, gesturing with his head, and we all run out of the marquee, searching all over for them.

"Shayla?!" I call out into the dark as I run around in search of her. As the minutes tick on, I'm more convinced something is wrong, and the dread in my gut grows tenfold. She's been gone for over an hour. I run toward the car park, looking around frantically. I race down the path and stop when I see Alaia's pink blanket that Shayla had her wrapped in lying on the floor. I sprint toward it and pick it up and look around. "SHAYLA?!" I shout, panting, and look down at the blanket in my trembling hands.

"Cole," I turn when I hear Josh and see him jogging toward me. "She's not here." He pants and looks at the blanket I was holding.

"Alaia's blanket," I whisper, my voice breaking. "Shayla had her wrapped in this blanket. Josh, something's wrong." I tell him uneasily, and Josh sighs, rubbing the back of his neck, his blue eyes looking around.

"Let's not think the worst. We're going to find them, bro." Josh assures me, squeezing my shoulder. "I'm going to go speak to the manager and see if I can get access to the security cameras. You keep looking." He says, and I nod numbly.

My eyes roam around in the dark. "Shayla, where are you, baby. Where are you." I sigh helplessly, and I run around the car park, looking around frantically. She's not here! We would have found her if she were —I'm going to lose my mind. Where would she go? She came with the wedding cars. It's not like she jump-started a fucking car and took off.

I find Sam running toward me from the other side of the Marquee. "I can't find her. She's not here, man. Isn't that Laia's?" He questions, pointing at the blanket.

I nod, looking at it. "I found it on the floor in the car park. Shayla had this wrapped around her."

"Fuck." Sam curses, placing his hands on his head as he paces back and forth. "We need to call the police, Cole. Something has happened to them. Shayla wouldn't take off without a word, bro." I feel my heart fill with trepidation at his words. He's right. She would never disappear like this.

"Cole?" I whirl around when I hear Aimee behind me. She takes one look at Sam and me, and her blue eyes fill with concern. "What's going on? Any news?"

"Shayla and Alaia have disappeared," Sam states, pacing back and forth. "Something's happened to them. I fucking know it!" He shouts angrily, and I bite my lip hard, staring down at my daughters' blanket. Oh God, please, please let them be safe. If anything happens to them, I won't survive.

"Oh, my God." Aimee gasps, looking around. "Don't say that. They're fine. They're around here. They have to be!" She shrieks. I stood immobile as all hell ensued around me. Jo and Aimee cry, holding each other. The worst one of them all was her mother. When she found out her daughter and grandchild are missing, she collapsed into Sam's arms. I sink to the floor, clutching my wife's shoe and my daughter's blanket to my chest. I couldn't breathe. I felt like my lungs were collapsing.

"Cole." I lift my eyes and see my mother's worried gaze. She takes my tear-stained face into her small hands and brushes the endless tears that fall from my eyes. "Somethings not right. Where are they?" I whisper. "Where are they, Mum?!" I sob, tightening my hold on the shoe and blanket I kept clutched against me. My head falls against her chest, and she holds me while I cry helplessly.

"We're going to find them, darling." She assures me, stroking my head. "They're both fine. You'll see."

"I should have gone with them," I say, sitting up and looking down at the blanket. I bring it to my nose and inhale deeply. It smells like Alaia, and I sob when my insides ache. "I shouldn't have left them alone. I should have gone with them." I whisper wretchedly.

"Sweetheart, you weren't to know this would happen." My mother states, rubbing my back comfortingly, but I shake my head.

"I'm her husband! I'm supposed to protect them!" I shout hotly. "I couldn't protect them. It's all my fault."

"What do you mean it's been erased?!" I look back when I hear Josh shouting. "A mother and her baby are missing, and you're telling me the footage has been erased!" He growls, grabbing the manager by the collar of his suit. "What kind of an establishment are you fucking running here?!" I hand the blanket and shoe to my mother before I get up and walk over to where Josh was with the manager of the venue.

"Where's my wife." I hiss furiously. Josh lets him go when he sees me striding toward him. "WHERE ARE THEY?!" I roar, grabbing him by the collar of his jacket and bringing his face close to mine, glaring menacingly at him.

"Look, I told your friend already. I don't know about any woman and her baby!" He shouts, trying to push me off him, but I clench my jaw tight and glare at him hard.

"You or someone on these premises have taken them! That's why you deleted the fucking footage! I'm not leaving until I find my wife and daughter, you hear me?! I want every square inch of this place searched until you FIND THEM!" I scream at him and push him so hard he falls back on the floor. "Anything happens to my family. I will rain all of hell on you, do you hear me?!"

"Cole, come on." I hear Josh behind me. He pulls my arm as I continue to glare at the manager. My whole body was shaking. "If they're here, we'll find them."

"Call the police. I want every inch of this place searched. I want no stone left unturned. Do you understand me?" I utter, and Josh nods and watches me walk away toward the marquee. Everyone had already started to leave, and it was almost empty. I see Shayla's bag sitting on the table we were seated at. I pick it up and open it. Her makeup, her phone, her keys to the house, it was all here. She's not gone anywhere on her own free will—they've been taken. Somebody has abducted them. I press my hand to my mouth and close my eyes. Who the fuck would take them and why? It's been two hours, and my mind's reeling. What if I never see them again. What if something happens to them. With a growl, I kick the table over and watch everything fall and smash on the floor.

"Cole, the police are here." I turn and look at Josh; he gestures for me to follow him, and I do. There were four police cars and two vans. This all feels like a terrible nightmare I'm trapped in and can't seem to wake up from.

"Mr Hoult, I'm Detective Chief inspector Scott. Can we ask you a couple of questions?" I nod silently. "Before we launch an investigation, we usually wait twenty-four hours before filing a missing person's report. Would your wife have any reason to take your daughter and want to disappear?"

I frown and shake my head. "No. She hasn't left me. They've been taken! She went to the bathroom to change our daughter, and they never came back. I found one of her shoes and my daughters' blanket on the floor." I explain, raking my fingers through my hair in frustration.

Detective Scott nods and takes notes. "Why would your wife and daughter be taken? Do you have anyone that you can think of that would wish you or your family any harm? Has there been anything suspicious following up to the abduction of your wife and child? A note? Phone calls? Anyone following you?" I shake my head and shrug, rubbing my temples, trying to think of something, but it all came up blank.

"No, there's nothing. Everything was normal as it always is. There was nothing out of the ordinary, and I don't have anyone that would want to hurt them. Not that I know of anyway." I explain with a sigh. "Shayla wouldn't leave without a word; she wouldn't. Someone's taken them by force. I know it. The footage of the moment she disappeared is also gone. Someone in there knows something, go and do your job and find them!" I mutter angrily, and Detective Scott nods.

"Mr Hoult, I understand you're worried, and we will do everything in our power to find your wife and daughter. However, cases like these are more common than you think. It wouldn't be the first time a wife up and leaves without a word. We must follow procedure and consider all aspects before we can say for certain that they have been abducted." He explains, watching me as I pace back and forth. "My team is searching inside and the perimeter of the establishment. If they're here, we will find them." He assures me, and I shake my head. "I know it's difficult, but I need you to stay calm and by your phone in case she or anyone else contacts you. If it is an abduction, it's usually for ransom, and they will be in contact with you."

My heart hurt, just thinking about them hauled up someplace scared or hurt made my stomach clench painfully. "Find them, please find my wife and baby. I'll pay whatever they want. I'll give them everything I have—just find them, please." I cry, and Detective Scott nods and squeezes my shoulder.

"I know this is not what you want to hear, but I have to ask, could your wife have been involved with another man? Could she have left with a lover?"

I scowl at him and shake my head. "My God, no! Shayla would never do that. We love each other fiercely. She would never cheat on me, and I would never cheat on her. I'm telling you she hasn't left me. She's been taken." I insist and look at Josh, who was scowling at the detective also. "You don't think *Blake* would..."

Josh looks at me, and his frown deepens. "Nah, why would Blake kidnap Shayla and Alaia? Not for the money, the guy's loaded." Josh states warily.

"What if it's not for the money, Josh. They were close while Shayla and I were broken up after I lost my memory. What if he's pissed off about us getting back together, and he's taken them out of spite?" I clarify, and Josh blinks slowly. I can see the wheels in his head-turning.

"Cole, he seemed to care about her genuinely. I don't think he would do anything to hurt her."

"Exactly! Maybe he cares a little too much! He's definitely got the motive and the resources to pull something like this off!" I shout hotly. "I'm going to kill him," I growl, pacing furiously.

"Mr Hoult, please calm down. Who is this Blake, and what is his association with your wife?" Detective Scott questions, looking between Josh and me inquiringly.

"Blake Bryant. He's one of the investors for a project we're working on. He's always had a thing for Shayla. I saw the way he would look at her. After my accident, I lost my memory. Shayla and I broke up for a while, and they got close; they even kissed once, but then we got back together, and Shayla cut him off to focus on our marriage." I explain, clenching and unclenching my fists. "If anyone has a motive and is responsible for this, it would be him."

Detective Scott nods while writing. "We'll look into Mr Bryant, and I'll bring him in for questioning."

"I want to be there when you question him," I state, and Detective Scott shakes his head.

"You can't be there, Mr Hoult. I know this is difficult, but please let us do our job, and under no circumstance do you approach Mr Bryant personally. Leave it to us, and if he is the one responsible for abducting your wife and daughter, he will slip up, and we'll get him."

"I can't just sit around and do nothing!" I exclaim.

"We'll be in touch as soon as we know something. In the meantime, as I said, keep your phone on, and if anything feels off or you get any calls or notes, let us know right away. Do not try and handle anything on your own because you will only put your wife and child's life in danger along with your own. I'm going to have your house on twenty-four-hour surveillance just to be safe." I heave a sigh and nod.

"Detective Scott." I turn when I see one of the officers walk up with a young lady in a waitress's uniform. She has a cut on her fore-head. "This is Miss Jones. She was working the wedding this afternoon when she saw Mrs Hoult and her baby get dragged away into an unmarked van. She was knocked unconscious and stuffed into an outdoor walk-in fridge behind the kitchen." The uniformed officer explains, and my heart rate slows drastically. I knew it. I fucking knew it!

"Oh my God," I whisper and turn my head when I feel Josh's hand on my shoulder. We share a fretful look, and I see the worry in the depths of his blue eyes. "What did you see?" I ask, taking a step toward the girl, and she winces.

"Um, I went to get some strawberries for the fruit platter when I saw one of the bridesmaids, holding a baby walking out the back of the build-ing. I didn't see who took them, they were dressed in all black, and their faces were covered, but someone grabbed them from behind and covered her mouth. She tried to scream, and she was struggling until she passed out, and they dragged them away to a black van and sped off. I ran out to tell someone what I saw, but I got knocked out, and when I came too, I was in the fridge. I'm so sorry." She cries, shaking her head. I crouch with my head in my hands.

"Take Miss Jones's statement, and I want a copy of all the security footage for the whole week. This was clearly premeditated, which means they would have had to come and skulk the place out. I want the names of everyone that works here, new and old." The officer nods before he leads the girl away, and Detective Scott turns and looks down at me.

"Mr Hoult, we're going to do everything in our power to find them and get them back home to you safely." He reassures me, but it falls on deaf ears.

My wife and baby have been abducted. They could be anywhere. They could be hurt or worse, and I'm supposed to just sit around and wait. "Come on, bro, let's get you home." Josh pulls me up to my feet.

"Josh," I whisper, lifting my tear-filled gaze to him. Josh nods and squeezes my shoulder, and pulls me in for a hug.

"I know. It's going to be okay, bro. We're going to find them. I swear to you." He sighs, and I sob helplessly into his shoulder.

"What's going on, baby?" I hear Aimee's voice behind me. Josh and I pull apart, and I keep my eyes cast down, tears of despair streaming endlessly down my face. Sam and Jo follow Aimee.

Josh heaves a sigh and rubs the back of his neck. "Shayla and Alaia have been kidnapped. A witness saw them being dragged away into a van." He explains sullenly, and Aimee gasps, covering her mouth with her hand.

"What?" Sam stammers, staring at Josh, utterly stunned. "What do you mean they've been kidnapped? By whom?!" He asks angrily. "Who the fuck would want to kidnap my sister?!" He exclaims irately and looks at me. "Cole, say something?! Whose taken my fucking sister?!"

"I don't know!" I shout, lifting my gaze to his. "I don't know."

"Oh, my God." Jo places her hand on her forehead and paces. "What would anyone want with her and Alaia?" She asks, and I lift my gaze to the dark sky. I just kept picturing Shayla alone and frightened, and it's killing me.

"Did Shayla ever mention anything about Blake to you two?" Josh asks the girls, and they exchange looks of concern and look at him again.

"Blake?" Aimee intones, wiping away her tears. "You think he's behind this?" She questions, and Josh shrugs, pulling her into his arms.

"We don't know. Cole thinks he might have something to do with it. He was close with her until Shayla cut him off. Maybe he got jealous and couldn't stand seeing her happy with Cole?"

Jo shakes her head. "I warned her. When we ran into him at the mall that time, and he was holding Alaia, I warned her that he was going to be trouble, she waved it off, and now he's—"

My head snaps to her, and I frown. "He held Alaia?" I ask, and Jo nods sullenly. "I fucking told you!" I shout, looking at Josh. "There was something I didn't like about that guy. I had a bad feeling the moment I met him. That mother fucker, I'll fucking kill him!"

"Who the fuck is Blake? Why are we just standing here? Let's go fucking find him and get him to talk!" Sam exclaims angrily. "I'll beat

him to an inch of his fucking life. Where the fuck does he live, tell me?!"
He shouts, grabbing me by my suit jacket.

"Josh, can you get your guys to find where he lives?" I ask him in a
flurry, and Josh sighs, closing his eyes.

"Cole, you heard the detective. If we all go and ambush him, it could
put Shayla and Alaia's lives at risk. The police—"

"Fuck the police!" Sam roars hotly. "By the time they get their
fucking heads out of their arses and get the warrants they need to search
his place, he could be doing all sorts to her man!" He shouts, pacing, and
stops to look at me. "Cole, if this guy is crazy enough to kidnap them
think about what he will do to her!" He shouts, grabbing me by the
lapels of my jacket, and I stare at him in horror.

No.

He wouldn't.

I turn my gaze to Josh, who stares back at me. "Oh, God," I whisper
and felt my stomach lurch unpleasantly. I run off and lean over,
throwing up everything I had consumed earlier. If he lays his hand on
her, I will rip him limb from fucking limb. I feel a hand on my back and
take the handkerchief Jo was holding out to me. I stand up straight and
wipe my mouth.

"Don't think the worst. When I saw him with her, he seemed to
genuinely care about her. I don't think he would hurt her or Alaia,
Cole." She tries to assure me, and I look at her.

"How could you possibly know that? If he's twisted enough to
kidnap her and my baby, what makes you think he wouldn't try and..." I
squeeze my eyes shut and choke on a sob. "I'm going to lose my mind, Jo.
She must be fucking terrified. This is all my fault. I was supposed to
protect them." I cry, falling to my knees, and she hugs me.

"Cole, this isn't your fault," Jo states while rubbing my back, and I
shake my head.

"It is my fault. If I never lost my memory and said all that shit to her
and broke her heart, she wouldn't have given that son of a bitch the time
of day." I sob, pulling away from her embrace.

"Cole, none of us could have ever seen this coming, babe. Shayla's a strong girl. She'll protect Alaia with her life, and she's going to find a way back to you. I promise you."

I tried to find comfort in her words, I did, but how strong can she be against a man that's bigger and stronger than her. I can't just sit around and let that son of a bitch hurt her. I won't.

I get up and storm over to Josh. "Call your guys. I want to know about every single piece of real estate Blake has ever purchased. I'm going to get my girls back."

Chapter 25

SHAYLA

I GROAN when I feel a sudden ache in my head. My head felt so heavy, I could barely lift it, and my neck was aching terribly.

I peel my eyes open and blink a couple of times until the blurriness clouding my vision clears, and look around the darkroom I was in. Where on earth am I? I wince when I feel a pinch on my wrist and my fingers felt numb.

I glance down and see my arms are bound to the armrest of the chair I was sitting in. I was still in my bridesmaid dress—Aimee and Josh's wedding. I was at the wedding. How did I end up in this dark and dingy room? Sheer panic rises inside me when I remember Alaia was with me before everything went dark around me. I look around the room frantically, my heart racing a mile a minute. Where's my baby? Where's Alaia?

"Alaia." I gasp and lift my eyes to the door. "ALAIA!" I scream, tugging on my restraints. I sob, trying to wiggle my wrists free, but they were bound so tight the rope burnt my skin. I try to move my legs, but they were tied to the legs of the chair. "ALAIA!" I shout, sobbing frantically. "Where's my baby?!"

What is happening? Where am I? Where's Alaia? Why am I tied to a fucking chair? "Help! Somebody, please help me?!" I cry, looking around the room. There were no windows, only a dirty bed with a paper-thin mattress in the corner. I felt like I was in a prison cell, and it smelt rotten. "Can anybody hear me?!" I call out again. "Cole?!" I wail, letting my head fall forward. "What's is happening?"

I jump, and my head snaps up to the door when I hear it unlock. I shrink back into the chair when a tall, stocky man walks in, his face covered. My heart was hammering against my chest so hard that I thought it would stop altogether. I lift my gaze up to him. "Who the hell are you?" I ask, my voice raspy from lack of water and shouting. "Where's my baby?"

"Your baby is fine, stop screaming, or you won't fucking be." He threatens. His voice was deep and menacing.

"I don't believe you. I want to see her." I cry, looking up into his steely eyes. "Please give me my baby," I whimper, pleading. "I'll be quiet. Please, just give me my daughter back."

He stood still, staring at me, and nods once. "H, bring the kid!" He snaps, and I see another masked man walk past the door.

"What do you want with us?" I ask, and he turns and looks at me again with a glare that made me recoil. Whoever this man was, he was dangerous. His whole demeanour was terrifying.

"So many questions, Cupcake. You'll find out soon enough if you stay quiet and be a good little girl, and if you don't..." He snarls and leans in close and waves a pocketknife in front of me before he runs the cold blade down the side of my face. "I'll slit your throat and shut you up indefinitely. Got it." I stare into his cold, unyielding grey eyes and nod slowly. "No one is going to hear you, so I wouldn't bother screaming for help. If you want your precious baby to keep her adorable little head intact, I suggest you cooperate and stop talking." He growls, snapping the blade shut. "I don't like talkers." He hisses, standing straight and looming over me. I gasp when I hear Alaia crying. The other masked man walks in holding her, and I sob when I see her.

"Alaia." I instinctively go to lift my arms to reach for her and wince when the rope pinches my skin. "It's okay, baby, mummy's here." I whimper when she reaches out for me crying. I could tell she's been crying for hours. Her eyes are puffy and red, her beautiful face tear-stained. I look up at the man beside me. "Please, give me my baby. I need to feed her; she's hungry. That's why she's crying." I sniffle. "I'll do whatever you want, I swear." I plead, crying, and he looks at Alaia.

"She refused to take the bottle. She's been screaming for fucking hours."

My heart shatters at his words. "Because she's still breastfeeding. I'll keep her quiet, I promise." I say earnestly and look at Alaia, who was crying so hard she was hiccupping. I sigh when the tall man beside me cuts the ropes with his knife. I rub my wrists and see they're bruised, and my skin was raw with rope burns. I hold my arms out and take Alaia from the other guy when he holds her out to me. I wrap my arms around her tight and hold her against me while I sob. "Oh, thank God you're okay. It's okay. It's okay, baby, I'm here, I've got you, mummies got you now." I whisper, kissing her face. Alaia stops crying, and her little body hiccups in my arms, and she whines a little. "Oh, I know, I know, shhh baby." The men walk out, slam the door shut, locking it behind them. I exhale and kiss my daughter's head, rocking her as she calms in my arms. I loosen my dress and warily pull out my breast to feed her. Alaia latches on and sucks at my nipple hard and gulps hungrily. She was starving, and that thought alone made me sob silently. What did these people want with us? What are they going to do with us?

As I watch Alaia feed, my mind wanders to Cole. He must be worried sick, wondering where we are. I'm hoping and praying he will find a way to find us wherever we are. If I know Cole, he will find some way to save us. He won't leave us here. I had no choice but to hold onto that hope for dear life. I was terrified— not for me, but for my baby. I don't care what they do to me, but if they hurt Alaia. I close my eyes and push that thought out of my mind. Cole won't let anything happen to us. "Daddy's going to save us, baby. We just need to stay strong long enough for him to find us." I whisper, brushing my finger over her cheek, and she sighs, looking up at me with those beautiful green eyes—eyes that are identical to the man I love. I close my eyes, and hot tears roll down my face. "Cole, please save us." I breathe, my voice quivering. "Please, baby."

Hours go by, and I must have cried myself to sleep on the bed because I jump awake when I hear the door unlock, and I tighten my hold on Alaia, who was asleep in my arms. I hear muffled voices from behind the door, and a second later, the same man as before walks in, likely to check on us to make sure we were still alive. I look up at him as he walks over to me, and I sink further against the wall. We stare at one another for a long moment. I had a million questions, but I was too scared to open my mouth in fear of what they would do to Alaia. "Hand me the kid." He commands, and I hold her tighter against me and shake my head.

"No, please, please, I'm begging you don't take her from me," I beg him, tears filling my eyes, and he only stares back threateningly.

"You'll see her when she needs to be fed. Hand her over." I look down at her asleep in my arms, and I press a kiss to her head, inhaling her scent before he pulls her from me. I whimper as he takes her away.

"She'll need to be changed soon," I say, and he turns and gives me a dark look before he walks out and locks the door. I choke on a sob and bury my face in my arms as I cry. How long were they going to keep me captive? Are they going to kill us? I was driving myself crazy, wondering the same questions repeatedly. I pace the small room back and forth restlessly. I had no idea what time it was. Was it night-time or day? I felt like I was trapped in that room forever. They would bring Alaia to me when she was restless and hungry or needed to be changed before taking her away again. I didn't understand why they wouldn't just leave her with me. I only left the room when I had to use the bathroom, and I was blindfolded until I got to the toilet. There were no windows in there either.

I was anxiously shaking my leg sitting on the bed when the door unlocks, making me start, and the two men from before walk in at the same time. I glare up at their masked faces, and the taller one points at the chair. "Sit." He commands, and I get up, my knee's shaking as I walk over to the chair and sit down. I see the rope in his hands and pull my wrists to my chest.

"Why are you tying me up again?" I ask, my voice quivering, and he glares at me hard wordlessly. I close my eyes and place my arms on the armrest and wince as he ties me up tightly. "How long have I been here?"

"Three days." He mutters as he ties my ankles to the chair. Is that it? It feels like weeks to me. "You'll get your answers shortly." I watch him as he stands and takes a couple of steps back. They don't leave. They just stand there, leering at me like I was a piece of meat. I frown when I hear footsteps on the gravel. I lift my gaze slowly, and my eyes go wide, almost bulging out of my head. No fucking way.

"Oh, my God," I whisper, horrified as I stare at the person standing before me. My vision blurs with tears as I watch Sophie hold my daughter in her arms. "You did this?" I ask, and she smirks icily, bouncing Alaia in her arms.

"Surprise bitch." She utters, holding my daughter's hand. "Oopsie, I should learn to watch my language in front of the baby."

I fight in my restraints as I glare at her. "Sophie, give me my baby." I hiss, looking at Alaia, tears rolling down my face. "What do you think you're doing? Have you lost your goddamn mind! Give me my baby!"

Sophie narrows her blue eyes at me and laughs. "Your baby? Oh sweetie, she's my baby now—or she will be very soon." She states coolly, and I gape at her aghast.

"What the fuck are you talking about, Sophie?!" I shout, tugging on my restraints, not even caring about the burns it was leaving on my wrists. I look up at the guy beside me. "Untie me, please, untie me goddamn it!" I cry helplessly, and he rolls his eyes with a sigh. "What's your plan? Are you going to kill me and raise mine and Coles baby yourself? Are you fucking insane?!"

Sophie hands Alaia to the other guy standing beside her and gestures her head to take her away. My eyes follow Alaia until she disappears out of sight. Sophie walks closer to me and smiles showing her pearly white teeth that I had the urge to headbutt right into her fucking skull. "Myself? Oh, honey, no. I wouldn't dream of keeping her away from her father." Sophie drawls, staring into my face, and I fist my hands tightly. "Alaia will be going back home to her Daddy today." She tells me, and I release the breath I had been holding. Thank God. She wasn't as batshit crazy as I thought she was.

"What's the idea here, Sophie? Are you going to pretend you found Alaia and hope that Cole will fall in love with you?" I ask bitterly, and she grins maliciously. "You're fucking crazy." I hiss acidly, tugging on my restraints again. Sophie holds her hand out to the tall man, and he drops a knife in her hand. I recoil and look at the blade when she holds it open in front of my face. I watch her closely and scream when she impales the knife into my thigh and twists before she rips it out. I sob at the red-hot pain that shot through me when she stabs me.

"You have no idea just how crazy I can be, Shayla." Sophie calmly states like she didn't just stab me in the fucking leg. "Tristan and I were always meant to be together. If it weren't for you, showing up and confusing him, he would have come after me, and we'd be together right now. You ruined everything!" I cry out when she slaps me hard across the face. "If I can't have him, neither can you, nor anyone else for that matter."

I lift my eyes and look up at her, horrified. "Oh my God."

Sophie takes hold of my face and looks into my eyes. "I tried to warn you, but you didn't listen. My warnings fell on deaf ears, so this is on you. You brought this on yourself."

Tears blur my vision as I peer up at her. "The plane crash...it was you. You tried to kill him!" I pull my face out of her grasp, yanking on my restraints, desperately trying to break free so that I could tear the bitch limb from limb.

"You were supposed to be with him on that plane!" Sophie shouts. "After all the pain you put me through, you both deserved to die, but then I found out he went alone, and when he survived and lost his memory, that was my chance to win him back, but you..." I wince when she grabs me by the throat and squeezes tight cutting off my oxygen. "You manipulated him and stole him from me *again*!" Sophie barks, digging her nails into my flesh before she lets go, and I suck in a lung full of air.

I glance down at my leg, panting through the searing pain of my stab wound and the lack of oxygen in my lungs. I see blood seeping through and staining my dress.

This lunatic is going to kill me. I'm not making it out of this. I lift my tear-filled gaze to hers and glare at her. "This time, you won't be around to screw with his head. If it weren't for you, *I* would have been married to him, and we would have been happy with our baby boy." She states, looking at the blade in her hand stained with my blood.

"That baby wasn't Coles. Do you think he wouldn't have found out eventually? I walked away from him countless times so he could be with you, but he didn't want you then, and he won't want you now. Why don't you understand he doesn't love you, Sophie!" I shout in her face, and she presses her lips into a thin line and looks at me.

"Oh, but he will." She replies with a pout. "When he gets that call informing him that they found his dear wife's beaten, dead body on the side of the road, Cole will need someone to comfort him through all of that grief." A gradual, knowing smile spreads across her plastic face while I look at her in alarm. "And I'll be there every day, consoling him and taking care of your beautiful daughter until he slowly but surely falls in love with me again." She grins, biting her glossy lips. "It's a good thing Alaia is so young because she won't remember you. She'll grow up and love *me* as her mother." I stare at her, tears rolling down my cheeks.

"You're delusional. Cole got his memory back, he remembers everything." I whisper icily. "He will never let our daughter forget me. Even if he did, my family will not. You will never be her mother, you psychotic bitch. Your own child couldn't bear to be yours and died before he was born. Probably a good thing too, because you clearly don't possess a maternal bone in your body—" I whimper when she slaps me again.

Sophie grabs my face and turns me to face her. I open my eyes and stare at her, wincing through the painful throbbing of my cheek. "You can kill me all you want, but I will always be there, in Cole's heart, living on through my daughter. You will never have them. Ever!" I exclaim, spitting in her face, and hiss when she slaps me once again with the back of her hand. The metallic taste of my blood makes my stomach churn whilst she wipes her face and glowers at me.

"It's only a matter of time, Shayla." Sophie drawls and smirks darkly. "We have a special connection Tristan and I. He's never been able to stay away from me for too long. Did he tell you that he made love to me after he left you? While you were falling apart, he was in my bed, making me come again and again." She claims, and I stare at her, and despite my crippling distress, I laugh haughtily while she watches me, a look of surprise on her face.

"Oh my God, you're so pathetic, Sophie." I chuckle, shaking my head. "A special connection? Do you seriously believe the shit that comes out of your mouth? You and Cole have nothing, you didn't then, and you don't now. He told me he didn't lay a finger on you while we were broken up, so your pitiful attempt to hurt me is all in vain. You're nothing but a manipulative, bitter shrew."

Sophie stares at me for a long moment before she rolls her eyes. "Any last words?"

"Fuck you!"

Sophie smiles malevolently and looks over at the two men in the room with us.

"She's all yours, do what you want with her." She tells the taller one, who turns his dark gaze to me when Sophie spins on her heels to walk out the door. "Just do me one favour..." She looks at me and grins darkly. "Make it hurt." I stare at her retreating back and jump when the door slams shut behind her. I lift my gaze to the men in the room with me, shaking my head, and finally allow that strangled sob to escape me as they advance toward me.

"COLEE!"

Chapter 26

COLE

"COLEE!"

I jump awake and sit upright, panting into the darkness. I reach over and turn the night lamp on, blinking till my eyes adjust to the light. I look back when I feel a warm hand on my shoulder and close my eyes, biting my lip.

"You okay, baby?" I heave a sigh and turn my head to look at my beautiful wife blinking up at me sleepily. I pull her into my arms and hug her tight.

I sigh, closing my eyes while I inhale her scent. "Thank god. I just had a horrendous nightmare that you and Alaia were kidnapped, and you were crying, pleading for me to save you." I exhale, and Shayla pulls back a little, looking at me with those gorgeous green eyes of hers.

"It was just a dream, baby," Shayla assures me, her hand stroking my face lovingly. "I'm right here, and look—our daughter is asleep in her bed." She says, looking over at Alaia, who was indeed peacefully asleep in her crib beside her. I take her face into my hands and kiss her again and again.

"Thank God. I was so scared, baby. I thought I lost you both." I whisper, pulling back to look into her eyes, and she smiles at me affectionately.

"I'm going to be with you forever, baby. I'm locked away in your heart, remember?" She declares, rubbing my jaw with her soft fingers, and I close my eyes, leaning into her touch.

"Of course you are. Please don't ever leave me, baby." I beg, looking into her beautiful face, and she grins, kissing me softly.

"I'll be with you for as long as you love me, honey." I smile and brush my nose over hers softly.

"Good, because I'm going to love you forever." Shayla laughs and curls her fingers around my neck, and draws my lips to hers.

"Shayla." I jump awake and look around the empty living room and sigh, closing my eyes when that ache in my chest returns full throttle. It was just another dream; they're not here. I've been having the same reoccurring nightmare for days. I keep seeing Shayla crying while holding Alaia and calling out for me to save her. I look over at the clock on my phone, and it's showing 6:25 am. It's been four days, and still no word on their whereabouts. The police have no leads and no clue why someone would kidnap Shayla and Alaia and have not asked for money yet. I found Blake, and I went over there with Josh and Sam the night before. I know the police said not to, but I couldn't just sit around anymore. It was driving me crazy. I didn't even care if I got arrested.

As soon as his housekeeper had opened the door, we all stormed in. "Where's Blake?" I barked at her, and she jumps back, terrified, and points down the corridor.

"In his study." She replied in a thick foreign accent. We stormed over to where she was pointing, opening every door till I found the one I was looking for. I barge in with Sam and Josh hot on my tail. Blake turns and looks at me first, then Josh and Sam with a frown. He hangs up the phone as I stride over to him.

"Where is she?!" I bark, grabbing him by the collar of his shirt. "Where's my wife?!"

Blake looks at me, his scowl deepening. "Cole, I don't know. I honestly don't. I haven't seen or spoken to Shayla since Christmas when I saw her at the mall." He explains, and I search his face. "Why would I kidnap your wife and baby. I have my own daughter to think about."

"You're lying!" I hiss through clenched teeth, and he sighs, closing his eyes. "I saw the way you look at her. You pretended to be her friend so that you could get close to her, didn't you? Huh, didn't you?!"

"Where the fuck is my sister, you little prick!" Sam bellows, fighting in Josh's hold to get to Blake, who opens his eyes and looks at me.

"Cole, I get your upset, and you're right; I was attracted to Shayla initially, and did I hope we could have been more. Yes, I did entertain the thought for a minute or two, but she's in love with you man, she made that clear to me from the beginning. Why the fuck would I waste my time kidnapping a girl who is in love with another man and will never love me. I have a daughter myself. I'm all she has. I would never do that to her; she's my whole world." Blake explains, and when my hold loosens on his shirt, he pushes me off him. "The police are already investigating me, and I'm cooperating and ready to do whatever it takes to help them find Shay and your baby. I have nothing to hide. I didn't kidnap them, I swear." He adds earnestly, and I back away from him. If it wasn't Blake, then who the fuck has them?

"If it wasn't this dickhead, who the fuck was it then?" Sam snaps agitated as he paces back and forth. "Where the fuck are they, man." He groans, rubbing his head irately.

"Cole, I care about Shayla, she's an amazing person, and if there is anything at all I can do to help, all you have to do is ask." He offers as I stare at the ground numbly.

"I don't understand." I utter, shaking my head, my eyes drowned in tears. "I just want them back."

Blake nods and puts his hand on my shoulder. "I'm so sorry, truly I am. Shayla is the last person to deserve this. I'm going to do whatever I can to help you find them." Blake says, and I lift my gaze to look at him.

"I appreciate it, thank you," I reply, and we shake hands before I turn and walk out of his office toward the front door. I stop when I see a little girl in the housekeeper's arms in the living room as I pass by. My heart clenches painfully, and I bite back the sob and rush out of his house.

I rub my hands tiredly over my face and stare up at the plain white ceiling. Four days—

that's all it's been, but to me, it feels like four years. This house is too quiet without them, the silence is deafening, and I feel like I'm drowning slowly. My phone suddenly rings, and I jump and snatch it off the coffee table—an unknown number. I press the green button and answer it hurriedly, my heart pounding. "Hello?"

"Good Morning Mr Hoult. I'm calling from the Chatham police station." My heart rate accelerates. Oh, God. "We need you to come down to the station immediately. We found a baby, and we believe it may be your daughter." The man on the other end says, and I feel a flood of relief wash over me.

"Are you sure?" I ask, my voice barely an octave over a whisper.

"Yes, sir, there's a note here to call you. If you could make your way down to the station, and you can identify the baby."

I stand up and nod, "Oh my God, I'll be right there." I grab my keys and run out the door. I stop when I see photographers at the gate. They start shouting and snapping photos as I rush over to my car.

"Move!" I shout as I try to drive out of my gate. The police officers guarding the house rush over and push the photographers away from my car. "Fucking vultures." The news of Shayla and Alaia's disappearance was all over the media, an urgent appeal with photos to anyone who might have seen or have any information on their whereabouts to get in touch with the police.

I call Josh as I'm driving. "Cole?" Comes his sleepy voice. "What's wrong? Any news?"

"They found Alaia," I tell him and hear him shuffling on his end. "I just got a call from the police station in Chatham. They found her with a note to call me."

Josh stays silent for a beat. "Really? Bro, I'm so relieved. What about Shayla?"

My heart sinks at the mention of her name. I shake my head as I stare ahead at the road. "They didn't mention her."

Josh sighs, "Do you want me to come to the station?" He asks, and I shake my head again.

"No, it's fine. I'm anxious to see my baby, but I'm so terrified at the same time. I'm scared I'm going to go there, and it's not going to be Alaia like someone's playing a sick joke on me."

"It's going to be her. Call me as soon as you get her or have any more information. Aimee and I will come over in a couple of hours." Josh sighs, and I nod, chewing anxiously on my bottom lip.

"Okay, I'll keep you updated." I end the call and release a shaky breath, a million thoughts going through my mind. Why did they agree to let Alaia go? Nothing about this makes any sense. What would they want with Shayla? If they don't want money, what do they want from us? I pull up at the police station and race inside toward the reception. "Cole Hoult, I got a call they found my baby," I say in a flurry, and the girl at the desk asks me to take a seat while she gets someone. I pace frantically, running my fingers through my already messy hair repeatedly.

"Mr Hoult." I turn when I hear my name and see Detective Scott motioning me toward him. "I got a call early this morning and came over right away." He says as we walk through the barriers further into the station. "We had a doctor come out and look her over. Your daughter hasn't been harmed in any way. She's perfectly fine." He adds, opening the door, we walk into a room, and my heart thumps when I see Alaia in the arms of an officer.

"Alaia!" I cry out, rush over to her, and take her into my arms. I kiss her beautiful face as I hold her tight against my chest. "Oh, baby, thank god." I sob, burying my nose into her hair. "You're okay. You're okay, baby girl. Daddy's got you now." I pull back and look at her, my heart racing a mile a minute. I'm so relieved she's okay. "Where did they find her?" I ask Detective Scott, and he sighs.

"She was dropped off at the station early hours this morning." He explains, rubbing his forehead. "She was left outside the station. The security team saw someone dressed in all black with their face covered leave the car seat by the steps and took off running. We sent a patrol out to scan the area, but they were gone. CCTV is being checked now to see if we can track them down. We'll find them, Mr Hoult."

"What about Shayla?" I question cagily, rubbing Alaia's back, and

Detective Scott rubs the back of his neck. "Why would they let Alaia go if they're going to ask for money? It makes no sense."

"It's hard to say, could be many reasons why they let the baby go and kept your wife. Taking the baby may not have been part of their plan. Shayla seems to be the target from the beginning for whatever reason. The fact they haven't made any contact or demands yet is unsettling. It could also be a possibility that Shayla made some sort of deal with her abductors."

I blanch at his words and look down at Alaia, who fusses in my hold. "Are you saying..."

"She may have sacrificed herself to protect her baby." Detective Scott states sullenly. I still at his words, and dread fills my gut. Tears blur my vision as the realisation that Shayla might be dead hits me like a tidal wave. Of course she sacrificed herself; that's why they let Alaia go. Oh, God. "Cole, listen to me, don't think the worst just yet. It's only been four days. It's just speculation at this point, all right. We're going to find her."

I look down at Alaia, who looks up at me, and I see Shayla staring back at me. My heart quivers. "Get your baby home and try to get some rest. We'll be in touch if we find something." He says and squeezes my shoulder. I nod numbly and take the baby's changing bag Shayla had with her when she went missing and strap Alaia into a car seat. I pick the note up they found with Alaia and look at it. My name and phone number were typed across the paper. I squeeze my eyes shut and swallow the lump in my throat.

Please don't leave us, Shay. Just hold on, baby. Wherever you are, please hold on.

I carry Alaia to the car and strap her into the passenger seat beside me. I kiss her hand a couple of times and close the door. I get into the car and sit there, staring ahead. I bite my lip hard, and in a rage, I punch the steering wheel a couple of times; choking on a sob, I press my head to the wheel and cry forlornly. God, please protect her, please bring her back to us safely. I don't want anything else. Just get her back to me.

Once I pull myself together, I drive back home. Alaia asleep in the car seat beside me. I sigh when I see the photographers were still camped out outside the house. The police officers usher them out of the way as the gate opens, and they snap photo after photo of me as I pull Alaia out of the car.

"Tristan, is there any news on Shayla?!"

"Tristan, where did they find Alaia? Where is Shayla?! Is it true that she's been killed?!"

"Get them out of here!" I shout angrily at the officers, who nod and start ushering them away from the house. I ignore the questions they were screaming at me and rush Alaia inside the house and lean against the door for a couple of minutes. She's not been killed. She's not. I set Alaia's car seat down on the floor and unclip her, gently lifting her into my arms. I kiss her head and sit on the sofa with her curled up on my chest. I take out my phone and call Shayla's mother and brother to tell them I have Alaia. Sara burst into tears sobbing uncontrollably on the phone and said she would be right over with Sam.

"Where's your Mummy, Alaia. What are they doing to her?" I whisper into her hair. I have to find her, but I don't know where to look. I've been racking my brain for days, trying to figure out why anyone would want to hurt Shayla. I feel so powerless. I have all the money in the world and no clue what I can do to find her. I wish they would just call and ask for money in exchange for her life. I'll give them everything I have, the clothes off my back, only to have her home safe. I look down when Alaia suddenly jumps startled in my arms and makes crying sounds and sniffles in her sleep. It was such a heartfelt cry it broke me. "Shhh, what's wrong, baby. It's okay. It's okay, sweetheart." I whisper, rubbing her back soothingly, and she settles, sighing and whining in her sleep. I wonder if she's having a nightmare or if she's just missing Shayla. There is no stronger bond than a mother and her baby, after all.

"Mummy will be back with us really soon, baby, I promise you." I sigh, kissing her head and closing my eyes. I sniff Alaia and frown; she doesn't smell like her usual herself. She smells like perfume and not the kind Shayla uses. It smelt familiar to me, but I couldn't remember where I had smelt it before. It definitely wasn't Shayla's perfume. She hates heavy floral fragrances. The ringing of the doorbell distracts me and starts Alaia from her sleep, and she starts to cry. I sigh and get up, rocking her gently while I walk to the door. I open it and see Shayla's mother and Sam at the door. Sara was a wreck. Her eyes were rimmed red and swollen, her face blotchy and tear-stained. She takes one look at Alaia and starts sobbing. Reaching out, she takes her from me and hugs her tightly, kissing her hands.

"Oh sweetheart, thank God you're okay. Oh, I prayed and prayed for you both to be found safe." She cries, kissing her forehead again and again. I close the door once they walk in and sit on the sofa, my head in my hands.

"Where did they find her?" Sam asks, sitting opposite me. I lift my head and look at him.

"They dropped her off at the police station early hours this morning with a note to call me to collect her."

"And Shayla?" Sam whispers, his voice strained, and I shake my head slowly.

"No word on her yet. They think she..." I say and bite my lip hard, swallowing my next words, unable to say them out loud.

"Think she what, Cole?" Sam questions fretfully, and I stare at him, tears rolling down my face.

"They think she might have made a deal with whoever took her. Her life in exchange for Alaia to be returned home safely." I sigh, dropping my gaze to the ground; I couldn't stand the look of despair in her brother's eyes as the possibility of his sister being killed dawns on him.

"Nah, nah, nah." He shakes his head vigorously and stands up, his hands on his head. "I refuse to believe that she's gone. She's fine, you hear me. SHE'S FINE!" He shouts, breaking down, his shoulders shaking as he sobs uncontrollably. "We can't lose her too!"

I hear her mother's sobs behind me as she hugs Alaia. "Your sister will come back to us, Samuel. She will. She has too." She cries, walking over to us. "Pull yourselves together. We have to stay strong for her and pray that she finds her way back home to us. Alaia needs to be fed and bathed. Does Shayla have any more of her milk frozen in the freezer?"

I shake my head sadly. "I don't think so."

"Sam, go out and get some formula," Sara tells her son, who nods, wiping away his tears. "We will not fall apart. Do you understand me?" Sam and I nod, and she gestures with her head for him to go, and he walks to the door. "Ask them what the best one is for three-month-old babies."

Sam opens the door, and I hear muffled voices. I look back and see Aimee and Josh walk in. Aimee runs over to Alaia and starts to cry when she sees her. "Hi Princess, I'm so glad you're okay."

I sigh, closing my eyes. My head was thumping unpleasantly, and Josh squeezes my shoulder, taking a seat beside me. "How are you holding up, bro? Is there anything you need me to do?" He offers, and I shake my head silently.

"I just want her back, man. Why aren't they calling? What the fuck do they want with her? I'm trying to make sense of all of this in my head, but nothing adds up. It makes no sense. Why would anyone want to hurt Shayla? Is someone trying to hurt me? I don't understand Josh, help me figure this out, bro. I'm losing my fucking mind." I cry helplessly, and Josh hugs me.

"We're going to figure it out, bro. One way or the other, the people responsible will be found." He assures me, and we pull apart when the door chimes again.

"I'll get it," Aimee announces and walk to the door to answer it. "Uh, Cole?" She calls out to me, and I stand up and walk over to the door and see a police officer holding a box in his hands. "Looks like a package."

I frown and eye the box. I didn't order anything— unless Shay did. She's always ordering something for Alaia. "This was just delivered for you, sir." The officer says and hands me the box before he turns and walks away.

I walk over to the sofa with the box and use the letter opener to rip open the tape. I open it, and my blood runs cold in my veins. I stare at the box unblinking before I stand up and reach inside with trembling fingers and pull the dress out of the box and hold it up. "Oh, my God."

"Is that...that's Shayla's dress," Aimee states, horrified, and clamps her hand over her mouth. "Is that blood?!"

"Oh, fuck." Josh mutters, staring at Shayla's torn and blood-stained dress. I drop the dress like it burnt my fingers, and it falls to the floor at my feet. I stood frozen in my spot, unable to move or make a sound. Josh runs out of the house to probably tell the officers to catch the person that delivered the box. I hear Aimee's whimpers of despair as I stood there completely and utterly numb. I can hear my heart rate slow drastically and beat deafeningly in my ears. If I didn't believe it before, I believed it now. Shayla wasn't coming back. They sent me her dress only to confirm my suspicions. I felt my stomach lurch at the thought of Shayla being hurt or worse. I run to the sink in the kitchen and dry heave. I had nothing in my stomach to throw up. I slide down to the floor, panting forcefully. She's not coming back. It wasn't until a little while later I heard Shayla's mother's scream when she saw her daughter's dress.

I couldn't believe it— I didn't want to. I didn't want to accept that my Shayla was gone. She couldn't be. "Cole." I blink, and tears fall from my eyes when I slowly lift my eyes to look at Detective Scott and Josh standing in front of me. Josh was crying behind the Detective, and I stare at him. "A body has been discovered matching your wife's description."

Chapter 27

COLE

"COLE." I lift my gaze and look at a teary-eyed Josh and shake my head from my position on the floor. We were at the mortuary, and I had to go in and identify the body. As soon as I see a body on that table, covered with a white cloth, my back hit the wall, and I slid to the floor with my head in my hands.

"I can't do it." I sob uncontrollably, shaking my head. "That can't be her lying there, Josh. it can't be!" I cry, covering my face with my hand as I weep. "I don't want to remember her like that. I can't do it." If I see her lying there, lifeless and cold, that's how I'll remember her. That image will haunt me forever.

"Cole, you have to. I know it's hard, but she's suffered enough. Let's do this so we can put her to rest if it is her."

His words wrecked me. *Put her to rest.* I don't want to put her to rest. I want her to wake up, so I can take her home with me, back to our baby girl who misses her terribly, back to her family who needs her.

"I can't, Josh, I can't. I fucking can't!"

"Come on, bro. I'll be right there with you." Josh assures and lifts me to my feet, and he pulls me toward the table. My heart was beating wildly in my chest, making it impossible to catch my breath. We wait while the man pulls the cloth back slowly. I take one look at the body, and I fall to my knees, screaming with my head in my hands.

Josh kneels beside me and wraps his arms around me while I cry uncontrollably. He looks up at the man and shakes his head, wiping away his tears. "It's not her." He rubs my back and presses his head to mine. "It's not her, bro. It's not her." Josh keeps repeating, reassuring me as I sob wretchedly. "Let's go, come on." Josh helps me up to my feet again, and we walk out of the morgue. I was so relieved it wasn't her lying in there, but that doesn't mean she was alive either. It could only be a matter of time before I'm back in there, and what if it is her next time? The fear alone of losing her is gut-wrenching, but the reality is much, much worse than I could have ever imagined.

"I'm so sorry you had to go through that, Cole, but this is good news. It means your wife could still be alive." Detective Scott says as he follows us out of the room.

"Could be," I mutter sullenly. "What are you waiting for? How long till I'm hauled back in there, and it is Shayla lying dead on that table? They could be doing anything to her, she's obviously hurt, and you're still sitting on your thumbs! Do your fucking job and find her before they kill her!" I shout angrily, glaring at him.

"Cole, we're doing everything we can; we're following every lead possible to find them. They're still looking through the CCTV footage, but it takes time. I assure you we are all working very hard to track your wife down."

"While you're working 'very hard', they're holding her captive doing god only knows what to her. They're sending packages to the house, dropping the baby off to your doorstep, and you still can't find a damn lead as to where they're keeping her?" Josh questions, his brows fused tightly. I close my eyes and rub my temples agitated. The more I think about them hurting Shayla, the angrier and more powerless I felt.

"There has to be something we could do. Anything is better than sitting around, waiting, and wondering. Every second that passes by is a second longer Shayla suffers." Josh states, and Detective Scott nods.

"Unfortunately, there isn't anything you can do. Other than pray and hope someone comes forward with some information, or we catch a lead. We have to be patient." He claims, and Josh looks over at me. "We've sent the dress off to forensics to be tested. We'll find something.

In cases like these, something is always overlooked or missed, and I promise you, we will find it soon."

"By the time you find whatever you're looking for, they could kill her and dump her body someplace and disappear!" I hiss through clenched teeth and rub my hands over my face shaking my head. "I can't. I can't be in here anymore. I can't fucking breathe." I storm off outside and suck in a lungful of air. I lift my gaze up to the sky and bite my lip hard. Where are you, Shay. Where are you love of my life? Please, sweetheart, find your way back to me. Don't leave me here to go on without you, please. Just hold on for me, hold on for us. I look back when I feel Josh's hand on my shoulder.

"Let's get back." He sighs, and I nod, following him to his car. I sit in the passenger seat, staring up at the gloomy grey sky as the rain hits the window. I lose myself in the memories of Shayla and me. This isn't how it's supposed to go for us. We're supposed to have more babies and grow old and grey together. We're supposed to share our messy love story with our grandchildren while we're sitting in our rocking chairs at eighty, just like she promised me. I still have so much I want to do with her, so much of her I haven't even kissed yet, so many things I haven't said to her. Please, don't let this be the end of us. I can't live without her. I don't know how to. "Stop," I gasp suddenly, sitting forward when I see a church. "Stop the car!" I tell Josh, and he looks around frantically and slams his foot on the brakes.

"What is it?" He asks quickly, and I push the door open and run across the street toward the church. I push the door open and walk inside. I'm not a religious man, but she was, and if anyone was going to help her right now, it was God himself. I walk down the aisle toward the prayer desk and look up at the statue of Jesus Christ staring down at me. I fall to my knees, lace my fingers together, and close my eyes.

"God, I wasn't raised to believe in anyone other than myself. I know, I probably have no right being here and asking you of anything, having no faith— but my wife has always had faith, and she prays and is a good person. I'm desperate, and you're the only one I can turn to for help and guidance right now. I'm begging you. Please help Shayla, please keep her safe and give her the strength to keep on fighting and find her way home to me and our baby girl. I'll do anything. I'll come to church every Sunday. I'll donate more money and time to those in need. I'll give up everything I have, just please, please help me find her." I cry in despair. "We only just found each other again. Don't take her from us," I whisper and lift my gaze to the statue again. I get up and wipe my tears before I turn and walk past Josh, standing there watching me pray, his blue eyes swimming in tears.

We get back in the car and drive back to the house. There were even more people loitering outside the house. As soon as we approach, Josh's security team clears the pathway to the house. He rolls down the window as we drive in through the gates. "Stay alert, and if anything suspicious catches your eye, you call me, understand?" He commands, and the boys nod in response. "Everyone needs to be checked and cleared before they come near the house." He adds before he drives toward the house and pulls up. I look at the paparazzi and frown. I get out of the car and walk over to the gate. "Cole? What are you doing?" Josh asks, grabbing my arm, and I turn to look at him.

"If they won't call me, I'll reach out to them. I'm going to get my wife back, whatever it costs me." I pull my arm and gesture for them to open the gates, and Josh follows me and stands beside me, his eyes scanning every face in front of us. The cameras flash in my face blinding me momentarily, and I blink a couple of times. "I have a message to the people who are holding my wife captive. I don't know why you've taken her or what you want, but please, I am begging you, don't hurt her. If it's money you want, I'm ready to pay whatever it is; just let her come home. I'll give up everything I have; please don't hurt her and get in contact with me. Shayla, if you see this, please hold on, baby. I'm going to find you whatever it takes. I love you more than anything. Please come home to us." I cry and allow Josh to pull me back toward the house while everyone screams and shouts questions at us.

As soon as we walk into the house, everyone gets up to their feet and looks at us. Each person was looking more wrecked than the next. "It wasn't her," I announce and watch the flood of relief that washes over their faces. Mine and Shay's mother sob and sink onto the sofa. Sam kneels with his head in his hands while Jo consoles him crying, and Aimee runs into Josh's arms, sobbing. My Dad walks over to me and pulls me in for a hug, and I cry into his shoulder.

"She's going to come home, son." He assures, rubbing my back. "Don't give up hope. Shayla's a strong girl; she won't give up without a fight."

"I don't know how much longer she can hold out for Dad. God knows what they're doing to her." I sigh distraughtly, wiping my eyes, and walk over to where Alaia was asleep in her bouncer, her little arms wrapped around one of Shayla's t-shirts.

"She cried herself to sleep. She's not feeding Cole. She's refusing to take the bottle with the formula milk. We couldn't get her to stop crying until we gave her a t-shirt that smelt like Shayla, and she finally fell asleep." Sara tells me, sobbing into her tissue, and I look down at my baby and close my eyes.

"She misses her. Oh, God, what am I going to do?" I sob, curling my fingers in my hair and rocking back and forth. "She won't take anything but her mother's breastmilk. How am I supposed to feed her? She's going to starve."

"I've called a paediatrician. They'll be here soon to help find a solution. If she refuses to eat, they might have to take her into the hospital and feed her through a tube till she takes the formula." My mother explains, and I shake my head sullenly, brushing my thumb over her little hand. I'm not the only one suffering and missing her. Alaia's sensing it too.

The doorbell chimes, and I look back at Josh, who goes to answer it. He pulls it open and scowls. "The fuck? What do *you* want?" Aimee utters icily while walking over to the door. I wipe my eyes and walk over to the door and scowl when I see Sophie standing there. She's the last person I expected to see.

"Sophie?" I mutter, looking her over, and she looks at me, her blue eyes apologetic.

"Tristan, I heard about Shayla and your baby getting kidnapped and wanted to come and check up on you and see if there's anything I could do to help?" She claims, walking into the house, but Aimee blocks her path.

"Yeah, you can fuck off back to whatever hole you just crawled out of." Aimee hisses, and Sophie turns her gaze to Aimee and looks at her sadly.

"Look, I know Shayla, and I never saw eye to eye. And I'm not without my mistakes, but I wouldn't wish this on my worst enemy. It's truly awful, and I can't even imagine how concerned you must all be feeling." Sophie asserts, sweeping her blonde hair out of her face and tucking it behind her ear. She looks at me and tries to take a step but stops when Jo puts her hand up, stopping her, coming to stand beside Aimee, both girls glaring at her. "I just wanted to make sure you were okay and offer my support. Please, Tristan, let me be there for you? We were friends before anything else." She says and looks at Josh pleadingly. "Josh?"

"He doesn't need your support, you little wench. I had a feeling you were going to come out of the woodwork again, you've sniffed out an opportunity to dig your claws into Cole, but I won't let that happen." Aimee says, taking a threatening step toward Sophie, who looks at me ruefully.

"Aimee, Jo, let her through." I sigh tiredly, not having the energy to fight. Aimee looks at me sharply, and I nod slowly. The girls back away, letting her pass, although they didn't take their eyes off her for a second as she strolls over to me.

"I'm so sorry, Tristan. You must be beside yourself with worry." She offers, rubbing my arm supportively. "Have you heard anything at all? Are they any closer to finding her?" She asks, and I sigh, rubbing my forehead.

"No, nothing yet. They're searching, and we're all here waiting for some sort of news." I explain and walk into the kitchen. She follows me and watches as I lean against the kitchen island. "I just don't understand what they want with her."

Sophie walks over to me and nods slowly. "Tristan, don't think the worst, they'll find her, and she'll be back home with you where she belongs, sweetie. Whoever took her returned your baby safely. They might let her go too."

I look at my feet and sigh. "It's been four days since they took her. They sent us her dress, which was torn and covered in blood. Wherever she is or whoever she's with, she's not safe. I know that for sure." I say, tears spilling over and running down my cheeks. "I just want her home alive and well."

"Oh, sweetie, she will be," Sophie assures me, wrapping her arms around my neck. "It's going to be okay. If you need anything, all you have to do is ask. I'm here for you always." I sigh, closing my eyes, and wrap an arm around her waist. I open my eyes and turn my head when a familiar smell hits my senses. I know that smell. That floral...perfume. The scent on Alaia. I pull back from the hug and look at her for a long moment. No, Cole, stop being stupid. Sophie would never do something this crazy. I blink and clear my throat.

"I'm going to use the bathroom. Why don't you grab yourself a drink? I'll be back in a second." I tell her, and she nods, smiling a little. I watch her as she walks over to the fridge as I walk out of the kitchen. "Josh," I call out, and he looks at me from the sofa. I gesture for him to follow me, and he gets up, following me as I run up the stairs to the bedroom.

"What's wrong?" Josh asks, watching me as I rummage through Alaia's laundry basket. I pull out the outfit she was wearing when I got her and sniff it. I pull it away from my nose and pull my shirt and sniff the perfume that had rubbed off onto my shirt. It's the same smell.

"Smell that." I give him Alaia's outfit, and he sniffs it and looks at me, his eyes narrow a little. "Now smell this." I pull my shirt, and he leans in closer, sniffing before he pulls back, looking at me bewildered. "It's the same smell, right? I'm not crazy?"

Josh looks at Alaia's outfit and then at me and nods. "Yeah, it's the same for sure. Why?"

"When I picked Alaia up from the station and brought her home, I smelt this perfume on her clothes," I explain, and Josh frowns. "I knew it was familiar, but I couldn't place it. It's not Shayla's smell. She hates perfumes with strong floral smells; it gives her a headache. It wasn't until Sophie just hugged me that I placed the smell. It's Coco Chanel, I know because it's Sophie's favourite perfume. I bought it for her." I explain quietly, and Josh's eyes grow wide. "Think about it? Why would Alaia come back smelling like a perfume that's not her mother's? And who hates Shayla and would benefit from her disappearance?"

"Sophie," Josh utters, his eyes narrowed. "Surely she wouldn't go this fucking far, man. That's some fucked up accusation, Cole. We're talking about kidnapping and possibly manslaughter; she couldn't have fallen that far off the reserve surely." Josh whispers furiously, watching me as I pace frantically.

"Josh, think about it. No demands have been made for ransom. Sophie doesn't need the money she's loaded, so she's got the resources to hire people. Alaia's returned safely, but Shayla isn't, and she shows up the same day as the baby and the dress?"

"No, you're right. It's too much of a coincidence. I'm going to tell the police outside and call the detective. You keep her here." He says and runs out of the bedroom. How the fuck did I not even consider Sophie. I'll fucking kill her. I exhale deeply and rush downstairs. I see her sitting on the sofa gazing down at Alaia, smiling knowingly. Goddamn psychotic bitch. I stride over, grab her by the arm, and lift her to her feet, dragging her to the foyer.

"Where is she?!" I shout, glaring at her. Everyone gets up to their feet, watching us. "WHAT HAVE YOU DONE WITH HER?!" I roar in her face, and Sophie looks up at me, startled.

"Tristan, what are you talking about? Done with who?" She asks, looking up at me, her blue eyes wide. I grab her by the throat and slam her hard against the wall, and she cries out.

"I'll fucking kill you, Sophie, I swear to GOD! Where's Shayla?!" I bellow, glaring stormily at her.

"Cole, what's going on?" Aimee asks, coming up behind me.

"It's her! She's the one that's kidnapped, Shayla!" I growl, tightening my grip on her throat and her eyes go wide, and she gasps, trying to pry my fingers from her throat.

"Tristan, I can't breathe." She gasps, and I loosen my hold, not wanting to kill her before telling me where Shayla was.

"I know it's you. Alaia came home smelling like your fucking perfume! You fucking psycho, where is she?! TALK!" I roar, looking into her wide blue eyes as she stares at me. I'm ripped away from her, and she falls to the floor, coughing and gasping. Police officers hold me back as I go for her again.

I watch Aimee as she walks over to Sophie and grabs her by the hair, lifting her back to her feet. "I should have fucking known it was you! What did you do with her? I'll fucking rip your head off bitch, what have you done with Shayla?!" She screams before she punches her in the face, and Sophie hits the floor with a whimper. Josh grabs Aimee and lifts her into his arms as she goes for her again.

"I don't know what you're talking about?!" Sophie cries, wiping the blood seeping from her mouth. "Why would I kidnap Shayla? You're all crazy." She cries, getting up to her feet.

"If anyone would want her gone, it's you! You'll do anything to get Cole back! That's why you're here, after all, aren't you? Your puny little brain thought if Shayla were out of the picture for good, Cole would come running to you! Didn't you?!" Aimee screams, and for a fleeting second, I see Sophie's guise slip, and the evil shone in her eyes before they went back to the usual rueful façade she was putting on.

"I only came here to check on a friend. Since when has that been a crime!" Sophie argues, brushing away her crocodile tears. "I'm going to have you arrested for assault." She cries, looking at the blood on her finger when she touches her lip.

"Good! I'll fucking finish you off on the inside then, you crazy bitch!" Aimee sneers, fighting in Josh's hold.

"Sophie, where is Shayla?! What have you done with her?!" I growl, trying to break free from the officer's hold on me, and she looks at me shaking her head.

"I can't believe you would accuse me of such a thing, Tristan. I came

307

here with good intentions, and look at how you're treating me. I can't believe I ever loved you!" She sobs, trying to walk out, but Jo steps in her way and glares at her.

"You're not going anywhere bitch. You better start talking, or I'm going to rip your hair from your head and punch those veneers so far down your throat you'll be shitting out teeth for the rest of your life." She threatens, advancing toward her. "What have you done with my best friend?" Sophie backs up against the wall.

"I haven't done anything to her! I don't know anything about her kidnapping, I swear."

"Stop lying!" Jo screams and slaps her hard across the face. "If you thought for a second, we would have ever allowed you to get close to Cole and Alaia, you're dumber than you fucking look."

"Yeah, over our dead bodies, bitch!" Aimee hisses in Josh's hold. Sam walks over and pulls Jo away from Sophie, and glares at her darkly. He's unusually calm, which is never a good sign.

"Where's my sister?" He almost whispers to her, and she backs away from him and throws me a beseeching look. "Look at me when I'm talking to you!" Sam snaps, making her jump. "You better start talking and tell us where my sister is, or I swear to God I will do far worse than kill you. I know people in dark places, and I will make you disappear quicker than you fucking blink." He tells her calmly, and tears roll down Sophie's face as she stares at him.

"I didn't do anything." She whispers, shaking her head, terror evident in the depths of her blue eyes. Detective Scott walks into the house and pulls Sam away from Sophie.

"Sophie Turner, I am arresting you on suspicion of kidnapping, you do not have to say anything, but it may harm your defence if you do not mention when questioned something you later rely on in court..."

Chapter 28

COLE

"I'M GOING to ask you one more time." Detective Scott sighs tiredly. "Where is Shayla Hoult?" I watch behind the glass as Sophie rolls her eyes and shrugs her shoulder.

"I don't know. How many times do I have to keep repeating myself? I don't have anything to do with her kidnapping. Those people are all crazy, and they've poisoned Tristan against me. If anyone should be arrested, it's him. He was trying to kill me. They all were!" She shrieks, sitting forward in her seat. "I'm going to press charges on every one of them." She mutters, touching her swollen lip.

"Miss Turner, I don't think you've quite comprehended the gravity of the allegations and charges you're facing here. You had an innocent woman and her baby kidnapped and helped captive. You're facing some serious charges, two counts of kidnapping with intent to cause harm, false imprisonment, and manslaughter. We've got evidence that proves you're guilty of the charges against you, so the sooner you tell us where you're keeping, Shayla, the less harsh your sentence will be. However, if you continue to be uncooperative, I'll personally make sure every hour that Shayla is kept captive adds on another year to your sentence." Detective Scott informs her, and Sophie blanches and looks at her lawyer, who clears his throat.

"Detective, please refrain from threatening my client. Where is this so-called evidence you speak of?" He asks, and Detective Scott pushes a file toward him, which he opens and reads.

"Your client's perfume matched the one all over Alaia Hoult's clothes down the to the last note. We also found a strand of your client's hair on her clothes when she was dropped off at the station. Which the lab has confirmed matches the one we took from you at the time of your arrest. Your fingerprints have matched up to the ones on the car seat. Do I need to go on?" He adds, leaning back in his chair, his arms crossed. "Where is she?"

Sophie exchanges a glance with her lawyer, who nods and leans in to whisper something in her ear, and she frowns; a look of horror crosses her features, and her shoulders fall. "She was taken and being held at a house in Canterbury." She confesses, fiddling with her nails. My heart thumped hard in my chest, and I place my hand on the glass as I glare at her through the window, my fist clenching and unclenching. They took her all the way to Canterbury. That's fucking miles away. "I left her there with the two men that I hired to abduct her. I highly doubt she's still alive. I paid them a lot of money to make sure she wasn't." I gasp and place my hand over my mouth, and tears blur my vision. *Oh, God, no.* She better be fucking lying, or I will kill her with my bare hands.

"You better pray she is alive, Miss Turner. Or else, you'll be facing a hell of a sentence.What's the address to this house, and who are these men you hired?" Detective Scott questions, leaning forward.

"I don't know them. I found them through some people I know. I don't even know their real names. One calls himself H, and the other goes by Big Q. They're not exactly what I would consider the friendly types." Sophie explains, and I hang my head biting back a sob, and shake my head when I feel Josh's hand on my shoulder.

"The *Smith* brothers?" The detective stands and shoves his hand through his unruly blond hair while he paces.

"Oh, *fuck*. She just fucking left her there with two dangerous men." I cry, biting my lip, all sorts of horrific images rushing through my head.

"Cole, I'm fucking scared for her, man. I'm scared of what state we're going to find her in." Josh admits fretfully, tears streaming down his face. I squeeze my eyes shut and sob, punching the wall beside the glass.

The door opens, and Detective Scott walks in holding a paper. "We've got the address. We're going to get her."

"I'm coming too." I declare, wiping away my tears, and Detective Scott shakes his head.

"Cole, you can't come. It could be dangero—"

"I don't give a fuck! I'm coming!" I shout and walk out of the room with Josh following me.

"We're done sitting around and waiting. We're coming...with you or by ourselves." Josh declares and Detective Scott sighs and nods, gesturing for us to follow him through to the back of the station. Officers were running into cars and vans, and they were alerting the ambulance service to be on site.

"You need to stay in the car. These men are twisted and dangerous. They're wanted for a long list of crimes. We don't know what we're walking into, so please let us handle this and trust that we will get your wife out safely."

"All right! Let's just go!" I shout impatiently, and he hands us bullet-proof vests to put on, and we get into the car with the Detective, and we drive, speeding the entire way, blue lights flashing, sirens blaring. It felt forever, the drive to Canterbury was over an hour and a half usually, but with the police cars, we got there in forty-five minutes. I'm coming, Shayla. Just hold on, baby. This place was literally in the middle of the sticks. It was a deserted house and looked like something straight out of a horror movie. Josh and I exchanged concerned glances. The house was surrounded. If the men that took her were in there, they had nowhere to run.

"Stay here and stay down." Detective Scott instructs us, and we nod. He gets out of the car and closes the door.

"Detective, the black unmarked van is parked outside the back door of the house." A voice comes from the radio, and I stare at the house, my leg shaking wildly. I just want to run in there to find Shayla already. I silently pray that she's alive. Please, God, let her be alive. Josh and I watch as they burst through the front door, and we can hear shouting and banging. I shake my head, not being able to sit in the car. I push the door open and get out of the vehicle.

"Cole, don't." I hear Josh as I walk around the car, my eyes glued to the house. He grabs and pulls me, holding me back while I fight in his hold.

"Get the fuck off me. I have to go to her." I hiss, trying to break free, but he holds me tight. I stop when I see the two men being brought out in cuffs. Josh lets go of me, and I race over to them. "Stop!" I shout and look at the men that held my wife captive. They were tall, built, covered in tattoos and scars. The taller one looked me in the eyes, and a slow dark smirk appeared on his face. "You son of a bitch!" I punch him so hard across the face, I felt his jaw crunch and dislocate. He turns his dark gaze to me and winks before they haul them into the van. I push aside my anger and run into the house, followed by Josh. I look around and almost threw up. The place was disgusting, and there was a putrid smell. I push through the police officers to the back of the house.

"Get me something to cut these! And get the paramedics in here now!" I hear Detective Scott's voice shout, and I push through the officers and run into the room and stop. I saw her bloodied feet first, and my blood ran cold. She was tied up and lying on the floor.

"Oh my god." I hear Josh whimper from behind me. I rush over to her, pushing officers out of my way until I saw her on the ground. "Shayla!" I scream, fighting in the officer's hold to get to her. "Let me go!" I growl, shoving them off me, and I move closer to her. She didn't look like herself. She was covered in bruises, bite marks, and cuts. Her hands bound together. Her beautiful face was swollen and covered in bruises like she'd been slapped hard or punched. I fall to my knees beside her and smother the scream that escaped me when I saw her. My entire body was shaking.

"Oh baby," I cry, reaching over to brush my fingers through her damp hair. Her usual soft silky hair tousled. The detective stops me before I could touch her. He shakes his head as he cuts the rope off her wrists, and he winces when he sees the rope burns.

"Don't touch her. Forensics need to take DNA samples. She's alive...barely, but she's alive." He tells me, and I look down at her pale and bloodied face. She was in a black oversize t-shirt and her underwear as she lay unconscious on the floor. Everything inside me ached. I knew she was hurt, but I didn't...I couldn't even imagine it being this bad. What have they done to her?

"Shayla, I'm here. I found you, baby. I'm right here." I cry and move aside when the paramedics come to check her over. They place an oxygen mask over her face, and they lift her eyes lids to check her pupils. Her eyes are bloodshot. I push myself up on my trembling legs and look around the room. I felt sick to my stomach. This was all my fault—this happened to her because of me. I look on the floor and see a pool of her blood by the chair she was probably tied to. I feel Josh's hand on my shoulder and lift my gaze to look at him.

"Josh, what have they done to her?" I cry, looking back at her, and Josh shakes his head sullenly. He visibly paled when he saw the state of her.

"She's alive. That's all that matters right now. Everything else will heal, Cole." He tries to assure me, and I swipe his hand off my shoulder.

"Will it?" I whisper sceptically. "Maybe on the outside, her scars will heal eventually. But will it heal here?" I question, pointing to my temple. "Will it heal here," I point to my heart. "She'll never recover from this, not ever, it will always haunt her forever, and it's all my fucking fault." I cry, shaking my head and walking out of the room, not having the stomach to be in there anymore. I run out of the house and see the van was still there with those fuckers in it. I run over to it and the officers guarding it catch me before I rip the doors open.

"Whoa, easy, buddy." The officer holding me back says, wrapping his arms around me. I see their smug faces looking at me through the caged glass, and my anger flares even more.

"WHAT DID YOU DO TO HER!" I scream, punching the door hard. "YOU SICK SON OF A BITCH! WHY?!" I sob, screaming as I push the officer off me and go for the doors again, but they grab me and haul me away.

"Calm down, or I'll be forced to cuff you and put you in the car." The officer warns me, and I shake him off me.

"You're going to pay! Do you hear me, you sick fucks! You're going to pay for everything you did to her! I'm going to make sure you never see the light of day again!" I threaten, pointing at the rotten bastard who smirks and blows me a kiss. "You and the psychotic bitch that hired you!" Josh drags me away from the van. I was seething. Every time I saw their faces and Shayla's state flashes in my mind, my anger fires up all over again.

"Cole, calm down, or you're going to get yourself arrested. They're going to get what's coming to them, bro. We'll see to that, don't you worry." Josh reassures me, glaring menacingly at the offenders in the van. I turn when I hear voices coming out of the house. They're rolling Shayla out of the house on a stretcher, and I run toward her. "You go with her, and I'll go back to the station and get the car. I'll tell everyone she's been found, and I'll come to the hospital, all right?" Josh says, and I barely nod as I watch them push her into the back of the ambulance. I climb in and sit down on the seat beside her.

"Is she going to be okay?" I ask the paramedic girl worriedly as she puts a cannula on her arm for an IV drip.

"She's in pretty bad shape, but she's hanging in there. Your girl is a fighter. You'll know more when they examine her more extensively at the hospital." She explains, and I lift her hand to take it into mine. "Avoid touching her for now. Police will need forensics to take swabs for any DNA." She explains, pulling her hand away and placing it on her stomach. I nod and wipe away the tears that spill over and run down my face. Shayla coughs a little and groans. I lift my gaze and look at her.

"Shayla?" I lean close, looking at her bruised and bloodied face, and she whimpers. "Baby, can you hear me? I'm right here, sweetheart.

You're safe now." I tell her and wait for her to open her eyes, but she doesn't.

"She's been through quite an ordeal. She's taken a couple of hard blows to her face and head, so she's a little concussed." The paramedic explains, and I sigh, closing my eyes. "How long have you been married?"

"Which time?" I say, not wanting to get into the whole story. "We were married for six months, got divorced, and got married again eight months ago. We've had a very rocky relationship, but I have never loved anyone more than I love that girl right there." I admit, and the paramedic smiles sadly.

"I hope you don't mind me saying, but I'm a huge fan of both you and your wife. I used to see your pictures in the papers or social media all the time and always wish to find someone to look at me the way you'd look at each other. I could just feel the love through the screen of my phone." She states with a smile, and then her face falls when she looks at Shayla. "Then I read about her being abducted and now seeing her like this..."

I look at her, frown and, sit up straight. "Please don't say anything to anyone about what she's suffered. I don't want the papers to find out about what she's gone through and have it all over the internet. It would destroy her even more."

Her brown eyes go wide, and she looks at me, surprised. "Oh, no, I would never. I'd have to be completely heartless to do such a thing. I've always idolized her and hoped I'd meet her one day, but I obviously didn't ever dream it would be like this." She replies woefully and shakes her head.

"I would appreciate your discretion, and so would Shay. I don't want her to suffer any more than she already has." I sigh, leaning forward and rubbing my hands over my face tiredly.

"You've had a tough time lately, huh, first your accident and now this. It's like a bad omen." She utters with a little frown. Jesus, she really was a fan. She wasn't wrong, though. Maybe we do have a bad omen; that's why we can't seem to just be happy.

After what felt like forever, we finally make it to the hospital. They wheel Shayla into the A&E department, and the doctors come running over as the paramedics list the injuries she's suffered and what they've treated. I see four police officers and a woman dressed in plain clothes waiting with them as they roll her into a private room. The doctor looks at me questioningly. "I'm her husband, and no, I'm not leaving her side for a second," I state firmly, and he nods, relenting. I stand in the corner of the room while they examine her. The blinds go down, and the woman walks in with a briefcase waiting for the doctors to finish examining Shayla. They roll up her shirt, and I wince, closing my eyes when I see more bite marks and bruises on her ribs.

"Possible bruised and broken ribs." The doctor runs his hand down her ribs, and she jumps and whimpers in protest. I take a step forward, my heart up in my throat. "Order a CT scan for the ribs and her head."

"Am I okay to take photos and do my examination before you take her away?" The woman asks, and the doctors nod and leave the room. She looks at me and blinks. "I'm going to need you to leave the room for this." She informs me, and I look at Shayla lying unconscious.

"Please don't hurt her." I request, and she shakes her head comfortingly. I walk out of the room and close the door behind me. I anxiously paced back and forth. I had a splitting headache, and I was worried sick about Shayla or how she would react when she wakes up. The examination felt like it took forever. Once that was done, they took her to have her CT scans. She had two fractured ribs, and thankfully, her head was fine. Her brain wasn't swollen, her skull wasn't fractured; she just had a cut on the side of her head, which would heal in a week or two. She had a stab wound on her thigh, which needed stitches, but fortunately, no long-term damage has been done...physically speaking anyway.

Two hours go by, and I sit by her bedside, her dainty hand in mine, waiting for her to wake up. The doctor said she was very malnourished. She hasn't eaten or had anything to drink in days. They're going to pay for everything they've put her through. I'll make sure of it. I feel her fingers twitch in my hold, and I open my eyes and look at her. She's stirring awake. I brush my hand over her forearm gently in an attempt to comfort her, but she jumps, ripping her hand away from my touch with a pain-filled whimper. "Shayla," I speak softly and reach over to touch her face. Her eyes flicker open, and she screams, or at least she tries; her voice was gone. I pull my hand back and stand up. "Shayla, it's me, it's me, baby, it's me," I say, reaching out to take her hand, trying to soothe her. Shayla looks around the room, and her eyes turn to me. "It's me, sweetheart, you're okay, you're safe now, you're safe," I reassure her, kissing her hand, and her eyes fill with tears as she looks at me, her lips quivering. "I found you, baby. It's over." I reach out to touch her face, but she shrinks away and starts to cry, her frail body shaking with hoarse sobs as the reality of what she's suffered hits her.

"Sophie." She cries, shaking her head.

"I know baby, I know, the police have her, and the two men have been arrested too. It's over. You're safe."

I press my lips to her hand and couldn't contain the sob that erupted within me. I was supposed to be strong for her, but I couldn't. I was so relieved she was alive but so angry at what she's been through; the fear in her eyes broke me. When I sit on the side of the bed beside her, she turns her face away from me. "Why did you save me." She asks weakly, her voice strained and croaky.

I frown, "Shay."

"You should have let me die." She whispers vacantly, facing away from me.

"Baby, please don't talk like that. I was going out of my mind trying to find you. We all were." I tell her, kissing her hand softly, but she pulls it away and rests it in her lap, her fingers trembling. "Shayla, look at me, please?" I cry, but she stays silent and continues to stare out of the window to her right.

"I can't."

"You're right to hate me. It's all my fault. I'm so sorry." I admit dropping my gaze. "If anyone deserves to die, it's me, not you. I wish I had died in that crash. This would never have happened to you if I had died. She would have left you alone."

Shayla finally looks at me, but she doesn't hold my gaze as she used to. She wouldn't look me in the eyes. "It was her. The plane crash. It was Sophie."

I stare at her wordlessly, my mouth agape while I let her words sink in. Sophie was the one responsible for my plane crash? "What? I don't understand. They said it was turbine engine failure." Shayla shakes her head meekly.

"It was her. She tried to have us killed, Cole." She croaks and drops her gaze to her hands, an endless stream of tears falling from her eyes.

Jesus Christ.

"Here, drink this." I pour her a glass of water, and she takes it from me and drinks it and sighs, wincing a little. I take the empty glass from her and take her hand into mine again. She doesn't pull away this time.

"How's Alaia?" She asks, lifting her eyes to look at me for a second before she looks away again.

"She's at home with your mum. She's okay; she wasn't hurt. They left her outside a police station with a note to call me to collect her." I explain, and she closes her eyes and cries.

"Thank God. I was so worried she had done something horrible to her." She sniffles, looking at the rope burns on her wrists. "When she said she would return Alaia to you, I was so relieved, but I didn't trust her not to hurt her."

"Alaia's fine, baby; she misses you so much. She's refusing to feed on the bottle, she wouldn't drink the formula milk, and the only way they got her to stop crying is with your shirt." I state, and Shayla sobs, covering her face with her hand. "I'm so thankful you're alive. We both need you so much, baby. We wouldn't survive without you, not for a second." I cry, pressing my forehead to hers.

"I didn't want to survive, Cole. I didn't want to wake up and face you after what they..." She winces and squeezes her eyes shut, shaking her head.

"Hey, look at me," I lift her gaze to mine gently. "There is nothing so big you and I can't work through. We're going to get through this together. You've got a big family who loves you and will do anything for you, and you've got me. I love you so much baby, please don't shut me out."

"Cole," She whimpers wretchedly, shaking her head.

"They're going to pay for what they did to you. I swear to you, baby. I won't rest until they suffer ten times what you did. All three of them." I promise her, and she releases a quivering breath.

"The police are outside waiting to speak to you. To get your statement, are you up for it?" I ask, and she sighs, and I feel her body start to tremble in distress. "You don't have to if you're not ready. They can wait."

"No, it's okay." She breathes, pulling away. "I'll speak to them, but I want a shower first."

"Okay, I told Aimee to bring you some clothes on their way over. I'll call them and see where they are." I say and hand her another glass of water. "Drink that. The doctor said you're dehydrated." Shayla takes the glass and sips the water. I watch her as I call Josh to see where they are.

"Hey bro, is Shay okay?" He asks as soon as he answers. I look over at her and bite the inside of my cheek.

"Not really. How long till you get here, she wants to shower?" I ask with a sigh. "Aimee did pick up some clothes for her, right?"

"Yeah, we're about five minutes out. I've got Sara and Alaia. Jo and Sam are behind us. We'll be there soon." I nod and utter an okay before I hang up the phone.

"They'll be here in a few minutes. Your Mum and brother are coming too." I inform them while I sit on the chair beside her bedside, she stares up at the ceiling and nods.

"I don't want to see anyone," Shayla whispers, tears rolling down the side of her face. "Especially my mother. Please." I nod and lean in to kiss her forehead, but she pulls away and shakes her head, squeezing her eyes shut as if it pained her. "Don't."

I push aside the sting of the disappointment of not being able to touch her and nod, fisting my hands by my side. She's suffered so much. It's only natural for her to close off. I'll be patient, however long it takes.

I'm going to do everything I can to erase those horrific memories from her mind, even if it takes the rest of my life. I will do it.

A knock sounds on the door, and it opens abruptly, causing Shayla to jump startled and gasp sharply before she starts to sob. I jump up to my feet and take her hand. "It's okay, baby. It's just the police officer. It's okay." I assure her and scowl at the police officer, and he looks at us apologetically.

"I'm sorry to disturb you, but there are some family members out here that would like to see her." I shake my head.

"No, keep everyone out. I'll be out in a second." I instruct him, and he nods and closes the door. I look at Shayla, who had her eyes closed and panting to catch her breath. "Are you okay?" I ask, brushing my thumb over her bruised knuckles, and she nods. "I'll be right back, sweetheart." I walk to the door and look back at her once more before I slip out of the room. I close the door and lean against it closing my eyes. I release a painful breath that was choking the life out of me.

I want to scream and break everything in my fucking path.

"Cole." I open my eyes and see everyone in the corridor, waiting anxiously. I walk over to them and kiss Alaia's head in my mother-in-law's arms, looking at me with red-rimmed and worried eyes. "How is she? Can we see her?" Sara asks, and I exhale deeply and shake my head.

"She doesn't want to see anyone or doesn't want anyone to see her in that state. She's not okay at all. She just wants to shower, and the police are still waiting to take her statement."

Sara sobs shaking her head. "Please let me see her, just for a second."

"You don't want to see her like that, trust me. Maybe after she showers, she might feel a little better. I'm going to take Alaia in for a bit to see her." I explain and take Alaia from her hold and take the bag of clothes from Aimee.

"We'll be here waiting to see her. Tell her we love her." Aimee says, brushing away the tears that roll down her cheeks.

"I will." I turn and walk back to the room Shayla was in. I make sure I open the door slowly, not to startle her again. Shayla takes one look at

Alaia in my arms and bursts into tears. She pushes herself up to sit and cries out, holding her ribs. "Take it easy, baby. You have two fractured ribs; try not to move suddenly." I tell her, and she winces, her eyes on Alaia. "Do you want to hold her?" I ask, and she shakes her head.

"No. I just want to shower." She cries, reaching out to touch Alaia's hand that was stretched out to her; her fingers tremble, and she pulls them back. "Okay. Do you want me to help you shower, or shall I get Aimee and Jo in to help you?" She looks at me for a second, and I see the fear in her eyes, and my heart tightens painfully in my chest. She doesn't want me to see her naked. "I'll get the girls, okay?" She nods meekly and lowers her gaze. I take Alaia back to my mother-in-law. "Girls, can you help her shower," I request, and they nod and get up to walk to the room, but I stop them. "She's fragile and really scared. Please be careful with her. She jumps at every loud sound, so open the door slowly. She's not in good shape, so when you see her, don't freak out. She hasn't seen how bad she looks yet." I state, and both girls exchange looks, and their eyes fill with tears, which they blink away and exhale. I watch them as they walk toward the room.

They hesitate for a moment but push the door open, and I hear them gasp sharply.

Chapter 29

SHAYLA

I STARE out of the window at the gradually dimming sky. The sound of the rain hitting the window and the distant rumble of the thunder was soothing.

It gave me something else to focus on, other than the ache in my body, my wrists' stinging, and the crippling fear that had my heart racing a mile a minute. I didn't think I would see daylight ever again.

The scary part is that I was okay with that. In fact, I was welcoming it. I gave up fighting after the third time. I begged them every hour to just kill me, but they didn't. Sophie wanted me to suffer, and suffer I did. I can still feel their hand's all over me. I can feel their long beards dragging along my skin, making every hair on my body stand with disgust. I thought I was broken before—I was wrong. Now, I'm broken and damaged beyond repair. I don't want to be here. I don't want to breathe. I don't want to live in this body. It doesn't belong to me anymore. I feel dirty and tainted.

Every time I close my eyes, I see their faces walking toward me with those dark and leery eyes. I was terrified of falling asleep because I'm afraid I'll open my eyes and see his face close to mine. Being woken up by the foul stench of his breath. The dark, chilling smirk. His voice whispering in my ear that I was worthless now as he yanks my legs apart and forces himself into me.

I don't want to live with those memories for the rest of my life. I couldn't bear to look Cole in the eyes. I feel ashamed and unclean. I don't feel like his wife anymore— I don't belong to him. I don't want him to touch me. I don't want anyone to touch me ever again, not after they robbed me of my pride, my self-worth—my life.

I don't want to live.

I flinch, and my heart starts to race when the door opens slowly. I'm safe. They can't hurt me anymore, but every time I hear that door open, in my head, it's that very door to that room opening, and I expect them to walk in and hurt me again. I lift my eyes and see my two best friends standing at the door. I sigh in relief, but my heart refuses to settle. Fear still consumes me. They gasp when they look at me, their eyes fill with tears, and they look at me in horror and pity. I haven't looked in the mirror in days. I don't need to because I can see the terror in the eyes of those I love the most. I'm a monstrosity, and I feel it. I drop my gaze, not having the stomach, to look them in the face.

They walk over to me, and I sob silently while they crawl up on the bed to hug me, but I shrink away from them, and they back away, "Shayla..." Aimee whispers, her voice breaks, and I squeeze my eyes shut. "We were so worried we'd never see you again." She cries, reaching out to touch my hand, but I move it, and she sighs dejectedly.

"Shayla, we know you're terrified, babe, but please don't ever think you're alone. Aimee and I are here for you if you need to talk. We're here for you, babe, always." Jo tells me, and I shake my head slowly.

"I don't want to talk. I just want to shower. I can still feel their hands, their saliva..." I close my eyes and wince. "All over me. Please, please just help me wash them off me." I sob helplessly while they cry with me.

Aimee sucks in a deep breath and exhales, wiping away her tears. "Okay, come on." She stands and holds her hands out to me, and Jo walks around the bed to help her. I hesitate, but I slide my hand into hers, and they help me out of bed. I cry out when a sharp pain shoots up my leg and ribs. "Lean on us, Shay, don't put weight on your ribs." I shake my head, unable to move. It hurt—every step I took hurt.

"I can't. I can't walk. It hurts." I sob pathetically, and they exchange looks.

"Shall we get Cole to carry you to the bathroom?" Aimee asks, and I cry. I don't want him to see me like this, but I don't have a choice. I have to shower. I nod and hold on to Jo when Aimee opens the door and sticks her head out to call for Cole. He comes rushing over and looks at me; our eyes meet, and the despair in his eyes every time he looks at me makes me want to die even more. "She can't walk. Can you carry her to the bathroom?" Aimee asks, and he nods and walks over to me. I look up at him as he stares into my eyes.

"Can I?" He asks, gesturing to his arms, and I nod timidly. I hiss when he lifts me into his arms so carefully like I was a fragile china doll he was afraid he would break with the barest pressure. He walks to the bathroom on the other side of the room. We walk in, and he sets me back down on my feet again slowly. "You okay?" Cole asks when I whimper and hobble, trying not to put pressure on my leg that was stabbed. Cole takes hold of my hands, and he guides me slowly toward the shower when I look up and catch my reflection in the mirror. I gasp when I see the state of me. I had two black eyes, my lips were dry and cracked, and I had a deep cut on my temple. My face was swollen on one side when I'd been punched while trying to fight them off me. My neck was bruised, where they gripped me tightly and held me down. I had a bite mark just below my collar bone. I choke on a strangled cry and collapse into Cole's arms, screaming as loud as my lungs would allow.

Cole gathers me into his arms and holds me as I weep defenceless into his chest. "Why did you save me? Why didn't you let me die? I was ready to die! I don't want to live. I don't." I sob into him, and he tightens his hold on me.

"Shayla, please don't talk like that. You're going to heal, baby. In time it's going to get better."

"No, it's not! It's not ever going to get better—it's not. They robbed me of my life! I belong to them now, and I can't live with the image of them in my head. I can't, Cole, I can't!" I scream, hitting my head, and Cole grabs my hand, stopping me.

"Get the doctor. Now!" Cole shouts at Aimee, and she runs out of the room as I cry hysterically.

"Let me die, please just let me die!" I sob, shaking my head. I see images of them walking toward me, and I scream, closing my eyes. "Get them off of me, Cole, please get them off me!" I try to scream, but nothing came out. I tremble frantically in his arms. Cole lifts me into his arms and hits the water, and steps under the shower with me.

"It's okay, baby, shh, shh, it's okay. They're gone, they're gone." Cole assures me. He lifts my head and lets the water run over my face as he brushes the dried blood away. "You don't belong to them. You're mine, and you always will be." He tells me, pressing his forehead to mine, and I shake my head, sobbing. The doctor comes running in, and I jerk in Cole's arms while he holds me. "They're going to give you something to relax. It's okay, sweetheart."

"No! I don't want to sleep! I don't want to sleep!" I scream terrified. If I sleep, I'll see them, and I don't want to. "No, please! Please." I sob, shaking my head vigorously.

"All right, all right. He's gone, he's gone, baby." Cole shakes his head, and the doctor backs away, and I whimper, panting. Aimee and Jo had run out of the bathroom, sobbing when they saw me in that state. "I got her. Leave us." The bathroom empties, leaving me alone with Cole. He holds me until my sobs ebb away, and silent tears remained. "Let me take these off you, baby, and we can clean you up properly." I pull back and allow him to undress me slowly. "Keep your eyes on me, okay." I try to look down at myself, but he lifts my gaze to his. "On me, sweetheart." I nod and keep my eyes on him as he washes my body gently.

"Harder," I whisper. "Scrub me harder."

"Shayla—"

"Scrub me harder!" I sob, and he nods and scrubs me with more force, and I wince, watching his face as he scowls, his jaw clenched tight and throbbing. I wanted to rip my skin off. Every part of me they touched, I wanted to burn. I wash my hair and turn the dial making the water hotter until it burned my skin. I hear Cole hiss when the hot water hits him, and he reaches to turn it down, but I stop him.

"No," I whisper.

"Shay, you're going to scald yourself. It's too hot, baby."

"Leave it." I hiss, closing my eyes as I stand under the spray. I wanted it to burn. I needed it to burn; maybe that would wash away the stench of shame they've left on me. "I can't get clean." I whimper weakly, and Cole draws me into his arms and kisses my forehead.

"Baby, you are clean. If you keep torturing yourself like this, you're letting them win. You're letting that bitch Sophie win. What happened to you doesn't define you, do you hear me? You're the strongest, most beautiful girl I have ever met. It's going to take time, but you will beat this, and I'm going to be there by your side every step of the way. I'll be your strength through all of it. If you keep it locked away in your head, it will haunt you forever. Talk to me, talk to the girls. I'll find you the best therapist out there. You're going to beat this." Cole affirms, and the water shuts off before he helps me out of the shower.

After he helps me dress in my clothes, he lifts me into his arms and carries me to the bed again. I look down at him as he sits me down gently and kneels in front of me, his green eyes filled with concern as he gazes up at me. "Alaia needs to be fed, Shay. She's not feeding on the bottle. She won't stop crying." Cole tells me and sighs, rubbing his forehead. "Will you be up to feeding her?"

I look down at him, and my vision blurs with tears, "Of course." Cole smiles a little and helps me back into bed. He leaves to get Alaia, and I can hear her screaming as soon as the door opens. I get visions of when she was screaming like that when we were abducted. I shake off the thought, and Cole walks back in with her in his arms.

"I know, sweetheart, look, it's mummy, princess." He says, kissing her head as he walks over to me. He hands her to me carefully, and I hold her against my chest and close my eyes, biting back the sob that was itching to escape from within me.

"Hi baby, oh, I know you're hungry," I whisper and lay her down; I unbutton my shirt and gasp when I see the bite mark on my breast. I hesitate and close my eyes wincing. I force away the images that flood my mind and push my nipple into Alaia's mouth. She latches on and sucks hungrily, gulping quickly while she blinks up at me, tears rolling down the side of her face. I brush her tears away and watch her as she feeds. Cole sits at the end of the bed, by my feet, and watches me feed her.

A knock sounds at the door, and I pull the sheet over Alaia, covering myself while I feed. Cole opens the door, and a man in a suit walks in with two police officers, both women. "Hi Cole," They shake hands, and he turns his attention to me. "Hi Shayla, I'm Detective Chief Inspector Scott. I'm the Detective assigned to your case. Is this a good time to ask you a couple of questions?" He asks hesitantly, and Cole interjects, but I nod.

"Sure." I sigh, and he nods, the door closes, and he takes the seat beside my bed.

"How are you feeling?" He questions, narrowing his chocolate-coloured eyes at me. He looked to be in his late thirties. Clean-shaven, hair cut short and styled neatly, greying at the sides.

"I've been better," I answer and look down at Alaia, who was still sucking at my nipple hungrily. I dread to think about how hungry she was.

"I know what you've suffered isn't easy, and I want you to know that there is help available to you should you need it. Just remember that you are not alone, even though it may feel like you are." He says, and I nod numbly. "Reliving what you went through is going to be tough, I know, but we need to take your statement now, while it's still fresh in your mind, so we don't skip over any important details that might help your case and incarcerate those that did this to you." He explains, and I nod. "Are you happy for your husband to be in the room for this?" He questions, looking over at Cole, watching me.

"You don't have to stay," I tell him, and he shakes his head. "Are you sure?"

"I'm not going anywhere," Cole assures me, and I sigh and look at the detective, who nods.

"Can you start from the moment you were abducted?" He asks, and I nod, licking my lips.

"Uh, I was at my best friend's wedding, and I went to the bathroom to go and change my baby. After I changed her, I got a little lost and ended up at the back of the building. We walked out of the main building, and that's when someone grabbed us from behind. My first thought was that it was Cole, but they covered my mouth and nose and dragged us away. They knocked me out, and the next time I woke up, I was tied to a chair, alone in that room." I explain, and he nods while the women behind him write down what I was saying.

"What happened after you woke up?"

I frown, thinking back to the moment I woke up. "Uh, I started screaming and shouting, asking where Alaia was because she wasn't in the room, but I remembered having her with me when I was grabbed. That's when the taller one of the two walked in and told me to be quiet, or he would slit my throat and silence me indefinitely. They were in black masks at that point, so I didn't see his face. Only his eyes..." I continue to explain what they said to me and what they did with Alaia and me until Sophie walked in.

"So three days later, Miss Turner walked in holding Alaia, and that's the first time you saw her?" He questions, and I nod.

"Yes, she told me that Alaia would be her baby soon. Then the shorter one took Alaia away, and Sophie came over to me. I asked her what her plan was, and she said she was going to have me killed and thrown on the side of the road to be found while she was consoling my husband." I explain and look at Cole, who watches me, a deep scowl on his face, his chest rising and falling quickly. "Her whole plan was to get me out of the way while she worms her way back into his life. She confessed to being the one responsible for his plane crash. She tried to have us killed, and when she found out I wasn't on the plane with him as she had planned..." I glance down at Alaia asleep in my arms. "She told me if she couldn't have Cole, then no one could," I sigh, wiping away the tear that rolled down my cheeks. "I told her she was crazy, and she stabbed me in the leg and slapped me a couple of times. She told me she would take Alaia back home to Cole, and before she left, she told the two men that I was theirs to do with what they wanted and to make it hurt. I never saw her again after that." I tell him.

"What happened after?" I stare at my hand, my vision blurring as I relive the moment they stripped me down. "Take all the time you need, Shayla."

"After she left, they both took off their masks and kicked the door shut before they walked toward me and untied me from the chair. I fought them as they took my dress off. The taller one picked me up and threw me down on the bed." I whisper, closing my eyes. "I tried to fight him off. I scratched and kicked, hitting him wherever I could, but he was too strong. He grabbed me by the throat and punched me hard in the face. I was in a daze, but the other one held my arms down while the bigger one took my underwear off." I explain and choke on a sob. "They raped me." I cry, shaking my head. "I screamed the whole time, begging them to stop, but they didn't. They took turns assaulting me, biting, and grabbing me until I was screaming, and they would laugh, enjoying the pain they were inflicting on me. Every time they forced themselves on me, they would whisper that I was worthless, that I was theirs now." I sob despairingly into my hand.

"That's enough," Cole growls, walking over to me, his eyes swimming in tears. He wipes his eyes and points to the door. "You can continue later." The detective gets up, and they leave the room. Cole tries to touch me, to soothe me, but I push him away, turning my face away from him.

"Don't...please don't." I sob, closing my eyes. "Just take her and go." Cole takes Alaia from me, and I weep into my hands, my entire body shaking as I'm stuck reliving that moment again and again. Cole sighs and leaves the room. They say it's over, but it's not. It's over for them. It's not over for me, and it never will be. I still have to relive those painful moments to give my statement, and then I have to stand in court and relive it again with them in the same room. I don't have the strength for that. Their faces, their voices, and their touch have been burned into my memory forever.

I wanted to forget. I was hoping that if I slammed my head hard enough into the concrete floor, I could lose my memory, but it didn't work. I'd give anything to lose my memory right now. Just to have a moment of peace.

I spent two days in the hospital, I gave my statement, and they said they would be in touch if they needed anything else or I should call if I remembered something relevant to help the case. I was discharged and allowed to go back home. Cole helps me into the house and lays me down on the sofa. I was tired, drained, too scared to sleep. I force myself to stay awake. Jumping awake every time I doze off because I'd see their faces.

"Shayla, please get some rest, darling. You need to get some sleep. I'll make you some soup, and you can eat it and get some sleep." My mother says, walking over to me. She's been crying since she set her eyes on me at the hospital. I'm sick of all the sympathetic looks I keep getting from everyone. They're all fussing over me, and I just want to be left alone. I don't want to talk. I don't want to sleep or eat. I just want to be alone.

I heave a sigh and rub my forehead. "Mum, I'm fine. I'm not hungry." She sighs, relenting when she detects the bite in my tone. She goes off to check on Alaia. A couple of minutes later, Aimee and Jo come over to check on me.

"Do you need anything?" Aimee asks, and I shake my head silently. "Why don't I make you a nice tea?" I sigh and pinch the bridge of my nose in agitation.

"Tea? Is it a magical tea that will wipe away all the horrible memories in my head? Please, just leave me alone. I just want to be left alone in peace. Please!" I exclaim, irritated and regret it instantly when I see the tears in their eyes. I watch them as they get up and walk away, and I sigh, squeezing my eyes shut. They all mean well, I know that, but I feel like I'm suffocating, and they don't understand what I'm living through every day. It's not something a bowl of soup and a cup of tea is going to fix. I want to lock myself away from everything and everyone. The house finally clears a couple of hours later, and I curl up on my bed. Alaia asleep in her crib beside me.

I stare at her while she sleeps. I was lost in thought when I feel the bed dip behind me. I roll over and look at Cole sitting there watching me. I lay on my side, ignoring the ache in my side where I was pressing against my ribs. Cole lays down on his side, facing me. We lay there looking at one another. I hadn't noticed I was crying until I felt him brush away the tears with his fingers. "Do you want to talk?"

I release a quivering breath and shake my head. "No."

Cole's eyes rake over my face, and he reaches over and takes my hand in his and presses my fingers to his lips. "Baby, don't bottle things up. Talk to me, tell me what you're thinking, what you're feeling."

I sigh and bite the inside of my cheek. "I was thinking that I shouldn't be here. I don't feel like I belong anywhere anymore." I admit and lick my lips. "I feel broken, and I feel angry and nothing like myself."

Cole's eyes water as he looks at me, his thumb brushing over my fingers soothingly. "I wish I could take all the pain away with one swipe, but I can't, baby." He declares, gazing at me lovingly. "In time, I will, if you let me. I will fix all the broken pieces inside of you..." He whispers, kissing my finger. "One kiss at a time." He adds, kissing another finger. "I'm going to shower you with my love until that anger you feel ablaze inside of you burns out." He kisses my palm. "Even if it takes the rest of my life, I swear to you, I'm going to fill your beautiful mind with so many happy memories all the bad ones will diminish in comparison." I gaze at him wordlessly for a moment, and my insides ache.

"How can you still want me after everything they did to me?" I cry, and he looks at me woefully.

"Because I love you, you silly girl." Cole whispers, and the sincerity in his eyes made my heart flutter. "You're the last person in the world to take any blame for any of this. I'm to blame. I should have left you alone and just married her. You would never have suffered like this if I had just listened to you." Cole admits miserably, and I sigh, shaking my head.

"No, but you would have. Neither of us could have ever imagined she would do something like this. I knew she was delusional, but to go to such lengths. She's truly deranged. I can't get the crazy look in her eyes after she stabbed me out of my mind. And the fact I have to face them in court is just..." I sigh, closing my eyes.

"They'll be lucky to make it to court." I open my eyes and look at Cole questioningly.

"What does that mean?" I ask.

"It means they're going to get what's coming to them. All three of them."

I lift my head and look at him warily. "Cole, what have you done..."

Chapter 30

COLE

As I LAY there watching Shayla, she's gazing at me inquisitively, her eyes searching my face. "Cole, what have you done?" She queries, and I kiss her palm gently before I shake my head.

"I told you, they're going to pay for everything they did to you," I explain, and her brows knit tightly. "Sophie is facing fifteen years, and those fuckers are going down for twenty years at least. Detective Scott said they've got a shit ton of offences they're wanted for. They'll be lucky if they don't get life." Shayla's eyes water as she looks at me. "They're going to suffer every single day for years."

"What does that even mean?" Shayla queries while I brush my fingers along her jaw, and she flinches, shrinking away from my touch.

"You don't need to worry about the specifics, baby. Just know that they will endure ten times the pain they inflicted on you. You're not the only one that's got that rage burning inside of you. I punched that fucker so hard I dislocated his jaw, but that knowing smirk he gave me makes my blood boil every time I replay it in my mind." I express, my jaw twitching with agitation. Shayla closes her eyes and sighs.

"I see that dark smirk and hear their grunting and laughs in my head constantly. I don't know how I'll ever forget it." She whispers, her voice quivering with trepidation.

"In time, you will. It's all very fresh in your mind right now." I reassure her, brushing my fingers over her knuckles. "I know you don't want to, but please try and get some sleep, Sweetheart. You're going to make yourself sick if you keep forcing yourself to stay awake."

I see her eyes go wide in alarm, and she shakes her head quickly, her chest rising and falling rapidly as her panic grows. "No, no, I can't, I can't." She whimpers, terrified, and I lean up and look down at her.

"Okay, shh, it's okay, it's okay, baby. You don't have to sleep, it's all right. I'm sorry." I try to soothe her, but she covers her face with her hands, sobbing quietly. I can't stand to see her like this. It's killing me. I feel so helpless; I don't know what to do to help her through any of this. "Let me hold you, baby," I whisper, brushing my fingers through her hair. I pry her hands away from her face, careful not to touch the wounds on her wrists. Shayla looks up at me apprehensively. "It's okay," I assure her, and she hesitates, almost as if she's trying to convince herself that she can trust me not to hurt her. I lay back and hold my arm out, and she slowly scoots closer and lays her head against my chest. I don't pull her. I just let her nestle herself against me until she relaxes before I wrap my arm around her. Her entire body was trembling against mine. I turn my head and press my lips to her forehead. "Your safe, baby. I will never let anyone hurt you ever again." I promise her, and she sighs.

We lay there together in silence. I run my hand up and down her back gently in an attempt to soothe her. I can feel her heart pounding against my chest, and I look down at her and see she's finally dozed off. I watch her closely, keeping still, so I don't jolt her or frighten her while she's asleep. Her brows are fused tightly, and she has tears rolling down the side of her face, soaking my t-shirt. I want to wake her; she looks scared, but she needs to sleep, or she'll make herself ill. My heart pains to watch her in this state. She's the shell of the strong woman I love at the moment, but I know she will bounce back from this. I fell in love with her strength, and I know that girl is still in there. As broken as she is at the moment, she's going to be okay. She has to be.

I fight the sleep that was begging to take me. I haven't slept much the past week, and having Shayla safe in my arms, I think my mind and body are finally ready to shut off. That was until I feel Shayla jerk in my arms, and she let out a shrill scream that almost made my heart stop. I shake her as she fights in my hold, seemingly trapped in her nightmare and reality of everything she's suffered. She kept screaming the words 'no' and 'stop' and 'please' over and over again. "Shayla, hey, it's okay." I try to shake her awake, but she fights in my hold, trying to hit me. Her nails catch my face just under my eye, but I shake it off and focus on waking her up. "Baby, baby, it's okay, it's okay, it's just a dream, baby, it's just a dream," I tell her, and she whimpers, opening her eyes, and looks at me, panting. "It's me, sweetheart. You're okay...you're safe." I whisper, brushing fingers through her sweat-damp hair. Shayla starts to sob, rocking back and forth. I kiss her temple, unsure of what else I can do to help her. "What can I do, sweetheart. Tell me what I can do to help you." I sigh, stroking her hair while she cries.

"Nothing." She sniffles, shaking her head. "I have to live with it for the rest of my life." She states and turns her bloodshot eyes to look at me. Shayla frowns, and her lips quiver when she notices the scratches on my face. "Oh, God, I hurt you." She cries, reaching out to touch my face. "I'm so sorry."

"Shh, baby, it's okay. It's nothing; I'm fine, don't worry about me." I say, kissing her fingers while she looks at me distraughtly. "Are you okay? Do you want to talk about it?" I ask, and she sighs, closing her eyes.

"I was just reliving the moment they..." She winces and shakes her head. "I'm okay. I'll get something for your face. It's bleeding." She whispers, trying to sit up, but I stop her.

"Shayla, come here." I wrap my arms around her and kiss her forehead. "I think I know how I can help you," I mumble against her temple, and she frowns.

"How?"

"As soon as your ribs are better, we're doing some boxing. It always helped me when I'm angry or hurt. I think you need to focus all that anger inside if you on something and let it out." I explain, and she lifts her head and looks at me.

"Can we start tomorrow?"

"No, baby, you'll hurt yourself. You're still injured, and your body is too weak to take on exercise right now." I look down into her eyes and smile, stroking her jaw. "Soon, okay?" I promise her, and I see the disappointment shine in her eyes, but she nods. I wasn't going to risk her getting hurt. "Josh and I will teach you." She silently nods, and we lay down again. She fell into a restless sleep, jerking and twitching, waking up every hour in a cold sweat.

It went on like this for weeks, and I could see her sinking deeper and deeper into depression and reclusion. She shut off from everyone around her. Even me. She's angry and resentful, and every day that passes, I feel like I'm losing her.

"What are you thinking, man?" I turn and look at Josh while I pace in the kitchen.

"We need to pull her out of this, Josh. I can't stand to see her like this anymore. She won't talk to anyone. Not the girls, not her mother, not me. She won't even open up to the therapist. I tried to take her to one of those group therapy meetings, where she could sit and be with people who have suffered as she has, but she got up and walked out after ten minutes. That's not Shayla up there, and I'm scared if I leave her alone for a moment, she's going to do something stupid or hurt herself." I tell him frenetically, and he watches me sadly.

"The girls are here. They can watch Alaia. Let's take her to the gym, as you said before. This could be the only way to get that anger out of her." Josh suggests, and I run my fingers through my hair and nod.

"Yeah, yeah, you're right. She's healed now; let's do it. At this point, we've got nothing to lose." Josh nods, and I skip up the stairs to the bedroom where Shayla was. I knock, announcing myself before I open the door and see Shayla lying on the bed with Alaia. She looks up at me when I walk over to her, her eyes cold and distant as she watches me.

I keep my eyes on hers as I sit on the bed. "You up for a little outing?" I ask, reaching over and rubbing Alaia's stomach, and she giggles.

"Outing?" Shayla inquires, and I nod slowly. "Yes, remember a couple of weeks ago I told you I wanted to take you to do some boxing? Well, you're healed now, so Josh and I are taking you to the boxing club. The girls will watch Alaia for an hour or so." Shayla sits up, and I can see she's about to refuse. "Please, baby. For me?"

Shayla looks down at Alaia and bites her lip, mulling it over before she nods. "Okay." She agrees. I offer a little smile, and she slips off the bed to change. I pick up Alaia and take her downstairs to the girls who were excited to see her.

"Hi, baby girl. Oh my god, you're so big, and I only saw you a week ago." Aimee chirps excitedly, kissing her forehead.

"When are you going to cook me one of those?" Josh asks, resting his chin on Aimee's shoulder, who giggles and slaps his head playfully.

"When you take me on honeymoon and put one in me," Aimee replies, and Josh narrows his eyes at her.

"I'll fly you out tomorrow." He whispers and kisses her softly. I sigh, watching them, and it hits me how much I miss Shayla and how we used to be. I miss her touch, her kiss, and most of all, I crave to hear her laugh again. Amid all the chaos, it completely slipped my mind that I would surprise Aimee and Josh with a honeymoon. They've been an absolute rock for Shayla and me, and I know Shayla feels awful for everything that happened at their wedding. Even though it wasn't her fault, she still feels terrible about it.

Once Shayla got ready, we drove to the gym, which was ten minutes from our house. Shayla looks around the gym at all the men, and I can see the dread in her eyes. "Out." Josh orders when he too noticed the panic in Shayla's eyes, and everyone clears out, leaving us alone. Josh was part owner of the gym. He and our mutual friend Murray opened the place five years ago. It was a boxing and mixed martial arts club where I often come to train with Josh and Murray— a Muay Thai instructor.

"You trust me, right?" Josh asks me, and I nod, my eyes on Shayla, who was looking timidly around the gym.

"Of course."

"I need to push her. It's going to be hard to watch, but let her be, don't interfere." Josh tells me, and I swallow hard. "Warm her up."

I exhale and walk over to Shayla, and Josh goes to the equipment and pulls an impact vest on. I help her pull the gloves on and teach her how to throw a punch while holding the pads. "That's good, baby, now harder, push your fist like you want to go through the pad," I instruct, and she punches hard. I talk her through the sequences of punches and follow my movements and instruction. "Right hook, Harder." She hits the pad, concentration on her face, flushed and sweaty. "Josh is going to take over now, okay, baby?" Shayla nods silently, and I back away from her as Josh walks over. Josh places his hands on her shoulders, and she flinches slightly but keeps her eyes on his.

"Do you trust me, Shay?" He questions, and she looks at him vacantly for a long moment but nods. "You know I would never hurt you, right?" She nods again. "Okay, I need you to hit me." He tells her, and she shakes her head, scowling. "It's okay. This vest protects me. You won't hurt me, but I need you to give me everything you've got inside you. All right?" Shayla looks over at me uncertainly, and I nod, urging her on silently. Come on, baby. You got this.

"Okay." Shayla sighs and punches Josh in the chest gently.

"Harder Shayla," Josh says, and she puts more force into her punch. "Harder!" Josh shouts, making her jump, and she glares at him. Josh takes a step toward her, and she jumps back. "Are you weak?" he hisses while advancing toward her, and Shayla backs away, shaking her head. "Are you weak?!" Josh yells again, and she looks up at him, her chest rising and falling quickly, her eyes drowned in tears. "Hit me!" When he reaches to grab her, she shoves him back.

"NO!" Shayla screams, and he grabs her arm and pulls her against him. Shayla whimpers and punches him in the chest over and over again.

"Is that all you got?! Come on, harder! Hurt me, Shayla! HIT ME!" Josh barks, and she sobs, hitting him repeatedly. I watch her as she relives the moments those bastards hurt her. Josh did it—he got her to open up that box she's been trying to keep locked away. Josh let her hit him and took each blow, each punch she wished she could have delivered to them. Shayla was screaming and sobbing, and it took everything in me to stay back and not take her into my arms. She has to feel this. In order to heal, she has to get the rage she has festering inside out of her.

Josh pushes her back, and she attacks him again. In her mind, it wasn't Josh anymore; it was her captors. It was written all over her flushed face. She was gasping for breath, but she didn't stop. I watch as Shayla delivers a swift punch to Josh's face, and I take a step to intervene, but he holds his hand out, stopping me. My heart was up in my throat. I've never seen her like this. She held so much hatred and rage in her eyes. "Hurt me, Shayla, come on! Just like I hurt you." He goads her, and she punches him in the jaw again. Josh shakes off the blow, his nose was bleeding, but he didn't seem phased. He's a fighter, after all. That would have felt like a slap to him. Shayla wasn't strong enough to hurt him, but he wanted her to feel like she was. "Are you a coward?!" Josh shouts, shoving her back again.

"NO!" Shayla screams, hitting him wherever she could. Josh grabs her and wraps his arms around her tight—holding her against him.

"It's over now," Josh tells her while she fights in his hold. "You're stronger than you know, Shay. You're stronger than them." He speaks in her ear, and she sobs helplessly. "You're sick of everyone treating you like you're made of glass but you're not. You're a fighter, Shayla. You're not weak. Those bastards are." Josh directs her toward the boxing bag. "Show them you're not a weakling. Fight back!" He shoves her into the bag.

"Ahhhhh!" She screams, her head pressed against the bag. I take a step to go over to her, but Josh pulls me back, shaking his head.

"Leave her." We stood watching her as she punches the bag. Letting out all her anger and frustration until she fell to her knees, panting to catch her breath between her anguish-filled sobs. Her cries echo in the empty gym. Josh walks over to her and lifts her face so she could look at him. "You're the strongest woman I know. The only way you will let them win is if you give up being you and hide. Don't give them or anyone that power over you ever. They can't hurt you anymore. No one can." Josh tells her earnestly, brushing a strand of hair away from her face, and she stares at him.

"Teach me. Teach me how to fight." Shayla says, her voice raspy, and Josh nods.

"Of course, but you have to promise you'll stop hiding away and shutting everyone out. We're all here to help you heal." Shayla nods and averts her gaze to me, and I smile at her.

"I promise." Josh hits her shoulder playfully with his pad.

"You owe me a nose job. I think you broke my beautiful nose. Who taught you to swing a punch like that, pretty girl?" Josh chuckles, and she looks at him and laughs sadly.

Ahh, there it is. There's my beautiful wife. I walk over and kneel in front of her. "My brother." She whispers and looks at me. "And my husband."

I smile and rub her jaw gently. "She always had a mean right hook on her. That was all her. Believe me. I've seen the bruises on my body to corroborate it." I tease, and she smiles weakly. I feel my heart flutter when she smiles. As cheesy as it sounds, it does light up my whole life.

"I'm sorry about your nose." Shayla apologises to Josh, who shakes his head.

"Don't be, I'm fine. I was just joking. It takes more than a punch to break Josh Matthews nose."

"Yeah, it takes a Cole Hoult." I joke and shove him, so he topples over onto the mat and chuckles, kicking me over. We look at each other and hurl ourselves at Shayla, who gasps when she falls back on the mat. She laughs while we playfully punch her.

"You want to train with me. You need to get tough quick, Shay." Josh tells her, and Shayla scowls and slaps him with her boxing glove, and he groans, rubbing his forehead. "Ow."

Josh scampers off to the office when Murray walked in. I lay down beside Shayla on the mat and look over at her. "You okay?" She turns her green eyes to me and sighs heavily.

"I will be." I lace my fingers with hers and lift her hand to my lips, brushing a kiss on her knuckles.

"That's my girl." Shayla looks over at me, and I hold her gaze intently. "No one can break you unless you give them the power too, Shayla Hart."

Chapter 31

SHAYLA

"Are you sure about this?"

"Yes."

Cole and I stare at one another for a beat before he nods and turns his gaze to Josh, who watches us silently, a stoic look on his face.

"The last thing we want to do is set you back, Shayla. You've been pushing yourself too hard. Do you really think you're ready for this? What if it triggers you, and you go right back to the state you were in?" Josh questions, concerned, pulling his knees to his chest. I look at him and wipe the sweat that had gathered above my top lip.

"I have to do this. Otherwise, what am I killing myself for?" I utter, looking between him and Cole, who share a look. "What am I fighting for if it's not to face my fears."

"The trials will start next week, baby. You're going to face them there. Don't put yourself in a position where you'll be vulnerable before you take that stand." Cole voices, reaching over and rubbing my ankle. We just finished another training session, and we were sitting in the middle of the boxing ring, having a discussion.

"Cole, I'm ready." I press, holding his gaze so he could see my determination. "Can you make it happen or not?" I ask them both, and Cole nods with a heavy sigh.

"Yes. We can make it happen if this is really what you want. If it's going to help you put this nightmare behind you, I will do everything in

342

my power and put you in a room with them so you can face them." Cole states, and Josh nods slowly, though neither of them looked pleased about it.

"Good. Do it." I mutter and push myself up to stand. Cole and Josh look up at me, and I catch the concern in their gaze. "If I'm going to bounce back from this and put this to bed, I need to face my fears, and I can't do that because they're locked away with them." I roll my sore neck and sigh. "They need to see that they didn't break me." I point out before I climb out of the ring and jump off.

Cole and Josh stand and climb out of the ring too. "We'll make it happen," Cole says and brushes a kiss to my sweaty temple. I turn my head and lift my gaze to him, and he looks into my eyes.

"Thank you," I whisper, and he holds my gaze, and his lips twitch a little. We hear Josh groan from beside us.

"All right, kids, you two are at it again with the intense stares. I'm out of here. Shay, you're kicking arse, girl. If I'm late for dinner again, Aimee with chew mine out and hand it to me. Lock up before you go." He says before he grabs his gym bag and walks to the exit. Cole and I mutter a bye and wave him off as he walks out.

"Shall we head out?" Cole asks, those emerald green eyes looking over my face intently. I bite the inside of my cheek thoughtfully. Things have been real tense between Cole and me the last couple of months. We're both frustrated, sexually and emotionally. I have desires and urges now that I didn't have before, but what felt natural before feels wrong to me now. I feel like I don't deserve to have these urges anymore, and I'm scared of what will happen if I do get intimate with Cole. Does he still want me as he used to? Will I feel different to him now? Will he enjoy it knowing those animals have tainted me. I'm still crazy about him and still want him, but I don't know how to express myself anymore because I don't feel sexy or attractive. I don't want him to touch me and think about them while doing so.

I'm driving myself crazy with this, and I don't know what to do. I miss him. I miss us. I miss me and how I used to be. It's been four months, and we've not even kissed. I can see he wants to, but he's just as scared as I am, and neither of us will make a move. That's what Josh meant about the intense stares. It's happening more and more frequently, and I feel like I'm back to when we first started living together all over again. My mind is in disarray, and I can't seem to make sense of anything.

"No," I answer after I realise that he had asked me a question, and I was just staring at him while my mind was running amuck. "Let's train a little longer. Is that okay?" I question, and he nods slowly.

"Sure. But are you not tired? You've pushed yourself quite a bit today." Cole points out, and I shake my head.

"Are you afraid you'll get your arse kicked by a girl half your size, Hoult?" I ask with a smirk, and his eyebrows go up in surprise. It's been a while since we've made flirtatious remarks at one another and his lips curl into an amused smile while he stares down into my upturned face.

"The way you've been training, you best believe I am." He replies, his eyes on mine. "But I'll let you kick my arse all day, every day, baby, and enjoy every second of letting you do it."

I lean in close, holding his gaze. "Oh, will you now?"

Cole smirks devilishly and licks his lips. "Mhm, you're fierce, and I love it." He whispers, walking around me until he was behind me. "It's sexy as fuck." He murmurs in my ear, and my insides clinch when I hear my attacker's voice instead of Coles. I squeeze my eyes shut and push the images away and release a slow breath while I keep reminding myself it was Cole. It was Cole's lips brushing against my ear like he has many, many times before. He grabs me, wrapping his arms around my neck suddenly, and I open my eyes and remember the months of gruelling training I've had with Josh.

"Every instinct will tell you to be afraid, you'll freeze, and for a moment, your fear will take over, and you'll forget everything you've learnt. You'll want to panic...*don't*. Your training is all up here." Josh told me, tapping at his temple while he held me down by the throat. "Push aside that crippling fear and fight back."

I place my hands on Cole's forearms around my neck and pull as he tightens his grip and drags me back. I step forward and twist my body quickly and pivot out of his hold before I swipe my leg and take his legs out from under him, and he falls back on the mat with a grunt.

"Fuck." He chuckles, looking up at me. I step over him, each foot on either side of him, and look down with a smile while he peers up at me proudly. Cole leans up and grabs me by the waist, and pins me down on the floor, straddling me with my arms pinned to the ground. "I've got you now." He drawls, smirking arrogantly.

"Do you?" I chuckle and thrust my hips up and pull my arms down swiftly, causing him to fall forward and let go of my arms to brace himself before his face hits the floor. I grab his torso and hug him tight before I use my arm to fold his, forcing him to roll onto his back and straddle him. Cole groans and grins looking up at me.

"If you wanted to be on top so bad, all you had to do is ask, baby." Cole teases me, and I smile, leaning down close to his face.

"Where's the fun in that?" I ask softly while looking over his handsome face, and he bites his lip, watching me closely before his eyes drift down to my lips as I pant softly.

"If you want control, baby, you better be prepared to take what you want." He whispers, looking up at me. I swallow hard, and we stare at one another heatedly. Coles hands come up and hold my hips. My heart starts to race the closer our lips inch together. I stop just before our lips touch, and he stills, making no move, watching me, waiting patiently to see if I'll close the gap and kiss him or pull away. I keep my eyes open and force myself to close the gap and kiss him. My eyes close the moment our lips touch, and he moans throatily.

Cole lets me control the pace of the kiss; his hands remain on my hips, thumbs stroking the exposed skin just above the hem of my yoga bottoms. I drag my tongue lazily along his bottom lip, and he parts his lips with a throaty groan, giving me access to deepen the kiss. The kiss starts off slow but grows hotter, dirtier while our tongues duel as we continue to kiss hungrily. I hadn't noticed Cole's hands travelled from my hips and was now curled in my hair while his mouth ardently attacks mine.

We pull apart, only to fill our lungs with desperately needed air.

Foreheads pressed together, panting to catch our breaths. "You okay?" Cole breathes, dropping soft, affectionate kisses on my jaw.

"Yeah." I nod, and he smiles a little, brushing his fingers through my hair.

"Christ, baby, you have no idea how desperately I've been wanting to kiss you again," Cole admits gruffly, his thumb stroking my bottom lip.

"So was I," I whisper, biting my lip, trying my best not to blush under his intense stare. "But I was scared you wouldn't want to." I finally admit, and he pulls his head back and frowns, his green eyes looking over my face.

"How could I ever not want to kiss you, sweetheart?" Cole questions, taking my face into his large hands. "Your lips are my holy grail." He adds, dragging his nose over mine, and I sigh, fighting back the tears I feel coming.

"Do you still want me?" I question hesitantly, dropping my gaze from his, terrified to see the look on his face, but he lifts my head and lowers his so he could catch my eyes.

"I've never stopped wanting you, baby. I want you just as badly as I did when we first met. That will never change." Cole affirms, caressing my face devotedly. "I'm just patiently waiting for you to be ready so I can make love to you like I've been longing to."

"Cole, I'm scared." I breathe, closing my eyes.

"I know you are, baby, but it's okay. I'll continue to wait for as long as it takes for you to be ready."

"What if..." I bite my lip, swallowing the lump forming in my throat. "I feel different."

Cole looks at me, his brows fused together. "It's not possible." He assures me and draws me close for a gentle kiss. "You pushed out a six-pound baby and still make my head spin when I slide inside you. I promise you...you'll feel perfect like you always do."

God, I love him so much. How did he get to be so damn wonderful?

"And you're sure you can wait? I completely understand if you—" I question warily, and he smiles.

"Shayla."

I stop rambling and look at him. "What?"

"Shut up and kiss me." I laugh a little, and he grins, watching me as I lean in and kiss him. Cole moans and wraps his arms around me tight, pulling my body against his. Oh God, I wish I could find some way to rip this anxiety out of me and just give into him, but I don't know how to.

After we make out for a little while longer, we go home and shower together, where we kissed some more. I had a mini panic attack when things got too heated, and Cole's hands grabbed my breasts a little too roughly, and I backed away from him. He apologised repeatedly, and I could see the anguish in his gaze when I backed up against the wall and shielded myself away from him. As strong as I was feeling, I still had bouts of sheer panic from time to time. I'll learn to control it better eventually.

A couple of days later, Cole and Josh told me they had arranged what I had asked for, and here I was, sitting in the passenger seat while Cole drove us to the prison where they were keeping Harvey and Quinton Smith. Just hearing their names gave me chills. It's incredible what money can buy you. Cole wouldn't tell me what it cost him, but I could imagine it would have been quite a bit to get me in a room with the bastards that stole everything from me. I stare out of the window silently, mentally preparing myself to face them again and going through everything I wanted to say to them.

Cole looks at me, "Shayla. We can turn—"

"No." I cut him off firmly and turn my gaze to him. Cole holds my gaze and frowns a little before he nods and looks at the road again. I look at the prison up ahead, and my hands fist tightly in my lap.

"Hey," I look back at Josh when he leans closer to speak to me from the backseat. "We'll be right there, and guards will be in the room too, so don't be scared, okay." Josh clarifies, and I shake my head.

"I'm not scared," I stare up at the prison as we drive through the gates. "I'm anxious."

"Remember what I taught you about your fear. You control what you feel, not the other way around." I nod slowly, and we get out of the car once we park up. Cole goes and speaks to the guard at the main gate before he waves us over, and we follow a guard through the prison. It was eerily quiet as we walk through the courtyard. I could feel my anxiety spiking, but I force it away. A guard comes out and greets us, shaking Cole's hand before he looks at me, and I stare at him.

"You're one brave woman." He states, and I look at him wordlessly. "There are guards in the room with you. They'll be chained so they can't hurt you."

I lick my lips, shaking my head while we stop outside a door. "There isn't anything left for them to hurt anymore," I say, and the guard narrows his blue eyes at me for a moment but nods, gesturing to the door. I turn and look through the glass and see them sitting in the room, chained to chairs.

"Whenever you're ready." The guard says, and I lift my eyes to Cole, who was looking at them through the glass, his chest rising and falling, his gaze stern and menacing.

"Stay here," I tell him, and he looks down at me and frowns deeply.

"Fuck no, you're not going in there alone." He argues firmly, and I glare at him.

"I am. I spent four days alone with these bastards. I need you to stay here. I have to do this on my own." Cole tries to argue but whatever he saw in my eyes made him relent. I turn and slowly exhale as I reach for the door. My fingers tremble as I slide the handle down and push the door open. Their heads lift when they hear the door open, and I walk into the room. Quinton's steely eyes find mine, and we stare at one another. That slow smirk appears on his face, makes my stomach clench painfully, making me want to turn and run, but I shove it away as I turn and close the door. Cole and Josh come closer to the glass, watching me like a hawk. I lock eyes with Cole, and he nods slowly, silently encouraging me.

"Hi Cupcake," Quinton drawls when I turn and face him. "Did you miss me?" I take a step forward. Inside I was screaming, but they won't ever know that. They leer at me darkly and bite their lip. I look over at Harvey, and he winks at me. I felt sick to my stomach at the sight of both of them. Moments they were holding me down, and my screaming flashes through my mind.

"No." I hiss, taking a step closer to Quinton, who watches me closely. "I came to wipe that smug smirk off your face, you sick fuck."

"Is that right?" He sneers, biting his lip as he leans forward in his chair, his chains rattling as he does so. "Are you going to hurt me, Cupcake?"

"What could possibly hurt sadistic fuckers like you?" I ask, looking at him, and he chuckles perilously. The same chuckle that haunts me to this very day.

"I think about you every night when I lay in my bed, Cupcake. Your taste—" I punch him hard across the face, he turns to me sharply, and I see the fire go up in his unyielding grey eyes. "Of all the women I have taken, *you*...were my favourite. So fucking tight..." I punch him again, and he growls and looks at me, blood dripping from his lip. "Keep hitting me, Cupcake. You're only turning me on."

"She's a feisty little bitch." Harvey laughs as I move over to him, and he smiles darkly, watching me. I lift my foot and kick my heel into his face, hearing his nose crunch on impact. He roars in pain, and I soak up the sound. It felt like music to my ears.

"You think you broke me, but you didn't." I spit gravely, looking at them both. "That's what you feast on—the fear. You think you're all-powerful because you can take what you want and strip away the life of innocent girls, but you can't, not this time...not with me. You will never do to another girl what you did to me." I declare, glaring in Quintons eyes, and he smirks. "I came here to take back what you took from me! My life." I lean in close and look at his loathsome face. "I'm not afraid of you. I will not give you that kind of power over me ever. You're going to pay for what you did to me and all the girls before me, one way or the other." I step back, and they watch me. The door opens, and Josh walks in with Cole, and they stand on either side of me.

Josh rolls his sleeves up as he glares at Quinton. Cole looks at the guards and nods. They walk over and unchain Quinton and lift him to

349

his feet. Cole takes the baton from the guard and walks over to Quinton, who glares at him, pushing his chest out and making himself big.

"You think about my wife while in laying your bed, do you?" He questions coldly. "Next time, you can think about this." He growls and swings the baton hard into his groin. Quinton howls in pain and keels over. The guards lift him, and Cole hits him hard in the groin again before he swings the baton and strikes him with force across the face. "That's for laying a finger on my wife! You fucking bastard!" He swings the baton and hits him on the other side of the face, and Quinton hits the floor in a pool of his own blood.

Josh waves off the baton Cole holds out to him as he walks over to Harvey, who looks up at him, his eyes wide as the guards unchain and pull him to his feet. Josh walks over to him and punches him hard in the face. I hear a crunch, and I'm sure I saw his jaw dislocate. Josh kicks him in the knee, and I listen to it crack when it snaps, and he screams in agony. "Where you're going, they don't like rapists, I hear. You won't need this anymore." Josh states calmly, kicks him hard in the groin a couple of times. Josh takes the baton and swings it at his face as Cole did to Quinton.

I watch as the boys beat them and while it wasn't quite the same as what I suffered, that fear that I had eating away at me disappeared. They no longer had any power over me, and for that, I was thankful.

I'm a survivor, and that's one thing no one can ever take away from me.

Chapter 32

COLE

I watch Shayla as she walks out of the doors to the prison ahead of Josh and me. "I'm so fucking proud of her," I tell Josh with a sigh, who smiles, nodding.

"Me too. She's a warrior," Josh squeezes my shoulder, and I look at him appreciatively.

"I don't know how I'm ever going to thank you, Josh. You've helped me with her so much the last couple of months. If it weren't for you, she'd still be a wreck."

Josh shakes his head. "I didn't do anything, Cole. I just pushed her into facing her fears. She did the rest. You know I've always got your back, brother."

"I know, and I've always got yours, brother." We share a smile and fist bump as we walk over to Shayla. "One last stop. I don't know how I'm going to face that bitch and not want to kill her for everything she's done."

"Shay's got her bro, leave her to it," Josh mutters as we walk outside. Shayla had her gaze up at the sky, and she released a long breath, her shoulders which were tense before was more relaxed now.

"You okay?" I ask, taking hold of her shoulders, and she looks at me and nods.

"Yeah. I'm good. Facing them again brought up so much for me, and I wanted to turn and run the moment I walked in, but that's exactly

351

what they want. They want me to be scared and weak because that's what makes them feel powerful, like they have control over me, like in some twisted way their victims belong to them." I explain, shaking my head. "I would rather die than give them the satisfaction of thinking they've broken me. They haven't, and they won't. That was enough to put out that rage I had burning inside of me." I kiss her forehead, rubbing her arms.

"You're damn right they have no control over you," I proclaim and cup her face with my hands. "I'm so proud of you, baby. You walked in there with your head held high when most would have crumbled. Your strength and courage are astounding, honey, and I can't wait to watch you raise our beautiful daughter to be just as strong and brave as you are." I declare, brushing my fingers through her hair while she gazes into my eyes.

"Oh, you guys are giving me all the feels over here," Josh mutters, pretending to sob. I throw my head back and laugh. "Someone cue the sappy music!"

"Fuck off, arsehole." Josh laughs and runs off when I chase him toward the car. Shayla laughs, watching while I chase Josh around the vehicle. "Don't make me leave your arse here, you little shit. Get in the fucking car." I chuckle while Josh keeps mocking me for my speech.

"Oh man, that sounded like something you would hear at the end of a cheesy rom-com movie." Josh continues to laugh heartily, holding his stomach in the back seat. I lean over and punch his leg hard, and he groans. "Ow, you fucker." He grumbles while rubbing his leg with a scowl.

"You two are impossible." Shayla laughs, getting into the passenger side, and watches us bicker amusedly.

"You ready for the next stop?" Josh asks, sobering up from his laughter, leaning forward, and Shayla nods, looking at me.

"Oh, you better believe it."

"Bro, don't you think Shayla looks like one of the Power puff girls?" Josh chuckles, and Shayla whips her head and looks at him with a scowl.

I laugh and look at Shayla, who was glaring at Josh. "Yes! The one with the big green eyes. What was her name?"

Josh cracks up laughing when Shayla reaches over, smacking him. "Buttercup!" He chirps, and Shayla pinches his thigh. "Ahhhh, fuck!" Josh howls, slapping her hand away.

"I do not!"

"You really do, baby." I laugh, and she turns her glare to me. "Come to think of it. Aimee is bubbles with her blonde hair and blue eyes. Jo is Blossom with her brown hair and brown eyes, and you, my love, are Buttercup. You three *are* the power puff girls!"

"Yes! Oh my god, it makes perfect sense. Sugar, spice, and everything nice." Shayla leans over and hits Josh, who cackles.

"Will you shut up! I'm more concerned about the fact that you both know so much about the power puff girls." Shayla points out, and I grin at her while she pins me with a pointed look.

"Who's got the power?!" I sing.

"We got the power!" Josh sings back, and Shayla couldn't hold in her laughter anymore.

"Ohh yeah!" We both shout together, singing the theme song. Shayla shakes her head, rolling her eyes while grinning.

"You're both idiots," She mutters, crossing her arms over her chest and looks out the window sulking.

"Oh, my Buttercup." I coo, reaching over and squeeze her chin. Shayla slaps my hand away and glowers at me.

"Cole, I swear to God." I laugh, amused, and poke her a little.

"I love you, Buttercup," I mumble, leaning closer to kiss her once we stop at the traffic lights, but she flicks my forehead, and I jump back. "Ouch!" I scowl, and she smirks.

"Bite me."

"Just say where baby," I murmur in her ear, making her smile, and she nudges me away with her shoulder. I chuckle and take her hand, kissing her palm before I place it on my thigh. Considering she's on the way to face Sophie after the hell she's put her through, she's in good spirits.

"So, have you given any thought to what you're going to say to Sophie when you see her?" Josh asks from the back seat, almost as if he read my mind. Shayla's face falls at the mention of her name, and the playful expression on her face disappears, and an icy exterior takes its place.

I glance at her, and she turns to look at me. "I've been picturing what I would say to her for months. I'm going to hit her where it hurts." She explains, holding my gaze, and I nod. "You might want to sit this one out," Shayla says, turning to face Josh, looking at her questioningly.

"When you say, 'hit her where it hurts,' you don't mean in the literal term, I take it?" Josh questions warily, and Shayla looks at me before she shrugs and faces the front again. "Please tell me you're going to slap the bitch around a little bit?"

"I'll decide when I see the deranged bitch." Shayla mutters acidly, her hands fisting in her lap.

The women's prison was an hour away in Maidstone from where those sick fucks were being kept. I tried so hard to keep it together and not kill that fucker. When he said those words to her, how he thinks about her while he's in bed, Josh had to hold me back. I was ready to rip his fucking head off. Well, his dick will no longer be functional...or exist for that matter. Best eight million I have ever spent. Thankfully, the system is corrupt, and it didn't take too much to get them to agree. Every time they look down and see their dismantled cocks, it will be a reminder of what they did to my girl. I wince just thinking about the pain they will suffer. Imagine having your dick shredded to pieces. I could have had them be taken care of, but dying is just not an option for them. I want them to live in fear, every single day for the rest of their lives.... they will suffer and get fucked up by someone ten times more twisted than they are.

We pull up at the women's prison, and we make our way through the gates where the guards lead us to where Sophie is being kept. Shayla, Josh, and I walk through the back, and they take us to a room isolated at the end of the building. Two guards stop outside the door, and they look at Shayla, who stares at Sophie through the glass. She had a busted lip and a black eye. They chew up and spit out pretty girls like Sophie in places like this, and she's clearly suffering if the state of her is anything to go by.

"What happened to her?" Shayla asks, looking back at the guard who eyes Sophie sitting cuffed to a chair.

"She got roughed up by one of the big girls in here. Pretty, spoilt, rich girls aren't liked very much around here—especially when they found out what she did to you." Shayla nods and pushes the door open before she walks into the room, and Sophie looks up when she hears the door open and her blue eyes go wide with surprise when she sees Shayla and I walk in.

"Surprise bitch." Shayla utters, standing in front of her. I lean against the wall, and Sophie turns her gaze to me, and I glower at her. Shayla whistles and takes a step closer to Sophie, following her gaze to me, and looks at her again. "He looks good, doesn't he?"

"You should be rotting six feet under right about now." Sophie hisses her frosty eyes on Shayla, who smirks.

"And you should be sipping champagne in some pretentious restaurant, but... here we are," Shayla mutters, crossing her arms over her chest. "Orange really isn't your colour. All though it does go well with the black eyes you're sporting there." She pushes her finger against it, and Sophie hisses and pulls her head back.

"Is that why you're here, to give me fashion tips?" Sophie snarls, and Shayla shakes her head.

"No, I came here to tell you personally that you failed, and your little plan tanked just like I told you it would."

Sophie grins, biting her lip a little. "Maybe, but it wasn't a complete failure. I hear those brothers fucked you up real good. If you're alive and standing there today, it's because of me." She hisses haughtily. "If I hadn't told them where you were, you'd still be rotting in that little room. You owe your pathetic life to me. I should have known those two idiots would get too distracted and greedy, making you their little whore and not kill you right away. I should have finished the job myself."

Shayla grabs Sophie by the throat and shoves her back while she leers at her. "You should have."

"I'll get it right next time," Sophie whispers, glaring up at Shayla, who licks her lips. "After all, I have nothing but time to plot your demise, you little whore."

"Give it your best shot. I fucking dare you." Shayla utters gravely. "You don't have what it takes to hurt me, Sophie. I bet you lay there in your infested cell thinking you broke me. Well, I have news for you, honey. You only made me stronger." Shayla says and steps back before she punches Sophie hard across the face. Sophie cries out, and her nose starts to bleed. "That's for laying a finger on my daughter, you psychotic bitch."

Sophie shakes off Shayla's punch and lifts her eyes to her again before she looks at me, smirking. "How does it feel, Tristan, knowing your perfect little Shayla is tainted and damaged. That purity that you loved about her is no more. I bet it haunts you, doesn't it? Every time you touch her or kiss her, you see them all over her. Do you taste them on her skin? Does she flinch when you touch her?" Sophie grins wickedly, and I straighten from my leaning position, staring at her angrily.

"Oh, you pathetic bitch. Is that what you think when you're locked up in that dingy cell all day? Is that what helps you get through the nights?" I question, walking over. Sophie watches me closely as I near her. "There is no force strong enough to ever put me off Shayla."

I smirk. "I could so easily beat you to an inch of your fucking life, but those wounds will eventually heal. No. I'm going to hit you where it really fucking hurts, you sadistic cow. While you're lying there night after night staring at the walls in your cell for the next twenty years. I'll be in bed, in the arms of the man you so desperately love." Shayla declares, lowering herself to Sophie's eye level. "I'm going to burn an image in your twisted brain, so you see it every time you close your eyes." She adds and smirks before she turns to look at me.

I dismiss the guards in the room, and they walk out, leaving us alone in the room with Sophie. I lick my lips and take a step, drawing Shayla against me. She looks up at me, and I smile before I kiss her long and deep, making her moan when I suck her tongue teasingly. I moan and pull back, pressing my forehead to hers while she pants. "I'm *hungry* baby," I growl, staring lustily into her gorgeous green eyes, and she grins.

"Are you now?" She drawls, raising a brow, and I bite my lip and nod, staring at her lips. "I have something I just know you would love to eat." My brows go up with interest, and she smirks and turns her gaze to Sophie, who was watching us in horror, her blue eyes drowning in tears. I brush my lips against the shell of Shayla's ear and nip gently.

"You sure?" I whisper, and she nods, looking up at me, a devious look in her eyes. Shayla wants me to eat her out and have Sophie watch. That's very twisted and cunning, but I love it. Sophie had this coming. She needs to see that she hasn't broken us, and maybe that will wipe the smug smirk off her fucking face.

I pick Shayla up into my arms and kiss her hungrily before I lay her down on the table in front of Sophie, whose face was contorted with disgust. "What the fuck is this?!" She screams, pulling on her restraints. "Guard! Get me out of here!" Sophie shouts, tugging on her cuffs wildly.

Shayla looks at her with a grin. "Shh, they can't hear you." I kiss Shayla's thigh as I peel down her jeans and underwear. Is it wrong that I'm rock hard right now? "Bon appetite, baby." She moans, her eyes on Sophie. I lick my lips readily as I look at her perfect pussy.

"Christ baby." I groan as I lower my head between her legs and lick slow and luxuriously up her slit. Shayla moans, curling her fingers in my hair. Sophie had a perfect view of Shayla's face so she could watch while she climaxes.

"Ohhh baby, yes, right there." Shayla moans, rocking her hips up as I suck her clit hard. She whimpers and writhes as I flick my tongue against her clit teasingly. It's been a while, so she won't take long to orgasm, and she's going to come hard. I moan appreciatively as I continue to devour her pussy.

"Guard! Hey! Get me the fuck out of here right now!" Sophie shouts, whimpering, pulling hard on her cuffs. Shayla and I were too engrossed in one another to even acknowledge her. Shayla starts to shudder as she nears her release. She stills and grips the edge of the table she was lying on.

"Uhh Cole, yes, I'm coming, baby. Oh, I'm commming! Cole!" Shayla whimpers, and I lift my eyes to Sophie's as I give Shayla that final lick, and she goes over, crying my name as she orgasms. I groan, lapping up her honey while she quivers and pants to catch her breath.

"I'm going to kill you, you dirty fucking whore! You're going to pay for this! I'll make sure of it!" Sophie screams, sobbing. "GUARD!"

Shayla chuckles, panting. "Mmm." I lick my lips and lean over, grinning down at her while she looks up at me. "I want more later." I burr brushing a kiss on her lips.

"Count on it, stud." Shayla breathes, kissing me back passionately before she pulls back from the kiss and looks at Sophie. "Oh, were you saying something. I couldn't hear you through the mind-blowing orgasm my husband was giving me." Shayla retorts and turns her head, and kisses me again, making me moan into her mouth. My woman is dynamite. I'm the luckiest son of a bitch on this planet. I help Shayla dress and lift her off the table.

"You've got the cheek to call *me* sick? What the fuck does this make you? You're disgusting, the pair of you!"

Shayla walks over to Sophie and leans over to look her in the eyes. "Revenge is a dish best served cold Sophie. I hope you enjoyed it... because I fucking did." She sneers and pats her cheek a couple of times. "Have fun in here. I hear you've made some really nice friends. I'll see you at the trials."

When Shayla steps away, I lean in close to Sophie and blow in her face, so she smells Shay's scent. Sophie winces and turns her head away. "Smell that, Soph? That's what a perfect pussy smells like. And believe me when I tell you she tastes even better. I could eat Shay's pussy all day, every day for the rest of my life, and never get enough." I stand up straight and smirk when she turns her distraught gaze up to me. "And I plan to. I'm obsessed with her."

I pull Shayla to me before I sweep her into my arms bridal style, and she gasps laughing. "Arrivederci, you psycho." Shayla wags her fingers and kisses me as I carry her out of the room. We grin against each other's mouths when we hear Sophie scream as we walk out.

"Take me home, Stud," Shayla whispers against my lips, and I nod.

"Right away, Buttercup." I grin and hiss when she flicks my forehead again. "Ow."

"Remind me again why I married you?" I laugh, and she looks at me, eyes twinkling like jewels while she grins impishly.

"Uh, because you had no other choice." I tease and brush my nose over hers. "And—you're heel over arse in love with me." Shayla throws her head back and laughs with gusto. I absorb the sound of her laughter, and it makes me feel all frivolous inside.

"You're such an idiot." Shayla giggles hysterically.

I sigh longingly as we walk out of prison. "An idiot in love."

Chapter 33

SHAYLA

"I don't fucking care!" Cole shouts, livid, as he paces back and forth in his study. "I want the head of whoever this fucker was that went to press with this, do you understand me?" I watch Cole as I sit curled up on the sofa, my knees pulled to my chest. We're a week into the trial, and someone has leaked information about my case, and the media are going nuts with it. News reporters and paparazzi were camped outside the house trying to get pictures of me.

"Tristan, we're looking into it, but I told you as soon as it goes to court, someone would leak information about what happened to her. It was inevitable."

"Inevitable? What the fuck do I pay you for Lucy?! It's a fucking media frenzy out there. You're the head of public relations. You were supposed to keep this under wraps. I told you to keep a tight lid on this." He shouts at Lucy—his publicist, and she watches him pace restlessly back and forth. "I want the name of the reporter who wrote the story and the publication that was bold enough to run it to be dismantled, you hear me?!" Lucy nods.

"Tristan, I will find the person responsible, but the cat is out of the bag now, and you know better than anyone that this isn't going to just go away if we ignore it. It's front-page news, and my phone hasn't stopped ringing; they want to hear Shayla's story."

"Like fuck I'm going to let that happen. She's suffered enough. Get a handle on this and get those fuckers off my property." Cole growls, rubbing the back of his neck in agitation. Lucy closes her laptop and brushes her fingers through her hair before standing. I get off the sofa and walk to the office. Cole has his back turned to me, his shoulders tense as I lean against the door and look at over Lucy, who smiles apologetically at me.

"I'll do it," I tell her, and her perfectly shaped brows go up. Cole spins and looks at me sharply, his brows knitted together tightly. "After the trial is over, set up the interview with whoever it is you want me to share my story with, and I'll do it."

"Absolutely not," Cole angrily growls as he strides over to me. "Not a snowball's chance in hell I'm letting you face those vultures."

I sigh and look at him tiredly. "Cole, I'm going to have to live with this for the rest of my life. Am I happy it's out there? No, of course I'm not, but it's out there now, and as Lucy said, we can't just shove it back in the box and ignore it in hopes it goes away."

Cole's eyes were filled with rage before they soften a little while he looks into my own. "Shayla, listen to me. I'm going to fix this. The stories are being pulled as we speak. You don't have to do this. They will break you apart, baby." Cole tells me dejectedly, taking hold of my upper arms. I close my eyes, resting my hands on his chest.

"What good is pulling the story now it's out there? People know what happened to me, Cole." I lower my gaze. "As much as I want to crawl into a hole and never come out, I won't. I have nothing to be ashamed of, right?" I ask him, and he shakes his head, his hands coming up to cup my face.

"Of course not, baby, but they won't care about that, Shayla. They will dig and poke at you until you break. They're ruthless. You know this." Cole tries to talk me out of my decision, but deep down, he knows once I make up my mind, I'll stick to it.

"I would rather tell my story how it happened than have them speculating and throwing false information around. Maybe if I share what happened to me, it will encourage others to do the same and not be afraid or ashamed for something they had no control over. If some good can come out of this whole nightmare, it will be worth it. I don't want people to feel sorry for me or think I'm ashamed when I'm not." I express. Cole exhales, closing his eyes briefly when I turn my attention to Lucy, who was watching us closely. "I want to put this behind me, and unless I give them what they want, they'll keep chasing me around. Tell them I'll do it, but after the trials are over." I tell Lucy, and he nods, casting a wary look at Cole, who nods, giving in.

"For what it's worth, I think you're exceptionally courageous, Shayla, and the world will see that too and commend you for it. You're truly an inspiration to every person who has suffered any form of assault." Lucy declares as she walks over and hugs me. "I admire your strength. I really do."

"Thank you." I offer a weak smile when she pulls away from me, and Cole dismisses her before he pulls me into his arms, his lips pressed to my forehead.

"I'm so sorry, baby," He mumbles, kissing my forehead softly. "I thought they had a handle on this. I've got the right mind to fire every single one of them for being so fucking lax." I feel the agitation thrumming through him, and I lift my gaze to his.

"You're not firing anybody," I say firmly. "How long could we have kept this under wraps for anyway? It was bound to come out eventually. I'll do the interview and tell them what really happened, and we can finally put this whole mess behind us because I'm tired, Cole." I exhale, and he nods, kissing my temple. Cole's arms tighten around me, and I rest my head against his firm chest. "I just want to go back to enjoying my life with you and Laia."

Cole kisses the top of my head. "Oh Shayla, I want that more than you could ever know, honey." He affirms with a long, drawn-out sigh. I honestly couldn't wait for some form of normalcy. So much has happened I've forgotten what 'normal' feels like anymore. I'm exhausted, and I know he is too. How much more could we possibly put up with before the strain gets too much and break us again.

I gaze up at him, and he looks into my eyes. "Always you and I, baby." I declare lovingly, and he smiles handsomely, brushing his nose over mine affectionately.

"Always, baby." He whispers, tucking his slender fingers under my chin and tilting my head up so he could brush a spine-tingling kiss to my waiting lips. I moan and part my lips for him to deepen the kiss, but Alaia's cry from the baby monitor interrupts us. We pull back, and Cole chuckles, shaking his head.

"Impeccable timing as always." He groans, watching me pull away from him to go and check on her. I look back at him once I reach the stairs, and he grins sexily, licking his lips. "I'll be coming for that kiss, Hart."

I smile and send him a flirtatious look. "I'll be waiting, Hoult," I reply and jog up the steps to check on our daughter. I walk into the nursery and pick her up from her bed. "Hi baby, how was your nap." Alaia stops crying once I pick her up, kissing her beautiful face. She's seven months old, and she's growing so much every day. Her first word was Dada, for which Cole was over the moon. He cried, hearing her on the monitor while she was babbling away in her bed. Cole sat up in the bed, his hair a mess, eyes still closed. "Did she just say...Dada?" He muttered, and I looked over at the monitor to see her smiling away, calling for her Dada at 6:30 in the morning. "She just said DADA!" I laughed when he fell out of bed and ran to the nursery to pick her up.

I smile fondly, remembering how excited he was. "How about we have a bath? Would you like that, princess?" I kiss her head of dark hair and walk to the bathroom to run us a bubble bath. She's obsessed with bubbles at the moment.

While Alaia and I were enjoying our bath, Cole wanders in and grins. "Oh, you two having a bubble party without Dada." He crouches beside the tub and flicks a little water in Alaia's face, and she giggles. She literally lights up whenever she sees him, and it's the most beautiful thing in the world. "You cheeky little monkey." Cole scoops up a handful of bubbles and places it on her head, and laughs. "Oh, that's just precious." He takes out his phone and snaps photos of her like the proud Daddy he is. I watch him playing with her, and my heart swells with such love. Despite all the shit that's happened in the last year, we're finally in a good place. Granted, we're still not intimate other than kissing. We've not done anything since that whole stunt we pulled with Sophie. Cole has been so patient with me. I know he's sexually frustrated if the 'long' showers he takes every morning and evening are any indication.

Cole catches me watching him, and he smiles, resting his chin on his hand that was holding on the side of the tub, and looks at me with those piercing green eyes which made something deep inside me quiver with need. I was in a daze picturing all the things I want him to do to me. "Honey."

"Hm?"

"If you keep looking at me like that, I will not be held accountable for my actions." He admits looking over at Alaia, playing happily with her bath toys and bubbles before he slides closer to me.

"I'll readily take full responsibility for your actions," I reply, holding his gaze, and he licks his full lips, a spark of desire ignites in his eyes, and I feel my lady bits flutter and throb with desire. Cole smiles and dips his hand into the water, his fingertips grazing up my stomach, which twitches under his touch. While his fingers leisurely drag up the valley between my breasts, I gasp when he circles my hardened nipple with the pad of his thumb. It's been such a long time since I felt his touch. I felt like I would come apart there and then just by him teasing my nipples. Cole leans over and brushes a kiss to my lips, his eyes on mine.

"Later." He promises, sucking my bottom lip before he stands, leaving me yearning desperately for his touch, his phenomenal taste. I smile when he winks and walks out of the bathroom—my entire body pulses with want. I groan and let my head fall back against the tub.

I look at Alaia, who was sitting in her chair with bubbles on her head. She lifts her big green eyes and looks at me, splashing the water, babbling excitedly, trying to tell me something. "Hey, don't judge me. He's hot, okay." I grin, leaning forward and kissing her little nose, and she giggles, displaying the dimples she got from her father. She's so freaking beautiful. "Who said you could be this cute, huh?" I smile as I wash her body. "You're going to keep your Daddy busy chasing away all the boys that will be going crazy for you. Yes you are." I smile as I lay her down on the bed after we were finished with our bath. Cole scowls from his position on the bed and snorts, putting his tablet down. "Boys?" He shakes his head. "No boys will get within two meters of her. I'll make sure of it." I watch as he crawls over to look down at her.

I laugh. "Oh, you better start preparing your little heart, honey, because whether you like it or not, she's going to be bringing home boyfriends and going out on dates. She might even come home married one day, who knows?" I tell him with a teasing smile, and his face falls while he looks down at her.

"Alaia Mae Hoult, you better not." Cole scowls at her, and she smiles, reaching up to grab his nose, making him melt instantly, and he kisses her fingers.

"Look at you. She's got you wrapped around her little finger." I chuckle, leaving her with him while I get dressed.

Cole picks her up and lays her on his chest. "You're not having a boyfriend till you're at least thirty. You hear me, princess?" Cole says, poking her softly while she slaps his face. He growls at her playfully, and she cackles. "You really are your mother's daughter. Look, she's abusing me already." Cole utters, laughing as she squeezes his cheek. "If any boys touch you, you do this to them too, baby girl, kay. I'm going to get Uncle Josh to train you so you can be a badass just like your Mama."

I look over at them while I brush my hair and smile. My only wish is that her fate is not as cursed as mine was.

I leave Cole with Alaia while I go and prepare her food. She's eating solids now and absolutely loves it. It's upsetting that she's weaning off my breast milk now she's eating proper food three times a day. I only give her my milk at bedtime, which I read was more comfort than her needing it. She grew in the blink of an eye, and she'll be a year old in five months. That's crazy to me. Cole plays with her on the floor in the living room while I prepare dinner. I can hear her laughing while he does the tickle monster on her. He's such a goof. Cole takes her upstairs when she starts to rub her eyes tiredly. It was past her bedtime, and if she doesn't sleep on time, she'll get cranky. I watch on the monitor as Cole lays her down in her bed and kisses her forehead, she starts to cry, and he rocks her gently. "Shh, oh I know, you're tired, sweetheart." He whispers, rubbing her back gently.

I stir the sauce to the carbonara pasta I was cooking while watching him with her. I pick up the monitor when he starts to sing to her. "Sweet dreams, baby girl." He whispers when she falls asleep and kisses her head. I dry my eyes before he sees me crying when I hear him coming down the stairs.

I stood in the kitchen, watching the sauce bubbling away for a while. Oh, stuff the food. I turn the cooker off and walk out of the kitchen. I see him sprawled out on the sofa, his long legs spread wide in that sexy, lazy manner men sit while he's watching tv—my mouth waters at the sight of him. Cole was topless in only a pair of grey tracksuit bottoms. Come on, Shay, don't lose your nerve now. I stroll over to him, and he looks at me as I straddle him. "Oh, hello." He smiles handsomely, placing his hands on my hips.

"Hi," I whisper before I press my lips to his, kissing him hot and needy. Cole moans throatily, his hand coming up to my nape, deepening the kiss.

"You're driving me, crazy baby," He groans, dragging his lips up to my throat. I tilt my head back, giving him more space to lick and nip at my neck. My head went dizzy with desire, especially when he tore my top off and his mouth was on my nipple, biting gently, licking, and tugging.

"Cole." I moan, curling my fingers in his hair, my body arching up into him, needing more of him. "I need you." I breathe, and he lifts his eyes to mine and brushes his fingers through my hair. His eyes search mine for a long moment, silently checking to make sure I was certain. I cup his face with my hands and lick my lips while I look into his eyes. "Make me yours."

Cole's eyes close, and he presses his forehead to mine, biting his lip hard. "Fuck baby, I've been aching to hear those three words from you again," Cole whispers, drawing my mouth to his. We kiss fervently while we undress one another. It felt so damn good feeling his lips on me, his hands caressing my body, his hard body pressed against mine. I shift between his legs, and he watches me eagerly as I grasp his manhood in my hand. Cole hisses, his mouth hangs open when I lick up his length. "Oh Shay, fuck baby." He moans gutturally, his eyes staring into mine while I suck him deep into my mouth. "Oh, Jesus..." He breathes, his eyes closing while his fingers brush my hair away from my face as I swirl my tongue around the length of him. His hips rock up, moans growing louder the closer he comes to his release. I want to taste him. I was aching to feel him throbbing and pulsing in my mouth. I find a rhythm, and he watches heatedly as his cock disappears into my mouth, and I suck up slow and hard from base to tip, flicking my tongue against the ridge, which causes the muscles in his abdomen to clench. Sexiest thing ever.

"Christ baby, stop, stop, I'm close, you're going to make me come." Cole groans, his fingers tightening in my hair when I look up at him but don't stop, I suck him harder, and he growls, gripping the back of the sofa. Biting his lip, "Oh *fuck*. You want my come, baby." He breathes, watching me avidly while I nod, moaning in response. I brush my fingers over his balls, and his hips jerk up at my touch, and I feel him grow harder, hotter in my mouth before he starts to throb and his balls tighten. "Oh fuck, Shay, I'm coming. Oh Shayla, yes, baby, uhh!" I soak up his moans while he thrusts his hips up, pushing himself deeper until he spurts his hot seed down my throat, biting his lip hard as his body shook with each surge of his orgasm, his chest heaving with frantic breaths, "Christ, baby." Cole pants breathless, opening his eyes to look down at me before he pulls me up, so I straddled him again and kisses me hard and deep, moaning at the taste of himself on my tongue. "That mouth of yours is something out of this world Shayla Hoult." He bites and tugs at my bottom lip. "My turn." With a devilish grin, he lays me down on the sofa, kissing his way down my body until he settles himself between my legs, and they fell open shamelessly for him.

I watch him, desire coiling deep in my belly when he lifts his eyes to mine just as he licks slow and lasciviously up through my slit, teasing me, taunting me, making me quake with each stroke of his velvet tongue on my nub. I circle my hips, rocking against his hot mouth. My body was begging him for more. I was panting and moaning wildly for him, aching for that sweet release. "Jesus, Cole." I moan, arching up when I feel that familiar, delicious heat spiral through me.

"Give it to me, baby, come all over my tongue." The vibrations of his deep voice sent a shiver through me, pushing me closer. Cole sucks my clit tirelessly, and I still panting as he flicks his tongue over my clit, driving me over the edge.

"Uhh, Cole, I'm coming," I whimper, curling my fingers in his hair.

"Look at me, baby, let me watch you come." I force my eyes open, and I hold his hungry gaze, unable to look away as I climax with a throaty cry; pleasure pulsed through me, leaving me trembling and gasping for air. "Uhhhh, Cole!" I vaguely hear him moan through the blood rushing in my ears. I collapse on the sofa, and he continues to lick and kiss my mound gently as my body settles down. I grab his head and pull him up, melding our lips together urgently. "I want you inside me... now." I moan into his mouth, and he groans in response; nudging my legs apart, I feel him pressed against my entrance, and I look up at him while he stares down into my eyes. My stomach clenches tight in hesitation for a second, and my mouth goes bone dry as I wait for his reaction while he watches mine sliding into me slowly, first the crown then inch by inch, until he was completely immersed to the hilt, deep inside me. I release the quivering breath I had been holding, and his eyes close.

"Oh my God, baby, I've missed your pussy so fucking much." Cole gasps, nuzzling his nose over mine. The look on his face as he slid inside me was all I needed. Cole didn't falter for one second, and his body still trembled when he pushed himself in like it always had. That and the moans and desire in his eyes was enough to force me to finally let go of the last bit of fear and doubt I was feeling of not being good enough, especially when he whispered...

"You're mine."

Chapter 34

COLE

ANOTHER GRUELLING DAY OF WORK. That office is unbearable without her. I'd rather stay in bed with Shayla. Actually, I'd rather stay *anywhere* with Shayla would be the correct term. Despite the stress of the trials and court Shayla is finally back to her usual self. Justice had been served. Sophie got twenty-five years, and the two fuckers got life in prison. It was over. I was worried she would go spiralling back to her depressive state while she was forced to relive the moments they tortured her. They offered to shield her away so she would face them, but she declined. The prosecutor tried to break her, blaming her for Sophie's mental state because of our relationship's breakdown, which resulted in her 'momentary lapse of judgement' and wanting to hurt Shayla. She even dared to stand there and lie that she was provoked, that Shayla threatened her first, and I was volatile and abusive to her throughout our relationship, which only worsened her mental state and drove her over the edge. According to Sophie, Shayla told her she would live to regret it if she didn't leave me alone. Absolute horse shit. I had the urge to jump over the seating area and strangle the crazy shrew. Sophie denied confessing to Shayla about being the one responsible for my plane crash. Another lie, but that investigation is still ongoing. The truth will come out, it always does.

The whole thing was absurd, they angled for a temporary insanity plea, and the judge dismissed it, seeing right through her bullshit. Once they were sentenced, Sophie kept screaming that she would finish the job the next time as they carried her kicking and screaming. I'm thankful it's all behind us now, but I'm still worried Sophie might find a way and come after Shayla or Alaia again. I wasn't about to make that mistake twice. I bought a new house with high-end security, and we are due to move. Shayla will have a bodyguard with her when she's alone while I'm at work. She downright refused, saying she could protect herself, but I was having none of it.

"I understand that you want to move and have the house guarded and protected, but I don't need a bodyguard, Cole. I can protect myself." She argues, glaring at me in that sexy way she does when she's fuming. I feel my cock twitch, stirring under her fiery gaze.

"You're wasting your breath, Shay. I'll be damned if I risk yours or Alaia's life again. We don't know what that lunatic is capable of. I'll die before I let anything happen to either of you." I tell her as I stand from my desk in my home office and walk over to her. "Don't fight me on this." I plead, taking hold of her face, and she looks up at me, her eyes fiery. "I want you safe— and seeing as I can't quit my job to ensure your safety personally twenty-four-seven, this is the next best option, this or I lock your arse away in the house. Which would you prefer?" I question, raising my brow inquisitively, and she narrows her eyes at me stubbornly.

"Neither." She hisses, pulling away and folding her arms over her chest. "I don't want someone tailing and following me around every time I want to go out. She's locked away, Cole. She can't hurt me."

I roll my eyes, "Shayla, there's no saying what that lunatic will do, we can't take her threats lightly. I'm *not* taking that fucking risk again. Do you understand me? You'll have close personal protection, whether you like it or not. If you don't, you can sit your butt at home. End of discussion." I declare firmly, and she shakes her head, averting her gaze from mine. I sigh and pull her close to me. "Stop sulking." I reach up to turn her head to look at me, but she pulls her face from mine, leering at me. "You're sexy as fuck when you're angry." I drawl, stepping closer to her while she continues to glare daggers at me. I reach for her, and she slaps my hand away with a scowl and steps back. I don't know how she does it, but this girl still drives me insane with desire, especially when she's got that fire burning in the depths of her gorgeous eyes. I grab her wrist and yank her against me. "Keep looking at me like that, and I'll bend you over this desk, sweetheart," I whisper, leaning closer to her lush pink lips.

Shayla's mouth curls into a slow smirk. She curls her fingers around my tie, licking her lips alluringly. "Call off your security detail, and I'll willingly bend over the desk for you." She states sultrily, and I stare at her.

"Not a fucking chance." I hiss, pressing my forehead to hers, my hands grabbing her hips, and she sighs, her temper flaring again.

"Well, in that case, honey, the only arse gracing your desk will be your own." She bites and tries to pull away, but I circle my arm around her waist and pull her against me again.

"Don't provoke me, Shayla. We've played this game many times, and I always win." I whisper, dragging my lips against the shell of her ear. "I'll have you on your knees sucking my cock so fast your head will spin." I groan, and she stares up at me, green eyes wide, her luscious lips parted.

She grins wickedly. "Mm, we shall see who'll have whom down on their knee's first then, big boy," She purrs—*fucking purrs* up at me, and I clench my jaw tight, staring into her eyes, fighting every urge in my body to not fuck her raw up against the wall. "If you succeed, I'll stop fighting you on this security obsession of yours. If I succeed, you call it off. Deal?"

It's adorable that she thinks she has what it takes to fight off my sexual advances. "Deal. Kiss to seal?"

"Dream on." She mutters, blowing me a kiss before she spins on her heel and sashays out of my office. I watch her sexy arse as she walks away and suck my bottom lip. She doesn't stand a chance. I give her a week at most before she caves.

After Shayla and I finally had sex after months, we've been at it like rabbits, unable to keep our hands off each other. As messy as our relationship has been, that raw magnetic pull we had from the very first moment I laid my eyes on her has never wavered. I'm still as obsessed with her as I was then—if not more. We're entirely in sync when it comes to the act of love. These little games we play with one another keep that fire inside us raging. I can't imagine spending my life with anyone else. She keeps me on my toes in every aspect of my life, and I love her madly for it.

Two weeks go by, and after a long stressful day at the office, I was happy to be home, and the smell of her cooking makes my stomach growl in recognition the second I step in through the threshold.

"Baby, I'm home," I call out as I close the front door. I drop my briefcase on the sofa and see Alaia in her bouncer, bouncing away while she watches Moana again for the millionth time. I walk over to her and kiss her chubby cheek. "Hi, sweetheart," I murmur against her cheek, inhaling her beautiful baby scent. "I've missed you so much."

"Has Daddy missed me, too?" I hear Shayla ask from behind me. I turn to look at her and do a double-take when I see her in *nothing* but her apron and red 'fuck me' heels with chocolate smeared over her thigh.

Oh, fuck me, indeed.

After the day I've had, a wild night between my wife's gorgeous legs was precisely what I needed to blow off some steam. I rise to my feet and let my eyes skim over her perfect curves. "Like you wouldn't believe." I gulp, walking over to her, then I remember our little bet and smirk as I advance toward her. She almost had me. I was ready to spread her out on the kitchen island and tongue fuck her tight pussy till she was screaming. I tower over her, and she cranes her neck to look up at me. "What are you doing to me." I husk, backing her up against the wall, and she gasps a little when her back meets the cold tiles.

"Me?" She intones, feigning innocence, but I see the mischief in her eyes. "I made a real mess of myself while I was baking brownies," Shay tells me smoothly and lifts the spoon she was holding covered in melted chocolate and licks it, deliberately smearing it over her lips. This woman is going to be the death of me. I sigh, staring at her lips, and swallow the saliva that had gathered in my mouth. "I've got chocolate...*everywhere.*"

I smirk, tilt her head up a little and suck the chocolate off her bottom lip and moan. "Why don't I help you clean up..." I whisper, swiping my tongue along her lips. Shayla sighs, parting her lips for me, but I nip at her bottom lip gently as I lift her hand and suck the chocolate smeared on her fingers. "After the long, stressful day I've had at work, all I dreamt about all day was coming home and falling into your arms," I admit taking the spoon from her fingers and dragging it down her neck. "Then I see you greet me like this..." I lick the chocolate off her neck, stopping to suck her pulse point, knowing it makes her crazy. Her head tilts back, and she moans. "Now, all I can think about is spreading you out, slathering your pussy in chocolate, and spoiling my appetite before dinner," I murmur in her ear while I untie her apron, and it falls to the floor at her feet. "If you weren't so damn stubborn, I would have my tongue all up inside you, driving you wild. You'd be begging me to make you come while you sit on my face and ride my tongue." I smear chocolate over her nipple before I grasp her breast in my hand and dip my head, licking it off, sucking her hardened nub while she hisses and arches up, pushing her breast up into my mouth.

"Fuck, Cole." She moans, curling her fingers in my hair.

"Oh, baby, I want to. I want to fuck you so hard." I take her hand and press it against my crotch. "All night long," I growl when she strokes me through my trousers. "In every position, I can get you into." Shayla whimpers, her face flushed when I brush my fingers through her folds, and her hips jerk at my touch. "Fuck, you're *so* wet." I hiss, pressing my forehead to hers. "Please, baby, give into me and let me have you," I fiercely whisper while I brush my fingers against her clit, she quakes visibly.

"You're playing dirty." She moans, opening her eyes and looking up at me, hot and needy.

"And you're not," I question, dragging my lips over hers as I speak quietly. "You know what those heels do to me—you're making me crazy, sweetheart; I can't focus on work. I dream about fucking you every night. Give into me already, and let's stop this fucking game."

"You give into me, and I will drop to my knees right now and suck you off so good, so hard, I'll lap up your cream as you explode in my mouth." Shayla groans stubbornly while she unbuckles my belt, and I bite my lip hard, watching her longingly.

"You're killing me." I almost sob, looking at her. I grab her hands, stopping her as she unzips my trousers. "You're not going to break me. Not with this." I tell her earnestly, placing my hands on either side of her head on the wall and stare intently into her eyes. "I'd rather go without sex and jerk off for the rest of my life than ever take the chance and face losing you and Alaia again," I add and push off the wall. Shayla watches me, her brows fused as I back away. "I'm going to shower." I turn and skip up the steps to the bedroom. While I stood in the shower, the hot water beating down on my aching shoulders, I hang my head, my palms pressed against the wall. I was feeling frustrated beyond belief. I get why she's resistant to not wanting protection. It can be gruelling having someone follow you around constantly like a shadow, but those threats Sophie made keeps replaying on my mind, and I'm scared shitless she will try and hurt them and succeed this time. Maybe I'm being irrational and overly protective, but I just can't risk it. I won't survive if anything happens to them. She's lucky I haven't up and packed us up to move to a different country where she can't find us.

I was lost in thought and didn't even hear Shayla step into the shower behind me. I felt her hand run up and over my back. My semi-erect rod springs back to life at her touch, and I close my eyes, groaning when her lips follow her hand. I straighten and sigh, tilting my head back while she peppers kisses along my shoulders which tense under her lips. "Shayla." Her hands sneak around, and she caresses my stomach, running her fingers over my abs. I cover her hands with my own. "You're not going to break me." I hiss when she wraps her fingers around my cock. My head falls back as she strokes me slow and steadily. "Ah, Christ, Shayla. You're killing me, baby." I moan and curl my fingers around her wrist before I pull her in front of me. Shayla lifts her green eyes, looking up at me sultrily, licking her lips before she slowly kneels, her eyes on mine.

I couldn't contain the grin that spread across my face as I look down at her. "You caved."

"I don't need a bodyguard, but it's clearly important to you, and if it's going to give you peace of mind and make you happy, I'll do it." I close my eyes and sigh in relief. I feel my entire body relax. I lean over and pull her up to her feet and take her face into my hands. "I was being unreasonable and inconsiderate by disregarding your feelings on the matter. I'm sorry."

"You don't have to apologise, baby. I get your reasons for not wanting a bodyguard, but my priority is always you and Alaia first and foremost." I explain, brushing my thumb along her jaw, and she smiles beautifully, caressing my chest.

"And you are ours." She whispers before I lean down and draw her in for the slow, hair-raising kiss I've been dying to give her all day. Shayla moans audibly. Her silky-smooth tongue sinks into my mouth, teasing my own as I back her up against the wall kissing her urgently, covering her body with my own. "At this rate, we don't need to worry about that lunatic killing us—Oh God – we're going to end up fucking each other to death." She gasps when I attack her neck, sucking and biting.

I groan, "It's a good way to go." I pin her arms above her head, bruising her lips with another hard and wet kiss, savouring in her heavenly taste. I lift her into my arms, pressing my forehead to hers, my cock at her entrance. I moan when she rocks her hips and slides down the length of me, her pussy swallowing me up greedily as I push in to the hilt. I held my promises to her and fucked her hard in the shower, then on the dining table after dinner, then we made love in bed until the early hours. Two whole weeks of sexual frustration, and we well and truly made up for it in one night.

"So..." I pull my gaze from Shayla standing in the kitchen talking to Jo and Aimee to look at Josh, who was sipping his beer, a grin smeared across his face. "I take it things are going well with you and Shay?"

I smirk and take a long chug from my bottle of beer. "You could say that." I lick my lips and glance over at her again. I scowl when Sam throws a cushion in my face laughing.

"My little sister has got you whipped, bro." Josh chuckles, shaking his head when I throw the cushion back at him.

"I'd tell you the reasons why bro, but I'm afraid you may need therapy after." I tease him with a grin, and his face twists in disgust.

Sam shudders, "I don't need to be hearing that shit, brother. That's just wrong." Josh and I laugh in response.

"You should have considered that little detail before you decided to fall in love with one of her best friends. You'll just have to grin and bear it because I listen to you two dickheads go on and on about how great your sex lives are. It's only fair I get some bragging rights, too." I retort mockingly, and Sam glares at me, not so amused. I love winding him up. I would never share any intimate details about our sex life with anyone. That's our business, and I love that Shay is just as passionate about our privacy. We hear the girls squeal with excitement over something in the kitchen, and I chuckle, watching Shayla laughing. She was glowing and happy.

It's been a while since we all hung out together, and after everything we've been through, we needed some downtime. Shayla invited Josh, Aimee, Sam, and Jo over for a movie night. We ordered Chinese food, and the boys and I were supposed to pick a film to watch. We have yet to do that. Sam leans over and taps my thigh. "How is Shay after every-thing? Is she coping okay?" He questions, glancing over at her. I follow his gaze and nod.

"Yeah, she's good. She has days where she feels down and just wants to be alone, but other than that...she's back to her usual self." I explain, watching her, and she catches me staring and holds my gaze, puckers up her lips, and blows me a kiss. I grin and wink at her, making her blush a lovely pink when the girl's awe at her.

Ah, fuck, I love her like crazy.

Two years and I still make her blush just like the day we first met. I'm hoping to make her blush like that when we're old and grey too.

"She seems happy, and that's all that matters to me," Sam smiles and pats my shoulder. "You're a good man, Richie Rich."

"Thanks to her." I sigh contently. "I'm the man I am today because of *her*," I say, watching her as she walks over to me, wine glass in her hand and a bowl of sweet popcorn in the other. I pull her in my lap, and she kisses me softly. "Hi," I mumble against her lips.

"Hey, handsome." She grins when I nuzzle her nose with my own.

"What are we watching then?" Aimee says, settling in Josh's lap in the other round loveseat. Jo and Sam take the long, crushed velvet sofa so she could be comfortable being six months pregnant. Sam kisses her forehead and rubs her round baby bump lovingly.

"We actually couldn't decide," Josh admits sheepishly, and Aimee rolls her eyes smiling.

"What did I say?" She pipes up, pointing at Shayla and Jo, who chuckle. "I'll pick something. And if I hear any of you testosterone-bearing schmucks complain, I will kick you where it hurts. You'll be first Hoult." She adds, giving me a side glare while I was nuzzling Shayla's neck.

I scowl. "What did I do now, I'm just sitting here," I complain, and she narrows her blue eyes at me playfully. "I know you love me, really, Aimes. It's written all over your face." I tease, throwing popcorn at her, and she flips me off, grinning.

"I really hate you, you smug git." I laugh and nestle myself into Shayla's chest with a moan.

"Protect me," I whisper to Shayla, who giggles and kisses my temple lovingly. Aimee and I have a love-hate relationship. She pretends to hate me, but I know deep down she loves me, really. She's like the sister I never had, she and Jo both are, and I love them dearly. Once the movie was picked, Aimee chose Pearl Harbour, we ate our food and pretended to watch the film. Not one of us was watching.

You know when you go to the cinema with your friends and girl-friends, and you all just start making out, yeah that was us. Like a bunch of teens in heat instead of the grown adults that we were. I think Shayla and I started it by whispering naughty things to one another about her fantasy of me being in a uniform, and it went on from there.

Josh and Aimee were kissing rather passionately in their love seat. Jo and Sam were too engrossed in each other to acknowledge anything around them, and Shayla and I were flirting shamelessly, teasing one another relentlessly until I was rock hard and throbbing, and she was wet and aching. We sure do make a fine pair.

God, I love my life.

Chapter 35

SHAYLA

"Okay, we're going to try this one more time."

I hold the spoon to Alaia's mouth and feed her the vegetable medley. Her face goes sour, and she spits it out with a shudder. "You really don't like this, huh?" I utter, putting her plate down with a sigh, and Alaia blinks at me and smiles showing her one tiny tooth she sprouted out of nowhere. "Don't give me that smile. You need to eat your vegetables, young lady."

"Why are you scolding my daughter?" I hear Cole say behind me as he walks into the kitchen. He leans over and drops a kiss on my neck and one on Alaia's head before he goes to the coffee machine.

"She's being stubborn and not eating her food." I hold the spoon to her mouth, and she turns her head, shaking it. Cole sips his coffee and leans against the kitchen counter, watching us with a smile.

"Wonder who she gets that from." He mutters, looking at me pointedly over the rim of his coffee mug.

"I love my food, actually." I point out, casting him a playful look, and he grins back sexily. I love the way he looks in the mornings. His hair is all tousled from sleep and a night of passion. Wearing only a pair of white Calvin Klein boxers, Cole stood there, looking like a sexy model, all hard and muscular. I don't know what's wrong with me. I'm lusting after him like a randy teen does her celebrity crush. I just can't seem to get enough of him. I read an article that said victims of sexual assault often go through stages where they either don't want sex or can't get enough of it. For me, it seems to be the latter. It's a coping mechanism;

the feeling of being loved helps overcome the bouts of anxiety that fight its way to the surface from time to time. Cole didn't seem to mind at all. Whether it be night or day, he's always up for the task of pleasuring me.

"I was talking about the stubborn part." He grins when I give him a wry look and retakes a sip of his coffee.

"Hey, you wanted her to be just like me." I utter, getting up and picking up the plate of food and walking to the sink beside him. "You got your wish."

"I'm not the one complaining, baby," Cole informs me, his eyes playful as he sidles close to me. His bare shoulder brushing mine as he leans closer, the warmth of his body spreads through mine.

"You're not complaining *yet*." I smile sweetly. "You will see when she's older and becomes a teenager, and you two start butting heads." Coles smile fades, and his brows knit together. He looks over at Alaia, who was cooing and playing with her toy in her highchair.

"She's going to be a good girl, just like her mother." He states, and I chuckle, washing her plate.

"Good girl, huh?" I intone wetting my lips. "That's not what you were saying last night." I remind him, and a slow, knowing smirk spreads across his gorgeous face before he sets his coffee down and curls his fingers around my wrist, pulling me against his hard burly body. Cole's green eyes glitter as they skim over my face.

"You're a good girl with very bad intentions, Shayla Hoult." I smile when he circles his arms around my waist, a mischievous glint in his eyes. "The perfect concoction of angel and devil in one beautiful package. You have the hottest kind of fire in you, and I just love to burn in it."

I feel my cheeks grow hot under his gaze, images of the night before filling my mind. "You ignited that fire in me, Cole." I declare, running my hands over his perfectly cut biceps. "I don't know what you've done to me, but I just can't get enough of you," I whisper against his lips, and he groans lowly, his hands cupping my bum and squeezing. "I'm worried you're going to get sick of me."

Cole frowns. "You must be joking. I'm obsessed with you." Cole whispers back, gliding his velvet tongue across my lips teasingly. I feel a hot desire course through my body and pool between my legs, making my knees wobble and womanhood pulse. "I'm addicted to you." He moans, tugging my bottom lip before he coaxed my lips apart and sinks his tongue in my mouth in search of mine. I greet his tongue with a gentle stroke of mine over his, and he groans zealously, tugging me against him roughly. "*Fuck.* Do that again." Cole breathes, squeezing my hips. I slide my hands over his strapping chest and glide my tongue over his smoothly with a breathy moan. I can feel his erection, hard like stone, pressed up against my belly. "You are insatiable. As soon as Laia is down for her nap, I'm going to fuck you wild." Cole growls possessively and kisses me hard and dirty, landing a hard slap on my bum and squeezing after, making me cry out in pleasure and just a touch of pain. Cole made it a point to christen our new seven-bedroom home as soon as we moved in.

Though it was insanely big, ten thousand feet, the house was exquisite, a half-acre plot with three floors. Cole and I fell in love with it the moment we saw the house from the outside. It was built on a private road in-country, secluded and peaceful. It has seven bedrooms, eight bathrooms, and five reception rooms. The kitchen was my favourite, it was spacious, and it had a big while granite island in the middle and the units was a dark walnut colour with three built-in ovens. There was a huge splashback mirror where the sink was located, which brightened up the whole room. To the back of the kitchen, there were white French doors to access the patio garden. Our master bedroom was so big it had five separate rooms in it. It had his and hers ensuite bathrooms, a living room, and two separate dressing rooms with a sun terrace overlooking the beautiful garden.

"What do you think?" Cole whispers in my ear, drawing me back against his chest as I stood in the walk-in dressing room.

"It's incredible, but it's so big, baby." Cole spins me around and looks down into my face. "It's only three of us. We'll get lost in this house."

Cole grins delightfully, "Three of us...*for now.* We're going to fill this home up with our babies." He murmurs, kissing me softly. "Besides, we're going to need the extra bedrooms for housekeepers and a live-in nanny." I pull my head back and look up at him with a frown.

"Live-in nanny?" I intone, and he nods slowly. "Why would we need a live-in nanny?"

Cole brushes his fingers through my hair. "Well, you are going to come back to work eventually, right? I don't see you being the kind of girl to want to give up your career to be a stay-at-home mum." He explains, and I chew my bottom lip. That thought hadn't even occurred to me. Cole noticed the saddened look on my face and tilted my head up so I could look at him. "Hey, what's with the sad face?"

"Cole, I don't want another woman raising our kids," I tell him ruefully, and he brushes his thumb along my jaw, his mouth set in a thin line.

"Of course you don't, baby, but what about your career? You worked so hard to get your degree. The last thing I want is for you to be unhappy." Cole expresses thoughtfully, and I sigh, my shoulders dropping. "Honey, I was raised by a nanny, and I turned out fine." He specifies with an assuring smile. "I want you by my side at Cult. We have an empire to run, baby,"

"I know, but I don't want a live-in nanny," I say, peeking up at him through my lashes, and he smiles dotingly. "We can have a nanny to watch the kids while we're at work, but when we come home, I want it to be just us. I want to come home and cook my husband and kids a home-cooked meal. I want to take care of my family, not have someone else—especially other women doing it." I clarify, brushing my fingers over his tie to smooth it out. "I don't want random girls living in our house."

Cole tilts his head to the side and regards me curiously with his eyes narrowed. "Shayla, this isn't a movie or a porno. I'm not going to screw the nanny or the housekeeper's sweetheart."

I scowl at him and pull my head back. "Won't stop them from wanting to screw you, though? If I were a maid working in your house and I saw you day in day out, I would definitely fantasise about screwing you."

Cole throws his head back and laughs with gusto. "Honey, if *you* were a maid in my house, I would screw you, no doubt." I hit his arm, and he chuckles, tightening his arms around me. "Oh God, I've got a semi just thinking about it." Cole groans, brushing his lips along my jaw. "Do you think we can role play that later?" He murmurs in my ear, making me flush ten different shades of red.

"Cole!" I rebuke, trying my best to look affronted, but my lips curl into a smile when he looks at me with eyes full of desire.

"What?" I stare at him, "Don't tell me you're not thinking about it. You're all red." Cole grins, wagging his brows at me suggestively. I was thinking about it. I curl my fingers around his tie and yank his face close to mine.

"You're a dirty man." I purr, and he responds with a throaty groan, his hands wandering down to my bum while his mouth snatches mine, drawing me into a feverish kiss.

"Keep talking to me in that manner, and I'll fuck your brains out right here in this dressing room, Gorgeous girl." Cole hisses against my lips as he backs me up against the mirror.

I grin against his mouth. "You fuck, you buy, Mr Hoult."

"I can't put a price on your pussy, baby." Cole moans, gathering my arms up over my head and licking down my throat. "But it will most definitely be worth the fifteen million."

"That's one expensive fuck." I grin, and he smiles naughtily while hiking up my skirt.

"And you're worth every penny." Cole moans as he hoists me up into his arms and slides into me hard and deep. The estate agent showing us the house was around somewhere and could catch us having sex any moment, but neither of us cared about anything but each other. Cole was pounding into me so hard I couldn't contain the whimpers of pleasure as I reach my climax. Cole covered my mouth with his hand smothering my moans. "Ahh, fuck!" He growls when I clamp down on him, and he nears his own release. I cover his mouth with my hand, silencing him, and we come together in heated bliss.

"You're trouble, Cole Hoult." I grin, panting when he removes his hand from my mouth. What am I going to do with this man?

"And you love it."

I really did.

I love being reckless with him. We've had such a troubled relationship. We never really enjoyed being together and doing things most people who date do. After Cole told the agent we're buying the house and to send him the paperwork; he took me out to lunch to celebrate our new beginning.

The following two weeks were spent packing the old house to move to the new place. Cole was at work, so the girls came over to help me pack.

"Jesus, I thought I had a lot of crap." Aimee huffs, settling a box down on the floor, and winces.

I smile sheepishly. "It's mainly Cole's stuff. All my stuff I fit into like four boxes. The rest is all his, Alaia's and kitchenware." I sigh, looking around the house sadly. "I can't believe we're moving again. I feel like that's all I've done lately, packing and moving from one place to another. I moved out of the apartment to Coles, then back to the apartment, then back to Coles, then here, then back to the apartment, then back here again and now to a whole new place."

Aimee blinks at me and sighs. "I'm exhausted just listening to you say that sentence, girl." She grumbles sitting on the floor, and she smiles when Jo comes waddling over. "That better be pillows in that box."

Jo smiles and sets the box beside the others. "It was." She replies and comes over to join us.

"How's my nephew?" I coo, reaching over and rubbing her bump. She beams at the mention of her baby boy.

"He's good, growing well and very active, so much so that he doesn't let me sleep at night." Jo pouts, moving my hand to a spot where I can feel him kick. "Between the baby and your brother's horrific snoring, I'm exhausted."

I laugh, "Yeah, Sam's snores still haunt me to this day. I could hear him through the wall; how you manage to sleep next to him fascinates me." Jo rolls her eyes, shaking her head.

"I wish you would have warned me before I got myself involved with him." She whimpers mockingly, and I grin.

"I would have, had you told me you were thinking about sleeping with him?" I point out, and she grins sheepishly and winces.

"You got me there." She laughs a little. "The sly bastard charmed me with his dirty mouth and sexy muscles." I roll my eyes with a grin.

"I'm starving," Aimee complains, rubbing her flat stomach with a pout. "All this hard work has got me famished. Let's order Chinese. I could devour some kung pao chicken and sticky rice."

I moan at the thought of food; I was hungry too. "We ate a sandwich an hour ago, but that sounds too good to pass up. I'll order it." I get up to my feet and sway when my head spins. "Whoa, head spin."

"Shay, you okay?" Aimee asks, concerned, and I nod when it subsides.

"Yeah, I got up too quick, I think. I'm good." I take out the Chinese menu and order our food. We sat around the kitchen island, eating our food and discussing our men. "Should I be worried?"

Aimee frowns, shaking her head. "No, of course not. Every man has fantasies about screwing a nanny. It's right up there with the maid and nurse. How was it, though?" She asks, her eyes glittering as she looks at me curiously.

I smile and pick up a piece of chicken with my chopsticks. "Amazing, but our sex life always has been," I explain, biting my lip. "I've been crazy randy lately. If I see him topless and walking around, I get the urge to jump him. I'm worried he's going to get sick of me if we keep humping like bunnies."

"Mm, I was like that with Sam. He'd come home after a workout and just looking at him all sweaty drove me crazy." Jo explains, chewing on her chicken. "Then I found out I was pregnant, and it turns out it was my hormones running wild."

Aimee grins, leaning back in her chair. "Josh and I have been at it like crazy too, so you're not alone, girl."

I laugh, "You would be. You're still in the newlywed phase. I couldn't get Cole off me after we got married." I sigh longingly. "I love that he still wants me after everything."

"Did you have any doubt?" Jo questions dubiously, and I shrug. "Cole is crazy about you, Shay; nothing will ever change that," Jo assures me, and I nod, pushing away my self-esteem issues that were creeping up to the surface.

"Damn right, he looks at you like he's fascinated with you," Aimee states, biting into a prawn cracker and chews gingerly until her face falls. "Oh, crap." Her blue eyes go wide, and she covers her mouth and runs off toward the bathroom. Jo and I watch her run off, and her retching echo's in the house. We look at one another, and Jo's brows go up.

"Could she be..."

My mouth falls open as I look at Aimee, who comes back muttering to herself. "Aimee? You okay?"

She sinks into the chair and nods, pushing her food away with a grimace. "That was gross." She shudders and sips her water, looking at Jo and me over the rim of her glass. "What? Why are you looking at me like that?"

"Aimes, are you pregnant?" I ask, and she chokes on her water and starts coughing hysterically. I reach over and pat her on the back. "Easy girl."

"No," Aimee croaks, clearing her throat. "I don't think so. I had my period..." She stops and frowns. "When did I have my period?" Jo and I smile at one another. "You and I are on the same cycle. Have you had yours?" She asks me, concerned, and I shake my head.

"No, I haven't had mine yet. I should be due soon, though." Aimee relaxes a little while I load up the app on my phone, and I stare at it unblinking. "Oh God."

"What?" Aimee asks, sitting forward.

I lift my eyes and look at her. "It says I'm two weeks late?" Aimee visibly pales, and so do I as we stare at one another.

"Oh, my God! A double pregnancy!" Jo chirps excitedly, bouncing in her chair. "Our babies will be best friends!"

"I can't be pregnant!" Aimee and I cry out together.

I feel sheer panic, and I get up and pace back and forth. "Alaia is not even one yet! Oh, my God! I can't be pregnant. I'm on the pill."

"I'm not ready to be a mum!" Aimee whimpers. "We've not even been married a year."

"Uh...guys." Jo chuckles, watching us. "You should take a test before you panic."

"I have tests," I gasp, looking at Aimee, who nods, and we all hurry to the ensuite bathroom in the master bedroom.

"You first." I hand one to Aimee, and she looks at me, her blue eyes showing her concern. She shakes her head and looks at the test in her hand.

"No, you first."

"Oh my god!" Jo gets up from the bed. "You two are killing me. Why don't you do it together? Aimee, use the other bathroom, Shayla you go in here. Go!" Aimee and I jump, and I hurry into the bathroom while Aimee leaves the room to go to the guest bathroom. My fingers were trembling as I ripped the test open. I can't be pregnant again; it's not possible. I pee on the stick, wash my hands, and leave the bathroom. I place the test on my nightstand, and Aimee puts hers beside mine. We look at each other. I hold my hand out to her, and she takes it. Aimee was shaking too. We wait anxiously for three minutes.

"It's time," Jo says, looking at the watch on her wrist. Aimee and I walk over to the nightstand.

"On three?" She whispers, and I nod. We exhale and lean to look at the test. I stare at the word **'Pregnant'** numbly. Well shit. I look over at Aimee, who had the same look on her face.

"I'm pregnant." She whispers.

"Me too."

"Guys! This is so great! Why aren't you excited? All three of us are pregnant at the same time. How incredible is that!" Jo exclaims, hugging us both. It was incredible, and I know Cole will be over the moon when he finds out, but Alaia is still so young. *I'm* still young. Two kids before I'm thirty.

"Have you discussed kids with Josh?" I ask as we all sit on my bed. Aimee stares at the test in her hand, chewing her lip nervously.

"Yeah, briefly, but we said after a year. We were careful. I don't understand how this happened." She sighs dejectedly.

"I was on the pill, and that fertile freak still got me pregnant," I mutter bitterly, looking at the monitor at Alaia, who was asleep in her bed. Both our tests say 3-4 weeks pregnant.

"Are you going to tell the boys together?" Jo asks, grinning. She's excited enough for both of us. I place my hand on my flat stomach, and Aimee does the same to hers. We look at each other and laugh.

"Shayla, what the fuck? We're pregnant!" Aimee exclaims, still stunned.

"I know!" I groan and fall back on my bed. "Is it bad that I'm upset I won't get my brains screwed out by Cole anymore?"

Aimee laughs and lays down beside me, her head beside mine. "Bish, I'm right there with you." She laces her fingers with mine, and we sigh. Jo lays down on my other side, and I lace my fingers with hers.

"I miss getting fucked." Jo utters out loud after a while. We all break out into fits of laughter on the bed.

Aimee and I decided to tell the boys on the weekend, and of course, we had to have our JoJo there with us for the moment. We stood in the kitchen whispering to one another while the boys were playing UFC on the PlayStation in the living room.

"So, we just go over there and hand it to them?" Aimee says, exhaling nervously. I nod and push her wrapped box to her, and she chews on her full lips. We got baby grows made. Mine had 'And then there was four...' printed on the front and Aimee's one had, 'And then there was three' on hers. I was half excited and half nervous. My stomach was fluttering wildly. "Let's do this before I pass out." Aimee sighs, brushing her hair away from her face.

We walk to the living room, step in front of the screen, and the boys lean over trying to see the screen, scowls on their faces. "Girls, you're blocking the tv," Josh utters, moving from side to side, trying to see.

Aimee and I glare at them, and they lower the controls, watching us with wide eyes.

"Bro, what did you do?" Cole whispers, his eyes on mine, leaning into Josh, who shakes his head, his eyes on Aimee's angry gaze.

"Nothing. What did you do?" Josh mumbles back from the corner of his mouth.

"I didn't do anything, I swear," Cole utters, putting the control down. I fight the urge to smile and keep my face stoic, pretending I was livid.

"Oh, but you did. You *both* did something." I hiss. Cole and Josh exchange confused glances. We toss the boxes at them, and they catch them and look at us. They look at one another nervously once more and down at the box in their hands.

"I'm confused." Cole frowns, looking at me. "What's this?"

"Open it." I grouse, scowling. Aimee gestures to Josh, who casts another look at Cole before they tear the boxes open. They pull out the baby grows at the same time, brows knitted together. They read the front and their eyes lift to us. Cole stares into my eyes, "And then there was four? Shay is this..." Cole lowers the baby grow and shifts in his seat. "... what I think it is?"

"Aimes?" Josh utters his blue eyes wide.

Aimee and I look at one another, and we smile. "We're pregnant." We announce together, and the box falls off Josh's lap, and Cole's frown turns into a bright grin. The boys look at one another.

"YES!" They shout excitedly and hug each other before they fly off the sofa and rush over to us.

"Oh, baby." Cole wraps his arms around me and lifts me off the ground into his arms. I wrap my legs around him, laughing. "You're pregnant?"

"I am." I smile, pressing my forehead to his.

"But you were on the pill?"

I nod with a sigh. "I was, but much like yourself, your sperm also knows no bounds." I tease, and he laughs, pulling my lips to his for a long, passionate kiss. Josh and Aimee were also kissing.

"Yo!" Sam exclaims, throwing a cushion at us, grimacing. "We're still here! In case you all start stripping." Cole and I pull apart, panting, grins plastered on our faces.

"Shhh! Jo, shut your man up." Josh grumbles against Aimee's lips, who giggles. Jo pulls Sam down for a kiss, and he grunts, kissing her back quickly, forgetting about everyone else in the room.

"You've made me the happiest man in the world, baby." Cole groans, staring into my eyes lovingly, his fingers combing through my hair. "You're having my baby again."

"Let's pray this one goes better than the last." I sigh, brushing my fingers along his jaw. A sudden shadow falls over Cole's gaze as he remembers all the problems we had last time. We didn't get to enjoy the pregnancy the first time around. I pray this time will be different.

We've left all the bad memories behind us, remember?" Cole reminds me, and I nod, smiling a little. I didn't want to ruin this moment for us, so I push away all the negative emotions and focus on enjoying the moment.

"Absolutely." I grin, and he cups the back of my neck, brushing his lips over mine.

"Shay." He whispers into my mouth.

"Hm?"

"How about that nanny?" Cole drawls mockingly and laughs when I pinch his nipple. "Ow!"

"Bite me, Hoult."

"Just say where baby."

Chapter 36

COLE

"WE'RE GOING TO CHURCH?" I hear Shayla ask sceptically from inside her dressing room.

"Yes, we are," I answer, pulling on a pair of boxer shorts. Shayla pokes her head out and gives me a bemused look.

"Since when do you want to go to church? You don't even believe in God." I walk over to her dressing room and lean against the door, watching her stand there, her back to me while she looks through her selection of dresses in a matching pair of sexy black lace bra and panties.

"I do now." I declare, and she looks back at me over her shoulder.

"You do?"

I nod and stride over to her. Shayla turns and faces me while I place my hands on her waist and pull her against me. "The one and only time I have ever been to church was after you got kidnapped," I explain, gazing into her eyes. Shay's face falls at the mention of the incident. I lick my lips, brushing my fingers through her long dark hair. "They found a body that matched your description, and I had to go and..." I hesitate, shaking my head when I get flashes of that girl lying dead on that table.

Shayla notices the glum look on my face, and her brows fuse together. She reaches up and brushes her fingers over my face soothingly. "I was so thankful that it wasn't you. That was one of the worse moments of my entire life. On our way back home, I saw this church,

391

and I ran out of the car. I felt helpless and desperate, so I walked in there, and I prayed for God to help me find you and bring you back home to us. I made a promise that I would go to church if you came back safe and sound. And I found you. God brought you back to me." I explain, and Shayla closes her eyes and presses her forehead to mine.

"You prayed for me?" She questions softly, and I could hear the pain laced in her tone, which made me ache.

"I never stopped praying for you, Shayla. Even before I knew you existed, I must have unknowingly prayed so hard for you that you had no choice but to find me." I whisper, kissing her softly. "You not only taught me to love truly, but you also gave me faith. You taught me to believe." Shayla smiles, biting her lip a little.

"I love you, Cole," She sighs, trailing her fingers down my throat, her lips brushing mine as she speaks softly, sensually. "I love you so damn much."

I smile, dragging my bottom lip over her lips. "I love you," I murmur against her mouth as I gently part her lips. "I'm infatuated with you. Absolutely and completely besotted." Shayla moans when my tongue finds hers. We spend a good ten minutes kissing passionately, almost forgetting that we had to attend church until Shayla pulls away breathless.

"Stop riling me up. We're going to church." She scolds me teasingly, and I chuckle, dropping a kiss on the base of her neck. "I refuse to walk into church with damp panties." She utters with a sigh and tries to pull away, and I tug her back.

"How about no panties?" I suggest impishly, and she gapes at me apprehensively, her eyes go wide, her cheeks rosy.

"Tristan Cole Hoult, are you trying to get me sent straight to hell? I am not attending church commando." She hits my shoulder when I laugh. "You walk into church with lewd thoughts like that, and you may just spontaneously combust. You little devil."

"There's nothing little about this devil, baby." I drawl lasciviously, I spank her shapely bum, and she gasps. I press her hand against my crotch. "See."

"Behave." Shayla berates me trying to be all serious, but I see the glint in her eyes before she pulls away. "We're going to be late. Get ready."

Sunday morning service was quite lovely. I'm new to the whole religion thing, but it was very enlightening. I enjoyed it more than I thought I would. I sneak looks at Shayla, who looked like she was listening to the pastor intently with Alaia in her lap. Although she seemed lost in thought, her eyes glossed over. I still can't believe she's pregnant again. I'm over the moon. I missed out on so much of Shay's pregnancy with Alaia, and I'm determined to enjoy every second this time around.

After church, I took my girls out for brunch. We went to that cafe in Islington that Shayla took me to. Sunday was our day to spend together as a family. The weather was beautiful, bright, and not a cloud in the blue sky. It was the beginning of spring, so it was nice and warm out. We ordered the same as last time and ate our waffle in delight. Shayla even fed Alaia some, and she loved it, reaching out toward the plate in her highchair, opening and closing her little hand.

"Cole, don't give her too much," Shayla tells me off when I push a tiny piece into her mouth, and she smiles, chewing. "It's full of sugar, and she'll get all hyper."

"How can you say no to that face? Look at her. She looks just like you do when you eat something you love." I coo lovingly, reaching out to feed her more, and Shayla slaps my hand.

Shayla looks at Alaia and grins, "Of course, you don't eat your vegetables, but this you love, cheeky little madam."

"Do you think she recognises the taste from when you had it while you were pregnant with her?" I ask, scooping up some melted chocolate on my finger and holding it to her lips. Shayla sucks the chocolate off my finger with a moan.

"I don't think that's how it works, honey. The baby only gets the nutrients from what you eat. They can't actually taste what you eat." She explains, licking her luscious lips, "She's just like her mummy, hopelessly drawn to things that are bad for her." She gives me a pointed look, and I grin, taking her hand into mine.

393

"Oh, but I'm bad for you in all the right ways, sweetheart. Just like you're good for me in every possible way. I think we balance each other out quite well." I reply, leaning closer while my fingers play with hers.

Shayla leans forward, her eyes on mine. "I'm inclined to agree."

"That's a shame. I was hoping I'd have to convince you." I retort, taking her chin between my thumb and forefinger and brushing a kiss on her soft lips.

"Lucky for you, I'm easily pleased." She smiles, pulling away before I could deepen the kiss. I open my eyes and glare at her mockingly.

"Oh, okay, you're just going to leave me hanging like that?" I complain, and she laughs at my put-out look. "Kiss me, woman."

"No. You have to earn the pleasure." I groan, sinking back into my chair and look at Alaia chewing on her teething toy.

"Oh, here we go," I mutter with a groan. "What am I going to do with this mother of yours, hm? Tell me, princess." I ask her, and she squeals at me, and I nod. "Will you kiss Dada? Give Dada kiss Laia." I pucker up, and she leans forward, her mouth open, and kisses me on the lips. "Sweetest kiss ever." I coo, squishing her cheeks gently, and she hits my hands.

"She's such a Daddy's girl. Hey, what about me?" Shayla pouts, puckering her lips, and Alaia smiles at her, shaking her head. I laugh out loud and kiss Alaia's head.

"Daddy's little princess, come here." I lift her out of her chair and sit her on the table in front of me.

"This baby better be a boy," Shayla grumbles, sitting back and rubbing her stomach. "I'll show both of you."

"Stick your tongue out at Mummy," Alaia pokes her tongue, mimicking me, and I grin when Shayla throws a sugar sachet at my head. "That's my baby!" I growl, nuzzling her neck, making her giggle. Alaia's becoming more and more interactive with us, and I love it. She's crawling and pulling herself up to stand and gets all excited when you praise her for doing something. She's just growing into her own little personality now, and it's adorable.

"What if we have another girl?" Shayla asks, resting her chin in her hand while she watches Alaia and I play.

"Good, I hope we do. I'd love another girl." I tell her earnestly, and Shayla blinks. A look of surprise fleets across her beautiful face.

"Really? I thought you would want a boy." I shake my head, looking at her over Alaia's head.

"I don't mind what we have as long as he or she is healthy, but I love the idea of being a girl Dad," I explain, and Shayla smiles adoringly at me. "A boy doesn't need a Dad much, but a daughter will always need her father."

"Why are you so darn cute?" Shayla asks with a sigh, and I smile, resting my chin on Alaia's shoulder, looking into her eyes.

"Could ask you the same thing, Buttercup." I quip, and Shayla rolls her eyes.

"You're really not letting that nickname go, are you?" She huffs, sitting back in her chair. I laugh and shake my head.

"Not a chance."

"Excuse me?" Shayla and I look up at the young girl with blonde hair and grey eyes who timidly approaches our table.

"Yes?" I ask with a frown, but she was looking directly at Shayla. I didn't like the look in her eyes.

"I'm so sorry to bother you, but you're Shayla Hoult, right?" She questions, her eyes narrowing as she looks between Shayla and me. Shayla casts me a wry look before she nods and looks at the young girl standing before her.

"Yes..." Shayla replies cagily. I pull Alaia closer to me, my eyes watching this strange girl's every move.

"I just wanted to say thank you." I watch them closely. Shayla looks at her, confused.

"For what?" She questions, turning her body in her chair to face the girl who casts a look at me before she looks at Shayla again.

"Um, I saw your interview on TV, talking about what happened to you." Shayla's shoulders were tense as she looks at the girl standing before her. She couldn't be older than sixteen or seventeen. "I was being abused by my stepbrother." She adds in a flurry, and Shayla releases a shaky breath. "I was too scared to say anything in fear of him hurting me more than he already was." She explains, dropping her gaze to her feet as though she were ashamed, a look I've seen on Shayla many times. "But listening to you tell your story and how you chose to fight instead of giving them the power to destroy you..." She sighs, a tear rolls down her pale cheek. "It gave me the courage to finally tell someone what he was doing to me. You saved my life, and I just wanted to say thank you." Shayla stands up and gives the young girl a tight embrace.

"What's your name, sweetie?"

"Hannah." The girl cries into Shayla's shoulder while she soothingly rubs her back till her sobs calmed and she pulls Hannah to sit at the table.

"Hannah, I'm proud of you for finding the courage to open up. It's incredibly hard and scary, I know, but you did it. Did they arrest him?" Hannah nods, brushing away her tears with the back of her hand. "Good. You're safe now, and it's going to take time to find yourself again, but you will, I promise. It does get better. Just remember not to close yourself off because you can drown in that dark loneliness, and the voices in your head telling you that you're not good enough or that you're not worthy will kill you slowly every day. Don't let it." Shayla explains, brushing her fingers through her blonde hair. "You're going to be okay."

"Thank you so much. I'm such a huge fan of yours." She sniffles, and Shayla smiles, lifting her head so she could meet her eyes.

"Well, now you're my friend. Keep that beautiful head up, and don't you ever let it fall for anyone. Okay?" Shayla expresses warmly and hugs her once more after Hannah nods. She looks over at me and smiles shyly when I wink at her. "He's hot, right?" Shayla whispers, leaning toward her, and Hannah blushes profusely. "It's okay. You can say hi." She assures her, and Hannah lifts her gaze to me again and smiles.

"Hi Hannah," I hold my hand out to her, and she hesitates but takes it, her fingers trembling in mine. "It's a pleasure to meet you."

"Um, you too." She whispers and looks over at her friends, who were all looking over at us and whispering.

"Would you like to take a selfie with him?" Shayla asks, and Hannah's eyes go wide, but she shakes her head.

"Actually. Can I have one with...you?"

Shayla's brows rise in surprise, and she looks at me and smirks. "Wow, you hear that, Lord Hoult. She wants a selfie with *me*." She teases playfully, and I laugh heartily.

"Too right, you're more of an idol than I will ever be, baby." I tell her earnestly, and she smiles dotingly back at me, reaching out to caress my jaw.

"You guys are adorable together. My friends and I were watching you from over there, and you can feel your love just radiating through the whole room." Hannah states watching Shayla and I exchange loving glances.

"Thank you, I hope someday you'll find someone who makes you feel as special and wonderful as Cole does me because you deserve it and don't ever settle for anything less," Shayla tells her, and Hannah smiles, holding up her phone, she snaps a couple of photos with Shayla.

"Thank you so much." Shayla nods and watches her as she wanders back to her friends before she turns to me and sighs heavily.

"Baby, you blow me away," I affirm, lifting her hand and kissing her wrist. "Just when I think I can't possibly love you more, you prove me wrong once again. I'm in awe of you, the way you just lit up that girl's eyes and gave her hope and something to believe in, something to fight for. You're incredible, Shayla." Shayla's eyes well up, and she sighs casting a look at Hannah laughing with her friends.

"I only told my story, Cole. She did the rest. It takes courage to take a stand and not allow that darkness to swallow you up. It's scary how easy it is to give up, but when you have something worth fighting for, you find the strength to pick yourself up." She adds, gazing into my eyes. "You gave me that strength. You reminded me of who I am."

"Come here." I lean over the table and pull her in for a kiss, my fingers brushing through her hair as I deepen it, making her moan.

"Take me home."

After we get home, Shayla goes to change and put Alaia down for a nap, and I throw myself on the sofa with a sigh. I've got so many meetings lined up on Monday, and it's honestly exhausting just thinking about going into the office. I untie my tie, leaving it hanging on my neck, and unbutton my shirt, feeling too lazy to get up and get changed. As I mindlessly flick through the tv channels, I see Shayla coming down the stairs, and she's changed into a pair of grey, tight-fitted booty shorts and a white crop top. I smile up at her and toss the remote aside when she straddles me and kisses my chest. I pull her head up and curl my fingers at her nape, pulling her mouth hungrily to mine.

"Mm, baby, can we talk for a second," Shayla mumbles in between kisses. "As insanely sexy as you look right now..." She moans when I aptly flick my tongue over hers, her hands running over my chest.

"Mhm, talk. I'm listening." I groan, grasping her hips and rocking up against her hot core. She smells so damn good, all sweet and fruity my head whirls.

Shayla's head tilts back while I lick up her throat, stopping to suck her pulse. "Christ, Cole, I can't string a sentence together when you do that, let alone have a conversation with you." She purrs, curling her fingers at my neck, arching up into my touch as I grab and squeeze her breast. I smile against her neck, rocking up, grinding my erection against her eliciting a drawn-out sexy moan from those beautiful lips of hers.

"What do you want to talk about, baby?" I whisper, sucking on her bottom lip, my hands splaying out on her backside before I squeeze, and she rolls her hips, rubbing herself against my erection.

"Uhm, I was, uh...thinking that I... Oh, fuck..." She gasps sharply when I lift my hips and grind her down against me harder. Shayla quivers, pressing her forehead to mine.

"You were thinking...." I urge her on with a groan and her eyes close, rocking her hips slow and steady, masturbating against my hard cock.

"I was thinking that...Uhm, I would... uhh, I would be...fuck, oh, fuck..." Shayla pants with a shudder. I watch her in delight as she tries her best to have a conversation with me while she gets herself off by gyrating against my dick. She's so fucking sexy.

"You would be what, baby...." I whisper, dragging my lips over her chin, gripping her hips tight. If she doesn't climax soon, she'll make me come inside my boxers. She's pushing me closer and closer with each thrust of her hips. The friction was driving me mad.

Shayla leans forward, placing her hands on the back of the sofa while she moves her hips back and forth. I lean back, looking up at her flushed face. She wasn't thinking about anything but that orgasm she's building. "Cole," Shayla breathes against my lips, "Uh, I want to... Oh, baby, I'm gonna come."

I squeeze her hips hard and grind up against her faster, "Shayla, if you don't hurry up, you're going to make *me* come. Come for me, baby."

Shayla pants nipping at my ear before she dips her tongue, making me grunt, "Come with me, baby."

"Shayla, you're killing me. The last time I came in my boxers, I was thirteen." I growl, biting her neck. Shayla moans in my ear and rolls her hips which sent a jolt of pleasure through me. My balls tighten, and I feel that heat rush through me, my cock pulses. Oh fuck.

"Come with me." She moans breathily in my ear. "Come with me, now, uh, I'm coming, I'm coming..." She whimpers and stills as she hits the peak of her orgasm; she lets out the sexiest fucking moan I've ever heard, which spurs my own climax. I squeeze her bum and grind her down wildly as I come hard.

"Oh, fuck, fuck, yes, Shayla...." Shayla goes limp in my arms, panting heavily, while we gently rock against one another, riding out the last seconds of our climax as it ebbs away, "Christ, baby." I pant, kissing her shoulder. "That was a good talk. Best conversation I've ever had." I smile lazily when she chuckles against my neck. "You made me come in my fucking pants. That has never happened to me before." I admit, and she pulls back and looks at me, her eyes glittering, she licks her lips.

"Really?" Her chest was rising and falling while she catches her breath.

I nod, brushing her hair away from her face and tucking it behind her ear. "No other woman I've been with has ever brought me remotely close to having an orgasm while grinding on me like that," I confess, and she smiles a little.

"So, that makes me your first?"

I chuckle, rubbing her hips. "That makes you my first," I confirm, and she grins, leaning over to kiss me but stops just before our lips meet.

"Oh wait, we were supposed to talk," Shayla utters, straightening, coiling her fingers around the tie I had around my neck. I smile up at her and narrow my eyes a little.

"Can we talk in the shower? I'm literally sitting in my come, and it's grossing me out." I wince, and she laughs and slips off me. When I stand up, I pick her up and throw her over my shoulder while carrying her up to our bedroom. Shayla giggles and grabs my arse.

"Hey, Cole?"

"Yes baby."

"What were you doing that made you come in your boxers at thirteen?" Shayla questions curiously, I can hear the amusement in her voice, and I grin, biting her hip gently before I suck hard, leaving a nice love bite.

"What any horny teenage boy would do," I answer, rubbing her bum while I walk up the steps. "Humping."

I hear her giggle, "Humping what?"

"None of your business." I spank her, and she whimpers with a laugh.

"But baby..."

"It's private," I mutter, setting her down on her feet once we reach the bathroom. She looks up at me with those big green eyes, and I groan.

"I'll tell you if you tell me." She urges, raising her brow, and I look over her face while she pushes my shirt off my shoulder and drops a kiss on my chest, peeking up at me through her lashes.

"Tell me what?" I ask, intrigued as I unbutton my trousers. Shayla gets undressed and walks back toward the bathtub, beckoning me to her with her finger. I take my pants and boxers off and clean myself off with a washcloth before walking over to her. She runs the bath and turns to look up at me. "Tell me what?" I press, pulling her against me.

"The naughty things I did to myself." Shayla hums sultrily, running her fingers over my torso.

"Mm, you got yourself a deal," I murmur, drawing her lips to mine for a slow and deliberate kiss while the bathtub fills. Shayla whispers the things she did, and I found myself getting hard all over again.

"I'm going to need a visual. You'll be doing that again while I watch." I request lifting her into my arms bridal style and carry her to the bathtub.

Shayla laughs.

"Fine, but in return, you'll do your thing while I watch." She grins, and I frown, settling behind her.

"Really? Mine is nowhere near as sexy as yours."

"Maybe not to you..." She moans while leaning back against my chest. I look down at her, and she lifts her eyes to look at me.

"You're a really strange girl," I utter, kissing her temple, and she laughs, running her hands over my thighs. "So, what did you want to talk about?"

Shayla sighs, lacing her fingers with mine, and I watch while she plays with my fingers. "I want to help people." She states, and I frown a little, waiting for her to continue. "People like Hannah, to be precise. People who have suffered as I have."

"Okay, how are you planning to help them?"

Shayla twirls my wedding band, "I was thinking I could be an advocate for women or men, even children who have suffered assault and are struggling to open up like I was. It's scary the number of people that suffer or have suffered through some sort of assault. Thirty percent—that's really high."

"Are you sure you're up for it? It can be emotionally draining and might trigger your own fears and anxiety listening to others tell their story." I state, and she nods, brushing her lips over my fingers.

"I'll be fine." She assures me, "I've dealt with my demons."

I press my nose to her hair and inhale her scent, "If it's going to make you happy, I'll support you all the way with whatever you choose to do." Shayla looks up at me and smiles, lacing her fingers with mine. "You're going to change the world someday, Shayla Hoult." I declare with a smile, and she closes her eyes when I kiss her forehead.

"I doubt it but thank you for believing in me."

"How can I not when you've changed my whole world, baby. I have no doubt you'll do the same for others too, just as you did for Hannah today." I murmur in her ear affectionately, and she sighs, relaxing into me. I don't doubt for a second that she will succeed in helping people, she's the kindest person I know, and she has a light in her that people are drawn to.

I just hope she doesn't break herself again in the process.

"I hope so."

Chapter 37

SHAYLA

"ARE you going to find out the sex of the baby?" Aimee asks while she scoops up a piece of chocolate cake and eats it, followed by a delightful moan. I sip my mixed berry smoothie and nod.

"Mhm, for sure. Are you?" I ask her, and she nods enthusiastically, chewing on a mouth full of cake. "Does Josh have a preference?" I question curiously, and she nods, glancing over at him.

"He said he doesn't mind as long as it's healthy, but he'd like a boy." I smile and nod sipping my smoothie. We were having lunch before our appointments. "Can you believe how late Jo is? She's overdue by eight days."

I wince and nod, "I know. I spoke to her earlier, and she's very irritable. Sam said she keeps snapping at him. They're both on edge, just waiting for the baby to arrive. Even I'm getting antsy waiting for the phone call." I explain, fiddling with my straw, and Aimee sits back in her chair and rubs her baby bump.

"I hope I'm not overdue. I will literally rip Josh's head off and hand it to him." She mutters, brushing her golden hair out of her eyes and looking at her husband, who was in a deep conversation with Cole.

I watch Cole while he listens intently to whatever Josh was saying, nodding his head. "How are you feeling? Are you still being sick?" Aimee shakes her head and smiles.

"No, it's stopped, thank god." She replies and leans closer to me. "Are you still feeling randy? Because I can't get enough. I mean, I've always loved sex, but this pregnancy has turned me into a right little nympho." I grin and pull my eyes from Cole to look at her and nod.

"I feel your pain. I wasn't this bad with Alaia. I mean, I was a little horny at times, but this one's got me humping Cole like a bitch in heat." Aimee and I giggle, and the boys look over at us mid-conversation. I blow a kiss at Cole, and he winks at me. "It doesn't really help that they look like that now, does it?"

Aimee snorts. "Doesn't hurt either." She retorts, staring at Josh, who takes her hand and kisses her knuckles. "Have you thought of any names?"

I nod, smiling. "Cole is choosing this time because I chose Alaia's name. He's picked Aria if it's a girl or Rome if it's a boy." I tell her, and Aimee smiles, placing her hand on her chest.

"I love the name Rome. Rome Hoult."

I smile and sigh, rubbing my bump as I sink back into my chair. "Actually...it's going to be Rome Joshua Hoult."

Aimee drops her fork and looks at me wide-eyed. "Oh my God, are you serious, Shay? You'll give him Josh's name?" I take Cole's hand when he reaches out for me, and I look at Josh, whose blue eyes were just as surprised as his wife's.

"We'd like to if you don't mind?" I ask, looking between them and Josh shakes his head and smiles. "You've been our rock through so much, Josh. Cole and I could never repay you for everything, so we thought this would be a nice gesture."

"Are you kidding? I'm so touched. You really don't have to repay me for anything. You two are my family, of course, I'm going to help you if I can. I know you two would have done the same for Aimee and me without thinking twice. Thank you both so much. I'm stoked." Josh and Cole hug tightly, and Aimee hugs me.

When Josh comes over to hug me, Aimee throws a breadstick at Cole. "Don't go getting any ideas thinking I'm going to name my child after you now." She warns him, and Cole laughs, shaking his head and throwing a breadstick back at her.

"Wouldn't dream of it." After lunch, we go to the private hospital for our appointments. Aimee had hers at the same time as mine in the room next door.

"All right, let's see how the baby is doing." The sonographer smiles, pressing the receiver against my bump. Cole was holding Alaia in his arms while they both stood beside me. "Everything looks great. Your baby is growing perfectly. Are we finding out the sex of the baby today?" She questions, lifting her brown eyes to look at us, and we both nod. "Well, you're having a boy. Congratulations." I gasp and look at Cole, who grins and leans down, brushing a kiss over my lips.

"Look, Alaia, it's your baby brother," Cole says after he pulls back, bouncing her in his arms. He looks at me and bites his lip. "I'm having a son."

I lace my fingers with his and close my eyes when he kisses my forehead. "*We* are having a son." I scold him playfully, and he laughs, kissing me. "You already stole Alaia. This one is mine."

"You can have the next one." He murmurs against my lips with a chuckle, and I hit his shoulder. "You're carrying the heir to our empire, baby." I frown up at him.

"Why does it have to be an heir? Why can't it be an heiress?" I question, raising my brow quizzically, and he pulls back, his green eyes searching mine.

"Honey, I was kidding. I want all my children to run the family business as equal partners. Unless they don't want to, then we'll decide when the time is right." He explains and grins. "Now, retract those claws and stop glaring at me like that." I smile, shaking my head. Smarmy git. He knows exactly what buttons to push to wind me up. We walk out of the room simultaneously as Josh and Aimee were grinning lovingly at one another. "So?" Cole coaxes, and Josh smiles.

"I'm having a daughter," Josh declares and wipes a tear that rolls down his cheek.

"I'm having a son!" Cole exclaims, and they hug while Aimee and I just watch them shaking our heads.

"Excuse me, but what are we here exactly, just a couple of ovens with legs cooking up *your* buns." I proclaim, placing my hands on my hips.

Cole and Josh pull apart and look at us, glaring at them. "We're sorry?" Josh mumbles warily.

"What do you say? Shall we forgive them?" I ask Aimee, and she shakes her head.

"Nah," She looks at me. "I'm going to take *my* daughter and go shopping." Aimee smiles at me, and I look at Cole, who was frowning.

"And I'm going to take *my* son and join you." We link arms and stroll past the boys watching us as we walk away.

"You've been married longer. Do we follow them or..." Josh trails, looking at Cole, who narrows his eyes while Aimee and I wait for the elevator. He looks at Alaia in his arms.

"You're a girl, what do you think? Shall we go after them?" Alaia grins at him and grabs his nose with her fingers. "I'm going to take the nose squeeze as a 'yes Dada, go after them' then. Let's go."

I giggle watching Cole with Alaia. "I can't wait to see Josh holding our baby girl and being all cute with her." I hear Aimee sigh, watching him as he walks over to her. "How does your heart not explode with joy when you watch them together?"

"It does." I sigh longingly, and Aimee laughs.

"What the fuck happened to us, Bish. We were three fierce bitches, and now we melt like butter in the hands of these idiots." Aimee utters, nudging Josh away with her shoulder, and he licks his lips and gives her a look full of meaning, and her eyes go all soft.

"We married two of the biggest player's in the country, that's what." I answer, looking up at Cole, who gives me his signature 'I'm going to drive you wild' look. I raise my brow at him, and he smirks roguishly in return. Aimee and I look at one another and sigh.

"You also brought them to their knees," Cole mumbles in my ear, and I feel that heavenly warmth spread through me from head to toe.

Damn him. As punishment, we dragged the boys shopping with us to get a few things for the babies.

"I can't believe she's going to be one in two weeks." Aimee pouts looking down at Alaia in her pushchair. "You're growing up so fast, princess. I can't wait for you and Isla to be besties." She says, kissing her hand.

"It's actually worked out really well. Two girls and two boys in our group. Rome will have his cousin Treyson and Alaia will have Isla. How adorable is that?" I smile, holding up an outfit for Alaia.

Aimee smiles, looking at outfits for her baby girl. "I don't want to jinx it, Shay, but I'm just so happy. If it weren't for you and Cole, I wouldn't have met Josh. I'm so thankful I have you in my life, Bish."

I grin, looking at her over the railing. "It all worked out in the end. You, me, and Jo will always be in each other's lives, no matter where we are. We made a promise remember. Bishes for life!"

Aimee laughs, "Bishes for life."

Later that evening, Cole and I were sitting on our bed, me on my tablet and him on his, looking through emails. "Do you not think we're going a little overboard with this birthday party?" I ask, looking away from the tablet to him, staring intently at a document on his device.

"No," Cole utters, typing away on the screen. "What my baby wants, my baby gets." I frown.

"Cole, she's turning one, she doesn't have a clue what she wants. She's not even going to remember this." Cole looks at me and shrugs.

"She's aware of more than you realise." He replies, his brows lifting to his hairline. "Don't you see the way her little face lights up when she sees Moana on the screen?" I smile and nod, "Or the way she sways side to side when she hears the song."

"That is adorable." Cole nods, smiling, and leans over, puckering his lips for me. I lean in and kiss him softly.

"Let's give our baby girl the birthday she deserves." Cole mumbles against my lips, and I grin, "I can't wait to see her little face when the actress sings the song to her."

"Me either." I declare and pull away with a content sigh.

"Don't you think she kind of looks like Moana when she was a baby at the beginning of the movie," Cole utters, shutting down his tablet and looking at me.

I laugh and look over at him when he lays down on his side and rubs my bump. "I guess so. Only she's got big green eyes, like you," I state brushing my fingers along his jaw, and he smiles adoringly at me. "I hope our son looks just like you." Cole scoots closer and pushes my t-shirt up, exposing my stomach where our unborn son lay. He presses soft, loving kisses over my baby bump. "With your mesmerising green eyes," I whisper, gazing into his eyes. "Your sexy smile," I add, brushing my thumb over his bottom lip, and he kisses it. "Your adorable dimples." I grin knowingly, and he laughs a little.

"My tongue fucking dimples." He corrects cheekily, making me laugh. "That was one of our best moments."

I nod, smiling, "I agree." I brush my fingers through his messy hair. "And our trip to Nice."

Cole moans, closing his eyes, "God, yes, that's right up there with our honeymoon." He says, opening his eyes and staring into mine.

"I think I'm a little obsessed with you, Cole Hoult." I declare, trailing my fingers down the side of his face. His eyes light up, and he smiles up at me dashingly before he crawls up and takes the tablet resting on my chest, and sets it aside.

"Just a little?" Cole murmurs, grabbing my thighs and tugging me down the bed so I was entirely on my back. "Let me remedy that." Dipping his head, he kisses me deeply. I moan, curling my fingers around his neck, kissing him back amorously. I ached to feel his hard body pressed against mine, but that's the downside of pregnancy, the bump in between us. Cole had me naked and sprawled out on the bed in sixty seconds. Our tongues duelling heatedly, he flips me over onto all fours, and I gasp when I feel his hot tongue run up my spine while his fingers stroke my sex tantalisingly. I whimper when his mouth replaces his fingers. My mind goes hazy when his tongue slides inside me sensually.

We both groan when my phone starts to ring. I see Aimee's name on the screen and grab my phone. "Hello?" I answer, biting my lip hard as Cole continues to nibble my clit softly.

"Bish."

I pull the phone away and curse under my breath when Cole slides a finger inside me. "Yes?" I reply, desperately trying to keep the quiver out of my voice.

"Why do you sound...oh god...please tell me you're not fucking." Aimee utters, and I feel my cheeks go red hot. I bite my lip hard and fist the covers when Cole licks my clit slowly.

"We are not... *fucking*." I reply, trying to pull away, but Cole grips my hips tight and grinds me down against his mouth, and I lose my breath.

"You dirty little liar." Aimee laughs, and I hear Josh mutter something on their end.

"What's up, Aimes?" I ask, looking down at Cole, watching me from his position between my legs.

"Fuck my mouth." He whispers to me, and I almost lose my mind and moan audibly, only just catching myself in time.

"Jo's in labour, you hussy." She tells me, and I gasp and press my forehead to the bed.

"Really? Oh gosh, okay, we're on our way." I mutter, and Aimee laughs heartily.

"Uh-huh. Course you are. I'll see you in about half-hour, bish. Happy fucking!" I hang up and toss the phone aside.

"Oh god, baby, we have to hurry. Jo's in labour." I say, looking down at him, and he squeezes my hips and moans. The deep timbres of his voice send a shockwave of pleasure pulsing through me, and I rock against his tongue, rubbing my clit against his mouth over and over till I climax with an ear-piercing cry. Cole moans gutturally, drinking up my juice's greedily.

I look down at him, panting, while he rubs and squeezes my bum. "Fuck me," I demand, gazing into his eyes. Cole smirks, and in a flash, he was behind me. He curls his fingers at the nape of my neck and tugs me up so my back was pressed against his chest. His mouth hungrily seizes mine, and we kiss hard and dirty. His long fingers curl around my throat while he pushes himself into me, feeding me his manhood, filling me deeply, inch by inch, until he's buried to the hilt. I whimper in delight.

"*Fuck*, baby, your pussy is to die for." He nips at my ear as he starts to thrust slow and deep, his lips on my neck, biting and sucking hard.

"Uh, baby, yes." I pant, tilting my head back against his shoulder as he drives himself deeper into me with every hard plunge, pushing me closer and closer to sweet ecstasy, "Baby, you feel so good." I moan avidly, winding my fingers around the back of his neck. Cole growls, and I lean forward, pressing my palms on the bed, pushing my hips back against him, meeting his penetrating thrusts while he grabs my hips and squeezes hard.

"Fuck, you're so wet. God *damn*, baby." Cole growls, biting his lip, and he spanks my right bum cheek, squeezes hard, making me cry out fervently. "You're going to come for me, aren't you? I can feel your pussy getting tighter, wetter around my dick, baby." He pounds into me relentlessly. "Come for me, Gorgeous girl."

I whimper, fisting the covers as he drives me straight into the arms of that toe-curling release I was burning for. "I'm coming! Oh, God, I'm coming, baby." I cry out as I explode and flutter wildly around him. "Ohhh, Cole!"

Cole's head lulls back as he thrusts into me with slow and vigorous strokes, the force of my orgasm spurring his own. "Oh yeah, that's it, milk that cock honey, fuck yes! I love fucking this perfect pussy." He growls, squeezing my hips as he spills his seed deep inside me. "Ah, *fuck, fuck*, Shayla!"

My legs turned to jelly, and once Cole stills, we both collapse onto the bed, gasping to catch our breath. "Oh my God, I take it back. I'm definitely more than a little obsessed with you." I pant, looking over at him, and he smiles handsomely, his eyes closed.

"Right back at you, baby." Cole moans, slapping my bum.

"Where did you learn to fuck like that, my God." I moan, closing my eyes, and Cole leans up and kisses me slow and deep, sucking my tongue.

"Porn." He groans into my mouth, and I laugh.

"Dirty git." I grin up at him, and he chuckles, shaking his head. "Oh shit, Jo!" I sit up suddenly. "She's in labour!" Cole sits up and kisses my shoulder. "Come on, Adonis." I take Cole's hand and pull him up off the bed. After we got cleaned up and dressed, we drop Alaia at Cole's parents and head to the hospital.

～

WE SEE Josh and Aimee in the waiting room, along with Jo's father, "How is she doing? Any news?"

Aimee shakes her head. "Not yet. We got here not long ago." I sit beside her, and Cole walks over to Josh, talking to Jo's dad, Phil. "Did you look in the mirror before you left the house?" Aimee grins, her blue eyes raking over me.

"No, why?" I ask apprehensively and look down at myself.

Aimee laughs, "You look fucked out, girl. You could have at least run a brush through your hair." I stare at her dumbfounded and reach to comb out my hair with my fingers.

"We left in a rush," I whisper, unlocking my phone and loading up the camera. "Do I really look that bad?" I look at my reflection in the camera and gasp a little. My face was all flushed, my hair a tousled mess, my lips were swollen, and I had love bites all over my neck. "Oh shit." I curse, pulling my hair over my shoulder to cover up the love bites.

Aimee nudges me, grinning wickedly. When I look at her, unable to keep the smile from my face, she cackles. "You little slut." She teases, poking me, and I slap her hand away.

I giggle, shaking my head. "Shhh, you're no angel either, you little minx."

"Lord knows I'm a sinner. Especially for that man over there. On our way over here, he pulled over, and he gave me a good seeing to in the back of the car." Aimee explains, and we snicker like two teenagers sharing dirty little secrets. "He's going to be the death of me." She groans lustfully, and I nod, catching my gorgeous husbands' eyes while he was talking to Josh, and he gives me a smouldering look, which I return with a sugary smile.

It was past midnight by the time Sam had come out of the delivery suite, tears staining his face. I've never seen my brother cry, even when my dad died. We all stand up and walk over to him. "He's here." He sniffles, wiping his tears. "I'm a Dad." I hug him tight, and he sobs into my shoulder.

"Congratulations, Sammy. You're going to be an amazing father. How's Jo?" I ask once we pull apart.

"She's good. Very tired and emotional, but she did so damn well." He sighs and hugs the boys and Jo's dad. "They're cleaning her and the baby up. Once they're done, you can come and see him."

"Congrats, brother, welcome to fatherhood. There's no feeling like it." Cole states, slapping his back, and Sam nods.

"I've never fallen in love with another human being so fast in my life. It's crazy." He explains, and Cole nods in understanding. Sam went back into the delivery suite, and I step into Cole's embrace when he opens his arms up for me. I was emotional seeing my brother like that. Cole brushes my tears away and kisses my nose.

"Those better be happy tears, Aunty Shay." He scolds me playfully, and I laugh, nodding in response.

"They are." I sigh happily. "I can't believe I'm an aunt, and you're an uncle." Cole grins and kisses my forehead.

"We're going to be the coolest aunt and uncle ever." I smile up at him, and he nuzzles his nose over mine.

"I'm kind of fond of you, Mr Hoult," I whisper, and he kisses me.

"I'm *very* fond of you, Mrs Hoult." He murmurs, drawing me in for a passionate kiss.

Twenty minutes later, we were finally able to see Jo and the baby. I walk in and hug my mum, who was shedding endless happy tears. Poor Jo looked swollen and exhausted, but her eyes were beaming with such joy as she cradles her son in her arms. "Hi, pretty girl. How are you feeling?" I ask, leaning over to look at my nephew wrapped up in a blue blanket.

"Tired and sore," Jo replies, smiling, her voice raspy from straining for hours on end. "I can't believe he's finally here." She whispers, looking down at her beautiful baby boy in her arms.

"Oh, my goodness, he's beautiful." Jo holds him out to me and take him into my arms, and smiles. "Hi baby, I'm your Aunty Shay. Oh, I'm going to spoil you rotten." I brush a kiss on his forehead. "Welcome to our world, Treyson Richard Hart."

Chapter 38

COLE

"Happy birthday, princess." I croon, looking down at Alaia, who just rose from her sleep. She smiles up at me as soon as she sees me, displaying her two teeth. She's always so happy in the morning, and this morning was no different. She's just lying in her crib, kicking back with her hands behind her head. "Good morning, my sunshine." I pick her up and kiss her cheek affectionately. "Is my baby girl one-year-old today?" We walk out of the nursery back to our bedroom, where Shayla was still asleep. "Let's go wake up, Mummy," I whisper, kissing her temple and smile when I see Shayla lying on her front, peacefully sleeping. I crawl up on the bed and lay Alaia down on her stomach, and she immediately crawls over to her mother. I lay on my side and watch as she makes cooing sounds, pressing her hand to Shay's face, who stirs from her sleep and smiles.

"Mm, good morning, birthday girl." She sighs, lifting her arm and wrapping it around Laia, who tries to crawl over her. She looks over at me and grins beautifully. "And good morning to you, Stud." I smile at the nickname and brush a kiss to her waiting lips.

"Morning, Gorgeous girl," I whisper, pulling back and gazing into her eyes. "You've got ten minutes before we have to be up. The caterers and the event organisers will be here in half-hour." I inform her, and she nods, kissing Alaia's head when she rests it on her chest.

414

Shayla pouts. "Can we just stick her in a jar, so she won't grow anymore?" I chuckle, reaching over and rubbing Laia's back.

"Sounds tempting," I reply, scooting closer and laying my head beside hers while we watch our daughter move around the bed. "It feels like just yesterday she was born."

Shayla heaves a sigh. "I know, she's grown up in the blink of an eye. I want her to stay small forever so she will never leave us."

I smile fondly and lace my fingers with hers. "I'm not ready to think about that yet," I admit, leaning over, holding Alaia's foot and pulling her back to us before she crawls to the edge of the bed. She giggles and crawls off again. "Get back here, you little rascal." I laugh, pulling her back, and she cackles. "Soon, our home will be filled with the laughter and cries of our babies," I assure Shayla, and she lifts her eyes to look at me. "You promised me at least three babies." She laughs sardonically.

"We'll see." I pout, and she looks over my face.

"You can't backtrack now. You promised, and you're a woman of your word Shayla Hoult. Your word is your bond."

"Cole, I'm still in the process of cooking the last one you popped in me. I'm not a bloody machine." She squeaks when I grab her face and plaster my lips to hers.

"But baby, you make the cutest and sweetest buns, and I want more." I groan against her lips, and she laughs.

"Get off of me, you fertile freak." She grins, trying to scoot away while I nuzzle her neck, Alaia sitting between us, watching us goof around. "You're going to get me all fat and then leave me to be with your secretary."

I laugh into her neck. "Honey, you're confusing reality with porn again," I mumble, nipping at her ear. "I'm not going anywhere. You're stuck with me forever and then ever after that too."

Shayla sighs with a content smile. "That's an awfully long time to put up with your raggedy arse."

I gasp, affronted. "You love my arse," I growl, nipping at her lip, and Shayla beams up at me.

"Yes, yes, I do. You have a fine arse, Cole Hoult." She declares lovingly, and I smile, kissing her nose.

"As do you, my love," I lean in to kiss her, but she pushes me away and sits upright. She mumbles about her bladder being full before she rushes to the bathroom. I look at Alaia, who was lying down with my phone in her hand. I couldn't imagine living my life in any other way. I'm truly blessed.

An hour later, the house was bustling with people. The event organisers and the catering company for Alaia's birthday party setting everything up before family and friends arrive to celebrate our daughter's first birthday with us. The house was decorated to perfection, Hawaiian style. Everywhere I looked, I saw Moana and Maui and pictures of Laia we took of her growing up. Her birthday cake was four tiers, blue and white with shells, resembling the ocean with a chocolate mould of baby Moana sitting on the top.

Of course, our birthday girl was dressed like a baby Moana with a red crop top and white mini baby skirt, and a pink flower in her hair. She looked beyond cute. A couple of hours later, the party was in full swing. Good food, the company of those we love the most, laughter of children running around the back yard playing with the actors or jumping like crazy in the bouncy castle.

I watch Shayla as she sits with Alaia and the girls while the actress sings Alaia's favourite song, 'How far I'll go' to her, and the other kids gathered around, and Laia beams watching her, her green eyes vast and wonderous. "I'm going to go check on the boys, make sure everything is okay," Josh says, walking off toward the team of security guards scattered around the house.

After posing for the millionth photo of the day with Shayla and Alaia, it was time for her cake to be cut. I was holding her while Shayla brought the cake out, and everyone starts singing happy birthday to Alaia, who stares at the cake lit up with candles and a sparkler, the most beautiful smile on her face. "Let's get another photo of the three of you with the cake." The photographer says. Shayla wraps her arms around my neck from behind, and once the photographer got Alaia's attention, we smile for the camera.

Shayla and I lean over and blow out the candles for her. I look up at her, and she kisses me softly, her soft fingers brushing along my cheek. "Thank you for giving me the world's greatest gift." She whispers, gazing into my eyes lovingly.

"Are you kidding? I should be thanking you. You've filled my life with so much love, baby. I'm so thankful I got drunk and married you. You turned out to be the best mistake I have ever made in life." I declare, and she smiles, rubbing my jaw affectionately. "I'm crazy about you."

"I'm crazy for you too." She whispers, scooping up some icing off her cake and smearing it on Laia's little nose. "I'm most definitely mad about you too, princess." She coos lovingly, taking her face into her hands and kissing her forehead. "Happy birthday, sweetheart, be happy, and may that light in your eyes always shine bright, baby." She expresses to Alaia, who smiles up at her adoringly. Shayla is such an exceptional woman and mother. The rest of the party went by without a glitch, and Alaia was wiped out. Shayla and the girls took her upstairs to bathe her and put her down to sleep.

"That was a great party. I'm a grown arse man, and I had a blast." Josh chuckles, sitting back on the sofa, taking a sip from his beer. I smile and nod, looking over at my mother and Shay's mother directing the kitchen's cleaning crew. Sam comes across with baby Trey in his arms and sits on the sofa with a tired sigh.

"It really was. Shayla did a great job with organising everything." I tell him, and Josh nods, looking over at the baby in Sam's arms.

"How's fatherhood treating you, bro?" Josh questions putting his beer bottle down and taking Trey from Sam.

"Tiring man, but I wouldn't give it up for the world," Sam admits looking over at Trey curled up on Josh's chest. "To think I was terrified of ever having one of those, now I can't picture my life without him."

I smile in understanding. "Yeah, they really do change your life, especially if it's with the right woman," I state, and both men nod in agreement.

"I feel so left out. I can't wait to hold my baby girl in my arms and relate to what you guys are saying." Josh grumbles put out.

Sam and I laugh.

"Patience bro. Your time is coming." Sam assures him, and he sighs with a roll of his eyes. "I still can't believe you both got the girls pregnant at the same time. Did you guys plan it or something?" Josh and I chuckle, shaking our heads.

"Not at all. Shay was on the pill. We were planning to wait till Alaia was two to have another baby, but my boy just couldn't wait another year. An overachiever like his father." I state with a smug grin, and the boys laugh.

"Aimee wanted to wait at least a year before we started to try, but one night of passion changed that plan real quick," Josh utters with a proud smirk, looking down at Trey, who wiggles in his arms. "When are you planning to make an honest woman of JoJo then?" He asks, looking at Sam, who smiles.

"We're planning to have a wedding in December. Jo wants a Christmas wedding." He explains, sipping his beer.

"Anything you need, bro, we're here for you," I tell him, and he nods with a thankful smile. "Here's to married life with kid's boys." I toast, and we all raise our bottles, grinning before taking a long chug of our drinks. It sure was a good life. Once the cleaning crew and the parents left, Shayla finally joined us and collapsed on the sofa beside me with an exhausted sigh.

"Wow, I didn't realise how tired I was until right now." She huffs, closing her eyes, resting her head on my shoulder.

I smile and kiss her head.

"Shay, the party was amazing." Jo praises while she feeds the baby in the love seat, a blanket thrown over him. Shayla smiles tiredly and shifts when I wrap my arm around her shoulder, pulling her against me.

"Thanks, it was worth all the stress to see her little face light up." Shayla sighs happily while I play with her hair.

"This cake is fucking insane." Aimee groans, shoving a forkful in her mouth and moaning in delight. Shayla giggles when Josh tries to eat some, and she slaps his hand away and growls at him. "Mine. I'll kill you."

"Baby, how many slices have you had?" Josh asks her, amused, and she shrugs, cutting into the slice of cake and eating it.

"I don't know, like three pieces." She moans, licking her lips, and looks at Josh, who was watching her with a smile. "Blame your daughter. She's making me hungry." She grumbles, and when Josh gives her a pointed look, she rolls her eyes. "Okay fine, more than usual." We laugh, and he kisses her temple tenderly while she smiles happily and goes back to eating her cake.

We were chatting idly while I flick through the TV channels and stop when I see the news. I sit upright, and Shayla looks up at me confused, and her gaze follows mine, and she stares at the tv.

The room falls silent as we all listen to the news.

The headline read,

'Former Fashion Designer & Socialite—Sophie Turner found hung in her cell.'

I look at Shayla, who was staring at the tv unblinking while the news reporter tells the story of how Sophie had taken her own life by hanging herself in her cell after struggling to adjust to life behind bars. They found a suicide note on her bed with her final words scribbled on a piece of paper clearly directed at Shayla. *"I'll see you in hell, bitch!"*

"Shay, you okay?" Jo asks, concerned, and Shayla gets up without a word and walks out of the living room. I look over at Josh, who was scowling. I get up and go after Shayla as she pushes the doors open to the garden and rushes outside. She lifts her eyes to the sky and exhales slowly.

I walk up behind her and wrap my arm around her waist, pressing my lips to her temple. "It's over," I whisper, and she chokes on a sob and cries. I turn her and pull her against me, wrapping my arms around her tight. "It's over now, baby. She can't hurt you ever again." I press my lips to her head, and she nods, crying tears of what I'm hoping was relief into my chest. Josh, Aimee, and Sam come out looking concerned, and I look over at them, nodding my head, assuring them silently that she was okay. As strong as she's been through all of this, I know she was still on edge after the threats Sophie made. These tears were ones full of relief, her way of letting go of the last bit of apprehension she'd been holding onto. That little voice deep down nagging her, wondering, waiting if another attack would follow. Thankfully, it's over now. Sophie will burn in the deepest core of hell for all of eternity for everything she did to her.

Shayla pulls back and looks up at me, tears flowing from her beautiful eyes. "Did you..." She trails silently, asking me if I had something to do with her killing herself off, and I shake my head.

"No, I had nothing to do with that. She obviously couldn't handle being locked up. The warden did say girls like her are like fresh meat to a hungry lion." I explain, brushing her tears away.

"I did." I turn and look at Sam, and Shayla frowns. "I may have visited the prison. A guard there is a friend of mine, and when he found out you were my sister, he did me a favour." He explains with a shrug, stuffing his hands into the pocket of his jeans. "It wasn't enough that she was locked away, I wanted her to suffer, so I had my artist friend paint a photo of you and Cole kissing on the wall opposite her cell, she'd be forced to stare at it, be reminded every second, of every day that she didn't break you," Sam tells her. Shayla pulls away from me and runs into her brother's arms. Sam wraps his strong arm around her neck and kisses her temple while she sobs into his shoulder. "I'll destroy anyone that hurts my baby sister. I told her I would make her disappear, and I did."

Shayla pulls back and looks up at her big brother. "Thank you." She whispers, and he smiles playfully knocks his fist on her chin.

"Always got your back, kiddo." He declares earnestly, and she smiles with a nod.

"I know, and I love you for it." Sam kisses her forehead.

"And I love you, Sis." Shayla sighs, and Aimee slings an arm around her shoulder, and they walk inside.

"Hallelujah, the witch is dead!" Aimee chirps, making Shayla laugh. Sam and Josh turn to me, and I smile, watching her.

"Are you going to tell her you went to see Sophie?" Josh questions, and I shake my head.

"Nah," I smile and look at him. "Sam was right. The painting of us slowly drove Sophie crazy enough to take her own life, which is all I wanted. If she knew there was another threat to her life, she'd be living each day on edge." I explain, rubbing the back of my neck tiredly. "It's finally over, and she doesn't need to know what went on behind the scenes to make it happen. Thanks to both of you, we can finally put this shit to bed and enjoy the rest of our lives." I sigh, relieved, and they nod. We exchange hugs and all head back inside to our wives and kids.

As I sit beside my wife and pull her into my arms, I recall my final words to Sophie before I hung up and walked away from the cubicle. "You are, and forever will be my greatest regret." I hiss into the phone while glaring at her hatefully through the glass. "You have nothing left, Sophie. Good luck finding the funds or the help to see your threats through. The rights your father tricked you into signing over to him are now mine. That business you worked so hard to build is no more. It's crashed and burned just like your pathetic life. Your own parents, your brother, who are biologically wired to love you, have disowned you. You're going to rot in here all by yourself just as you deserve."

"You did this to me!" She shouts irately down the phone. "You ruined my life! You and that whore of yours!"

I laugh, amused, "You did this to yourself. Thank fuck I fell in love with Shayla and got a taste of what true love should feel like."

"You loved me first, and if it weren't for that tramp, you'd still be in love with me!"

"The fuck I did." I roll my eyes in disgust. "What the fuck do you know about love? You tried to kill me, you fucking lunatic! I never loved you, not really. What I thought was love for you fails in comparison to what I feel for Shay. Even after we got back together, every time I had sex with you, I was thinking of Shayla. In my mind, it was her, in my heart, it's *always* been her, and it always will be. Feast on that, you deranged trollop. I hope you burn in the deepest core of hell." I chastise and slam the phone down before I get up and walk away.

I blink when I hear a roar of laughter in the room and look down at Shayla grinning at something Aimee says. I press my lips to her head and inhale deeply, filling my lungs with her scent.

She's my everything.

Chapter 39

SHAYLA

"Shay." I lift my gaze from staring at my huge baby bump and look at my husband, who rolls over when I turn the night lamp on. "You okay?" Cole questions drowsily, and I glower at him.

"Why won't this baby come out." I hiss angrily, and Cole groans, leaning up on his elbow and looks at me, his green eyes narrowed.

"Maybe he likes it in there and isn't ready to leave just yet." He smiles, rubbing my bump, and the baby squirms inside me at his father's touch. My due date was six days ago, and this stubborn child is showing no indication of arriving anytime soon.

"I've had enough." I whimper, agitated. "I'm uncomfortable. I haven't slept a wink in days, and I'm swollen like a beached whale. Look at me." I complain, gesturing to myself, and Cole lets his eyes wander over me, and he smiles. "What are you looking at?"

He blinks, bemused.

"You just said—"

"You get this baby out of me right now." I huff, and Cole scratches his forehead, his brows fused together tightly. "You put it in me, and you're going to get him out."

Cole chuckles, "Honey, how am *I* supposed to get him to come out?" I glare at him, and his smile fades, and he looks at me sheepishly.

"I don't know Cole, how about you sing to him? I don't care *how* you do it. If you don't get this child out of me soon, I'm going to kill you." I grumble and push the covers off, and he watches me roll side to side, trying to get up. "You going to help me up or..." I sneer sardonically, and he takes my hand and pulls my arm, so I could get up and go empty my bladder for the fifteen times in one hour.

"Wow," Cole mutters to himself.

"I heard that!" I snap hotly, and Cole smiles, shaking his head before he falls back down on the bed, watching me while I shuffle my way into the bathroom to pee.

THE NEXT AFTERNOON I was pacing the kitchen; evidently, exercise helps bring on labour. I was thoroughly enjoying my packet of Doritos when it's suddenly plucked from my fingers, and Cole sets a plate of pineapple in my hand. I glare up at him, and he smiles warmly. "I was enjoying that," I complain, and he shakes his head, eating the tortilla chips himself.

"This..." Cole mumbles while chewing and holding up the packet of Doritos. "Isn't nutritional for you or the baby. It certainly will not help him come out any quicker. Pineapple helps induce labour naturally, eat up buttercup." I stare down at the chunks of fresh pineapple and sigh miserably.

"Why won't he come out?" I whine helplessly, and Cole sets the packet in his hand on the side and steps closer to me, his hands rubbing my bump soothingly.

"He will, when he's ready, baby." He assures me, and I sigh heavily when he picks up a piece of pineapple and holds it to my lips. I look up at him, sulking and eat it. "We'll go for a walk after you eat this. The midwife said the more active you are, the quicker the labour will be." I nod glumly, and he kisses my forehead sweetly. I've been so awfully moody with him this past week, but I can't help it. I'm just so uncomfortable and fed up with being pregnant. Aimee had baby Isla three days ago, and I'm still waiting for our little prince to make his grand entrance.

Two more days go by, and I'm now nine days overdue and extremely irritable. "Eat your curry," Cole tells me, and I sigh, forcing myself to eat the vindaloo I had sitting in front of me.

"This isn't helping. It's only going to give me heartburn later and likely set my arsehole on fire." I grouse, dropping my fork, and Cole shakes his head.

"You said you wanted to try everything. Stop complaining and eat your food." He says firmly, and I look at him. He's always sexy as hell when he's angry. Maybe that will spur him into having sex with me.

"This stupid curry isn't going to do a damn thing!" I gripe, and he scowls at me.

"Shayla, I'm fucking trying. I don't know what else to do to help you, babe!" He replies, standing up from the dining table. I smirk inwardly and watch him rub the back of his neck, frustrated. "I get it. You're uncomfortable and fed up. I'm doing everything I can to help you, but you just keep biting my fucking head off."

"Maybe because it's your fault." I retort, standing up and placing my hands on my hips while glaring at his muscular back. Cole spins around and looks at me hard.

"My fault?" He intones, and I nod. "How is it my fault you got pregnant? You were on the fucking pill!" He protests stormily, his green eyes boring into my own.

"It's kind of hard for the pill to work when you were pumping your spunk into me every five seconds!" I answer, and he scowls. I felt so bad goading him like this, but I was dying.

Cole takes a step toward me, his eyes hot on mine. "I didn't hear you complaining at the time." He drawls raptly. "In fact...as I recall, you were the one screaming *fuck me harder* and moaning in delight when I pumped my spunk into you." I look up at him and resist the urge to moan. "It takes two to make a baby sweetheart, and you're just as guilty as I am."

We stare at each other for a beat, and I couldn't take it anymore, so I curl my fingers at the nape of his neck and pull his mouth to mine. Cole groans and wraps his arms around me, and kisses me hard and deep as he backs me up against the wall. Clothes went flying all over the place.

Cole scoops me up in his arms and carries me upstairs to the bedroom, still kissing wildly. When he lays me out on the bed and looks down at me, I take hold of the chain around his neck and pull his face close to mine. "Get this baby out of me."

Cole smiles and brushes a kiss on my lips before he rolls me onto my side, settling himself behind me and buries himself into me slowly while he licks and kisses my neck. We rock together gently, the crown of his penis stroking that sweet spot buried deep leisurely while he increasingly builds my release. "You okay?" He whispers in my ear lovingly, and I moan, tightening my fingers around his when he laces them together, penetrating me steadily until I explode all around him and take him over with me. Cole whispers sweet nothings in my ear as I shudder in his arms. We lay there for a while until our laboured breathing and bodies calmed. I relax into Cole as he trails his fingers lightly over my side and stomach.

"I'm sorry for being a bitch to you earlier," I whisper, brushing my fingers over his, and he smiles, nuzzling my neck.

"Don't be," He murmurs, rubbing my hip. "You were trying to provoke me into having sex with you." When I chuckle he I feel him grin against my temple.

"You should have had sex with me when I asked then," I tell him, and he laughs deeply.

"Honey, as sexy and irresistible as you are, hearing the words 'Fuck me, or I'll kill you' makes it really difficult to get a hard-on. You're petrifying when you're hormonal *and* angry." I snicker and kiss his fingers gently.

"I just want him out already." I sigh sullenly, and Cole rubs my stomach before he rolls me onto my back and shuffles down to my bump.

"He's going to come out soon," Cole says reassuringly, and I sigh, watching him while he kisses my stomach. "Isn't that right Rome, you're going to come out real soon because we can't wait to meet you, son." I smile and brush my fingers through his hair while he talks to my belly.

After a hot shower, I hug my body pillow and finally get some sleep.

An ache in my stomach stirred me from my slumber. I roll onto my back and hiss when the pain gets stronger. I look over at Cole sleeping beside me and shift to get out of bed when I feel my pyjama bottoms were wet. My membranes must have ruptured while I was asleep. I reach over and gently shake Cole awake. "Hm." He lifts his head in the dark. "What's wrong, baby?"

I exhale slowly, and Cole sits up and turns the night light on, blinking a couple of times till his eyes adjust to the light. "My water broke," I tell him, and he shifts and pushes the covers off himself and gets out of bed. I watch him walk around the bed to my side, and he takes hold of my hand to help me sit up.

"Are you having contractions?" He questions, brushing my hair away from my face, and I nod. "What do you need me to do?"

I exhale slowly when another contraction comes. I wait for it to pass before I speak. "Call my midwife, then my mum. Tell her I'm in labour, and we'll drop Laia to her." I instruct him, and he kisses my forehead before he grabs my phone. While Cole was on the phone, I take off my wet clothes and change into a pair of grey comfortable tracksuit bottoms and one of Coles oversized hoodies. The pain was getting worse by the minute, and I was worried we wouldn't make it to the hospital. "Cole, we have to go. Like right now." I whimper, and he looks at me, baffled.

"I thought you said early stages of labour takes ages?" Cole utters, and I shake my head and whimper when another contraction hits, crippling me momentarily. "Shayla?"

"Cole, this baby is coming really soon. We need to leave now." I say through my breathing exercise, and he looks around frantically.

"Okay, uh, I'll get Laia and your bag. Can you walk?" He asks me, and I nod. "Okay, wait for me by the door. I'll be down in a minute." I watch as he rushes off to get Alaia and her bag while attempting to make my way downstairs, stopping every time another contraction starts.

Shortly after, Cole was driving us as fast as possible to get to my mum's to drop Alaia off. My mum comes out and kisses my head and tells me she loves me before taking Alaia and goes back into the house. The drive to the hospital from my mother's house was twenty minutes, and I could already feel that familiar urge to push, and I was trying so hard not to panic. I am not having this baby in the fucking car. "Hang in there, baby, just breathe. We're almost there," Cole reassures me supportively when I cry in pain, panting through the urge to push.

"Cole, I need to push." I whimper, and he shakes his head and looks at me before he looks ahead again.

"No, baby, you can't push yet. We're almost there. Just hold on, sweetheart," He pleads, driving faster. "I'm going to get you there." He promises, taking my hand and kissing my knuckles. I scream when pain rips through me, and I grip the headrest fighting the urge to push. "Breathe baby, breathe," Cole says soothingly.

"Oh, God! Please! I don't want to give birth in the car! Please hurry, I can't, I can't hold it anymore!" I cry helplessly, and Cole curses, and the car shifts faster. "Call my midwife, tell her the baby is coming!"

Cole looks at me, wide-eyed, when I start pushing. "Oh, my God. Shay, the hospital is five minutes away. Hold on just a little bit longer, baby. You got this." He says, looking at my phone and calling the midwife. I shake my head and grip the handle on the door tight. I couldn't fight it anymore; I give in and push through the contraction, screaming.

"Hi, it's Cole, Shayla's pushing. She said the baby is coming." He tells her in a panic as he tries to drive and keep an eye on me at the same time. "Like three minutes out. Shay, she said to take off your bottoms, baby." He instructs me, and I whimper, taking off my seatbelt and sliding my bottoms off with trembling fingers. "I'm going to put you on speakerphone," Cole tells her and sets the phone on the side as he drives and takes hold of my hand while I groan and push.

"Oh, my God!" I scream, "The head is out, his head is out."

"Shayla, listen to me, just breathe, sweetie. You're almost here; I'm coming out to meet you. Everything is going to be okay. Just focus on your breathing." My midwife says, and I cry, squeezing Coles hand. "You're doing great, sweetie."

"We're here, baby, we're here," Cole says as he pulls up outside the hospital. He rips his seat belt off and turns to face me, kissing my hand repeatedly. I sob when I feel another contraction, I let go of Cole's hand,

and the door is opened, and I see my midwife and two doctors. Everything was a blur after that. With one final push, I whimper when the pain finally stops. I look down at the baby in my hands, crying. Cole stares at him, unblinking for a few seconds. "You did it. He's here. Our baby boy is here." Cole cries, pressing his forehead to mine while I sob.

"Oh my god." I cry as the midwife takes him from me and wraps him in a blanket.

"I can't believe you just delivered our baby," Cole says, kissing my forehead. I lift my head and look over at my midwife and doctors checking Rome. "You're incredible, baby."

"Is he okay?" I ask in a flurry, and she smiles warmly at me.

"He's perfect." She replies reassuringly. "Good job Mama." I finally relax when I hear that he was okay. I was terrified something was going to go wrong. I don't know how on earth I managed to deliver him by myself.

"Are you okay?" Cole whispers, brushing my sweat-damp hair away from my face. I nod tiredly, and he kisses me.

"I cannot believe I just gave birth in the damn car." I croak, and he smiles, kissing my knuckles.

"You delivered him like a pro. Just when I thought you couldn't do anything more to amaze me, you prove me wrong once again. Your strength is truly astounding, baby." Cole declares lovingly, and I sigh, shaking my head.

"What strength? I was terrified something was going to happen to him." I cry, and Cole brushes my tears away.

"Hey, shh, he's fine, baby. You did amazing." He affirms, smiling handsomely. "I am so going to tease him about this when he's older." I smile despite the exhaustion and ache of my body. "He made us wait nine days but shot out of you within an hour. That's my boy." Cole adds proudly. The doctors get me on a stretcher and finally hand me our son as they wheel us into the maternity ward. I look down at him and smile. He was gorgeous and looked like a bigger version of Alaia when she was born.

"Hi, baby boy," I whisper, brushing my lips over his forehead. "I'm so happy you're finally here, and I'm so thankful you're mine, Rome Joshua Hoult."

"Hey, what about me?" Cole pouts, and I smile up at him as he walks beside the stretcher.

"Sorry, honey, but you'll have to step aside. There's another beautiful boy in my life now." I declare affectionately, and he grins adorably in return. After the doctors checked both RJ and me, they wanted to keep us in for twenty-four hours for observation. I sigh contently, watching Cole hold our son against his chest. He lifts his eyes and looks at me, holding my gaze.

"Like what you see, sweetheart?" Cole drawls with a knowing smirk, and I nod slowly.

"Very much," I admit with a smile. Despite all the horrific things we've suffered the past two years, I'm so thankful we made it through together. If I had the option to hit restart and have a do-over— I would still find and choose to love Tristan Cole Hoult, not because I need him or can't live without him...but because I don't want to.

Ever mine, ever ours.

Chapter 40

EPILOGUE

SIXTEEN YEARS LATER...

ON A BEAUTIFUL SATURDAY morning in the month of August, Shayla Hoult rolls over in the bed she shares with her gorgeous husband Tristan Cole Hoult and smiles contently.

At the tender age of forty-six, he was still every bit as handsome as he always was. She lay on her side and admired him while he slept. He still looked the same—but older with fine lines that came with maturity, which made him even sexier. The stubble of his beard had specks of grey, which she loved.

"Why are you staring at me?" Cole mumbles, his eyes still closed, causing his wife to start while she was lost deep in her thoughts. Shayla smiles, her cheeks flushing ever so slightly, and reaches over to brush her fingers over his cheek. Cole smiles, peels his eyes open, and blinks, looking at his beautiful wife smiling at him lovingly.

"How long have you been awake?" Shayla giggles when he wraps his strong arm around her waist and drags her closer till she's pressed up against him.

"Not that long." He groans, pressing a kiss to her forehead while she nestles into his warm embrace.

"How did you know I was staring at you then?" She mumbles

SHAYLA HART

against his chest and smiles when the rumble of his deep laugh vibrates against her lips.

"Because every time you look at me, my entire body tingles." He moans, kissing her pulse, and she sighs. Shayla pulls her head back and peeks up at him through her long dark lashes.

"How many girls have you fed that line to over the years, Lord Tristan?" She questions whimsically, while Cole grins toothily but groans when Shayla pulls his ear.

"Ouch...you...you...only you!" He grumbles with an amused chuckle while she glares playfully. Shayla lets go of his ear, and he rubs it with a pout. "Why are you abusing me at this ungodly hour?"

"Ungodly? It's nine o'clock in the morning." Shayla tells him and watches his eyes glow with mischief.

"It is?" He questions and rolls over on top of her. "I think it's definitely sex 'o clock." He strokes his nose over hers. Shayla runs her hands over his muscular back while he lowers his lips to hers.

"RJ!" The couple jump apart when they hear excessive knocking, followed by seventeen-year-old Alaia's shrill scream. "Get out of my bathroom, you doofus!" Shayla groans closing her eyes.

"Every bloody morning." She sighs, looking up at her husband, who smiles. "Eight bathrooms in this house, *eight,* and they fight over one."

"MUM!" Alaia furiously shouts while thumping her fist on the bathroom door. Shayla shakes her head while Cole chuckles.

"I don't understand why they never call for you. It's always Mum, why not Dad?" She complains while Cole rolls off of her onto his back.

"Because you're the mediator in this house, baby." Cole spanks her bum before she gets up, pulling her robe on and tying it up. "The Hoult family peacekeeper. It's a big responsibility."

Shayla rolls her eyes, exasperated, "Oh please. You just like being the good guy." She mumbles while walking out of the bedroom. Shayla follows the voices toward the bathroom on the third floor and comes face to face with a livid Alaia.

"What's with the screaming again first thing in the morning, Laia?"

She questions with a frown, and Alaia turns her emerald gaze to her mother.

"He's in my bathroom *again*." She complains with a huff, brushing her fingers through her sleep-tousled light brown hair in frustration. "He's got his own. I don't understand why he keeps using mine!"

"No one told you to steal the master bathroom, princess!" RJ's response comes through the door. Alaia growls and thumps her fist on the door again.

"Get out of my bathroom, you idiot!"

Shayla rolls her eyes, shaking her head. "Alaia, language and lower your tone. You'll wake up your sister." Shayla scolds her. "Rome Joshua Hoult, get out of your sister's bathroom."

"But Mum—"

"Now," Shayla orders firmly while staring at the white wooden door. The door opens, and RJ walks out with a towel wrapped around his waist, his dark green eyes identical to his mother's glowering at his older sister. Shayla glares at both her children. "I've had it with the two of you and this bathroom argument every morning."

"Tell your son," Alaia growls at RJ, who narrows his eyes at her mockingly. "Why do you insist on using my bathroom when you've got your own?" Alaia questions crossing her arms over her chest.

"How many times do I have to keep repeating myself. It's the only one in the house with a bathtub big enough to fit my six-foot-two arse in to have my ice bath

RJ explains with a roll of his eyes. "Why don't you just take *another* bathroom. We only have seven others."

"Because *this one* is closest to my bedroom," Alaia argues back.

"What is all this commotion?" Cole frowns, walking over to join his family. Alaia turns her gaze to her father and sighs.

"Daddy, can you please tell your son to stay out of my bathroom." Alaia gripes.

RJ crosses his arms over his chest and rolls his eyes.

"Will you tell your *daughter* to stop being such a princess and that I have to take an ice bath after my training." Cole and Shayla look at one

SHAYLA HART

another while they both continue to bicker. Cole scratches his head, unsure of what to do when Shayla looks at him expectantly.

"Kids, that's enough." He declares firmly. "Alaia, you've put a claim on the master bathroom sweetheart, from time-to-time other people may want to use it. If you want a private bathroom just for yourself, you can choose one of the others." Cole states and Alaia looks at him, her mouth agape while RJ throws his hands up.

"Thank you!" He exclaims with a victorious smile while Alaia glowers at him and turns her gaze to her mother.

"Mum, will you please say something."

Shayla sighs, rubbing her forehead. "Laia, be reasonable, honey. What have I always taught you both about sharing?" Alaia's shoulders sink when she catches the firm look in her mother's eyes. "You are both fortunate enough to live in a beautiful home like this, while some people don't even have a place to call home, let alone argue about who gets the master bathroom," Shayla explains, looking at both her children exchange glances. "I do not want to hear another word regarding this bathroom dispute, or I will ban you both from using it. Do you understand me?"

"Yes Mum." They both utter shamefacedly. Shayla nods and sighs, satisfied they both understood.

"Good." She looks between them. "You're both mature enough to figure this out without fighting. I'm going to get started on breakfast." She adds, turning back and walking toward her bedroom to get dressed.

Cole looks at his children, "Go get ready for breakfast." They both nod and scamper off to their bedrooms. Cole watches them pushing and shoving each other as they walk down the corridor to their separate bedrooms. Cole never had siblings of his own, but he'd imagined if he did, this is what it would have been like. Growing up, Alaia and Rome were continually bickering and finding something to fight over. While they love each other fiercely, they still annoy one another—well, more Rome getting on Alaia's nerves by being overprotective even though she's older than him by a year and a half.

Alaia has grown up to be as his father had always dreamed, a carbon

434

copy of her mother but with his eyes. She has long, naturally wavey light brown hair—which she also got from her father— that ends at her waist. She stood at five-foot-five and a slim athletic figure. Her personality was all Shayla, without a doubt, and Cole loved that.

Rome is a handsome boy, tall, athletic, and mischievous. Shayla swears he's a miniature version of his father, with his dark brown hair that's cut short on the sides and long on the top, just like Cole's. And then there's his little princess, eleven-year-old Aria Rae, who is a mixture of them both but is the sweetest, most loving little girl to have ever walked the earth—after her mother, of course.

Twenty minutes later, the house smelt sensational with home-cooked goodness. Cole strolls into the kitchen while his wife cooks pancakes. He wraps his arms around her from behind and kisses her pulse. "As good as this food smells, I can't wait to eat *you* later," Cole growls in her ear hungrily, making her grin.

"Shh, baby, the kids are going to hear you," Shayla whispers back, looking up at him, and he matches her grin leaning close.

"They're not even in here." Cole chuckles, kissing her softly. Shayla wraps her arms around her husband's neck and parts her lips when his tongue silently requests permission to meet her own.

"Oh, barf. Mum and Dad are making out again." RJ grumbles, walking into the kitchen, followed by Alaia, who grimaces as they take their seats at the dining table. Shayla and Cole laugh as they pull apart.

"Now you know how we feel watching you slobber all over your little 'friends' you keep bringing over." Alaia retorts, making air quotes with a roll of her eyes while picking up a piece of fruit and eating it.

"I'm with Laia on this one." Shayla chimes in, flipping a pancake.

"They are my friends— friends who happen to appreciate my awesome kissing skills," RJ replies smugly, tossing a grape at Alaia, who giggles and throws it back at him.

"Sounds a lot like someone else I know." Shayla quips, giving Cole a pointed look. He smirks at her from the dining table but suddenly frowns, looking around. "Hold it. Where's my mini princess?"

"Right here, Daddy." Aria chirps, bouncing into the kitchen to join her family. Cole holds his arms open to her, and she runs into him.

"Oh, here she is." He envelopes her in a hug and kisses her cheek. "Why are you the last one down? Usually, it's your lazy brother that comes down last."

Aria pulls away from her father's embrace and looks over at her big brother, who draws her to him and tickles her. "Are you becoming lazier than me, huh squirt!" Aria laughs, slapping his hands away as he tickles her relentlessly.

"No! You're still the laziest in the Hoult kingdom. Laia was doing my hair. Stop!" She giggles, fighting in his hold.

"Okay, I'll let you off, then squirt," RJ says, ruffling her freshly braided hair, earning himself a glare from both the Hoult sisters.

"Mum, RJ messed up my hair!" Aria grumbles, walking over to her big sister, who pouts and attempts the fix it.

"Rome, leave your sister alone." Shayla's firm voice comes from the kitchen.

"Tattletale." RJ scowls at her playfully, and she narrows her green eyes at him and scrunches up her nose. When RJ reaches out to tweak her nose, she slaps his hand away and glowers at him. Cole chuckles, shaking his head.

"Honey, are you planning on joining us for breakfast?" Cole calls out to Shayla, who laughs a little. "And why have you set the whole table?"

Shayla walks in with a plate of freshly prepared chocolate chip pancakes. "Because we have guests joining us." She informs them, and they all look at her expectantly. "Everyone's coming over for breakfast, remember I told you this last night." Cole blinks up at her and then frowns. "You didn't hear a word I said, did you?"

"Wait, is that what you were saying while I was rubbing..." He stops and looks around the table at his children. "... your foot?" He finishes widening his eyes, and Shayla glares at him while the kids exchange glances.

436

"Oh, hell nah," RJ utters with a grimace after he swallows his mouthful of apple. Alaia chokes on her hot chocolate and starts to cough hysterically. "I don't even want to know what the foot was a euphemism for."

"I think I just lost my appetite." Alaia shudders while Cole smiles at his wife sheepishly.

"I don't get it," Aria asks, looking around the table. "So what if Daddy was rubbing Mummy's foot? He does it all the time." She asks while looking around the table with her wide innocent gaze.

"Your brother and sister are being silly. Eat your breakfast, sweetheart," Shayla says, brushing a kiss on her youngest daughter's head. "Aimee and Jo's are coming over for breakfast."

"Like *all* of them?" RJ questions sitting forward, and Alaia watches him with amusement. Shayla looks at her son and nods.

"If you're asking if Isla is coming, the answer is yes." Shayla smiles when RJ looks at her and then down at himself.

"Why didn't you tell me before!" RJ complains just as the doorbell rings and his eyes go wide.

"I'll get it." Aria chirps, running to the door.

"Looks like it's too late to tart yourself up, little bro." Alaia teases with a laugh, and he growls at her. Shayla giggles and playfully hits Alaia's shoulder.

"Leave him alone." She scolds her eldest, who was teasing her brother about his crush. "You look as handsome as ever, honey." She assures him, kissing his cheek, and he smiles lovingly at her.

"Thanks Mum."

"Ugh, you're such a mama's boy." RJ gives her a side glare, and she pokes her tongue out at him. "Look, it's your girlfrie—ow." Alaia hisses when RJ kicks her under the table.

"Morning!" Aimee chirps, walking into the kitchen, followed by Josh, Isla, and their youngest daughter Zuri, who was one year younger than Aria.

"Hi, punctual as ever, Aimes." Shayla drawls sarcastically, and Aimee grins.

"Bish, don't even get me started on the day I've had," Aimee grumbles, sliding her sunglasses on top of her head.

"Yeah, please don't. I've only just gotten her to calm down." Josh says, giving Cole a handshake and taking a seat next to him. Shayla looks at her questioningly, and Aimee rolls her eyes with a shake of her head.

"I'll tell you later," Shayla nods, giving Isla and Zuri a hug before they go and sit beside the kids. The doorbell chimes again, and Aria runs off with Zuri to answer it. Jo and Sam walk in a couple of seconds later, followed by Trey and their youngest little girl Talia.

"Bish, why are you so late? I'm freaking starving?" Aimee scolds her, and Jo laughs as she walks over to sit on the other side of Shayla.

"Oh, pipe down. I just saw you pull up." Jo retorts, squeezing Shayla while she waves at her big brother, who winks at her and takes a seat by the boys. They all tuck in and eat their breakfast while conversing with one another. Shayla leaned back in her seat and took in her surroundings slowly. She looks over at her eldest, who was having a conversation with her best friend Isla, then she looks at her son, who was talking animatedly about sports with his cousin Trey. Aria was showing Zuri and Talia something on her phone, and they all giggle. Then she looks at her husband, who catches her eye from across the table. They share a knowing look, and he smiles at her handsomely.

"So, Auntie Aimee, what story are you going to tell us today?" Alaia asks, her green eyes glittering with curiosity. Aimee looks around the table at Shayla and Cole and grins widely.

"Have your parents ever told you about how they got back together and married the second time around?" The kids all shake their heads, and the adults around the table laugh. "Oh, this is good. So, they broke up, right, and your idiot dad was about to marry 'the witch,' while your mother was about to flee the country to get away from your dad. I will have you know that if it weren't for me...none of you kids would be here." She explains and cackles when Cole throws a grape at her.

"Hey! That's not true." Cole chides, laughing. "I found out the same time she did."

Aimee grins and throws at grape back at him. "Let me tell the story!"

She grumbles and turns to face the kids who are watching her curiously. "So, basically, I was working with a girl named Becky..." Aimee starts to explain. Cole looks over at his wife, laughing while Aimee describes how they were running back and forth, looking for each other. Shayla looks at him, and she gazes lovingly into his endless green eyes.

"Be mine forever?"

Shayla nods with a grin, "Okay."

The End.

Special Dedication

I WANT TO DEDICATE THIS BOOK TO THOSE WHO HAVE SUFFERED
ANY FORM OF ABUSE OR ASSAULT.
YOU'RE STRONGER THAN YOU REALISE.
YOU ARE NOT ALONE.
DON'T SUFFER IN SILENCE.
AND MOST IMPORTANTLY, NEVER GIVE UP BEING *YOU*.

Thank you
For Reading

DEAR READER, THANK YOU FOR TAKING THE TIME TO READ
LOVE ME AGAIN.
I TRULY HOPE YOU ENJOYED READING THIS BOOK, BECAUSE I
ABSOLUTELY LOVED WRITING IT AND SHARING IT WITH YOU. I
WOULD LOVE TO HEAR YOUR FEEDBACK AND THOUGHTS ON THE
STORY!
REVIEWS ARE AN AUTHORS LIFELINE SO IF YOU ENJOYED THIS STORY
PLEASE BE SURE TO DROP ME A REVIEW AS THIS HELPS OTHERS SEE
AND READ MY BOOK ALSO.
IF YOU DON'T ALREADY, BE SURE TO FOLLOW ME ON MY SOCIALS FOR
UPDATES ON UPCOMING BOOKS!
LOVE ALWAYS,

About The Author

Shayla Hart is a UK based contemporary Romance novel writer. Born and raised in London Shayla has a soft spot for steamy romances. She first started writing in 2009 as a means to escape and found she absolutely fell in love with it. They don't call her the CEO of love for nothing.

Shayla is currently working on a new title An Assassins Oath which will be out 31 March. Follow her for information and updates on her upcoming titles!

Printed in Great Britain
by Amazon